*Ironbark*

In 1862 the Colony of New South Wales
resounded with the name of Frank Gardiner.
Of the many bushrangers who then
terrorised the roads he was the most
notorious. And he alone was able to capture
the public imagination – with his dark good
looks, his swashbuckling manner, and his
impudent disregard for authority. Based on
true events, this is Frank Gardiner's
story told for the first time.

Colin Free was co-creator and script editor of the very successful television drama series *Ben Hall*.

# Ironbark

COLIN FREE

METHUEN PAPERBACKS

Eyre Methuen

First published 1976
Copyright © 1976 by Colin Free
Printed in Great Britain
for Eyre Methuen Ltd
11 New Fetter Lane, London EC4P 4EE
by Richard Clay (The Chaucer Press) Ltd
Bungay, Suffolk

ISBN 0 413 34730 3 (hardback)
ISBN 0 413 34740 0 (Methuen Paperback)

For Winifred Bayley

# One

She had never seen him stripped before, not to dwell upon. The sun came raying through the clustered vines and eucalypts, slanting through a fume of mist across the water where the early morning midges danced. You could smell the earth where she sat among the bracken and rocks and listless veils of maidenhair, and the forest was dense all around and filled with the cries of the whipcrack bird and the ringing tinkle of the bellbirds. Their trysting place was a watering hole along the Winooka Creek; you could see the roo marks and the cowpats and the hole in the bank where the wombat hid – wild animal country. Even the cattle were wild, as wild as the man she had waited for.

He stood belly-deep in water, and leaned and scooped the water in a sudden drenching glitter, his head back, snorting, teeth bared through the black of his beard, the water draining down him through the matted body-hair as he rubbed the sweat of the night away.

'Come on in!' he challenged her.

'Damn you,' she said, pulling the shawl about her.

The sun lit up his shoulders in a downy gilt and speckled his hair with gems. He was tanned as dark as a boot and maybe even darker, for there was a touch of the aboriginal in him, some distant and forgotten grandparentage from the First Landing, from the 1780s, back where it had all begun almost a century past. He had the amber eyes of the aboriginal, and the breadth of the nose and the gleam of the teeth and, yes, the earth-power, the earth-knowledge in his blood; he had the animal grace, and the blind patience of ancient rock. Yet he was a man built tall, and broad across the shoulders, the chest sculptured in planes to the belly where the hairs gathered to a vertical, flaring at the base. He was a hard, deep-veined, muscular man, as handsome as wild horses.

7

She stirred the fire and the smoke went up straight as a column into the vaulting trees. The sun was now a bright smoulder behind him and the first breeze of morning shifted back in the Valley somewhere, back where she lived. You could hear the breeze approaching with a rustling impatience, and then the foliage lifting about them, leaves falling in a dizzy spiral into the glass-smooth water.

She got up and threw a handful of tea into the billy and looked at him, at the thrust of his jaw, the hard, bold lines of his head, the eyes provocative, wicked. 'I have to go,' she said. But she wasn't going, not that moment, not when she felt the sharp drag of her body to his. She didn't care.

'Turn your back,' he called across the water. 'I'm coming out.'

She looked at him.

'I mean it,' he said.

He stared out of the water and she kept looking in a way that stirred him. She had the same fire and damn-all impudence that had kept him wanting her these whole five years – she'd been just a girl then, the best of three, Kate Walsh, the wildest, burning the way that sulphur burns, slow and secret, and he supposed he loved her.

'Well?' he asked, standing there at the water's edge.

'Not bad,' she said.

'The best,' he told her.

'You think so?'

She looked at him shamelessly – she'd come a long way from shame – at the water draining from his flanks, the hair matting, picking up the dance of light.

Then he had his arms about her and his hands against her flesh. His hands were ice-cold from the water so that the heat of her body received him like a branding. 'I have to go,' she told him, and, when he ignored her, 'I mean it, Frank, I have to.'

He stood back from her, a little below her down the bank, and his hands parted the unfastened dress and bared her breasts to the sunlight. Then he leaned over and kissed her once, then

8

twice, nuzzling at the hard knots of her nipples, his lips teasing, playful, and she pulled her hands behind his head and crushed him to her. A bright stillness gripped the forest; and there was the nod of wild-flowers and the plink of seed-pods in the water, and she saw the breeze create a dreamy undulation rippling down towards them. Then the hot air of a far-off desert was all about them, tossing her hair, stirring the leaves, and the blue smoke of the campfire uncoiled towards them, enveloping them. They made their way up the bank and she poured the black tea into the mugs.

'I used to pray a wicked thing,' she said, 'every night as I lay beside him. I used to pray I'd dream of you.' She blew on the tea and sipped it. 'But I hardly ever did.' She watched as he began to dress.

'That's the punishment,' he said, teasing, pulling on the heavy moleskin pants with the sawed-off ends.

'Did you? Did you dream of me?' she asked.

He didn't answer. He thought about it. He dressed carefully from the shin-high leather boots to the scarlet of his shirt, slipping on the leather waistcoat, knotting the speckled sweatband beneath his beard. 'I never dreamt,' he told her, thinking of the pitch-black lock-up and the thirty men, and the sweat and stink of thirty men, and the clockwork prowl of the guard, ten to the corner, ten to the door all through the night, and the murmur of the sea and the thunder in the rock you slept upon. 'I lay me down,' he said, 'and died until they woke me.'

She pushed her dark hair back from the wind and began to fasten her dress. The touch of his hand restrained her. 'Something to remember,' he said, as his eyes dwelt a moment more on the high thrust of her breasts, his gaze taking in the column of her throat, her winged lips parted, the moisture there, her eyes as dark as night and deep as pools, and a hunger lying sullen in them even now.

'Until tonight?' she said.

'God knows where I'll be then.'

'You're home, Frank. You've come back.'

9

He thought about it. Frank Gardiner was home again. This was home. It wasn't even on the map. Two hundred miles from Sydney town, and further than the moon. Home for the second time around – he'd been taken twice for horse-thieving, the first time put in the lock-up, the second on Cockatoo Island from which no man escaped. Now he was free, and it was legal.

He looked at her – Kate Walsh as she still was to him, but in truth, by the priest's blessing, Kate Foster. 'What did you marry him for?'

She looked away.

'Kate?'

' 'Cause I thought I loved him.'

'And you stayed true?'

'Till today.'

'What did you marry him for?'

'You were sent off for ten years, Frank.'

'Haven't you heard of good behaviour? I got my ticket of leave. I cut it in half. And I came back, didn't I? Like I said I would.'

'So I'm married.'

He drained the tea and stood up. 'Best you stay that way.'

She looked into the fire. 'I could always leave him.'

He started towards the horses and she got up and finished fastening her dress, her fingers angry at the buttons. 'Oh my Gosh,' she said. 'What's got into you? What did they do to you? I did exactly what you'd have done. I looked after myself. I bought my bed and supper. I found someone. I'm not a stick. God help me, what was I supposed to do?'

He soothed and gentled the horse, murmuring to it, then turned to her. 'I'm going into Ironbark, to show my presence to Sergeant Canning. Then I'm heading back to Carcoar to take up my trade.'

'Then we'll be three days' ride apart?'

She couldn't read him any more – not the way she used to. She couldn't tell whether it was truth or provocation.

'Butchering's steady,' he said. 'I was a damn' good butcher.'

'Well, I hope you have a fine old time.'

'Well, I won't swing for it.'

'Takes money, though. Where'll you get the money?'

'I'll get the money where I got the horse.'

Then it dawned on her. The old excitement gripped her. She knew him now, she recognised him, he hadn't changed, he was as wild as he'd ever been. She hoisted her skirts and ran to him and flung herself upon him. 'You black bastard,' she said. 'I thought you'd turned as straight as a stick.'

'I have,' he protested.

'With a duffed horse?'

'Oh, that.'

'Third time round, they'll have your head on a post. And you're riding him into Ironbark to see the Sergeant-in-command?'

He looked at her, her head thrown back with laughter – this was the wildness he loved. A dozen times he'd lain with others who, in candlelight, with great calf's eyes, would plead with him to mend his ways, sluts and school-teachers, Christians and pious little virgins, but this one, this crazy Kate, she wanted him worse!

'Damned if I can love a butcher.'

'You wasn't asked.'

'Listen,' she said, 'listen . . .' Bright in the eyes she unfastened the saddle-bag. 'I got something for you.' She brought out the cloth-wrapped thing, heavy and box-shaped, and put it in his hands. 'For coming home,' she said. 'I saved it.' He looked at her. 'Open it,' she said.

He took the package and pulled the wrapping off. He didn't know what to expect, some femininely useless thing perhaps. But the box, even the box was something. 'That's hand-made,' he said. 'That's brass hinges.'

'Open it,' she laughed.

He opened the box. 'Oh Lov',' he murmured. 'Oh, my God!' And the tears sprang to her eyes at his true reverence for what was just a gun, special and priceless as it may be, but bits of metal none the less. 'Do you like it?' she encouraged. And there was something special about her, then, that childlike, tippytoed-eager Kate, standing not much higher than his shoulder, her eyes immensely wide and vulnerable, her patchwork azure dress – the hem ripped, the seams a web of stitches – demanding the warmth of love and shelter.

He weighed the gun in his hand, truly unable to speak. He had never seen such a gun. It was a Navy Colt revolver, a single-action gun of the calibre that could slam a man to the ground the way you'd fell a steer. He looked up at her. 'That's a beautiful thing,' he said, fingering the octagonal facets of the barrel, a barrel that was a hand-span long at least, with a 7-groove twist he hadn't seen before. But he knew this much – it was worth half-a-dozen muzzle-loading pistols of the kind the traps carried : one gun worth half-a-dozen troopers. His hand gloved the rich wine-colour of the walnut grip, and the flange married to the heel of his hand and it became immediately his gun, wedded to him, part of him, a good gun.

'Don't, don't!' she shrieked as he levelled it.

'Where'd you get it?'

'I found it.'

'Where?'

She turned away with a touch of the coquette. 'People give you presents, you shouldn't ask.'

'Come on, where'd you get it?'

'I told you I found it – in an army captain's holster.'

'In a box?'

'On the mantelpiece.'

'In the bedroom?'

She got angry. 'If you like it, take it, and damn where it came from.'

'I like it,' he said, nesting it back in the velvet of the box. 'But what'll I use it for?'

'Oh,' she said, refusing to take the bait, 'doesn't a butcher have to kill the beasties in the yard?'

He gripped her arm, hard enough to leave a mark. 'I never shot a man in my whole damn' life.'

'Never said you was going to. But there's plenty good trade

on the road, Frank.'

'You'd have me hang, would you?'

He had never thought about the trade before, not so clearly. He had never thought about his future except for butchering; and he'd supposed the money would come from cards or some indulgent female – he wouldn't want that much. But the trade – the other 'Trade', he began to think of it – was not that much against the grain.

'There's gold on those roads,' she said, like a woman priming a lazy fire. 'All those fellers coming from the diggings, gold in their pockets, brand-new watches, solid gold.'

'Dammit,' he said, thrusting the box at her, 'whyn't you go on and do it?'

' 'Cause I want to be a kept woman,' she said with a teasing grin.

'Tell you what I'll do,' he said, jamming the box in his shirt, 'I'll think about it.' And he mounted the horse.

'Bring me something,' she said.

'No, I'll think about it.'

She went up to him, her hand along his thigh, exploring him, her head against his moleskins.

He looked down at her. She was the damnedest woman of them all; and he knew he should have bedded and broken her when she was in her teens.

## Two

'And what part of England do you hail from?' said the tireless Mrs Considine.

Frederick Pottinger, who was lost in a daydream, gazed up at his oppressor. The ample lady was framed by the curve of the open coach and shrouded by a cloud of dust from the wheels.

'India,' he said. 'I was born in India.' And immediately regretted it.

'You were born in India?' she repeated. 'Mr Pottinger was born in India, Clara.'

'Yes, Mama,' said daughter Considine in a whisper that was lost in the grind of the wheels.

'How extraordinary!' madam told him.

'Though not of Indian parentage,' he offered mischievously.

'I beg your pardon, 'ow's that again?' she asked, in a goggle of curiosity.

'Never mind.' He waved a hand at her. She was a large plum-pudding of a woman, her full, flowing roundness cruelly indented by stays, her face dusted white, rouged red, and aggressively hairy. The daughter, crushed by Mama's bulk, was built much finer, with the sharp, bright face of some forest bird, heavily feathered, as indeed she was, in pink and lace, buttoned up tight to the bottom of her jaw. In any case, conversation was impossible, and five hours of abortive forays were more than merely fatiguing. He spent ten to a dozen seconds examining the miserable countryside – the drained grey of the trees, the dung-coloured hills – and resumed his perusal of Clara Considine's wrist.

It was not an unusual wrist, but a delicate, feminine wrist of a creamy softness dimpled with the stretch of sinew, and veined with blue. Abruptly, as though invaded, Clara shifted in her seat and rearranged the volumes of her dress. How painfully intimate, she thought it was, to have her skirts grazing the gentleman's trousers. She looked at him with a little secret fluttering look, and then, to save herself: 'Mama, look – cockatoos!'

He was not a handsome man, she thought, but he was elegant, yes, though in a somewhat shabby way. His cuffs were frayed, and he kept trying to bury them, and his collar was grimed. He looked like a preacher, or a lawyer perhaps, he had the lawyer's bookwork nose and the penetrating eyes. But no, there was a wickedness, she thought, the entrancing wickedness of the predator, with eyes balanced like a hawk's above that impressive, impossible conk! 

She looked at him again, and he was looking at her, and quite rightly she divined, with a blush, his thoughts were not sublime.

'But you must,' said Mrs Considine, leaning forward with a gasp, 'have spent a deal of time in England?'

'Twenty years,' he yelled above the din – with such vigour that Dr Hudson woke with a glare of malevolence.

The Doctor was also on his way to Ironbark, to take up practice. He, like Frederick Pottinger, had joined the coach at Crossroads.

'Haven't I seen you before?' he accused.

'I'm a much-travelled man,' said Pottinger evasively.

'At Fivecrown – at the diggings? The goldfields?'

'Never,' said Pottinger, though it was a lie. He remembered clearly Dr Hudson extracting teeth and tucking sovereigns in his money-belt. He remembered the awful spill of mullock and mud. And one night a man was murdered in mud, drowned in it, and they'd played cards behind the canvas shelter because you didn't interfere, and the Cobbler had said to the dying man's cry, ' 'E sounds like a drain on a windy night!'

'At Fivecrown in the hollow,' the man persisted.

Pottinger sighed. Hudson's was a tedious game. And now the tiresome fellow was seeking an alliance with Mrs Considine. 'I do believe we have a man of mystery, Madam.'

'Do tell us at least,' she conspired, 'what you will do in Ironbark?'

'I shall live on my annuity,' he said, not without some truth, 'and I shall become a wastrel, a rapscallion.' That silenced them, at least. 'Why,' he went on, 'what else is there to do in Ironbark?'

'You could learn some manners for a start,' said Dr Hudson tartly and opened his book, which he could not read for the bounce and sway of the coach.

Pottinger now leaned forward to the girl and asked, 'What will you do in Ironbark, Miss Clara?'

His answer was a singularly stunning flush and he knew that in another place, other circumstances . . .

Just then the coach began to grind to a halt. Hudson stuck

his head out. 'Hi there, coachie, what's the trouble?'

'Battle Creek, sir,' the coachman said, and set about the crossing.

The sudden silence and the swish of water was hard on the ears after hours of unrelenting din, and they were suddenly aware of the high summer sounds: the piercing shrill of the cicadas, the lament of crows, and something deeper, less tangible – the mighty crush of heat that lay like molten iron above the plains.

Now the coach stood motionless up to the axles in the muddy water; and Dr Hudson turned again with the squeak of his coat against the leather. 'What's wrong? Why aren't we moving?'

'The horses are drinking,' Clara said.

'How long must we put up with this?' Hudson said petulantly.

'Most inconsiderate,' Mrs Considine muttered.

Pottinger knew what they were thinking, what all travellers thought – that any place of ambush was a dangerous place, that there were said to be some two hundred brigands on the road, and not all of them were gentlemen. There was a 'Mad Dog' Morgan, he believed, whose souvenirs included human heads. And wasn't there an aboriginal ...? Nursery tales, he thought, bedtime horrors. They were in it for the pickings, not the blood. And yet he felt a prickle at the scalp, a crawl of flesh. There was something, somewhere, and his body knew it.

He opened his eyes to Hudson's cry: 'Come on, coachie, that's enough.'

'Just let 'em cool their bellies, sir.'

'Get moving, man!'

But the coachman would have his way. And it seemed to Pottinger, gazing on the glassy water, that they were locked in a treacle of time, and he began to feel a growing certainty that they were waiting in a ferment of disaster, that the stubborn coachman could be in league with some ruffian horde.

'Last time we travelled, Clara and me ...' began Mrs Con-

16

sidine in a high, strained voice – but the coach moved off with a sudden lunging sway and she had to clasp the Doctor's arm for fear of pitching overboard. ''E might've give some warning,' she complained; and they climbed from the water with a great crashing and splashing, the whip-sound smacking in their ears like gunshots fading to a distant, rolling echo.

Mrs Considine was so relieved to resume the journey that she shared around her supply of mineral water, Pottinger declining, and there was a deal of merriment and camaraderie – from which he excluded himself – as they tried to fill the tiny metal cup.

He, for his part, was pleased to see the change of countryside. They had been climbing for the last mile or so almost imperceptibly, but climbing to a greener slope with the trees pressing in, until they entered a sapling forest of welcome shadows and hidden depths with a matted carpet of eucalyptus leaves. And finally, as they topped a windy rise, Mrs Considine announced, 'There – there's Ironbark.' And Pottinger, dutifully following the direction of her gloved finger, gazed across, expecting to see a cluster of shanties or a yellow, meandering road. But there was nothing, nothing that would stir the mind.

'Where?' asked Dr Hudson.

'There – in the mountains.'

Pottinger sighed. He couldn't even see the mountains. What he did see was an unlikely rise of landscape, three or four hills he supposed they were, swelling from a brown plain.

'The town,' said a voice, and he looked round into Clara's nutbrown eyes, 'is on the other side.'

'On the other side of what?'

'Of the Ironbark Mountains.'

He smiled at her disarmingly. 'And are you an Ironbark maiden?'

The only reply was a roaring thundercrack that seemed to split apart the little house they rode in, and he heard a startled shriek from Mrs Considine and there was a sudden wink of sunlight from the plush behind the Doctor, as though an eye had opened in the wall, and he knew, even before the rearing of the horses, that a ball had smashed clean through the coach and that they were under attack.

He looked out as the coach slewed to a stop, and couldn't see a thing, but then the shadow of the coachman flicked across his gaze and there was the fellow with his arms flung up.

'What's wrong? What is it?' Hudson cried, as the gun appeared at the window.

'Get down,' said a hairy man. 'Get out on the road.'

'Perhaps we should oblige,' said Pottinger to the others.

Pottinger and Hudson got out of the coach. Both gazed into a flintlock carbine, a shameful, rusted thing held by a toothless lag on horseback, an aging, asthmatic man wheezing his encouragement. 'Step out and empty your pockets. And the ladies. I want the ladies on the road.'

'Leave the women out of this,' said Hudson.

'I want the ladies,' said the other adamantly.

Pottinger turned to assist Clara from the coach.

'You there!' At the wheezy command Pottinger looked back. 'Leave her be, and spill out.'

Well, Pottinger thought, something to write home about. He watched Hudson plunging through his pockets, tossing wallet, watch, and snuff-box into the hat, with the dismal and secret knowledge that he, Pottinger, had next to nothing to offer. Nevertheless, he peeled off his rings, found two sovereigns in a twist of handkerchief, a gold fob-chain without a watch, and a five pound note, his worldly wealth, his only surety that he would not starve.

'Is that all?' said the hairy man, compounding Pottinger's embarrassment.

'Alas, that's everything.'

'Where's the watch?'

'With the sovereign case, with the wallet.'

'You sauce me, I'll put a bullet through your snout.'

'I lost at cards, old chap – a different kind of banditry.' Already he could feel the shrinking dismay of his fellow travellers; he was a mere pariah, a cardsharp. 'I do hope you'll understand,' he said.

'Get your boots off – both of you.'

Pottinger and Hudson dutifully complied. It was common knowledge that a wise man carried his wealth underneath his stockings. Hudson, tottering about, as awkward as an emu, glanced at Pottinger. Pottinger read the glance and shook his head. 'When I give the word,' Hudson murmured.

'I prefer not,' Pottinger replied.

He glanced at the highwayman – the bushranger was busy now receiving Mrs Considine's adornments – and, Pottinger perceived, there was some terrible danger here: the hairy man was more afraid than they were, and he could smell the fellow's sweat and see the tremor of the gun, and he knew that somewhere in this bright and stunning moment a speck of terror lay.

'I'll take that,' said the wheezy voice behind him.

'Never you dare,' said Mrs Considine, clutching her worthless beads.

'I'll take it. Or you gimme!'

'Now!' said Hudson in Pottinger's ear.

Pottinger's hand fell to Hudson's arm, and the Doctor's face looked back at this mewling treachery and twisted with contempt. 'You call yourself a man?' Hudson brushed past him and upended his boots. 'There – they're full of nothing.'

'The girl,' said the hairy man, 'what's she wearing?'

There was a thin gold chain at Clara's throat.

'No!' said Clara, retreating. It was a trinket from her only suitor.

'You gimme that.'

'You've got enough,' said Mrs Considine. 'Be on your way.'

'You gimme, or I'll blow it off.'

Would he? Pottinger wondered. Would he kill for a strand of gold? He began to feel a numbed detachment as this moment of bright horror swam upon him. He saw the outlaw dismount, the loot spilling from the hat, coins clinking on the shale of the road, and the hairy man was lumbering towards Clara Considine, who had thrust herself against the bright enamel of the coach, her eyes wide and the glaze of perspiration on her.

'Leave her alone,' Hudson said, his voice sounding far off.

And the hairy man reached out for the glint of gold, his stubby fingers clawed, his nails chewed down; and Clara made to scream, but no sound came. And the hand was at her, like leather against the silk of her flesh.

'Lord save us!' Pottinger said. But even as he urged himself to action, Mrs Considine had flung herself upon the man, with a reckless vaulting of her bulk, and the man crashed against the coach and the flintlock blasted like a powder barrel. Clara wheeled aside, her hands clapped to her ears, eyes fixed and staring. And for a moment nothing happened – some leaves fell down from where the ball had passed, and Mrs Considine turned back from her task with her chalk-white face on Pottinger.

Pottinger abruptly started towards the outlaw who, bent as a pin, was supporting himself by the handrail, his breathing now a rasping husk of life itself. And there, on the wrinkled parchment of his throat, Pottinger saw an improbable insect, a glistening, blackbellied thing with a tiny bubble of blood beneath. Mrs Considine had buried the length of her hatpin.

'Doctor . . .' said Pottinger like a fool, scarcely knowing what to do, but he had the dying man in his hands and the eyes were rolling up to his in pitiful complaint. The devil of a thing to die for, Pottinger thought – forty quid if he were lucky, and a woman's hatpin.

'The pin,' Dr Hudson said in official tones, 'has undoubtedly penetrated the windpipe.' And, leaning in for Pottinger's ears alone, 'The fellow is drowning in his own blood.'

Pottinger got to his feet to let death take care of itself. It was a rotten business. He heard Clara's rasping sobs as she retched by the side of the road. What with this and the wheeze of the dying man and the hum of the flies – he didn't have the stomach for it! He should go home! But home was in those little pipsqueak pimples on the plain, in Ironbark where he'd hoped to start anonymous and clean.

'Would you be so kind as to help me,' Dr Hudson said behind him, 'to put the deceased on the coach?'

But they couldn't get the body on the roof, and there was no coachman anyway – he'd fled, as many of them did.

'Can you drive a coach, then?' Hudson asked with a chill in his voice.

'I can make a stab at it.'

'Very well, you shall drive the coach.'

It was all arranged that Clara would occupy the seat beside him, and Hudson and Mrs Considine would share the interior with the corpse on the floor. 'I shall put my feet on 'im,' she declared. She was made of sterner stuff than most and, in her time, had fought off the blacks and slaughtered her own meat. 'And I shall take the blooming reward.' But there wouldn't be a reward. He was just old rubbish, this one.

They set off down the road to Ironbark with the outlaw's horse in tow.

For a moment, Pottinger placed his hand on Clara's. It was a comforting, supporting gesture, but she did not respond.

She was still hearing the shrill ringing of the carbine in her ears, and seeing the dead man dying, dying . . .


## Three

Frank Gardiner rode into Ironbark not long before the coach arrived. He tethered his horse outside the Irish Tavern – to which he would return. Oh yes, it was an Irish town, there was no mistaking that. They'd transported the Irish 'undesirables' along with the pigs and goats and English poachers seventy years ago, and, for them that cared to remember, the emerald isle had now become a rock in a thirsty plain.

It was a high, hot sun around eleven in the morning and there were few but diggers about. They'd worn a track through the town, to and from the goldfields. The town was built on gold, or the smell of it, and when the fields were done it maybe wouldn't be here – not even the banks, the pubs, the barracks, anything. It was what he liked about the land – you couldn't box it in : you walked a quarter-mile past the last shack and canvas humpy, and you were in the wilderness again; you couldn't even see the end of it.

He pushed out from the hitching rail and wandered on his way. Two amber-coloured mongrels threaded past him, yapping at the wagon in the road. A digger, drunk, fell out of Boots & Shoes. Gardiner kept going. It was a good, rich morning, rich with the smell of dust and horse manure and the elusive fragrance of the bush that drenched the air with oils of turpentine and eucalyptus.

The whole town lay stunned by heat and absent rain. The buildings pressed together on both sides of the rutted track, standing supporting each other, the clapboard, the wattle-and-daubs, the tinsheet tumbledowns like an avenue of tipsy travellers with no good place to go. Yet the bank was imposing as a bank was supposed to be, and the police barracks, a solid, once-white pisé wall peeling back to show its bones. It opened directly on to the street, and he paused to look through the well of darkness that was the doorway to the corridor. The corridor went clean through to the dusty brilliance of the barracks yard, and opening from it on one side was Sergeant Canning's office, and on the other the cells, the lock-up – or the 'logs' as they were called.

He stood for a time outside the barracks, slitting his eyes against the brutal white of the wall. He drew on the cigar which was now a stub and eased the gun into his belt and closed his coat about it. He felt himself divided – by the gun and the law, by Kate and an easy life in the slaughter-yard with the salt smell of the blood and the lazy hum of flies and the sharp knife peeling back the carcase. An honourable trade, he thought. He would be respected. He went in.

'Gardiner? Frank Gardiner?' Sergeant Canning asked, as though pondering some enigma.

'I didn't think you'd forget me, Sergeant.'

'Who asked you to walk in here? Where is the Trooper?'
And Canning sighed, perhaps at the futility of his question. The office was a humid box with an earthen floor upon which some tattered matting lay. Upon the matting a desk, two chairs, a chest of drawers, everything dusted by the powder of the street outside, by a kind of despair, a hopelessness – spiders in the corner, the lantern glass as black as ash. This was an outpost, the fretted end of the long red tape that represented bureaucratic law and order. And of course there was no trooper doing duty by the door, and of course there would be no reprimand. Discipline only resulted in desertion or worse, a spreading atrophy.

'So they turned you out, did they?'

'They couldn't stand the sight of me. Do you have a place for this?' said Gardiner, offering the butt of his cigar.

'You do not smoke in here,' the Sergeant said.

Gardiner dropped the butt and stood on it.

Canning clamped his jaws and sorted through his papers. He was a man of some forty years or more, too old for the game, with dreams of some small acreage on Ironbark Creek with Bess, his wife, and a run of fowls and the corn growing, and two good horses. There had been children, two of them, both dead of diphtheria and the doctor's helpless treatment of salts, senna and calomel.

Now he studied Gardiner's papers. 'You must have been on good behaviour.'

'No. Just scared of the sharks. Cockatoo's surrounded by the fiercest sharks in Sydney.'

'And what do you intend to do?' Canning asked with his fingers loosely knit together, resting on the paper.

'I dunno. Work, I suppose.'

'Work where? Doing what?'

'I dunno,' Gardiner said, truly not knowing for the first time. 'I might go back to butchering.'

'Take a bit of money, wouldn't it?'

'A bit.'

Canning got up from the desk. He was shorter than Gardiner,

23

built more solid, chunkier. His hair that used to be a sullen ginger was bleached out, mixed with grey.

'If you make trouble for me, I'll toss you in the logs so hard, you'll crack your skull. You stay out of trouble, you hear? I know your kind, I know the way you think. But I've fifteen, twenty men out there – and I'll put 'em on you like a pack of dogs the moment you look sideways. Is that clear?'

'Yeah, I believe I understand.'

'You'd better.'

Gardiner went outside.

Canning watched him – the dark shape of the bearded man outside the window, ruminating – and it gave him unpleasant, unbidden feelings. For this was a killing man, he knew, and the glass was like a membrane that could let the tide pour in.

Gardiner, as though divining the fear behind him, looked back once, smiled, and was gone.

At the other end of town across the bridge, the coach was coming in and he watched it pull up to the Irish Tavern and saw the nobs get out. And he saw Pottinger get down from the driver's seat and knew at once that something was wrong – and by the time he got there they were dragging the body out, and there were all these women and topers and kids rushing up from somewhere and he couldn't see a thing.

'What's up?' he said. 'Who's dead?'

'It's "Onepot" Wally Higgins,' someone said. 'They kilt him.'

Gardiner lit another cigar and steadied the flame as Pottinger elbowed past. 'What happened?' he asked.

'Ask him,' Pottinger said.

Gardiner gazed back into the dead man's eye.

And why not turn to the Trade, he thought, since he's left a place for me.

And that was when the gun felt good, tucked against his belly. The gun would get him two hundred quid, and then he'd be gone for ever.

24

# Four

'I want to try my gun out,' Gardiner said, sighting across the little cone of the front brass sight.

'But Frank, you don't need a gun, I mean, not for shootin'. A gun is to keep 'em in line, to make 'em behave. I mean, just any ol' gun'll do.'

'This ain't any old gun.'

'That's the point, Frank. The gun is too good for the game. Suppose you lose it?'

The authority was Johnny Piesley, a crooked weed of a man of twenty-three, built so skinny he could hide behind a sapling, with a head too large and decked with a polka-dot pattern of red-hot pimples and razor cuts, as though he'd attacked it. He was a sorrowful, self-pitying man in a strawberry coat and a lemon shirt, each garment stained and slack from his cavernous build, and he'd been on the roads since he was old enough to ram a pistol. In fact, he sported four guns, all muzzle-loaders, which he carried at the belt. They were at the creek, an un-named creek out of Winooka Valley, where Gardiner had found his partner. Winooka was outlaw country, limestone country full of caves, and every man who lived there had the shackles and the lash buried in his past.

'Me,' said Piesley, 'I use horse-pistols – and I haven't shot a horse-pistol in eighteen months.'

'They're going to be the death of you,' Gardiner said. 'They'll be all rusted up inside.'

'Frank, I been on the road for three years straight —'

Gardiner got up and filled the billy from the creek.

Piesley looked at him with a kind of despair. You couldn't reach Frank Gardiner, you couldn't talk to him, he took offence so easily. 'Have you seen Kate?' he asked as Gardiner came back up the slope.

Gardiner emptied the can of water over the coals and Piesley scrambled back from the splash of steam. 'What did you do that for?'

'What did I do what for?'

'You splashed me.'

'I'm putting out the fire.'

Piesley sulked. He couldn't help it; that was his way. It went with his almost beardless face. He was a child with four big horse-pistols, and by guess or God he was one of the best who ever worked the Trade.

'Sure I've seen Kate,' Gardiner said. 'She up and went and married on me.'

Piesley scrambled over to him, anxious to make amends. 'You know what you want to do, Frank? You want to mark her, you want to brand her so she knows it.'

'Is that what you'd do, Johnny?'

'By God, if she switched on me, I would.'

'Yeah, getting married, that's a terrible, immoral thing to do.'

Piesley laughed – which seemed the safest thing to do – and helped his partner scrub the fire out. There was going to be a hot west wind – you could tell by the dead stillness and the way the leaves hung vertical – and they didn't want to start a bushfire.

'What's the time?' Gardiner said.

'Half past eight,' Piesley said, screwing his face up. He had half a dozen elaborate gold watches, not one of them with his own name in it.

'Best we go, then.'

'Plenty of time, Frank. We'll just be kicking our heels about.'

'It's two hours to the Narrows, Johnny.'

'We're not goin' to the Narrows.'

'We're going to take 'em at the Narrows, Johnny.'

'But Frank . . .'

'Listen . . .' Gardiner moved up close to him. 'If you're going to ride with me, there's something we have to straighten out. I make the decisions.'

'Yeah, but Frank, I mean—'

'Stop whining, Johnny.'

Piesley swallowed hard. He couldn't explain. He had the words, but he couldn't get them out. It was he – Piesley – he was the professional. Frank had never stuck up so much as a rusty mug. What was he giving the orders for?

' 'Less you'd rather go it alone,' Gardiner said.

'I didn't say that.' He was sick of being alone; he didn't have a friend in the world. 'Let's see how it works,' he said.

'We'll make it work,' Gardiner laughed, scrubbing Piesley's hair.

'Don't do that!' Piesley yelped, backing off.

And Gardiner came at him and smoothed his hair in place, like you would for a child, both gentle and mocking – and Piesley felt a terrible conflict, an angry embarrassment and a melting compliance. The whole world knew that it took a man to ride with Frank Gardiner, and he was that man! 'Don't, Frank,' he pleaded. 'You'll make a sook of me.'

They rode straight out from the creek, across the foothills and into the mountain valleys. They climbed for the best part of an hour, and after an hour looked back on the little hills of Ironbark. They were in the deep mountains now, halfway up, fifteen hundred feet or more in eucalyptus forest, and there wasn't a track or a footmark anywhere and Piesley, though he'd never admit it, was totally lost.

'You know where we are, Frank?' he ventured.

'Right over there,' Gardiner said with a sweep, 'that's the Bathurst Road. That's the Narrows.'

'Hell of a way to get there,' Piesley grumbled.

'I start the way I mean to finish. There's police patrols down there – which is where I want 'em.' And he urged the horse along the neck of the ridge beneath the tree ferns and the mossy rocks. He knew the country from childhood as though it was laced with laneways, and what he didn't know, the dark blood of the aboriginal informed him.

He rode with a quiet certainty, with a kind of passion. Not a bad way to spend your life, he thought. Better than horse-stealing – with half a dozen angry men with shotguns breathing down your neck for the sake of some old nag.

They plunged into cool shadows, skirting the rotten hulk of some fallen forest giant decked with orange fungus flowers. The rocks dripped water, and green stuff grew on them. Sometimes in the deep of winter it snowed here, and there were springs above, and the water found its way to the Valley, to Winooka. But down there, this season, there was a blue shimmer of heat and crows wheeling above an unseen carcase. It was a January heat, the worst time.

They came out right where he'd intended, just above that press of rocks that squeezed the road, the Narrows. And they waited.

'What's the time, Johnny?'

'You'll have to get yourself a watch.'

'That's what I'm here for.'

But ten, fifteen minutes later, a great thundering clatter of wheels came up the road – from the wrong direction.

'You sure you got this right?' Gardiner accused.

They peered over the edge of the rock. It was a coach, all right, but embossed with Her Majesty's insignia, a big, lumbering thing with a sweating pair of chestnuts working hard. Preceding it were two redcoats, fully armed, and two more aft. The driver, good with the whip and words of rough encouragement, was partnered by another man – with a shotgun.

Gardiner, more to get a better view, got up.

'Not this one!' Piesley said, pulling at his coat.

'What's in that thing?' Gardiner said, as the coach rolled around the turn.

'That's the gold coach. No one touches that.'

'Why not?' Gardiner said.

'Frank, there's a dozen guns on that.'

Gardiner sat back on the rock and hooked his arms around his knees. 'Yeah, I see that.' But he was thinking: 'A dozen guns, that's the equal of two Colt Navy guns.' It was just arithmetic, he knew, but the thought appealed to him.

The coach was late and the sun got hotter, and they didn't

talk any more. A couple of travellers went past below – a little family with the dog, the kitchen table, everything.

'I hope you got this right,' Gardiner said.

Then they saw the coach, maybe twenty minutes away. You could see it coming as a puffball on the Clanville loop of road. There were two roads to Ironbark, one along the mountain way. Gardiner could remember the time there hadn't been a road at all.

'What you do,' he said, getting up, 'is go on down the way a bit – and when I take 'em, close in behind.'

'That ain't necessary, Frank. They can't turn round in the Narrows.'

'They can run, can't they?'

'Yeah, all right,' Piesley said, and hesitated at the horse. 'You forget I always used to do it on my own.'

'And how many did you lose in the scrub?'

'Yeah, yeah, I know,' Piesley said. He didn't give a damn about the runners. If they could run, good luck to 'em. But Frank, he was taking this so seriously!

Piesley waited in a shelter of rocks not far from the road. There was a big goanna halfway up a tree, pretending to be a branch, waiting for his supper. And Piesley, for no good reason, felt a sudden crush of sorrow for himself, waiting there with the sun heavy on his head and the horse-pistols leaden in his belt; he felt a fear upon him, a wash of dread, like a man who sees his own grave turning over.

The coach came crashing past abruptly and he pulled the guns, two of them, and moved out taking a quick measure of the passengers – three men and a single tart-faced woman, tart with the kind of vinegars that he remembered of his mother.

He heard the coach pull into a sudden, creaking silence, and kneed his horse and leaned into the sway of the gallop, and even by the time he got there, which was seconds, the men were tumbling out before the steady glint of Gardiner's gun.

'You ain't going anywhere,' Piesley told the driver, who sank back quietly in his seat.

Gardiner winked at Piesley, and Piesley felt a surge of certainty, the old feeling . . .

Two of the men were large and well-fed dignitaries of some kind, florid of face with a whisky flush, all satins and velvet, quite a catch. The third man had the smell of the stables, a horse-dealer down on his luck.

Piesley stuck a gun through the window. 'You, too,' he said.

'No, not the woman,' Gardiner said.

'She's wearing gold.'

'She's a woman.'

The three men stood sheepishly on the road. 'You're wasting your time,' said the foremost man, bald, with a skin like the shine of metal. He was Aubrey Holliday, the Governor's man, and by George he'd let them know it. 'I happen to be— we happen to be,' he said above the sloping plateau of his paunch, 'the Governor's representatives.'

'Aubrey, Aubrey . . .' chided the younger man, Cummings.

'This is a serious offence,' Holliday informed his captors, 'and I shall most certainly take steps.'

'Pull your pockets out,' Gardiner told him.

'Aye, well you're a bit late, lad,' said the horseman, heavy with accent. 'We've just been blooming well done.'

'Come on, don't give us that.'

'We've been done, I tell you, not more'n an hour ago. Some bleedin' lout with a gammy leg, he done us, took the lot. You can have my pockets, lad. You can have the lining.' And he pulled his empty pockets out.

'Don't waste your time, Thatcher. Do not converse with them,' Holliday said.

Gardiner looked at Piesley. He didn't know what to believe.

'Is that right, missus?' he asked of the woman in the coach. She wouldn't answer.

'Ma'am,' said Gardiner, removing his hat, 'I'm addressing you. Is it right that you've been robbed?'

'Yes, it is,' she said.

'Jumpin' Jimmy!' Gardiner cursed himself. 'What a way to start!'

'Now will you please remove yourselves,' Holliday commanded, 'and leave us to resume our journey?'

Gardiner scrubbed his beard. Something wrong here, he thought, the smell of money somewhere. Everything too neat and tidy, everyone balanced on the edge.

He dismounted and approached the anxious men. He could smell the anxiety, and see the little shift of Holliday's eyes.

'Aw, come on,' Piesley said, 'let's go.'

'No, wait a bit,' he said.

Holliday was like an animal lying doggo, pretending death. Then suddenly the Governor's man with an angry flourish pulled his coat apart to the ruby red of the lining. 'Look! Now do you believe it – no watch, no wallet, nothing!'

'Aubrey, Aubrey . . .' Cummings bleated.

Gardiner stood back and balanced his beard on his fist. 'I reckon you'd be a seasoned traveller, sir . . .' He saw the glances of the men. Somewhere in the forest a dead branch fell, and there was the departing thump of an animal, a wallaby, perhaps. 'Why don't you take your coat off?' he said. 'And your vest?'

'If you lay so much as a hand on me . . .'

'Why don't you do that?' Gardiner said, with the gun in the folds of the fellow's chin.

'This is an outrage,' Holliday said, beginning to disrobe.

'I hope so,' Gardiner told him. 'And you,' he said, moving the gun to Cummings, 'you're in this. Not you,' he told Thatcher. 'I know who has the money.'

'There is no money,' Holliday protested. 'We're cleaned out. We told you.'

'Get it off,' Gardiner said.

Holliday began to peel off his coat with infinite care. He knew what he was about. He needed time. There'd been a fifth man they didn't know about, a young fellow, a smithie's apprentice riding with the driver – and he had gone to report the first robbery. With any luck they'd send some men to scour the road.

'A bit faster,' Gardiner told him. 'You make me nervous. It's

31

the first time I've done this sort of thing.'

The two men took their coats off. A soft wind came up from the plain, a warm, caressing wind. Piesley's horse shifted. He looked at Gardiner. 'Whyn't we leave it?' he said. 'Before there's real trouble?'

'Go through the coats,' Gardiner said. 'Especially the lining.'

'There isn't time for this.'

'Do it.' Then Gardiner turned to Thatcher. 'Who was the man that done you in the first place?'

'That was the one we know as Happy Jack.'

Gardiner nodded. He knew Happy Jack the Sailor, and how he worked. He was a lightning thief, a twenty-second man only lifting what he could see. Not thorough. 'You, there,' he called to the driver, 'unpack the load and throw it down.'

Piesley choked back his feelings and allowed the single lament. 'There isn't time!'

'Ma'am,' said Gardiner, going to the window, 'how much would you be wanting for that brooch?'

'Don't touch me,' she whispered.

'I won't,' he said, 'I want to do a deal with you.'

The boxes, bags, and hold-alls began to thump down on the road. 'Open 'em,' Gardiner said to Piesley across his shoulder.

Piesley dismounted. It was like a nightmare. He couldn't believe it. No one took their time on a job like this; you wouldn't last five minutes. He pulled at the straps and ripped open the bags. The twine was tied in multiple knots. He couldn't break the twine. 'Gimme a knife,' he said to no one in particular.

Holliday glanced at Cummings. They were standing in little more than breeches and boots, a pitiful sight. The big wind came roaring up the road with yellow dust and leaves and branchlets raining down, and Holliday saw his brocaded silk ripping through the dirt with gloves and hat behind.

'Would you take five pounds?' Gardiner was saying to the woman. He didn't have five pounds, but at least it was an offer. 'It's for a lady,' he said. 'It's for someone special.'

'Frank,' said Piesley, moving close to Gardiner, 'you don't

understand. We have to get out of here. Every second we stay here—'

The wind tore at the trees about them, out of an empty sky. Only the coachman from his vantage point could see the approaching troopers, two of them, riding from the Clanville loop. He said nothing, and clenched his teeth against the knowledge, and felt for the gun that was tucked behind the seat.

'May we now be allowed to dress?' Holliday inquired ponderously.

'Turn around,' Gardiner said.

'I will not,' Holliday replied.

Gardiner seized him and sent him smashing into the coach with such a force that it rocked the springs.

'Oh my God!' Cummings breathed, shaken by the tremors he could no longer suppress. He was in a drench of fear for the sanctity of his skin, and shamefully moist at the crutch of his breeches. 'God help me,' he prayed. 'Do not let them make a fool of me.' And he saw the dark, bearded man at Holliday's back, and the flash of the knife. Cummings began to pass into a faint, then the wind struck him, and he merely staggered.

Gardiner looked back at him. 'I won't hurt him,' he said with a grin. And to Piesley, 'Get that stuff together.'

Piesley began to gather the takings, the cigar case, the boxed Havanas, the silver snuff-box. Then, 'Hey,' he said in sudden excitement, 'I got me some gold!' There was, indeed, a little chamois bag of gold.

'I'm not doing so bad myself,' Gardiner said, and the knife sliced through the stuff of Holliday's undervest – and there was the back pouch that Happy Jack the Sailor hadn't found. 'Sorry about your clothing,' Gardiner said.

By now Piesley was stuffing the saddle-bags with further treasure – the Webster duelling pistols, the silver inlay humidor, the Italian silk cravats. Quite a haul, he thought. He began to see the point.

'Now, listen,' Gardiner said to the woman in the coach, 'I'll give you seven quid.'

She shrank back from his undoubted malevolence.

'Ten. I'll give you ten.'

She began to fumble with the brooch, a floret of pearls and filigree gold, as Gardiner rifled Holliday's wallet for a ten pound note.

Piesley nudged him in the back. 'Better go,' he said.

'I'm going.' He took the brooch and put it in his pocket. 'Much obliged,' he said.

He walked back to Piesley, back towards the horses.

'We picked up nearly two hundred quid,' Piesley said, almost unable to believe it.

Gardiner looked back at the havoc they'd created. The dishevelled men, Holliday's undershirt flapping in the wind, his dimpled back naked to the sun, and all along the road a litter of worldly goods, the small things that amuse monied men, and the books and papers they put their faith in.

'Listen,' he said, turning back from the horse, and particularly to Holliday, 'if anyone is interested, tell 'em Frank Gardiner did it.'

Piesley was stunned. 'What did you tell 'em that for?'

'Because I done it.' And he put his boot to the stirrup.

The ball slammed into the saddle-blanket, then he heard the shot. The blanket ripped away as though a fist had bundled it, and he heard Holliday shout, 'Get down, get down!'

And, God help them, they were under fire.

'I told you!' Piesley said, and the second shot shaved his hair and he tangled with his own foot and hit the road.

The troopers were pulling their pistols, two apiece, and Piesley, halfway on his back, saw the coachman draw the gun, an ancient double-barrelled fowling-piece. And Piesley didn't even think about it; he cocked and fired the horse-pistol, the gun bucking in his hand, and he saw the coachman's shoulder open up, the cloth and flesh peeling back, and the second shot mashed his face, and he was gone, flailing backwards.

'I done him!' he yelled.

Then a bullet whipped into the road, inches from his boot and he rolled under the coach, and there was Frank, nursing the Colt revolver.

'Three more shots,' Gardiner said.

'What?' said Piesley.

'They got three more. Two,' he amended, as a bullet whined off the metal of the undercarriage.

'What are you waiting for?' Piesley struggled with the guns in his belt.

Gardiner put his hand on him. 'Get careful,' he said. And stuck his hat out and drew the remaining shots. He put his face to the wind and there were the troopers back some way, loading like the very devil. And he didn't know them, didn't want to, not their past, or how they looked, or who they were. They were just redcoats, lobster tails.

'Shake it up,' he called. 'I like to do it fair.'

And he didn't fire until he saw the flash, one, two, almost simultaneous, but he put in them a ball apiece with every reasonable care, placing the shots decent about the heart so that it was quick and clean. He heard the woman wailing, he thought, as they went down, and they went down very well, one like a cornsack dropping slow, and the other spilling over frontways with a terrible crack of his face on a rock.

Gardiner put his gun back in his belt and mounted his horse.

'That was murder,' Holliday said in something less than a whisper.

'That was for Cockatoo,' Gardiner said. 'I did it fair. You can't say less.'

'I think we better go, Frank,' Piesley said with a kind of deference.

'I'm going,' Gardiner said.

They rode out, back the way they'd come. Gardiner was silent, thoughtful. His technique was good, but much too slow. He'd have to work on it.

Anyway, he'd got the brooch, that was the main thing. He'd got something for Kate. He hoped she would like it.

## Five

Pottinger's dilemma was exactly to the measure of three and sevenpence. It was all he had until twenty-seven days had passed, till his annuity arrived. He could get drunk, he thought, or find a game of cards. Drunk, he thought, that was the thing, and he carefully set aside a sixpenny piece for a place to doss.

'Rum,' he ordered from Paddy Whelan, the innkeeper of the Irish Tavern. 'A double rum.'

Well, here he was, down on his uppers again. The going would be rough until the remittance arrived, but he supposed he could last the distance.

'Two troopers and a coachman,' a man was saying at the bar. 'All shot dead. Frankie Gardiner done 'em.'

'Gardiner wouldn't do a thing like that.'

'He done 'em. He said so.'

Pottinger tasted the rum. It was raw as a boot.

'Was you there, sir? Was you on the coach, one o' the gents on the coach that Gardiner done?'

He looked at the man at his elbow, a wizened shrimp of a querulous man. 'No, sir, I was not.'

'No,' the fellow echoed to his mates, 'Ay was not.'

They mocked his accent. They always did. He got up and walked outside into the inclement night.

The town of Ironbark was in a gloom of darkness and the wind had scarcely abated. There was the random wink of light and the screech of a swinging sign, and ... nothing. Where in God's name am I? he asked. And he tried to imagine the unimaginable, tried to place himself, to find the *raison d'être*, among this cluster of men and women in this abandoned landscape hundreds, thousands of miles from anyplace, stuck like gnats on a spinning globe, in the night, in the darkness, in the wind.

'Sit down,' said a voice behind him. 'It's sheltered here.'

He turned to see Sergeant Canning in the alcove, behind a thresh of leaves.

'A solitary drinker?' Pottinger said, accepting the offer.

'My office makes of me a public man,' the Sergeant said. 'If I drink at the bar, they're at me like a pack of bees.'

'I should have thought you'd do your drinking in the parlour,' Pottinger lightly chided.

'My wife does not approve of my single vice.'

Pottinger shifted uncomfortably. The man is in his cups, he thought, or given to self-castigation. In point of fact it was neither. In all the world, Sergeant Canning had no one to talk to. They used to talk – he and Bess – before the children died. Now they didn't.

The two men were silent, drinking as the wind worried at the peppercorn tree by the stables. Beyond the stables were the Travellers' Rooms – rather more de luxe than the Tavern itself – where, as Canning well knew, Holliday and Cummings were sound asleep.

More to change the drift of conversation, Pottinger asked, 'When will I get my money back?' He was thinking of his encounter with 'Onepot' Wally Higgins, the dead man with the hatpin in his throat.

'In due course,' Canning said. 'After declaration.'

'I've already declared.'

'There's some dispute,' the Sergeant confessed. 'Dr Hudson asserts that the five pound note was his.'

'That isn't true.'

'That, sir, is the nub of the dispute.'

'And what will be the outcome?'

'I imagine,' said Canning wearily, 'that Bathurst will arbitrate. Or Mrs Considine will recollect the sad event.'

Pottinger sighed. He was a man accustomed to the stubborn turn of fate, a bit of a philosopher.

'Until that happens,' Canning went on, 'until such time, you may have to draw on your banking funds.'

'Yes, quite,' Pottinger said.

There was a sudden roar of laughter and carousing from within the Tavern. Then the wind came up again and whipped the voices away with a cloud of dust, and the dust smelled of a desert far away, and burnt grassland.

'Can I buy you a drink?' Pottinger asked with the grace of the stony-broke.

'A diabolical day!' Canning said in an unexpected outburst. 'Three men dead.'

'Four,' Pottinger corrected.

'And Gardiner did it,' Canning went on, not even hearing his companion. He was still chafing from an hour with Aubrey Holliday, who had somehow brought him within the aura of blame. 'A ticket-of-leave man,' Canning lamented. 'Standing in my office. "What will you do?" I asked. "Work," he said, "at butchering." A proper turn of phrase, I must say!'

'I'm surprised you're not in pursuit.'

'The deed was done in Clanville. Not my Division.'

Pottinger laughed. 'The luck of the game.'

'But it will be my Division,' the Sergeant added with venom. 'Gardiner's a dog that dirties down the yard, and comes back to wipe his tail on the carpet.'

'Really?' said Pottinger, somewhat turned off by the metaphor.

'He'll come back,' Canning explained. 'He'll come back to Winooka Valley where his friends are. And I'll be expected to make the arrest.'

'To your credit, no doubt.'

The Sergeant gave the bitterest laugh. 'I doubt I can do it single-handed. I shouldn't say this,' he said; 'I wouldn't wish to make it public . . .' And he looked at the gaunt man in the dark, the stranger – could he trust this man? But the night lent itself. 'I shouldn't say it, but the Valley – Gardiner's Valley – is like a . . . like a . . .' He threw up his hands. 'We're out-numbered ten, twenty, fifty men to one.'

'Oh, come now. You're the law.'

'My men will desert,' he said bleakly, 'rather than go down the Valley. They'll be jumping the wall right this minute.'

'Desert?' Pottinger repeated, for it seemed to him an enormity.

'How long have you been out here?' Canning asked.

'Two, three years.'

'The rules do not apply.'

'The rules of the military are universal.'

'The rules do not apply.'

'I'd shoot a deserter,' Pottinger said.

Canning laughed. 'If you find him. And where do you find him? On the goldfields, yes, but where? The earth absorbs them, no one talks.'

Pottinger turned at a tiny, chipping sound beside him. The Sergeant was gnawing on his thumbnail.

'I believe I shall retire,' Pottinger said, rising, but really to escape the man.

'Join me in another one,' Canning said.

'Another time.'

Canning also rose. 'I've talked too much,' he admitted. 'Said things . . .'

Pottinger reassured him and bade him goodnight. Canning looked at the stillness of the Travellers' Rooms in the wind. Aubrey Holliday would make a deal of fuss for him, and the matter was already a good, stiff brew of controversy. 'I tell you, lad,' Thatcher, the horse-dealer had said, siding with Gardiner, 'he shot 'em down in self-defence. They opened fire without a word of warning, an' I'll testify!'

Damnation, Canning groaned as he started home for Bess.

Pottinger slept that night huddled to the wall of the Irish Tavern, slept on the floor in a scrap of blanket, wedged between two drunken diggers with the creep of mites upon his skin. All night another vagrant in the loft muttered in his sleep. The wind thundered in the roof and the dust rained down. Just before dawn someone, it seemed, strangled a dog – or that was the way it sounded – and he couldn't tell if it was dream or real.

In the morning, there was nothing to eat, and there was nothing ahead but an infinity of brassy days like this one. He splashed himself with water and took a stroll about the town. At half past seven, which seemed more than a reasonable hour, he presented himself at the barracks.

No one responded to his knock. He placed a finger to the door and the door creaked open on its hinges. A draught awoke along the corridor and puffballs of dust rolled up to meet him. He looked in on the desolation of the office – like a tomb waiting for the bier – with the hessian rolled down against the windows, and a spread of papers on the desk and 'Wanted' posters on the wall. John 'Blackie' Taylor, Thomas Sinclair, Shipton, Gilbert, Hodge – he read the names, all bushrangers, a great spill of ugly deeds between them.

He clasped his hands behind his back and strolled out into the welcome sunlight of the yard enclosed by walls. It was totally deserted, as though some calamity had struck, and littered by evidence of uncompleted chores – bits and pieces of carts and harness, wagon wheels, a broken shaft, a skeletal construction of bush poles and canvas, and everywhere the weeds growing, the rank grass climbing up the wall.

Eventually a couple of troopers in regimental disarray crawled out of the shabby quarters and made their way to the cookhouse. There was now a veil of smoke from the chimney, and the clash of pans within. Others shortly followed. A corporal with his tunic hanging loose was apparently rousing the men. Pottinger dimly wondered what had become of reveille, of the bugler and early morning parade – but even the flagpole, that great token of Colonial pride, was as naked as a stick.

No one took the slightest notice of him. He could have been invisible. He crossed to the stables and examined the mounts – not bad, not bad at all, he thought – and crossed back to the blockhouse, the street side again.

In the parade-ground a trooper was running up the flag. He was coatless, hatless, a disgrace. 'Is there no parade?' Pottinger asked, astonished.

The shabby fellow looked at him. 'When the Sergeant comes,' he said.

Pottinger turned abruptly back into the corridor, and there

was Sergeant Canning coming from the street, breathless, un-shaven.

'Pottinger!' he said, not displeased. 'How long have I kept you?' And immediately he turned into the office, fussing about, letting the light in, setting down his lunch, the hardboiled eggs and week-old bread. Then remembering the business that must be to hand, he declared apologetically, 'There is nothing, noth-ing, that I can do about the money, about your five pound note until ... until...' he tailed off lamely, because now, dammit, he couldn't find the paper, the report, the statements, anything.

'I was of the mind,' Pottinger said gently, 'to pitch in my lot with the troopers.'

'To do what?' said Canning, expecting a further problem.

'To enlist,' Pottinger said.

Sergeant Canning looked at him. 'Here? With me?'

'If I'm eligible.'

Canning laughed. 'Eligible!' And came across the room to seize Pottinger by the hand. 'The word, sir, is not "eligible", but welcome – welcome, Mr Pottinger!'

'I said I was of the mind.'

'Was?' And his eyes, which were of a peculiar milky blue, looked into Pottinger's as though asking for forgiveness or compassion. 'Enlist,' he all but implored. 'Let us make a go of it.'

Pottinger considered. He permitted himself a smile. 'Why not?' he said.

'Good. Excellent. We can make good use of you.' As indeed, he would, with at least one man presentable for the likes of Aubrey Holliday. And then, by God, he could build a force about this man, something to be proud of, the way it used to be.

'What rank would you have in mind for me?' Pottinger asked.

'Rank?' said Canning, rising. 'With a man of your experi-ence,' he said, taking the matter for granted, 'I should very well think — Well, let's put it this way – you'll be a corporal before the month is out. You'll be a trooper for the start – rules are rules, you know – but before the month is out...'

'From what moment do I serve?' Pottinger said.

'Now. This very minute. You simply sign the paper. Can you write?' he asked with a limping essay into humour.

'Where is the paper?'

Canning found the paper, and Pottinger signed. 'Sir?' he said to his commander.

Canning laughed. 'You're a stickler for formality, I can see that.'

'Could I have my orders, please?'

'Oh, come now...'

Something congealed between them, and some of the milk departed from the Sergeant's eyes. 'Are you a horseman?' he asked.

'It has been alleged.'

'Can you use a gun?'

'Naturally.'

Sergeant Canning turned to the window, to the wakening street, the shutters going up, the drift of diggers and vagabonds. 'Report to Corporal Lovatt,' he commanded. 'The Corporal will rig you out with uniform and arms. At the hour of ten' – consulting his watch – 'you will proceed under my command on your first patrol to Winooka Valley – there to apprehend the felon, Frank Gardiner.'


## Six

Sergeant Canning was correct – Frank Gardiner was in Winooka Valley and Johnny Piesley was with him. They were not only in the Valley, but in Walsh's house, at table, and Mrs Walsh was pouring coffee for her 'boys', as she thought of them though there was no kin and likely never would be now that Kate had married.

'So anyway,' Gardiner said, mopping up the bacon fat, 'I shot 'em. They asked for it, and I shot 'em.'

'By golly!' Walsh said, slapping his side, he was richly amused, 'you shot 'em!'

'Yeah, I said so.'

'The three of 'em?'

'Yeah, that's what I said.'

Mrs Walsh turned back from the stove. 'They wasn't rabbits,' she said; 'they was men.'

'No,' Gardiner said, 'they weren't men; they were troopers.'

'Right!' said Walsh. 'Troopers isn't men.'

'You fellers should read the Commandments,' Mrs Walsh said, and hefted the stewpot on to the stove. It had to cook slowly and it had to feed all comers. She was a small, spare woman shrunk to the bone, not much more than five feet of her, with quick, bright eyes as blue as lightning, matching her man's; but in John Walsh the eyes had not forgotten laughter, and he was taller, tougher, though only by an inch or two. They were quite a pair, these two, having melded to each other through the years, like a pair of Irish mannikins packaged in a splintwood house.

'What did you shoot 'em with?' Walsh asked, avid for the details.

Piesley pushed his tin plate aside with enough force to send it skittering. 'He didn't do 'em all,' he asserted. 'I did the coach-man. I did the first.'

'I never said you didn't,' Gardiner said.

'You never said I did.'

'I said we shot the three; that's what I said.'

It wasn't what he'd said, Piesley knew, but you couldn't win an argument with Gardiner.

'We better push on,' Gardiner said, getting up. 'We don't want to bring you any trouble.'

'Trouble!' said Walsh with a laugh. 'You're the only speck o' sunlight the Valley's seen in five long years. You never bring us trouble, Frank.'

Mrs Walsh gave him a look. 'No. Just three dead men, that's what he brought.'

'Two,' said Piesley. 'I did one.'

'Oh, Frank,' she said, in a despairing way. 'Oh Frankie!'

He went across and put his arms about her. She was just a tiny thing against him. 'What's there to fuss about?' he said. 'We never harmed no innocent men, now, did we? We only done the troopers. We only paid 'em back.'

'You killed 'em,' she said.

'I think you got a short memory,' he said.

But she remembered all right – remembered coming all this way, all those years ago in a creaky convict ship tossing like a splinter in a tub, and the whole world turned into ocean when the deepest water she'd ever seen before was in the village pond. Oh yes, she remembered, and a good deal more than that.

'You're still my sweetheart,' he said, putting his lips to her forehead.

'Oh, get off with you,' she said. 'You'd charm the pebbles in a field.'

'Johnny . . .' Gardiner said, and they both moved up to the door.

'Where are you staying?' Walsh asked.

'Up in the caves.'

'You got plenty to eat?'

'We got enough.'

They went outside, and Piesley went to fetch the horses from the yard. Gardiner lit his cigar and leaned against the bush rail of the verandah. He was looking out across the land that Walsh had claimed as his own – not good land, but land with rocks and stubborn timber in it, with a creek that dried in the heat of summer. Good land was at the further end, where the legal settlers were.

Walsh had been there a good long time and the land was a graveyard of dead intentions – the abandoned plough, the tipsy fences, the pig-run that the pigs had broken out of. Walsh was getting too old for it; he hadn't the heart for it. They'd cut the heart out of him on the flogging stand all of forty years ago; he'd been transported for the terrible crime of grubbing for food to save his life. It was something you had to teach an Irishman, that death was preferable.

'No rain,' said Walsh behind him.

'But it's going to. I feel it in my gun.'

'You're a devil, Frank,' Walsh laughed.

'I'm just an apprentice.'

Gardiner was looking at the little hut that stood across the way. The old man had had three daughters and he liked to keep them by. All married now – Kate and Helen and Biddy – they lived within the quarter-mile, and Kate, who'd married last, had stayed the closest.

'Is she in there?' Gardiner asked.

'Lend me your flintbox,' Walsh said, pushing a thumb in his pipe.

'Is she?'

'Frank . . .'

'John,' he said to Walsh, 'I've never been nothing but straight with you, you know that. And I can't help it, can I, if they stuck me down on Cockatoo? But I'd be the biggest liar in Winooka if I looked you in the eye and said I was done with her.'

'That don't make it any better,' Walsh said.

'Where's the husband? Where's Roy?'

'You better listen to me, Frank . . .' Walsh said.

Just then Piesley came up with the horses.

'Leave mine,' Gardiner said. 'You go on up to the cave.'

'Yeah, but hold on, Frank —'

'Do it. Don't make a speech about it.'

'I thought we was together,' Piesley lamented as he hitched Gardiner's horse.

'I got some business here,' Gardiner explained.

Both men watched as Piesley rode off with a heavy slump to his shoulders, his head nodding along. There was a blue smoke haze across the Valley, and that stillness in the air again. Both men momentarily gazed across. It was a stillness they knew about, the one before the hell of fire breaks loose.

'What I want to tell you,' Walsh said, 'is that me and Ma

45

talked about it, about you and Kate – and the only trouble we don't want, Frank, is that kind of trouble.'

'Where is she, John?'

'Best you forget about Kate.'

'That's an order, is it?'

Walsh banged his fist on the rail and a sprinkle of pipe-ash spilled across his hand. 'Dammit, Frank what're you trying to make me say? You're like my own given son. I don't want bad blood between us.'

'It's her, isn't it? It's Ma. She's complaining.'

'No, it's me. I might live here with four damn' women running me life and washing me socks, but I make my own decisions.'

'You're a liar, John.'

'You're a damned insulting bastard.'

Gardiner put a hand on the old man's back. 'You might have been a good many things, but, first thing always, you were a man. You know how it is with Kate and me.'

Walsh sighed and turned away for inspiration from the heavens. There was a spread of distant fleece against the blue down south, but close above them, spreading, the bruise-coloured smoke of a big, and unstoppable burn, and he thought he might remember what Ma had said last night that had sounded so right and proper and true. 'The fact is . . .' he began, but Gardiner was halfway across to the little hut, with the hens clucking off in all directions.

'Did you tell him?' Mrs Walsh said, coming to the door.

'Yes, I told him.'

Gardiner pushed against the door of the hut, and the door thumped against the bolt within. He knocked. 'Kate,' he called, 'Kate?'

He heard the bolt slide back and a pair of eyes appeared in the crack. 'She's not here,' Roy Foster said.

'Where is she?'

'She went into Ironbark.'

Roy started to close the door and Gardiner put his weight against it. Then both men were in the room. Roy was in his longjohns. 'What the hell?' Gardiner said. 'What time do you get going?'

'I got the grippe,' Roy said, sitting back on the screw of blankets he'd come from. 'I'm feeling poorly.'

'You stay there long enough, you'll likely fry in bed. The Western ridge is cooking up a treat.'

Gardiner looked at him – the man, or boy, who shared Kate's bed. He couldn't have been more than twenty-one or -two, and there was a kind of soft innocence about him with his soft, sandy hair and the dimpled chin. Gardiner said, 'Where the hell did she find you?'

'I did my own finding,' Roy said.

Gardiner pulled a chair out from the table and sat on it wrong way round. 'Tell me about it.'

Roy leaned back against the rough timbers, his face looking pale and the pimples showing. 'I got nothing to say to you.'

'I asked you a question.'

'I was working as a stockman down Pretty Gully way, down with the Dutchmen, with the Ouds. And I came up with Pieter Oud for the muster, to sort the strays and help with the branding. And anyway,' he said, thinking back a year or two, the way it was, the way it happened, 'anyway, I stayed.'

'My God,' Frank Gardiner said, shaking his head. 'And now you got the grippe?'

'I got something.'

Gardiner got up and put his hand against the young man's forehead. 'I don't think you got the grippe at all,' he said. 'I think you got the yellow fever – yellow in the gut. Is that right, Roy, is that what you got?'

Roy clamped his jaws like a child would, and gazed at the ashes of the fireplace and the big black kettle on the grate.

'You knew she was mine, didn't you, Roy?'

'I knew you were gone ten years for stealing horses.'

'And what did you think – that they'd do for me down on the Rock?'

'Ten years is for ever.'

Gardiner looked around the hut. They lived simply, and not

too tidily. There was her night-shift lying back across a chair, and there were burn-holes in it, old, undarned.

'The thing is, Roy, when something's mine...' He looked at the young man's face, pale against the timbers. 'I want to be real clear about this,' he said. 'You see this flintbox? I had it for a long, long time. When I went down to Cockatoo, I left it in Carcoar, with my things. When I got back a week ago, there it was, sitting winking up at me. Wouldn't you expect the same?'

'You got no right to Kate,' Roy burst out unexpectedly. 'You got no claim.'

Gardiner sat on the end of the bed. 'I'm glad to hear your side of it, Roy.'

'We're churched and married proper. She gave her word and ... and it was blessed,' he said. 'You got no right to say these things.'

'You want to fight me, Roy?'

'No, why the hell should I be fighting you?'

''Cause that's the way I feel. Can you use a gun at all?' Gardiner took out the Colt Navy gun and began to examine the chambers. 'Do you recognise this gun?'

'No.'

'Thought you might, that's all ... Where is she, Roy?'

'You better ask her Mum and Dad.'

'Don't tell me they're telling you what to do already, Roy?' he said, easing back the hammer with a gentle, caressing motion. 'You know this gun's been blooded?'

'Yeah, I heard about that.'

'Do you think I'd shoot a sick man in his bed?'

'I think you might.'

'Think I'd shoot you?'

'I don't think you'd have the guts,' Roy said after a pause.

Gardiner looked at him, at the hard, bright gleam of stubbornness behind the silky-lashed eyes. He laughed. 'I'm beginning to think you've got something going for you,' he said. 'So I'll tell you what I'll do. I'll just rest the gun on the footpiece here, and I'll just blow your big toe off.'

Roy swallowed. 'All right,' he said quietly.

'I mean to do it, Roy.'

'You better aim damn' straight,' Roy told him, 'or I'll likely lose my manhood.' But the sweat was breaking out.

'Yeah, I was kind of hoping for a ricochet.'

'Why don't you get it over with?'

'You don't think I'll do it, do you?'

'I suppose I'll soon find out.'

'And I won't do it,' Gardiner said, 'if you tell me where to find her.'

'Damned if I will.'

'You'd be the stupidest man I ever met,' Gardiner told him as his finger began to pull back on the trigger, and Roy Foster watched transfixed, watching the skin of Gardiner's trigger finger whitening with the pressure.

'Jesus God,' he gasped, 'what kind of man are you?'

'Damn,' said Gardiner. 'You broke my concentration.'

Roy Foster watched the round black mouth of the gun sighting up again, and he could almost see the bullet in it, then he gave a strangled yelp and plunged himself beneath the blankets and Gardiner heard him cry out, muffled, 'Just leave me alone!' He just got up and put his boot against the rump and said, 'Get out of there.'

Roy looked up, his stricken eyes just above the blankets, a real, true fever on him now.

'Where is she?' Gardiner said again. And he heard for the first time in the silence the distant pop and dull explosions of the bushfire, getting closer.

'I'm wasting my time with you. There could be a swarm of troopers waiting for me.' He put the gun right up hard where Roy could see it cross-eyed. 'Now tell me,' he said.

'She ... she's with her sister,' Roy burst out. 'She's with Helen.'

Gardiner stuck the gun back in his belt. 'You're damn lucky you still got two big toes,' he said, and he opened the door and he was gone, riding hard across the rise to Helen's place, to Jack McGuire's, a decent man, the father of two bright-eyed kids.

49

And the wind was coming up again, and it was rolling up the Valley, across the miles of scrub and forest, bringing with it not only the dust but the dense blue smoke, sweet with the tang of burning. Far off, from where the big burn was, nesting down behind the furthest ridge, came the furnace crackle of the blaze, like pistol shots, and now and then the dull thump of exploding trees. It could wipe them out if it got away.

'What do you reckon?' McGuire said, as Gardiner dismounted and moved across the yard.

'Be at the ridge in twenty minutes,' Gardiner said.

Both men stood watching the smoke-pall. Then the sun disappeared and the light became a kind of smoulder in itself. Pieces of charred bracken blew in about them, falling like snowflakes, black.

Ben Hall, Biddy's husband, rode in with Billy Dargin, the aboriginal. Hall was a tall, loose-limbed, mahogany sort of man, a horseman, his movements graceful, pared down and thought out. He wore a twist-tied shirt and ragged pants and gap-mouthed boots, and he was drenched from the sweat of work. He looked around, and took it in. There was a gradual drift of people brought together by the threat. And Helen came out of the house, the children gathered about her. 'I reckon we should damn' well run,' she said. 'We'll burn.'

The men conferred. 'What do you reckon, Billy?' McGuire asked. They always looked to Dargin in matters like these. He knew the land and its ways. It was a blood thing, they understood this, though he'd been brought up Christian and was more Christian than any one of them.

'We got about an hour,' he said, 'unless the wind changes.'

'Are we moving out, Jack?' Helen asked.

'Are we?' McGuire deferred to Billy Dargin.

'Damned if I know,' Dargin said, pushing back his hat, and worrying at the shock of shaggy hair.

'Better pray, Billy,' Gardiner said. 'Make it a double – one black and one white.'

Ben Hall laughed. Biddy came up and put her arm through his. 'Bettern't we go and fetch Pa?' she said.

'We're thinking about it,' Ben said. But he didn't tell her how bad it was. He didn't have to. Already, way off past her shoulder, he could see the flight of animals, one big red-feller kangaroo leaping wild, alight.

They all stood there in the wind, the women's hair streaming, watching this dun-coloured immensity of smoke and conflagration reaching out across the Valley. The truth was there was no good place to run to. The fire could move faster than a horse's gallop, and it was as skittish as a woman.

'While you're watching it cook,' Gardiner said, 'I'll go and get a drink.' No one heard him. He walked fast to the house where Kate would be, fast because the fire could cut him off from the caves, and he didn't care to be pinned down in case the troopers came.

'Kate!' he called. He saw Helen looking back at him; it was some damned family conspiracy, he thought. 'Kate, come on out.'

He heard the shift and trampling of horses from the shelter, and there she was looking at him, watching through the haze of smoke, her hair twined with sweat, face glossed, shirt unbuttoned and belly all but bare from the drift of her skirt.

'Who told you I was here?' she said.

'Your useless husband. What the hell is this about?' he said. 'What are you hiding for?'

'I'm not hiding, I'm visiting.'

'My God,' he said, exaggerating, 'I've spent half the day looking for you. First time, yesterday, I couldn't get clear of you, what have I done?'

'You killed two men,' she said. 'You and Johnny Piesley.'

'Three,' he said.

'That was a real good start, Frank.'

'So that's what it's about,' he said.

'No, it isn't!' she said with a high old flare of anger. 'No, it damn' well isn't.'

'Well, what is it, then?'

She turned away. 'You wouldn't understand.'

'Kate...' he said, taking her by the shoulder. 'Look,' he said,

'I brought you something. I didn't even snitch it. I bought it legal, special for you. Well, look at it, dammit. I didn't come all this way for nothing, did I?' And he gave her the pearl and filigree brooch.

'You bought it?' she said.

'I paid – I paid a lot of money for it.

Gently she placed the brooch to her lips – a fool of a thing to do, he thought. 'Thank you,' she whispered.

'She's away!' someone cried out from below, and Gardiner and Kate both turned to see the distant and topmost trees of the ridge ignite; it was a crown-fire, with the wind roaring at it, and the foliage was burning like molten gold draining down the slope. 'God help us,' Kate breathed. Then the length of the Valley was obscured by smoke; they were enfolded by it.

'I have to go,' Gardiner told her. 'Johnny's waiting for me in the caves.'

'I'm glad to see you, Frank,' she said.

He took her in his arms. Locked in the smoke, it was as though the rest of the world had blown away. 'I'll be back,' he told her.

She shook her head. 'No.'

'Are you scared of the law; is that what it is?'

'Damn the law,' she said.

'Is it your Ma, has she been at you, or Roy, or what?'

'It's the priest!' she burst out. 'I had to tell the priest. He come calling. And he heard me out. And I confessed, Frank, and I'm scared.'

'What of?' he said – but he knew. Priests and the promise of damnation were things he couldn't fight, and didn't understand. This, and the family, they'd claimed her – the immovable forces he'd never reckoned on.

'I love you,' she said, 'and that's a sin, that's a mortal sin.'

'I won't give up,' he told her, taking on that dark, satanic role assigned to him. He knew now he was committed, that, yes, he'd get together his two hundred quid or so, and he'd abduct her if he had to, and corrupt her if he had to; there was nothing and no one that could stop him. She had her Christ, and he had his temple – and she was the temple.

'You're not going to make it,' Billy Dargin told him as he mounted the horse.

'I'll outride it,' Gardiner said.

Ben came up. 'You can shelter back of my place.'

'No,' said Gardiner, with a clammy intuition on him, 'I've got bad feelings. I can smell a trooper in that fire.'

'They'll fry,' McGuire laughed.

He rode into the forest and the wind changed and the fire began to lap about him in a sudden, unnerving stillness before the big blow came. He rode downwind of where he reckoned the front would be, but no one could tell; you couldn't plot the path precisely. All he knew was that there was water in the gully, not much more than a splash of it, but water, and the horse knew it, nostrils flared at the smell of it and scarcely heeding the beckon of the rider. Nor was the sudden silence good; it was a tangible, threatening thing. The silence was part of the noonday twilight, the smoke fuming through the trees, and the little creep of fire behind him burning through the tinder of the forest floor.

He looked around him, the horse wanting to rear; he could feel the shiver in its flanks. 'Easy, boy,' he told the horse, reining in his own fear, afraid he might communicate it.

Then, all at once, the whole forest behind him peeled apart with a red-gutted roar of wind, the hot wind crashing down upon him and the flames fanning out with an orange incandescence, the flaming cinders streaming past. He heeled the horse and they went crashing down the slope, past the bracken sighing in the heat, the fringes curling and charring as they reached the flashpoint. They went pitching down towards the water lying like a pool of mercury in the sudden night of the burning forest. And he heard himself crying out encouragement, and then the topmost turpentines caught the blaze and a mighty blast of exploding heat scorched against him, and he felt the singe of his own hair as the horse stumbled, trumpeting with fear, and they both went down in water.

But water, dammit, wasn't the answer. This piddle of water

could boil a man alive. He got up, and the bloody horse was gone. 'Come back, blast you,' he yelled, and the fire was on him, his clothes alight, and he plunged himself in water and ran like hell upstream.

Now he had the horse again as the forest disintegrated behind him. The animal was trying to climb the rocks. He could see the burn marks raw on its back. He pulled his coat off, and the horse shouldered him head over heels, enough to break his bones. He came at it again. He could hear the clash of the hooves on the rock, the iron of the hooves striking sparks. A great, dead tree crashed down across the creek. Fountains of burning coals lit up the darkness. 'God damn you,' he said, as the hooves razored out across his face. And then he had the coat about its head, bundling the head, masking the eyes, and he wrestled the thing like a raging steer. I'm a thumping fool, he thought, to die for a horse.

He looked back, and he couldn't believe it. The fire was raging past the creek, across the other side. He wasn't that good a bushman – not in the Billy Dargin class – but he knew that if a man survived the firestorm, that two minutes of hell, he was standing in a burn-out, safe. And this was where he was, in the middle of a blackened landscape with the timber still popping around him, in a flaming colonnade of tree-trunks heavy with the fume of smoke.

He took the coat from the horse's head and cradled the head, offering comfort, murmuring, 'You great sook, you nearly killed us both.' They were standing in a forest pool of water, and it was hot as porridge and thick with ash and blackened debris. He began to examine where they were and the passage of the fire and the fading wind that drifted with it, and he thought with satisfaction: Kate's safe, she'll be all right. The fire was moving up along the Ironbark Passage, funneling through, as it quite often did, with a white-hot roar of intensity. Nothing there but the one road out, and heaven help the travellers on it.

'Good grief,' said a voice through the smoky haze, 'are you all right?'

Gardiner looked around. He couldn't see a thing except the blackened nightscape of the forest lit by stuttering flames and red-hot embers.

'Over here,' said the voice, and a rider appeared like a wraith through the smoke, the horse shying and plunging, but tightly controlled. 'According to the law of averages,' Trooper Pottinger said, dismounting, 'you should be done like a pig on a stick.' And he put his arm about the man, supporting him.

'I'm all right,' Gardiner said.

'If you don't mind my saying so, you look absolutely rotten. What the devil were you doing here?'

'I was lost. I lost my way.' And he put his hand up to his face to feel the sticky gum of blood from where the horse had slashed him, and the sickness rose and fell again. He was doubtless burned, but how badly he couldn't tell; the shock had numbed him. 'I'm all right,' he repeated.

Pottinger examined him, totting up the damage. 'I suppose you'll pass with a push,' he said. 'Are you far from help?'

Timber crashed behind them in the smouldering forest. Their eyes wept from the smoke, and Gardiner could feel the ash of his eyebrows. 'How come you missed the fire?' he asked the trooper.

'We were in the caves.'

'Oh,' said Gardiner. 'See anyone else up there?'

'Only Sergeant Canning.'

'I better go,' Gardiner said. 'People might be worried.'

'I'll lend you a hand.'

'Don't trouble. I can manage.'

Gardiner put his foot to the stirrup and the world wheeled over.

'Let me hoist you up,' Pottinger offered.

Gardiner shook his head to clear his focus. The pain was starting. 'Much obliged,' he said.

'Are you one of the Valley people?' Pottinger asked.

'You could say that.'

'Do you know Frank Gardiner? Have you seen him?'

'I've heard of him.'

'Been looking for him,' Pottinger said. 'Then the fire broke loose.'

'Could be anywhere by now,' Gardiner lamented. And as he eased the horse around, there was another, second redcoat moving through the trees. 'Changed my mind,' Gardiner said as he suddenly altered course.

'Here, have a care!' Pottinger cried, as the horse's head struck him and he stumbled.

'That's him!' Canning shouted.

Pottinger scrambled up, looking back.

'That's Gardiner.'

'Oh Lord!' Pottinger muttered, and even as he got his gun out, there was the sudden flail of hooves and he heard a sharp explosion and something slammed against his shoulder and he went toppling over, rolling, and a tree came up and smashed against him.

'Good God!' Sergeant Canning murmured. And, on the heels of that, 'You blundering fool,' he accused the stricken man.

He had just shot Trooper Pottinger.

## Seven

'Luckily, it's only a flesh wound,' Dr Hudson said with philosophic calm as Pottinger clamped down on the wooden peg between his teeth to stem the shriek of pain. 'We must cleanse the wound thoroughly,' the Doctor said, 'cleanse and scarify.'

The sweat poured off Pottinger. He was lying on a plain deal table covered by a filthy sheet – no less filthy than the Doctor's frock-coat, which was his badge of office. He lay there gazing at the ceiling of the Medical Hall. The ceiling was contrived of drooping calico with a panorama of ancient stains.

'If we do not scarify,' Hudson said, scraping away, grunting, sweating, 'we may live to regret it.'

Gangrene, Pottinger thought, in a fever of imaginings. It was 'only a flesh wound', that was a mercy, but Great God in heaven — 'No! Oh, no!' he cried out.

'Bite down,' Hudson said.

Pottinger gripped the bush timbers of the creaky bed.

'If you don't keep still,' Hudson said, 'the knife is bound to stray. Or do I have to strap you down?'

It's only a flesh wound. Pottinger instructed himself, but he'd seen the lacerations, the torn flesh, the passage of the ball ... He turned aside so as not to see the Doctor at his labours. There was a man, Tom Titmouse, grinning at him from his palliasse against the other wall. Tom had fallen down a mine shaft and they'd been forced to saw his leg off.

'You'll likely lose that arm,' Tom told him, 'once the rot sets in.'

The draught sucked in the canvas curtain to the street. Every so often the light stabbed in and there was the wink of the ochre road incised by the marks of carriage wheels, with puddles lying in between like a scatter of sovereigns.

'We shall now clean up,' Hudson said.

Pottinger removed the peg. It was almost bitten clean in half.

'What happened to the stiff upper lip?' Hudson asked.

But when he looked round, the patient was unconscious.

Pottinger revived at half past four in the afternoon to the sight of a pretty face.

'Miss Considine!' he said.

'Oh, you're awake.'

'Are you a part of this establishment?' he asked.

'I give my afternoons three days a week.'

'How splendid,' he said.

'Are you in any pain?' she asked solicitously.

'Oh, yes!' he said, and the pain repaid him for his trouble, and he subsided into fevered dreams again.

On the afternoon of the following day, Clara Considine returned.

'You really are a very pretty girl,' he said.

Clara coloured as she worked. She was cleaning the lamp and trimming the wick.

'Have you brothers and sisters?' he said.

'I have an older sister, Lettie.'

'Prettier than you?'

'Letty is short for Lelitia, not Letitia as most people think.'

'That would be Irish?'

'Papa is English. We grew up in England. He was a sailmaker. He employed four men.'

'Now he's a farmer?'

'Not a very good one,' she confided.

'Could you fetch me some water?' he asked.

She looked at him. 'I should have thought you were well enough to fetch it yourself.'

She brought the water to him. He took the cup in one hand and her wrist in the other.

'Please don't do that,' she said.

'You're built as fine as a bird,' he told her.

'Your behaviour is improper.'

She turned to her work again, assembling the lamp. Then suddenly looked at him, her eyes bright and direct. 'I think you should know that I'm spoken for. My young man, Michael Taylor, is not a dozen paces down the street.'

'Waiting in the rain?' he asked.

'He's a bank clerk for the Bank of New South Wales.'

'And are you betrothed?'

'That's entirely my affair,' she said.

But as the afternoon wore on and the rain poured down she sat with him in a mellower mood. Hudson was out sloshing through the mud somewhere, seeking a woman in labour, and could likely be trapped by the rising creek.

'I do so much miss England,' Clara said. 'I miss my friends, I miss the weather, I miss – oh, all kinds and manner of things …' She rose with a flounce to light the lantern, though it wasn't nearly time for it.

He got up, and when she turned, there he was behind her.

'Miss Clara …' he said, with a soft insinuating deference.

'What do you want?' she asked, retreating needlessly to the cupboard full of instruments.

'Must you dance about so much?' he said.

'What do you want?'

'Do stop cleaning and fussing,' he said, and took her hand and placed a kiss upon it.

'That was a disgusting thing to do,' she said, drawing back.

On the fifth day of his sojourn in the Medical Hall, he had a visit from Sergeant Canning. The room was now full of suffering men, two of them, one with dysentery, the other with a raging fever. 'I should like to return to duty, Sergeant,' Pottinger said. 'I'm quite certainly fit for all manner of things.'

But the Sergeant's eyes were full of a milky evasiveness. 'A few more days,' he said, 'would do you a power of good.'

'Good grief,' said Pottinger, vexed, 'men have fought in the battlefield with more than a blasted flesh wound.'

'Nevertheless —'

'I want to do my duty.'

'Shall we step outside?'

They went into the street. The sodden earth was steaming in the sun, and down past the General Store a wagon was bogged and several men were trying to hoist it out.

'You're a man of the world,' Canning said, with a peculiar sideways look.

'My solitary virtue,' Pottinger responded.

'I'm expecting a visit from Aubrey Holliday – who is the Governor's man – on the unfortunate business of the Gardiner affair.'

'I should think the Governor's man would have more on his hands than —'

'Frank Gardiner's been active on the roads. He's making a mock of my command. Three coaches, two wagons in less than a span of days.'

'A good score,' Pottinger said drily.

'But we ...' Canning said, leaning in, '... we could be held to blame.'

'On what grounds?'

'Why, for grief's sake, man, we let him slip through our fingers!'

And Pottinger began to wonder at the plural. *We* let him slip?

'We don't want,' Canning went on, 'a whole flock of awkward questions.'

'What kind of questions?'

Canning's hand went tenderly to Pottinger's arm, the one in the sling. It was a pathetic gesture. 'You're laid up, y'see? You're wounded. You're out of it.'

'I see,' said Pottinger.

And he saw with a particular clarity the interview he might have had — '*And Frank Gardiner shot you, Trooper Pottinger?*' — '*No, sir, it was Sergeant Canning shot me.*'

He looked at his conspiring Sergeant standing in the mud. The poor devil was contriving a false report in which the blame would be assigned to Gardiner; and he, Pottinger, for all he knew might emerge with a certain shine. 'I shall keep absolutely mum,' he said.

'Good chap,' Canning said with something perilously close to a wink.

'If you can grant me a certain absence?'

'A day or two, certainly. The lure and lights of Bathurst, eh?'

'Hunting,' said Pottinger, 'is more my métier.'

He did not say that the quarry was Clara Considine.


*Eight*

'What're we gonna do, Frank?'

'I don't know, feller.'

Piesley rolled over on his side. There they were, stuck on a rock on the top of a ridge like a pair of sunbaked lizards. It was the early part of afternoon, and they'd been there since noon.

'Have to do somethin',' Piesley said.

Gardiner looked at him through hooded eyes. 'What makes you say a thing like that?' He shifted the dead cigar from one side to the other. 'It's too hot. It isn't worth it.'

You could see right across the Plains from where they were, out into the deadland, desert country where periodically some damn' fool explorer went to find the place where death lived. And you could see the bruise of cloud way south of this, which would swell in a matter of hours into an afternoon storm. They'd had a run of storms since the fires went through. It was that time of year when a man couldn't move without the thought of weather.

'Just past two o'clock, Frank,' Piesley reminded him.

'Yeah?'

'So what're we gonna do?'

'I'll think about it.'

Piesley sighed loud enough to bend the twist of grass in front of him, and went back to flicking the ants away. They were coming at him in a column, and he kept flicking the leader, the scout off the edge of the rock.

'I'm a cruel bugger, ain't I?' he laughed.

Gardiner said, 'I see a wagon down there.'

Piesley scrambled up. 'Yeah,' he breathed. It was just an old wagon mooching along, but by God, it was something. 'We gonna do him, Frank?'

'No. I don't feel like it.'

Piesley hitched his guns in his belt. 'Well, I'm gonna do him.'

'Go ahead. I'll watch.'

'Frank! . . .' Piesley complained.

Gardiner shrugged. 'Enjoy yourself. I reckon you'd get all of half-a-dozen bags of flour, bit of treacle, maybe even spuds and rice. You could do real well, Johnny.'

Piesley subsided, 'I just want to do something, that's all.'

'Tell you what,' Gardiner said, leaning out and peering down, 'I'm going to follow the second feller.'

Maybe fifty yards behind was a horseman, dressed red as a beetle.

'That's a trooper, Frank.'

'Yeah. I know him.'

Piesley rubbed his eyes until they bulged. 'You know him? From here?' Hot damn, this man could see a gnat at fifty paces! 'Who is he?'

Gardiner got to his feet. 'The gentleman policeman. I wonder where he's going?'

Piesley trotted after Gardiner to the horses tethered to a banksia. 'You're going to follow a policeman?'

'Johnny,' Gardiner said patiently, 'you're getting the most terrible habit of repeating yourself. You think you could quit that?'

'I'm sorry, Frank.'

'Just thought I'd mention it.'

'How come you know a policeman?'

'I met him in a bushfire.'

'You met him in a bushfire?'

'Come on, feller,' Gardiner said. 'I think you got yourself some sunstroke.'

About fifteen minutes to three o'clock, Pottinger ran out of road. The bright vermilion just perished in the grass, twining into cartwheel tracks, the horse shying at a husk of snakeskin, headless. The sun smacked into his eyes, and the joggle of the ride pained his arm in the sling. Heaven help him, he thought, that he should ride to hell and back for the waggle of a woman's tail! Not that they'd come running in his former haunts, but it was usually no further than across the room. 'Move, move!' he said, heeling the horse. It was a rotten nag they'd given him.

At five past three he came upon the Considines', gazing down upon it from the rise, thinking, 'Not bad for a sail-maker!' And by Colonial standards with its several structures – the modest fenced house, the labourers' huts, barns, stables – it was positively grand. Though only, he sighed, if one ignored the perpetual summer death that lay over all, the dead grasses and barren fields, the hard-baked earth and the twine of dust that the wind picked up. And further to the right of it, a ringbarked forest, a thousand skeletons that Considine had killed in the name of pastoral progress. Unlike England, where the soil had been tilled for centuries, here the plough grubbed roots and rocks; it was the beginning, or the end, he could not be sure.

As he walked the horse through the gate, two brown, cadaverous hounds came snarling from the shadows and nipped at his boots with increasing yelps of dismay. He let fly with his boot and caught the cur on its snout.

'Would you call your blasted dogs off?' he said, turning away from the house towards the barn where Clara stood, sleeves rolled and hair pulled back.

'Juno! Vesta! Back, back!'

Pottinger dismounted, thinking how fine she looked on this summer afternoon, with the dome of her forehead smeared with dirt and glossed with sweat. More human, he thought, more ... approachable.

'Just paying my respects,' he said, crossing the dirt towards her.

Just then a young man came out of the barn and Pottinger's ardour immediately chilled. 'Michael Taylor,' he said, extending his hand.

'You know me?' said the youth.

'A policeman's intuition,' he smiled. But there was no mistaking the sharp and clean-cut features of this young man. It was a townsman's face with a touch of grace and education, and undeniably handsome, pure, with carefully-tonsured auburn hair and skin that barely even knew a razor. 'Pottinger, Frederick,' he said to the other, and they clasped hands.

'Come in, come in,' Clara said. She was not accustomed to receiving two *galants*. 'Come and see,' she said, urging Pottinger. 'We've been cleaning our Augean stable.'

They went inside.

'A sizeable stable,' Pottinger commented.

Clara laughed. 'That was just a figure of speech. This is really the woolshed.'

'Ah yes,' he said, removing his gloves. Thank heaven, it was mercifully cooler in here and they had even, for some reason, laid the dust with water.

'What do you think?' Clara asked, gazing down at the beaten floor.

'Excellent,' said Pottinger, though he had no idea. He was really thinking of this wasted afternoon, of how it might have been in the stillness of the house, his hand reaching for hers . . .

'Are your parents home?' he asked.

But his attention was drawn to Michael Taylor who was applying himself to a weighted drum through which a rope was passed, as a harness, so that he could roll the drum across the floor.

'I beg your pardon?' Pottinger said.

'They're droving.'

He looked at her, questioningly.

'Mama and Papa. Sheep,' she emphasised.

'Your mother?' Pottinger said, incredulous.

Clara laughed. 'Of course.'

Pottinger sighed, once for these rough colonial ways, and twice for the thought of Mrs Considine pursuing sheep on horseback. 'What is he doing?' Pottinger asked, observing Michael Taylor.

'Preparing the floor.'

'Yes, I can see that.'

'For the dance. The floor,' she said patiently, 'is spread with powdered cow dung, watered and rolled. And you must, must' – she clung to him – 'come to the dance.'

'Alas,' he laughed, raising his wounded wing, 'I'm a bit of a lame duck at the moment.' Even as he began to ferret for his watch and a reasonable excuse, Michael Taylor came up dusting his hands and declaring that the task was done, all but the ribbons and lanterns. So Clara gathered them arm-in-arm, the two of them, and said there would be tea and pastries.

They went in through the house gate beneath some golden

blossom, a native cassia, towards the orange-brick, iron-roofed structure. In this land this was wealth, as Pottinger very well knew; the corrugated iron and the fat iron water-tanks were luxury. He stood in the shade of the deep verandah, twelve feet width of it all around the house, with Michael Taylor, as Clara cleansed her face and hands at the tub.

'Very handsome,' he said of the house.

'Oh yes,' said Michael. 'Mr Considine has done his family proud.'

Pottinger examined the trim of wrought ironwork beneath the guttering. 'Mr Considine was, I believe, a sailmaker?'

Michael looked at him. He knew what Pottinger meant. 'A legacy,' he murmured. 'His uncle was in Iron.'

'Ah yes,' Pottinger said.

And shortly, when the young man had also washed, they went inside the house.


'They've gone inside the house,' Piesley said.

Gardiner gave him an acid look. 'Yeah, that was also my impression.'

The afternoon heat was now at its worst, and both men were unconsciously hunched against it. Even the leather of the saddle was hot to the touch.

'What're we gonna do, Frank?'

'I'm thinking.' He screwed around in the saddle. 'Looks pretty deserted, don't it?'

'I can't see anyone.'

'Nor me.'

Piesley looked at him. He'd got that way now, without even knowing it – he couldn't make a single decision for himself. 'What're you thinkin', Frank?'

Gardiner began to walk the horse. 'I'll let you know.'


Within the house, in the shaded kitchen with the moist, warm cooking smells, Pottinger was gazing on Considine's richest treasure, his elder daughter, Lelitia. Seen perhaps at her worst, Pottinger thought, with her apron, flour and dew of sweat, her dark hair straggling and a smudge on her chin – but ah, such a delicacy of features, the winged brows, the fine nose slightly flared, the fullness of the lips, the —

'Delighted,' he said truthfully with a modest bow.

'Oh Clara!' Lettie remonstrated. 'Look at the state I'm in.' She flushed with the crease of a frown, and turned with a fetching twist of slenderness: a fine-boned girl, he saw, taller than most, her cheeks and chin both dimpled fetchingly, the eyes bright and dark enough to mirror back the windows. 'Just look at me,' she wailed, challengingly. 'I'm not fit for callers.'

Pottinger flapped his arm in the sling. 'I'm not fit for calling.'

She coloured somewhat and returned to Clara. 'What will people think of us – entertaining in the kitchen?'

'Something's burning,' Michael said. She turned to the stove.

Pottinger settled himself unbidden at the plain deal table. He observed the bend of Lettie's body at the oven. What a pleasant way to spend a summer afternoon.

And despite the heat of the big black stove and the drum of the flies, it was cooler in the kitchen. It was built low with big, raw beams. The floor was earthen, or rather made from the clay of ant-beds culled from termite mounds, and hardened by time to a comfortable gloss. The room opened to a white-washed passage wherein, just visible, stood the greatest luxury, a bath tub, an iron tub boxed with timber.

'What are you making?' he asked Lettie as she brought the trays from the oven.

'Devil-on-the-Coals,' she said. 'For the dance. Are you coming to the dance?'

'No, he isn't,' Clara said inopportunely.

'What a shame.'

'Shall we go inside?' Clara asked.

Pottinger looked round at this distraction. Tea would be taken in the parlour. 'Of course,' he said, rising. He looked at Lettie as the others departed.

'No, I can't stop,' she said. 'You go ahead.'

He lingered, his eyes upon her. Extraordinary, he thought, feeling something pass between them, what a thoroughbred!

'Mr Pottinger!' Clara called from the parlour.

He excused himself reluctantly and made his way through the dimness of the passageway into a remarkably gracious room, for a settler's home, a room done out with black sassa-fras flooring, properly lined, fitted with cedar doors and windows, and boasting a fireplace of rough-hewn stone.

'Your tea,' Clara said unnecessarily, and he thought he saw in her eyes a light of impish tease.

'Thank you,' he said.

And the minutes swiftly became a tedium. The betrothed couple sat in murmured conversation that excluded Pottinger – about friends, and the friends of these, and so on, and so on.

'Then Henry Jolly said – and you mustn't repeat a word of it...'

Pottinger smiled politely. His mind was on that poor girl slaving two or three walls away. Was she spoken for? Was she perhaps even wedded? Lelitia Considine, he thought. Was there a touch of Spanish? No. But those coal-black, blazing eyes and the skin made olive by the sun. He looked at Clara and saw the shadow of Lelitia there, but fleetingly, and only in repose. They were sisters, yes, but from different planets, from some secret constellation in the womb.

'Perhaps your sister would appreciate some tea?' he asked of Clara.

'Oh, she never drinks it.'

'Let me try,' he offered graciously.

She looked up at him in a teasing way. 'All right.' And poured the tea.

'Excuse me,' he said, turning back towards the kitchen.

And he heard Clara's tittering laugh. 'I do believe the trooper is smitten!'

'I wondered whether —' Pottinger began as he turned into the kitchen. But it was all he managed.

The girl was standing rigidly, still as rock.

Lounging in the door was Johnny Piesley, and sitting at the table sampling Devil-on-the-Coals was Gardiner, with his gun on the pastry board.

# Nine

'Well, if it isn't Lord Henry Muck the Second!'

'Pottinger, actually.'

'Ectually, old boy, I know. She told me.'

Pottinger looked at Lelitia. 'Have these men been offensive?'

'Only just got here,' Gardiner said. 'Haven't had time to be offensive.' He glanced at the cup in Pottinger's hand. 'Do put it down, old love. Ai'm frightfully parched.'

There was a hiss and snort of laughter from the doorway.

'That there's Johnny Piesley,' Gardiner said. 'There's a price on his head, too.'

'Fifty quid!' Piesley said proudly.

'I come at a hundred,' Gardiner said. 'I kill troopers.'

Pottinger edged the teacup to the table, his eyes hard on Gardiner's.

Gardiner's hand fell lightly to his gun. 'No, I wouldn't do that – whatever you was thinking – 'cause I'd likely blow your tooter off.'

Pottinger looked at the girl.

'Go outside.'

'No,' said Gardiner, 'that would be rude. I'm the host, now. I'm entertaining you.'

'I have to inform you,' Pottinger said, 'that you're both under arrest.'

'Arrest?' Gardiner laughed, and shortly Piesley picked it up, embellishing the laugh with a high-pitched dingo howl, doubling over, holding his gut : 'Hoo! Ho, boy! Arrest? Ee-yah, you betcha!'

'Oh shut up, Johnny,' Gardiner said. 'Don't make a meal of it.'

'Who's that?' Clara called from the other room. 'What's going on?'

'Tell her,' Gardiner said. 'Tell her something.'

No one spoke.

'Tell her.'

'It's all right,' Lettie called. 'We're just —'

'That's enough. Who else is in there?'

'These are decent, respectable people,' Pottinger said. 'There's nothing for you here.'

Gardiner got up, scooping up the gun, glaring at Piesley. 'You'd laugh at a bent pin.'

Piesley laughed. 'Bent pin!' He pushed himself away from the door. 'I'm hungry. I haven't et since mornin'.'

'Poor feller's hungry, ma'am,' Gardiner said.

'I'm gonna get myself a piece of— Holy Christopher!' Piesley yelped, and even Pottinger winced as Lettie brought the savage chopper down a hair's-breadth away from Piesley's hand.

All wrong! Pottinger admonished himself as he crashed across the table and brought Gardiner to the floor – wrong timing, wrong moment – but the diversion had prompted him and now he grappled in a tangled darkness on the floor feeling a mix of whiskers, his own and Gardiner's, as they struggled face-to-face. Then something bright flashed out and a paralysing flame ignited in his head, and he rolled away with the sting of tears springing to his eyes. And 'Oh . . . oh . . .' he actually heard himself groaning.

'Golly,' he heard a voice lamenting over him, and Michael Taylor was collecting him like the pieces of a broken doll.

Pottinger looked painfully about. The situation was exactly as he'd expected, with Clara white in the doorway and the girl, Lelitia, pinned by Gardiner, his hand through the blackness of her hair and her head pulled back viciously.

'Let her go,' he croaked. He got to his feet feeling a warm spread of blood from the freshly-opened wound where Gardiner had smashed him with the gun-butt.

'I could have shot you dead,' Gardiner said.

'Let her go, old man.'

'Behave?' Gardiner asked her.

'Of course she will.'

Gardiner shoved her forward and she spilled across the table.

'Proper vixen,' Gardiner said. He eased back the hammer of the gun. 'She had no call to do that. We never even touched her.'

'She had no call,' Piesley echoed self-pityingly.

'Shut up, Johnny.'

'Ah!' said Piesley, and seized the chopper and slammed it into the wall hard enough to split the timber.

'You see what you done?' Gardiner said wearily. 'You've upset him. He just wanted something to eat. Get him something to eat. Both of us.'

'I'll do it,' Clara said.

'That's a good girl. You'll go a long way, love.'

Gardiner moved around and kicked the back door shut, parted the curtains and gazed outside. He had the feel of it now, he liked the feel of it, being in charge, boss and cock o' the walk, the air charged like you could hear their heartbeats. 'Where's your Mum and Dad?' he asked Lelitia.

'Down the creek,' she said.

'Down the creek where?'

'And likely back any minute with three of the men besides.'

'Oh yes?' Gardiner said, not believing a word of it. 'Where's the money?' They looked at each other. 'Look, I don't want to pull the house apart. I'm not in the mood.'

'The money's in the bank,' Michael Taylor said quickly.

'How do you know where the money is?'

'I work at the bank.'

Gardiner sat down again with a smile for this impetuous youth. 'What's your name, sonny?'

Michael told him.

'How much money does the old man have in the bank, Michael?'

'I'm not at liberty to say.'

'A lot or a little?'

'Mr Considine lives quite adequate.'

'I can see that.'

Clara put some cold meat and pickles on the table, and sliced some bread. 'Somethin' to drink,' Piesley said. 'Not tea, dammit.'

Clara went to fetch a small flagon from the shelves above the passageway.

'Now come on, you fellows,' Pottinger said, 'take your grub and on your way. You've got everything that's going.'

'Not everything,' Gardiner told him with his eyes on Lettie.

'You put your hands to me —' she said.

Pottinger stepped between them. 'Now then,' he said, 'no call for that. That is not Mr Gardiner's reputation.'

Piesley laughed, with his mouth stuffed with salted beef.

Gardiner looked up at Pottinger. 'Are you trying to make it hard for me?'

Pottinger sat in the adjoining chair, keeping his voice soft and controlled. 'Now do be reasonable. Go and ply your trade on the road. These are decent, law-abiding folk. You have no call to interfere with them.'

Gardiner wiped his beard and smiled. 'You know you're bleeding all over the table?'

Pottinger got up and went to the stove, resting against the mantelpiece. The four of them, he, Lettie, Clara, and Michael Taylor, watched the intruders eat. A perfectly disgusting spectacle, Pottinger thought, all this pushing, shoving and pawing of the food.

'I'll get you a mug,' Clara said.

'Nah!' Piesley told her as he unplugged the flagon and spilled it to his lips.

Lettie turned away, venting her feelings on Pottinger.

'How can you try to reason with them?'

Will you shut up? It was what he wanted to say. He felt like a man sitting on a kettle, suppressing the rise of steam. They, the two girls, he knew, still believed in the inviolate sanctity of their home, that they controlled the moment by right, or grace of station.

'Now will you go?' Lettie said, abruptly removing the plate.

'I haven't finished,' Gardiner said.

'Yes, you have.'

'I haven't had my drink. Stripe me,' he said to Piesley, 'ease up, leave a drop.'

Piesley slumped back in the chair with satisfaction, spread his legs and clawed his groin. 'Gees, that was good!'

'Something to drink out of,' Gardiner ordered Clara. 'I'm not a pig like him.'

Clara fetched the mug for him, and pushed the flagon down the table. As she did so, Piesley's hand clamped upon her rear.

She backed away so startled that she collided with the dresser and set the crockery jingling.

Piesley laughed. 'She's hot, ain't she? She's a real two-tooth.'

A 'two-tooth', as Pottinger knew, was a full-grown ewe, a young one, a virgin. He looked at Michael Taylor, who was white. And began a movement towards the door.

'Come on,' Piesley said to Gardiner, 'you've had your guzzle. Now it's mine.'

'Johnny,' said Gardiner, relinquishing the flagon, 'why don't you go and find the money?'.

'Because it's in the bank.'

'Don't you smell the money?'

'Yeah!' said Piesley, eyeing Clara.

'No, listen, Johnny – go and find the money.'

'Beast!' said Clara.

Piesley lurched out of the chair with the flagon in one hand, the other flailing towards Clara.

'No, you don't!' Michael Taylor warned him, stepping in between them.

Piesley looked at him, stunned as though his nag had talked.

'Dammit, leave her alone.'

Piesley bared his teeth in a grin. 'You want to watch your bloody language, son.'

'Johnny, will you go and find the money?'

Pottinger glanced down at the doorknob, almost within his reach. He could see the room and Piesley departing in the brass of the knob, and this little golden world looked so innocent;

and he was thinking, If I can get the door open, if I can reach the horse and get the gun ... Blast and thunderation, what a place to leave the gun!

'Wouldn't try that, Mr Pottinger,' Gardiner said.

'No?'

He turned and looked at the Navy Colt.

'Not that I've nothing against you personal, but I wouldn't try it. I mean,' said Gardiner, sitting himself on the corner of the table, 'why bother? What's it all about? Couple of fellers come in for a feed and a few lousy quid, what's the fuss about? These – what is it? – Considines have got it. They can spare it. Nobody's getting hurt. What's everybody so hot about?'

'You're a convict and murderer,' Lettie said. 'A mean, cruel, despicable man.'

'Ah yes,' Gardiner said agreeably, 'but it's the nobs that made us, ain't it?'

There began a splintering crash and ruckus from the parlour as though Piesley were brawling with himself.

'Oh, no!' Lettie said.

Pottinger caught her by the arm. 'Let it be. The man is drunk.'

'What's up, Johnny?' Gardiner called.

A further crash, and the tinkle of glass.

'Oh, Michael!' Clara sobbed, and threw herself into the young man's arms.

Just then, unexpectedly, the daylight was extinguished and the room turned sombre with a sulphurous penetration, half-light, half-presence, as though the evil of the moment had congealed.

'Blast!' said Gardiner, looking out. 'Now we're stuck.'

'Don't let us keep you, old man.'

'I'm not blooming getting wet,' Gardiner told him.

He parted the curtains, the filigree of lace, and the yellow light fumed in. 'Gonna be a crackler.'

Pottinger could see the heavy press of violet clouds against the phosphorescent landscape. Perhaps they'll hurry back, he thought, thinking of Considine and the hired hands. But what

73

if they did, what then?

'Johnny, what's goin' on?' Gardiner yelled.

There was for all of them a heavy, pressing silence thudding at the skull. The big black flies buzzed angrily at the window; you could hear the smack of their bodies at the glass. And the darkness grew in the kitchen. They waited silently for the first thrust of lightning. The iron of the roof began to pop as the metal cooled, creaking, lifting from the nails, and a few leaves fell with a sound like rodents scampering. Clinkers dropped in the grate.

The lightning tore through the air like the ripping of silk and the whole house shuddered with a thunderous detonation. Clara squealed, hands clapped to her ears, and even Gardiner breathed, 'Say a prayer, for Christ's sake.'

'My horse,' Pottinger lamented, gazing into the gloom.

Within moments the storm mounted with thrust upon thrust, the lightning dry and the thunder rolling in a barrage across the plains. Each of them now had turned to the windows.

The rain intensified, a fierce rain raining straight down, an unnatural rain as though each fat bladder of cloud was pierced with holes, and you couldn't hear a single raindrop, just the unbroken drumming of rain in a rising pitch that shortly grew to the racketing sound of hail.

'Just what we need,' Gardiner said glumly.

A further slash of lightning lit them with a white magnesium light, and Pottinger turned to see Piesley in the passage-way, the flagon hooked from a finger, his arms full of the pendulum clock from the parlour mantelpiece, and tankards and spoons and forks of silver.

Gardiner also turned.

'Lookit I got,' Piesley said.

'You what?'

'I got a clock,' Piesley yelled above the din of hail.

'You blooming booby, put it back.'

But Piesley dumped his haul on the table.

'That's Papa's things!' Clara cried.

And before Pottinger could stop her, she had flung herself upon the drunken man and there began something as wild, as brief as a tavern brawl, skirts flying like a harridan's and the nails clawing tracks down Piesley's face, and the man yowling, ripping at her – until Gardiner put a bullet through the roof, and the storm, the hail at least, obediently diminished.

'Get up,' he ordered Piesley. He was angry now. The whole thing had gone too far. 'We're going.'

Piesley's paw was at his face, and he pulled his fingers away to see the blood. 'Lookit she done to me.'

'Get up and get going,' Gardiner shouted.

A bubble of drunken lament broke within Piesley, and tears welled into his eyes.

Gardiner grabbed him and hauled him to his feet. He had nothing but contempt for this wet-pants weakling, and he wanted nothing more than to do undo what he had done.

'We're partners,' Piesley said. It was an appeal.

'Yeah, that's right, Johnny. Let's partner ourselves out of here. I'm sorry, miss,' he said to Clara. 'I'm real sorry.'

'Bitch!' said Piesley to her face. And his eyes grazed over the milk of her shoulder, bared now, where he had ripped the cloth.

Gardiner put a hand gently to him, sensing the danger. 'None of that, Johnny.'

Piesley's eyes remained on the girl. 'It's still raining, Frank.'

'I know that. Bit of rain won't hurt.'

For the first time, Piesley pulled the gun, the horse-pistol from his belt. 'You know what I'm thinking, Frank?'

'Yeah, I've got a fair idea. Come on, Johnny.'

'I'm thinking,' Piesley said, 'I'm gonna have a bath.'

'You're gonna what?'

'I never had a bath before. Not in my whole, entire life. Whyn't you fix me a bath?' he said to Clara.

'Because we're goin', that's why.'

'You back off, Frank! You've had your fun. Now it's my turn ... Come on, love. Fix me a bath. Why don't you do that?'

75

'Johnny . . .' Gardiner said.

'Fix it!' Piesley told her and, turning the gun on Michael Taylor, 'Else I blow his head off.'

Clara turned back to the room in agonised appeal.

'Do it,' Pottinger said. He turned at Lettie's gasp.

Gardiner laughed. 'I'm trying to get him out of here. You're trying to wash the brute!'

'Needs must, old chap.' He had seen in his mind a petrifying vision of the room attached to a burning fuse, worse than lightning, explosive. And he had also seen what the others hadn't – four, no, five horsemen approaching through the distant rain.

'Look, I'm going,' Gardiner said as Piesley began to pull off his boots.

'No, hang on, Frank, won't take a minute.'

'For God's sake,' Lelitia uttered as Piesley peeled off his pants.

'Well, don't look, then,' Piesley said.

She tried not to. And said to Pottinger, 'How can you let this happen?'

Five minutes, he was thinking. First, the dogs will bark, and then I'll get the gun.

'How's it comin', love?' Piesley said to Clara at the tub.

There was an inch or so of water from the rain tank in the tub. She looked at him, and down at him, and flushed.

'Hell an' dammit, Johnny,' Gardiner said, grabbing him.

Piesley backed off violently enough to topple Clara. 'Don't you mess with me, Frank.'

'You're drunk, mate.'

'I know I'm drunk. I like it.'

'Act decent, will you?'

'Gotta clean up first.'

'Put your pants on. You're coming with me.'

Next thing, in the abortive struggle, Piesley had sploshed over backwards into the tub with a startled howl. 'It's cold,' he yelped. 'It's wet.'

'Partners,' Gardiner sighed.

76

'Come on in,' Piesley said, grabbing Clara, and hauled her head over tail into the tub, and as she struggled to escape grabbed at the collar of her dress and ripped the dress to the waist, seizing her, fighting at her arms across her chest, her skin milkwhite, straining until they hurtled back to a splash of water.

Michael Taylor, lashed beyond caution, started out as Pottinger grabbed him. 'Wait!' he hissed.

Something in Pottinger's urgency alerted Gardiner, enough to ease back the hammer of the gun. 'What's going on?' he said.

'We don't want trouble,' Pottinger told him. 'We've got enough trouble.' He didn't dare to look behind at the tub where some form of silent struggle was occurring, the girl sobbing, the water splashing. But in the end, 'Leave her!' he commanded, and he had his arm, his one good arm about Piesley's neck and he was thinking as the outlaw threshed, Now I've bought it! And he saw with clarity, the Colt Navy gun pushing through the air in his direction, and the plop of water on the table where the bullet had pierced the roof, and then – great heaven! – the yelp of the hounds in the yard.

'Hell!' said Gardiner, wrenching the curtain aside. 'There's half the army in the yard.'

At that moment, Piesley crashed out of the tub and the detonation of the horse-pistol almost blew the room apart.

Pottinger saw Considine's horse rearing in the yard, and he dived down and pulled Lelitia after him.

'Get down!' he yelled.

Nothing happened, just the patient drip of rain and the distant jingle of harness.

'Clara? Lettie?' came Considine's voice.

And then, quite clearly in the cool of the fading afternoon, Mrs Considine: 'What's them horses in the yard?'

No one saw Piesley pull the trigger of the second gun, but the ball smashed through the window pane and took the curtain with it.

'Blooming idjut!' Gardiner remonstrated, and just as suddenly the room was full of flying things, pots clanging, urns

77

shattering under a reckless and unexpected volley of shots from the yard.

'Hold your fire!' Considine commanded.

Pottinger crept to his feet to see men with guns, three of them, and Considine and his lady, all looking towards the kitchen windows.

'We've got your daughters,' Gardiner yelled.

'Pull back,' Pottinger shouted. 'These are desperate men.'

'Look,' Gardiner asked him, 'who's running this?'

Two more shots blasted in the room. Clara screamed.

Gardiner turned angrily to Piesley. 'Will you just quit doing that?'

'We're coming in,' Considine called.

'No, you ain't,' Gardiner said. He sighed. 'We got what they call a situation here. And it's all your fault,' he accused Piesley. 'Go and put your pants on.'

'I got no more guns, Frank.'

'Well, that's a mercy.'

'I do believe,' Pottinger said, 'they've gone to get help.'

'Damn,' said Gardiner. It was true.

'Might as well turn in your gun, don't you think?'

'I got five bullets left in this. That's enough for you an' him an' them.'

'Would you shoot a woman?'

'You're damn' right I would.'

'I see.'

Gardiner turned on him. 'You give me a pain in the tail, you know that? You ain't being helpful at all.'

'Just give me the gun, old chap.'

Gardiner began to pace. He hadn't reckoned on this. He thought: maybe I could take a girl, the dark one, and push my way out through those guns. But he had Piesley to contend with. Piesley stuffed with a flagon of rum.

He looked out through the window, cautiously, sideways. The night was coming down. The storm was broiling off somewhere, heading north, and the sun had limned the clouds so that all the puddles in the yard were blood, as though some slaughter had taken place. He turned back to Pottinger. 'I'm in a bit of a fix, old boy.' And he looked at Lettie. 'I think I'll have to take your girl.'

Pottinger forced himself to examine his nails. 'Actually, she isn't my girl. I couldn't care a penny-farthing.'

'Well, someone does!'

'That's their worry.'

'I'll take you, then.'

'I thought you shot troopers?'

'Only when I'm in the mood.'

'I doubt,' said Pottinger facing a miserable truth, 'that they would trade my life for yours.'

There was a silence as Gardiner gazed out into the spectral light at the little knot of people in the yard – Mr and Mrs Considine and the two hired hands. The other man, the one missing had gone for help. And help couldn't be more than five minutes away.

'What do you reckon, Frank?' Piesley said, lurching up with dribble on his chin.

Gardiner turned back to the room, halfways in disgust. They were all watching him now – Pottinger, the boy, the women – to see which way he'd jump. Hell and blazes, how the hades had he got into this? Gardiner scrubbed his beard and turned back again, drawn helplessly to the window. There was an orange bloom of light upon the landscape and the shadows were a deep magenta. 'Park your guns,' Gardiner yelled, 'and we'll go peaceful.'

'Send the gels out,' Mrs Considine responded.

'Park your guns.'

'You lay a finger on 'em, an' I'll 'ave you knackered!'

'Now then, Moother,' Considine was heard to say in a ripe, rich accent.

The voices drifted through the stillness; you could almost hear a whisper.

'Are yez all right in there?' Considine bellowed.

'Oh, Papa, Papa!' Clara suddenly squealed, rushing to the window.

'Push off!' Gardiner said, shoving her aside. And only then did he realise that the group outside the house was three, not four. One of them had slipped around and — The bullet punched through the only pane of glass intact and he saw, even as he began to lift his hands protectively, the glass bellying in as slow as a dream, exploding with a powdery glitter, and he fell back, way back across the room with his face searing as though with acid on it and his skin peppered with blood. 'Jee-umpin' hell!' he said, and his teeth crunched down on bits of glass. But he still had the gun in his hand and the room where he wanted it. That was the one good thing about him. If he'd been a corpse, the corpse would still know how to pull the trigger.

'Y'all right, Frank?' Piesley asked in a worried voice.

He smeared his hand across his face. It was like the backside of a porcupine.

'Y'all right?'

'I thought your Dad'd play it fair,' he accused Lelitia.

'I wish you dead,' she said.

'Why don't you give me the gun?' Pottinger said, his hand extended.

Blood rolled into Gardiner's eyes. He felt as though half his face had been shot away. The room pitched over briefly and he had to hold the table.

'Someone's coming,' he heard a girl's voice say.

And Piesley's echo: 'Someone coming, Frank.'

'How many?' he croaked, or thought he did. No one answered.

'Give me the gun,' Pottinger repeated.

Gardiner looked at the trooper through veils of red at the blood-red uniform. 'Come here,' he said, and pushed himself off the table and made his way towards the bath tub. 'Get a rag,' he told him. 'Wet it.'

Gardiner pressed the cloth against his face. He looked in the mirror. He couldn't recognise himself.

'How many they got out there?' he asked.

'Nine, counting the woman.'

'I'm in a fix, ain't I? Tell you what I'm going to do, soldier ...'

Pottinger waited. It was best to wait. Time was ticking in their direction.

'What I'm going to do is...' Gardiner looked at Pottinger with the old grin returning. 'The moment those fellers start coming at the house, I'm going to shoot you, the banker, and those two girls – in that order.'

Pottinger felt the chill prickle down his back.

'Unless ...' Gardiner said.

'Unless what?'

'I got another plan.'

'Oh?'

'You're gonna march me out. Me and Johnny. You're going to arrest me. With this gun. Empty.'

Pottinger laughed. 'I hardly think so.'

'Think about it, old chum.'

Pottinger did – and began to see the merits of it. But Gardiner was there before him.

'And just so's you don't turn me in – bein' as I'm defenceless – I'm going to take the chopper. And if you so much as wink, I'll chop it through your skull.'

Pottinger moistened his lips. There seemed so many lives to consider.

'Well?' said Gardiner.

'Right,' said Pottinger. 'Give me the gun.'

Gardiner looked at him, measuring him. 'Now remember you're a gentleman.'

Pottinger pushed his hand out. Gardiner abruptly spilled the shells from the gun and put them in his pocket. He gave Pottinger the gun butt first.

'Let's move,' Pottinger said.

They went back into the kitchen.

'What's goin' on?' Piesley said.

'We're done, Johnny,' Gardiner told him. 'He turned the tables on us.'

'Golly!' Michael Taylor breathed. 'How did you do that?'

But Lettie, for one, didn't believe a word of it. Something, she knew, had taken place out there and her eyes burned into Pottinger's. 'Everyone stay quiet,' he warned, 'and let me do it my way.'

'Frank, Frank,' Piesley bleated, 'how did it happen?'

'Get your hands up,' Pottinger told Piesley. He didn't feel safe, not at all, even though they presumed he had control. 'Up, up!' he said in a more convincing voice.

Piesley put his hands up. His eyes were on Gardiner, and there were tears in them, brimming with hurt.

Pottinger glanced out into the yard. There was quite a bristle of guns.

'Tell 'em,' Gardiner said.

Pottinger moved a half-pace to the window. 'Hold your fire,' he called. 'This is Trooper Pottinger. I've made an arrest.'

'You've what?' said a voice that was clearly Considine's.

'They've surrendered. I'm bringing them out.'

Silence, and a whispered consultation.

'We're coming out,' Pottinger repeated. 'Open the door,' he told Michael Taylor.

Gardiner reached up and pulled the chopper from the wall. 'A little souvenir,' he said, tucking the thing in his shirt.

'Mr Pottinger!' Lettie commanded.

But the door was open and a fume of golden light spilled in with dust motes dancing in it.

'March!' Pottinger said, and they walked out into the yard.

Half-a-dozen men broke ranks and spilled towards them.

'Back, back!' Pottinger said. 'These men are in my care.'

'Good lad,' Gardiner told him.

But the men were pushing round and marvelling, and Considine was clapping Pottinger on the shoulder as Mrs Considine surged forward to embrace her youngest, Clara.

'Make way,' Pottinger cried.

They began to pace the long ten yards towards the horses, Considine stubbornly clinging, the men jolly, voices ringing in the stillness. 'Well done, trooper!' 'By goom, you'll cop a fair reward for this.'

Five yards. And the chopper in Gardiner's belt.

And Clara's wail. 'Mama, that man attacked me. He forced me —'

'Oh, my Gard!'

'— into the tub!'

Four yards, or even less, and the wink of sunlight on Pottinger's gun, loaded, waiting in the saddle. But he'd have to draw it, wouldn't he, and turn it round, and cock the trigger . . .

Then Piesley fell in the mud, straight down, flop!

'Get up,' Gardiner hissed.

'Shoot me,' Piesley urged. 'Don't take me in.'

'Get up, you great sook.'

'Tell 'em,' Piesley implored, 'I died game.'

God help us, Gardiner thought, he wants to be a hero.

'Get up!' Pottinger said, putting the boot in.

Piesley stumbled to his feet.

They were less than an arm's length from the horses when Lettie's voice shrilled out: 'That gun – it isn't even loaded.'

Pottinger felt his mouth go dry. This was the moment. He'd go down in history – with his head split open like a peach. 'Mount up,' he ordered the captives.

And heard a voice behind him. 'What's this, what's this?' Considine asked with a tangled furrow of his brows.

'Do not interfere,' Pottinger said, 'when I'm about my duty.'

'But the girl says, Lettie says —'

'I don't give a damn. Get out of my way.'

'Hold on, now . . .'

Pottinger climbed into the saddle. 'Do you honestly think I'd take them in with an empty gun?'

Considine looked back at Lettie.

Pottinger fixed her with his gaze. 'Thank you for your hospitality,' he said. He would remember her – like this – her face gilded by the dying sun, with his life, his honour depending on the stillness of her lips.

Then the three horsemen rode up the track, the horses dancing on the mantis shadows of their legs.

A mile or so away they stopped at the fork in the road. 'You done all right, trooper,' Gardiner said. 'I'll thank you for my gun.'

Piesley now grinned in the growing darkness; they'd let him in on the joke long before.

'In exchange for the bullets,' Pottinger said.

'And leave you with a loaded rifle?'

Both men did the gentlemanly thing and disarmed themselves. Gardiner offered his hand on the deal.

'I'll tell you this, Gardiner,' Pottinger said, as the horse grew skittish. 'I shall seek you out and pay you back. You made a fool of me . . .'

'It wasn't difficult.'

'. . . and I won't forget it. Next time you come at me, come shooting, because, by God, I won't play the gentleman.' He clamped his teeth and the words came through like knives. 'I'll shoot your heart out,' he promised.

He wrenched his horse around and rode away. He heard their laughter fading, and there was a jackass crying, settling for the night.

What the devil, he was thinking, will I tell the Sergeant-in-command?

## Ten

Kate Walsh had walked seven miles and it was almost noon. All she carried was the burden of her conscience, talking aloud sometimes as she toiled up the rough from the Valley, to the Lord on the one hand, and Old Nick on the other. She'd just got out of bed that morning and said she was going. 'Where are you going?' Roy had said. 'I'm going for a walk,' she told him. Roy immediately hitched his pants on and went over to old man Walsh's. 'Kate's gone walkin',' he told him. Walsh sighed in a way that pushed his brows up and went into the kitchen to tell Ma. 'Your daughter's gone walking again,' he said. She said a prayer on the spot and the ache began in her back again.

Kate began to climb into the bluff, almost down on her hands and knees. It was a hot, leaden kind of day with the air rich and moist bringing out the humours of the undergrowth. Her dress clung to her in big sweat patches; she had nothing on beneath. She climbed, clinging like a lizard to the rocks, the fabric clefting to her buttocks, hiking to her hard, lean thighs. She kept going, stubborn, and damn her cotton print, feeling the slide of the rock beneath her from her torso to her thighs. A rough lover, she thought, but made it to a slant of saplings where she rested.

There was, of course, an easier way to go – on horseback, for a start. But the troopers had been thundering up and down the Valley all week long and the story was that Gardiner had raped a girl called Considine, and been shot in the face, his face blown half away.

Now she wished she'd taken the horse and damn the troopers, but still and all they were using trackers and the only way you could fool a tracker was to think black and stubborn. She'd fool them all right, but maybe fool herself – chasing Gardiner was like chasing a willy-willy, that impish wind that spiralled like a spinning-top across the plains.

She'd gone to see Ben Hall. Ben Hall knew almost everything, and if he didn't, the abo Billy Dargin did. 'He's up top,' Ben said. 'But don't say I told you.'

She reached the high rock face when the sun was set so square above that she scarcely had a shadow. She'd done all this a hundred times from the time she was ten, but every single time it was a game of hide-and-seek. The cave had twenty, thirty ways to come upon it that they knew about, and the police preferred to keep away. You could take a dozen men up there and still be foxed, and likely leave a dozen dead. Of course, they always entered the easy way – where the river cut the cavern – for there wasn't a trooper born who'd care to lower himself into the chimney-pot and the darkness underneath. Once, they'd tried to smoke out Jimmy Moon and half-a-dozen others, and there was the mountain smoking twenty different ways like twenty different coffee pots, but they never got the rascal and never saw him since.

Kate now curved her body to an 'S' and sidled round a rock and vanished. Almost at once she was in darkness, or something worse than darkness, a cool, velvet thing, darkness you could touch, deeper than the night or the pitch-black pit of the graveyard hour, so dark it hurt the eyes. She traced her way along the wall, always keeping to the right. 'Think common-sense,' she urged herself against the rise of fright. 'Think —' But webs, and trails of webs entangled her, and some quick and rasping bug skittered across her hand. She stifled the yelp and kept going, seeing eyes and feathered, groping things, but always in imagination. 'Dear God,' she prayed, 'don't let me be lost.' But she knew where the rockfall was, and where the stone had shifted into 'London Bridge', as they called it, and how you had to crawl beneath into the Bishop's Cavern where the limestone had built upon itself, drop by drop for a thousand years, to form this giant pontifical throne. Then all at once the darkness heaved – she was prepared for it – in a huge, sweeping wave of bats' wings, like a musty cloak that stirred her hair. She couldn't help but cringe a little, and her skin prickled, but she pushed on, climbing now through grottoes ringing with the splash of water, guiding herself by the touch of tiny stalactites in the place they called 'John o' Lantern's Passage' where, as you walked, you could hear the tinkle of the dead man's bones, or so they said.

She hiked her skirts and clambered over rocks. She had her cave-sense now; and could 'see' the dark and feel the turns before they came. She stopped at a kind of crossways, hearing her breathing magnified like that of a beast in whelp, and called his name. 'Frank!' she called. And the name went bouncing round mad as a bat – 'Frankarankarank...' – down depthless sink-holes and limestone galleries and whispering walls, each name lapping at another's heels.

'God save us, love,' said a voice right in her ear, 'you sound like the twelve apostles.'

She spun about, almost expecting the touch of him, but it was just a trick of the caves and moments passed, a minute perhaps, before she saw the flicker of the lantern and his shadow dancing out before him.

'Are you alone?' he asked.

'Of course I'm bloody alone. And I'm cold, and I'm wet and you must've heard me coming, so why didn't you yell or something?'

She swept past him, even past his open arms, into the lair he'd made for himself – the scrap of bedding, and the bit of larder and the fireplace. She didn't see as she passed him, but he pulled a wry face. One of those womanly moods, he was thinking.

'Can we get a fire goin'?' she said, complaining, standing there with her arms wrapped about herself.

'Sure we can.'

He set the lantern on a ledge and set to work with a flint-box. Soon the fire was going. The smoke, they knew, was well dispersed – they'd given up the thought of it.

'How's that?' he said, looking up at her.

She looked at him in the firelight. The stories they told! His face was all of a piece, hardly a mark on it – and to think she'd wept for the thought of it. She moved up to the fire and knelt above it, pulling the front of her dress from her body to dry the sweat and water from the caves.

'Did you rape that woman?' she asked.

'What woman?'

'That ... Considine.' She said the name as though it were an animal.

' 'Twasn't a woman, it was a girl.'

'Did you?'

'Does it matter?'

'Look,' she said, glaring at him, the firelight in her eyes, 'don't you play funny with me. Did you, or didn't you?'

'Well,' he said agreeably, 'it was a long afternoon, y'see . . .'

She was on him – a hiss-and-spitting tiger, the claws out, the teeth bared, going for him, climbing up him like a tree so that they rolled in the dirt and sent the pans flying; and she was calling him all the names she'd ever heard of, going through the alphabet (the best girl-cusser he ever knew) as she snapped at him, actually snapped the way a wild bitch does defending the cubs. Then he had her by the wrists, right where he wanted her, and he felt the strength draining from her. So she brought her knee up, but he was ready for this, and rolled, and she rolled with him.

'Something's burning,' he said.

She looked down and snatched her skirt from the fire.

'Let me go,' she said.

'Not a chance.'

'Let . . . me . . . go!'

It was like trying to hold a piece of crooked lightning, her whole body arched and thrashed – and as the strength continued to drain, he felt it draining into him, powerfully.

'At least you come prepared,' he said, gazing down on the firelit gleam of her bared behind.

'Lemme go, Frank.'

'Katie,' he said, 'I never touched that girl, you know I didn't.'

She laughed, 'Now you say.'

'No, I never. Cross an' spit. Honest.'

'Why didn't you say so?'

'I was going to say so. You never let me.'

She looked at him, deeply into him. 'You didn't, did you, Frank?'

He shook his head and let her go, and his hand slid down to her shanks.

'Wait a bit,' she said.

She got up, and he tidied the spill of the fire. When he looked around, she didn't have a stitch on. 'Dammit to hell,' he said, 'that's a fair beautiful sight!'

He took her in both hands gently, the way you gentle a wild and skittish creature, and drew her to him. She dropped to her knees, supplying her body to his lips that moved across a known, yet newly-discovered terrain, across the places where the firelight licked, into the shadows and clefts of her secret, salt-tasting flesh. And shortly, she felt his thrust, long and fevered, and she locked her legs about him. 'Gentle does it,' he admonished. But he saw, though briefly, the whipcords of her throat, head back, teeth bared, and felt the iron-hard strain of her spine. 'Love you, Katie,' he thought he said, and she fought him, rolling, their bodies locked, fighting with a spitcat ferocity until he felt the scorch of the fire on his backside. 'Hot blazes,' he said, 'something's burning.'

'Keep going!' she demanded in a wild, throttled voice.

And he did.

When it was done, and done again, she lay back with the gleam of sweat on her, her skin gilded to a shine of amber and gold by fire and lantern light, the hair black as carbon with a pearly dew upon it. She gazed at the roof of the cavern where the cave spiders had stitched a constellation. 'Now I'll have to see the bloody priest again,' she said.

He also lay on his back, and turned now to reach across her for a twig to light his cigar. 'You see more of the priest than of me,' he said.

'If Roy was dead . . .' she said. 'I mustn't even think it.'

'Oh, give the feller a chance,' he told her. 'It's someone to warm your bed.'

'Don't you want him dead?'

'I'm an easygoing sort of feller.'

'He wants you dead. Said so often.'

'He knows where to find me.'

'Oh God . . .' she breathed in a way that signified half an hour of melancholy.

'Listen,' he told her, giving her a thump, 'I got a surprise for you. I think I got enough.'

'Enough what?'

'I'll show you.'

He gave her the cigar to hold and went across the cavern to fetch the rifle box, his treasure chest.

'What've you got?' she asked.

He looked at her. 'I haven't been idle. I've been on the job.'

'With Johnny?'

'With and without. Piesley's gone bush for a while. He's teamed up with Gilbert. Yeah, Gilbert's back,' he said. 'The old Flash Johnny.'

'Oh, Frank!' she laughed. 'Oh, my gosh!' She was pushing her hands through an assortment of watches, brooches, rings and ornaments, and sovereign cases, snuff-boxes, money-belts and money, little chamois bags of gold – she'd never seen the like.

'Been saving it,' Gardiner said. 'Didn't want to tell you.'

'What are you going to do with it?'

He scrubbed his beard and parked his cigar in his face. 'Gonna melt most of it down. I know a bent smithie, won't ask questions. Sell it up as ingots.'

'What'll it fetch, do you reckon?'

He put his arms about her and said it straight to her face. 'Enough to get us shed of the Valley, you and me. We're going, Kate, way up north where they never heard of us. We'll be Mr and Mrs Nobody, and I'll get back to the trade, back to butchering —'

'Oh, don't, Frank, don't ...' She had her head in her hands. 'I'm such a bloody fool, I am.'

'What's wrong, darlin'?'

'Nothing. Nothing,' she said, looking up at him, tossing her hair back. And her eyes had such a sparkle, and the tears were streaming; she was laughing and crying, all in one go.

'You like that, don't you?' he asked.

All she could do was nod.

'Thought you would.'

She lay back, flat out, with a kind of radiance upon her. She was going, she was leaving Winooka and Roy, and putting patches on his pants and grubbing for a living like a pig with its snout in the dirt.

Gardiner kissed her. 'That's what you wanted, ain't it?' he asked gently.

'All along, Frank.'

'Did it for you, Kate,' he said, which was partly the truth. 'Gonna make you mine.' And he planted two impish wedding rings, both of them pilfered, one about each nipple, and a nugget plumb centre in the middle of her belly.

'It's like an icicle!' she shrieked.

'Don't, don't, you'll upset the apple cart.' And he decked her with gold. And then it was the way it always was, their eyes questing each other's, the joke fusing into something deeper, urgent. His hands closed where the rings were, and she looked at him with a deep stillness, half-virgin, half-coquette, as she helplessly and eagerly received him.

Afterwards she dressed and cooked him a supper and they ate it by the embers of the fire. He kept looking at her with deep love-looks that made her stomach cave in, so she gave up in the end and turned her gaze into the wink of the coals. 'How much money would you say is in the box, Frank?'

'How much?'

'Melted down, and sold up?'

'Two, three hundred quid, I suppose.'

'Oh.'

'Why? What was you thinking?'

'Nothing.'

'Come on, tell us.'

Now she looked at him. 'It isn't that much, is it?'

'It's a blooming fortune.'

'Be gone in a year.'

He suppressed a wave of irritation with a sigh. Bloody women. You gave them too much loving, they started to think. 'I'll have my trade, won't I?'

'Butchering.'

'What's wrong with butchering?'

She shook her head. 'Nothing.' It was just and only for a moment – she couldn't see herself washing the blood from his duds and listening to the squeal of slaughtered beasts.

He got up and slammed the lid of the box. 'How much money do you want?'

'Don't get mad, Frank. I was just thinking...' – she made it up as she went along – 'suppose you get sick or something?'

Female arguments! 'I can get more, if that's what you want.'

'More watches,' she said.

'What else is there?'

She shrugged. 'Gold?'

He laughed. 'Yeah, I can see myself down on the diggings, shovelling up the mullock. I can just see myself.'

'On the roads, I mean.'

'Gold on the roads?' He wasn't dense, but he couldn't see what she was getting at.

'They fetch it from the diggings, don't they?'

'Of course they do. You bet they do. With a full escort with half a million guns.'

'How many guns?'

'What? Six. Eight. Must be ten at least.'

'Not that many.'

'Oh yes? Wait till you're looking down the barrel.'

She came over to him with an excitement he hadn't seen before, and took his hand. 'Frank, if we had one box, one solid box of gold . . .'

He reached across and tossed the Navy Colt into her lap. 'You do it.'

'You could get Johnny Piesley,' she said, 'and Gilbert and – oh, almost anyone. There's so much money in it. It's like – what they call investment. You could have so many men that the escort wouldn't dare to fire a shot.'

'I got a single Navy Colt,' he said.

'Get some more.'

'From where?'

'Oh, I don't know, Frank,' she said, annoyed. 'You must have some idea.'

He had some idea, all right. Those fellows – Piesley, Gilbert and the rest – they worked singly, or in tandem. You couldn't put their heads together, not even with a stick. As for guns . . . Forget about the horse-pistols and the fowling-pieces. They'd need Tranters or Spencers, long-range rifles, repeaters like the army had. And where the hell would you pick up a rifle?

'It was just an idea,' she said, opening a door for his escape. 'I didn't really mean it.'

'Yeah, I know,' he said.

'Frank, don't worry about it.'

'I'm not worried, darlin',' he told her, 'because I just ain't gonna do it.'

But he was. He knew he was. He was going to steal more gold than she could carry.

## Eleven

Frederick Pottinger, who was quite disgusted with himself, was lathering himself towards a sexual climax with all the tenacity of a man climbing some unconquerable alpine slope. He was grinding over the slackened flesh of a woman known as Dusty Mary who sold her accommodations for a florin. It's this or madness, Pottinger was thinking, uncertain of his preference. He was heaving upon a cushion of flesh, the skirts rolled up, and the body lay on sacking in a sagging tent hung with burlap. Outside, there was the snuffling of pigs and the gaggling cries of fowls. He looked down at the woman's eyes flecked with bloodspots and glazed by gin and tedium, and he screwed his own eyes shut and thought unashamedly of Lelitia Considine, conjuring up erotic pastures of nubile skin and compliant agitation.

'Ah . . . ah . . .' he said.

'You finished?' said the woman.

'No!' he gasped.

He redoubled his efforts. If he prolonged, would she ask for two and sixpence?

'Git at it, boy!' said a rough voice from the tent flap.

He couldn't wait. He didn't give a damn. And there – ah! – the foul deed was done.

'You're wanted,' said Corporal Lovatt.

'Dammit, do you have no manners?'

'Sergeant Canning wants you.'

'Blast!' He straightened his clothes. 'Do I look all right?'

'A bit thinner in the face.' Lovatt was watching the woman, who hadn't even bothered to close her legs. 'How was it?' he asked of Pottinger.

'I really must run along, old chap.'

'How much?' Lovatt asked the woman.

'Two shillings, five minutes.'

'Lend us two shillings,' he said to Pottinger.

Pottinger reluctantly pushed the coin into his hands. 'That's all I have till payday.'

'Push off,' Lovatt said, unfastening his trousers.

'You ready?' said the woman.

Lovatt laughed. 'Ready?' He dived upon her.

When Pottinger walked into the barracks yard, entering from the rear, he found Sergeant Canning waiting, pawing at the dirt. His face looked greyer than usual beneath the tan, and he looked at Pottinger with a peculiar sideways glance.

'Where have you been?' Canning asked in what was almost a whisper. 'The Governor's men are here.' And, to Pottinger's stare: 'Mr Aubrey Holliday and Mr Henry Cummings. They want to see you,' he hissed.

'Me?'

'It's like a visit from the Queen!' Canning husked.

'Is it about the Considines?' For weeks, Pottinger had been haunted by his failure. He had justified himself on paper but anyone, apart from Canning, could read between the lines. And Canning had believed it because he wanted to.

They started towards the office, the Sergeant's manner suppliant. 'Tell them the truth,' he advised, 'but not the unvarnished truth. Tell them the women were threatened with death, or worse, anything at all. Considine's complained, you may be sure.'

'I shall do my utmost,' Pottinger said wearily, pausing at the passageway.

'Because it reflects, y'see,' the Sergeant said, 'on me, on my command.'

'After you, sir,' Pottinger said.

'I'm not included,' Canning said bitterly.

No wonder he was worried.

'And how long have you been in the Colony?' Aubrey Holliday asked of Pottinger.

'Thirty-seven months, sir.'

'And how long have you served as a trooper?'

'Seven weeks, sir.'

'Do you like the life?'

'Yes, sir.'

'Not too hard, not too remote?'

'Sir?'

Holliday let the question lapse and he and Henry Cummings put their heads together. Holliday was seated in Canning's chair behind the desk, and Cummings was sitting at a corner with papers spread before him. He now passed a paper to Holliday and pointed to an item. Holliday looked up with false jollity. 'I see you tried your luck on the field. At Fivecrown.'

'There was an interlude,' Pottinger said, moistening his lips. And his heart was sinking, Now it was out, now he knew. Dr Hudson presumably had talked. There'd been that wench at the diggings, her death from abortion, her illegal burial, and the dog that dragged the corpse up. Most distasteful. And he hadn't been guilty. He'd only lent a hand and a one pound note.

'If you'll allow me to explain, sir ...' he began, but Holliday waved this aside with a cheery grin, got up from the desk and pushed his girth around the corner. 'No, no,' he laughed, 'it's I who should explain.'

Pottinger looked at Cummings, who was also smiling. A rum way, Pottinger thought, to haul a man across the coals.

'Fact is,' Holliday said, 'your little secret is out.'

'Oh, really?' Pottinger began to mentally dredge up a whole dross of unsavoury secrets, stolen amours, gambling debts, even the disputed five pound note. Was he to be accused of thieving his own money from the avaricious Dr Hudson?

Holliday, with a mischievous look, withdrew an envelope from his jacket. 'Your letter,' he said, 'was inadvertently forwarded from Fivecrown to the Sydney Barracks. It is the...' he searched the rafters for the phrase '... mode of address that intrigues us.'

'May I?' asked Pottinger, reaching for the envelope, tiring of this childish game.

Aubrey Holliday surrendered the letter. It was addressed: 'Sir Frederick Pottinger, Bart.'

'Good Lord,' Pottinger said, and sat down on the nearest chair.

Holliday laughed. 'So you are undone, Sir Frederick.'

Pottinger looked up as though someone had tweaked his nose. So he was titled – here – in Ironbark, in this hot, palpitating little town, in Sergeant Canning's earth-floored office with the cobwebs at the window and the hard sunlight shining through the smeared glass. People went past in the street. A wagonload of water barrels crashed and creaked its way along.

'Open it,' Holliday said cheerfully. 'Open your letter.'

Pottinger did so. It was a half formal, half commiserative letter from his father's lawyer in London. The news was so old, so stale from all those months on the oceans of the world, that it didn't seem real. His brother was dead from some obscure and unsuspected illness.

'My brother's dead,' he said. He heard a sound like dry leaves in the room as the two men moved with a shift of sympathy. Pottinger looked up at them. 'I'm touched,' he explained, 'but not that deeply. We were not that close.' And he thought of Francis, the elder brother, the gifted one, as he explained the lore of mathematical equation in the study room, saying in a high, papery voice, 'Freddie, you are such a dunce!'

'Such a loss,' Holliday was sighing. 'Such a long way from home.'

'A brother can never be replaced,' Henry Cummings said, rising now to gaze in a melancholy way from the window.

'Frankly, I detested him,' Pottinger said.

They looked at him askance. The poor man was undoubtedly in the twist of grief.

'Never mind,' Holliday burst out. And he seized Pottinger's

hand with such vigour that Sir Frederick was compelled to rise, his hand locked in a chubby squeeze. 'My sympathies and congratulations, sir. It's life, sir, the microcosm of life, joy and sadness all combined.'

'Thank you,' Pottinger said.

'I suppose you'll want to get home with all possible speed?'

Home? Pottinger thought. Home was thirty-seven months behind. Home to the manor house at Apsley Chase? 'I shall have to think about it,' he said.

'You're not determined?'

'Not entirely.'

'You prefer the Colony?'

Pottinger laughed. He could not explain, not to the Governor's men. The Colony was a ball and chain anchored in the mind. 'Such a devil of a journey home,' he sighed – and almost toppled from Holliday's exuberant clap upon his back.

'Excellent. What a blessing. We welcome you. A jewel in the crown of Empire, eh?'

'Welcome?' Pottinger thought. He hadn't been welcome at Fivecrown, or drunk at the Bull and Mouth, or blackening the tavern-keeper's eye in Sydneytown and jumping fences to escape the law. He'd been a bit of a rake, and enjoyed it, and this title, this damned title didn't become him at all.

'Your father would be proud of you,' Henry Cummings murmured.

Oh yes, indeed, the old chap, Sir Henry – British Envoy to China, Governor of Hong Kong, Cape Colony and Madras by turn – he'd do a cartwheel in his grave to think his hard-earned title had been handed down to the thorn upon his family tree.

'The thing is,' Holliday said, bundling up his papers, 'we must find you a decent sinecure, tucked away in Sydney. Something more than merely titular.'

'I shall not be going to Sydney,' Pottinger said.

There was a stunned silence in the room.

'I shall stay here.'

'Here? In Ironbark?'

'At my present post.'

Holliday looked at Cummings, and back to Pottinger. 'I'm afraid we can't have that.'

'Why not?'

Holliday looked at Pottinger, the dusty, dirt-streaked uniform. Was the fellow joking? 'You're a trooper,' he laughed. 'And a baronet. And a Guardsman. How can you stay here?'

'That's my decision,' Pottinger said. 'At least for the moment.'

Holliday gave a prolonged and windy sigh and slumped back into Sergeant Canning's chair. The chair creaked. 'Well,' he said finally, looking up, 'I suppose we shall have to work something out.'

'What happened?' Sergeant Canning asked anxiously twenty minutes later. 'What was it all about?'

Pottinger gazed at him. The Sergeant looked sick and pasty in the sunlight. 'There's been a bit of a turn-up,' he said. 'My brother's died in England.'

'Oh . . .' But the Sergeant couldn't hide his relief. 'I'm sad to hear it,' he said.

'And I'm a bloody baronet.'

Canning laughed uncertainly.

'I mean it. They've made me blooming Sir Frederick. I shall never get used to it.'

'You're joking.'

'Afraid not, old man.'

Canning, who was not without his humorous side, began to see the richness of it. 'What do I call you, then? Trooper Sir Frederick?'

Pottinger looked all around the barracks yard, seeing every inch of it in a different, crueller light. 'I'm afraid you'll have to think of something else to call me,' he told Canning, who stood there with his mottled face, his eyes transparent, trusting. 'They've just given me your job.'

## Twelve

'You get that holster for me?' Gardiner asked Old Jack Flynn.

Flynn turned around so fast he dropped half a keg of nails. It was early in the morning and he hadn't even put the blinds up, just opened the door and stuck the tub of brooms outside. 'Frank,' he gasped, 'you're a wanted man.'

'Why, what're you planning to do?'

'Nothing. I just mentioned it.'

'Well, did you get it, Jack?'

'What?'

'Did you get the holster for my gun?'

Gardiner took the Colt Navy out and put it on the counter.

Flynn shrank back, his eyes wide behind metal-framed glasses. He didn't trust his customer, never had, and especially not across a gun. He was a free settler from a grocer shop in Wicklow, and he didn't plan to end his days in Ironbark.

Just then, a patrol of troopers galloped past the door. Gardiner leaned against the counter to watch them go. 'Could have saved them the trouble,' he said. 'All that way to Winoka, and I won't even be there. Did you get the holster?' he asked for the third time.

'Yeah,' Flynn croaked. 'I got it.'

'Well, get it, then.' But Flynn was rooted to the spot. 'Don't wet the floor, Jack, just go and get the holster.'

While Flynn rummaged through the boxes, barrels, kegs and chests, sending linen flying, upsetting pots and pans, a pimple-faced youth came in, a new-chum trooper. Flynn looked up and turned white.

The boy said, 'Sir Frederick says to fetch buckets, brooms, and scrubbing soap.'

'Right. Yes. Help yourself,' said Flynn.

'Who's Sir Frederick?' Gardiner asked.

'That's old Pottie,' the lad said cheerfully. 'Fred Pottinger. They made him a Sir.'

Gardiner laughed. 'No, come on, now, what's the joke?'

'It's true. He's an English baronet. He runs the bleeding barracks, now.'

'What happened to the Sergeant?'

'Pottie's lapdog. Sits and bites his nails all day. Here,' he said with sudden caution, 'don't you go saying what I said.'

'No chance,' Gardiner said, and while the callow trooper stooped to gather buckets, lifted the boy's gun clean out of the holster.

'Gimme that,' the boy said.

'This what they fit you out with now? What is it?'

'It's an Enfield.'

Gardiner handed the gun back. 'You won't go far with a single-shot percussion.'

'It's what they fit me out with,' the youth lamented. 'They give the others Remingtons and Navies.'

Gardiner laughed. 'They're catching up with me. What's in the way of rifles?'

'Enfields. Five double-sevens.'

'Sooner use a stick. One dead shot and you're done. What else have they got?'

'Why?' said the trooper. 'Who's asking?'

'I'm a sort of gunsmith,' Gardiner said.

'They reckon,' the boy said confidentially, 'Frank Gardiner's got a forty-four Remington revolving rifle that fires six shots straight out.'

'Is that what they reckon?'

'I gotta go ... I gotta go, Mr Flynn,' he called. 'Sir Fred says to put it on the slate.'

Flynn came up when the trooper had gone and put the holster on the counter. He was sweating with big bright beads of sweat.

'That's real nice,' Gardiner said, handling the tooled leather, strapping it on. 'It fits real snug. How much do I owe you?'

'Take it,' Flynn urged him. 'With my compliments.'

'What do you think I am – a thief?'

Gardiner paid him for the holster, every penny, and bought a bag of lozenges of wintergreen. 'Have one,' he said offering the bag.

'Frank, it's going to be a very busy morning.'

'Mr Flynn,' Gardiner said, with his elbow on the counter, 'it's this way ... I'm going to need some guns, some of those Remingtons I'm supposed to have, and maybe half-a-dozen Colts. How much would it be for, say, ten, make it a dozen guns in all – six rifles, six Colts?'

Flynn said in a whisper, 'I can't do business with you, Frank.'

'Why not? I'm a cash-paying customer. Which his lordship Pottinger ain't. A baronet!' he laughed. 'I wish I'd known.'

'What do you want with all those guns?'

'Can you get 'em, Jack, that's all I want to know.'

Flynn began to pick worriedly at the frayed cotton of his sleeves. 'No. No, I can't.'

'What if I promise to cut your throat?'

'I can't do it, Frank. The army's got those guns. And Pottinger. He's got 'em all on order.'

Gardiner pricked his ears up. 'How many?' he asked.

'Two boxes. One dozen.'

'When?'

'Be here Tuesday,' Flynn said, wiping the trickle of sweat. 'Frank,' he whispered, 'there's people coming ... Good morning, Mrs Reynolds,' he said, 'and how are we today?'

'We lost another tooth,' Mrs Reynolds told him, dragging in a six-year-old.

'Be seeing you,' Gardiner told Flynn. 'Morning, Mrs Reynolds,' And he stooped to the child. 'Take a sweetie for your tooth.'

'Wasn't that Frank Gardiner?' Mrs Reynolds said.

Gardiner got on his horse and walked the horse out of town, choosing the longer way down past the barracks. Twelve guns, he was thinking. Arriving Tuesday. And what else would they have in the store? He slowed as he passed the barracks passage-way, hoping to catch a glimpse of the new baronet, but all he could see, quick as a wink, was men in shirtsleeves, or even undervests, swabbing down the walls. The place was as clean as a slaughteryard, or as clean as the customers thought it was. Then he heeled the horse and rode out of town. The sentry, the new one posted by the door, didn't even blink.

'Now the whitewash!' Pottinger commanded. 'Get them on the whitewash.'

'Whitewash!' Sergeant Canning barked.

A trickle of men slouched forward with brimming buckets.

'Move!' Canning roared.

'I want to see those walls white enough to blind me,' Pottinger said, patrolling, hands behind his back.

'Slosh it on!' Canning told them, his shadow on their backs as hard as a whip. Oh Lord, he was thinking, what a hell his life had become. In two weeks, less, the man had become a tyrant of cleanliness and order; they'd even dug latrines! And his office – Pottinger's office – they were putting floorboards in, and a desk twice as large, green-baize-covered on which the dust settled like talc and the orderly was forced to clean it twice a day. And when Canning now stood at the desk, on the wrong side of the desk, there was Queen Victoria gazing down. He'd started to think in his more melancholy moments that the Queen, his dear Queen with all her blind authority, had taken on the countenance of his carping, nagging wife.

'You think I am obsessed,' Pottinger challenged him as they stood in the yard to watch the troopers slaving.

'No, no, sir, of course not.'

'I cannot abide untidiness. Or filth, or sloth, or tardiness. Pride and punctuality, that's the thing.'

'Oh yes, quite so,' the Sergeant said, still sorting the virtues from the vices.

'As we learned in the Guards. As it was drummed into us.'

Canning nodded obediently, his face awash with tides of red and saffron; he did not feel at all well. His new commander had become a prig and a pompous ass, all in the time it took to rig him out in buttons and braid.

'Results,' said Pottinger, grinding his hands outside the

lock-up. 'Work achieves results – a fact not immediately evident, but cleanliness begets efficiency, and efficiency, results!'

The man's as pious as a Sunday parson, Canning thought. 'I agree,' he said. 'We've seen results already.'

It was true they'd netted a few alleged bushrangers – Paddy Oakley, the halfcaste Billy Jingles, and the Booters, Fred and Percy, but, oh my hat, you couldn't tell Sir Frederick they'd always been there for the taking. The bush was full of lay-abouts, all living on the shady side. You'd send them down to Bathurst and Bathurst would send them back again, stamped 'Insufficient Evidence'. It didn't make for good relations, though it made a decent tally in the book.

'I intend to make this outpost the pride of the Western Division. I intend to make my mark here, to do justice to my name. You will not recognise these barracks. They will be, Sergeant Canning, the Taj Mahal of the Western Plains. And I'll have the Governor here, by God I will...' And his face began to light up with the vision of it. He had a purpose now, a will, perhaps for the first time in his life. 'I'll have him in this office, the Governor and his lady. In a place more secure, more sanguine than Sydneytown. And the Queen will hear about it. I'm not a vain man,' he apologised, 'but I have a pride of Empire, and she should know, England should know, that Iron-bark is an arm of royal command.'

'I shall do my very best to assist you, sir,' Canning said humbly. 'May I go then, sir?' he asked.

There was no answer, not immediately. Finally Pottinger advised, 'There is a variety of armament on order, Sergeant – arriving Tuesday, I am assured. When we are thus equipped, I will lead a detachment of men personally, and bring back Gardiner – quite possibly dead. As an act of self-defence,' he amended thoughtfully.

'Excellent, sir.'

'You have my word, Sergeant. The brigand's days are num-bered.'

And there, for this day at least, the matter lay.

But in a not-too-distant place, across a sequence of ridges and valleys, the brigand himself was lighting a fresh cigar with a twig from Johnny Piesley's campfire, and he was saying in that twisted, convoluted way that drove the young man crazy, 'Tuesday. That'd be a good day for it.'

'A good day for what, Frank?'

'For what I'm thinking, Johnny.'

'Why, what're you thinking?'

Gardiner winked at him. 'I'll think about it.' He got on his horse. 'See you Tuesday. Keep yourself in nick. Get some sleep. Tuesday night we're going to light up Ironbark.'

Gardiner rode away into the shimmer of the forest. No man alive knew where he went.

## Thirteen

The evening at Considine's – what Pottinger whimsically and privately called his 'presentation' – was everything he'd fled from thirty-eight months ago. The only concession, he admitted, was that it hadn't been held in the woolshed. But here he was, the darling of the Ironbark 'aristocracy'. It was a joke. Such a raggle-tail he'd hardly met outside the stews of London, but they did have their pretensions, and their aspirations in this strutting game that besieged the whole damned Colony.

It was a stifling night, the last of summer, and he was drinking a sickly punch. There were fifteen people crowded in the parlour and most of them, it seemed, were pressed upon him.

'In forty-eight, no, 'nine it was,' Sir Godfrey Stockton was saying in a thin, septuagenarian's voice, 'we shed ourselves of the jolly blackfellers, man and boy alike. They were raiding the camp, d'you see? Pillaging the stores. And I said to my man, Croft – or was it Whittle? dashed if I know – "This can't go on," I said; "they're worse than a plague of rats." "Well, zurr," he said – he was a Northern country lad, no offence – "we'll treat 'em like the rats. We'll poison the water 'oles. And what we don't get done with strychnine, we'll drive 'em off with guns!' I want to tell you, gentlemen – and I see a lady there – that was the best bleeding hunt I ever had! We started out at six o'clock on a winter's day with a pack of hounds and half a dozen "monkey tails", breechloaders, the best black-catcher they ever made...'

Pottinger mopped his forehead with a handkerchief already damp and took tally of the 'aristocracy'. Apart from the elderly 'black-catcher' at his elbow, there was, of course, Mr and Mrs Considine and the daughters, Clara and Lelitia. Michael Taylor was tending his loved one even now, bringing her rose-coloured concoctions in quite elegant glasses rimmed with gold. A little to the rear, close by the spinet, the evening was also honoured by Aubrey Holliday and the self-effacing penman, Henry Cummings. They had brought with them, all the way from Bathurst, Pottinger's immediate superior, Captain St Clare of the Bathurst Detachment, a lean man of frosty manner and icy flesh, like the flesh of the dead. To the Captain's left, and hunched in a chair against the curtain, surely suffering an overindulgence of dinner wine, was the testy Dr Hudson, who all night had been trying to engage Pottinger in conversation. 'A word,' he kept saying, 'a word with you...' as Pottinger would be drawn away, or else deflected. And finally, there was Mrs Dwyder – Grace – the hairy widow from Toffee Hollow, made rich, it was alleged, by three husbands and fecund with three daughters, Angel, Ruby, and Cecilia who were ... homely was the kindest word. Cissy Dwyder had begun to play the spinet. Pottinger turned aside, setting his course for Lelitia Considine.

'If I could by any chance have a word with you...' Dr Hudson began.

'Later,' said Pottinger, shrugging aside the man's clammy hand. 'I've a desperate need for a spot of fresh air.'

And he fled from the house without so much as a glance at the dark-haired girl. It was pitch-black night outside, and the air was cool on his skin. The sky was brilliantly clear, and there was a pair of falling stars. Then he heard footsteps on the wooden treads, and turned expectantly.

'It's about that five pound note,' Dr Hudson said, looming up from the dark.

Pottinger was exasperated beyond all measure. 'Good heavens, man,' he said, 'I'm not in the least concerned.'

'No, but I felt I had to tell you. The matter's been befuddled down in Bathurst. And I wrote, you understand, to the Magistrate direct, but he referred me to the Constable, the Chief Constable and —'

'Please go away,' Pottinger said. And he set himself to listening to the thin plucking of the music, and when next he turned, the besotted Doctor had vanished like a wraith – though one who retched, miserably drunk, in the dark behind the stables. Well, Papa, Pottinger was thinking, so I landed on my feet after all – though it took two familial deaths and a trick of fate to do it. But the curious thing, the astonishing thing was that Pottinger found himself not averse to the little 'greatness' thrust upon him. He had warmed to his command, that much was obvious, and all that tiresome business of the Guards – from which he had ultimately escaped, and not with honour – had now borne fruit. A different kettle of herring, he thought, when one was dishing out the orders.

'Oh ... oh,' groaned the languishing Doctor in the distant night.

Pottinger strolled down by the woolshed, his pathway lit by starlight. There was an unexpected charm about the night. It was a paradox of this strange land, Australia, that its cruelty could turn to such a moist seductiveness, the air soft and damp, yet stunningly clear, bearing with it the spinet and the voices from the house, and the chatter of men in the huts as they bet their wages at a game of cards, and the snuffling of animals, asleep, in the pens. But alas, he sighed, he would be missed.

He turned back towards the house and saw her there, outside, framed by the door-light.

'Miss Considine,' he said, advancing.

She smiled in the dark. Her shoulders were bare to the night. 'We must close the garden gate,' she said, moving down to correct his lapse, 'or Papa will lose his treasures.'

They stood by an arching bramble rose which had been nursed in a tub all the way from England and now bloomed full-blown, the fragile petals peeled back to the dark heart of the flower.

'I'm a poor guest,' he apologised, 'but the air was stifling.'

'I thought it was the people?'

He laughed. 'It was the people.'

'You mustn't be too hard on us,' she said. 'We're a rough, raw lot, not like home.'

'I hadn't thought about it,' he lied.

Then she turned full upon him. 'You really are the most extraordinary man. And such a wicked man to conceal your true identity.'

'I thought it became me.'

'And you've made things exceptionally difficult.'

'Really?' he said.

'If a lady,' she mused in a mocking tone, 'were to betray some . . . interest in you after your unexpected elevation, she'd be dismissed, surely, as a selfish, grasping tart, would she not?'

'Tart?' Pottinger looked at her, at this vulgar word stemming from those perfect lips. 'Not at all,' he said.

'I've shocked you.'

'That would be impossible.'

'This is a plain land,' she said. 'I use plain words. I grew up with a convict nanny whose children taught me more things than I could learn in England.'

'You've spent your life here?'

'The last ten years of it.'

'Good Lord,' he said. A ten-year term, that was unthinkable. Only felons had to pay that price. 'But you must miss England, even so?'

'Not at all. Do you?'

Miss England? he thought. 'Yes,' he said, 'quite frequently.'

'You have a lady there?'

'No,' he said. And set himself to thinking: By Harry, these colonials were damned direct. 'Why do you ask?'

But no, she wouldn't play that game. 'What would you have done,' she asked, 'that afternoon in the kitchen, if Frank Gardiner had taken me hostage?'

'I should have punched his nose in.'

'But truly, what would you have done?'

He smiled at her. 'I should have looked the other way.'

'And if he had assaulted me?'

'I should have looked the other way.'

'What a despicable man.'

'I do my utmost.'

'Papa said you were not to be trusted.'

'That would be before my title?'

'Yes,' she conceded. 'Though what's a title?'

'You may call me Frederick.'

'No. Sir Frederick. I love your title. It gives you such an air. My sister Clara is quite beside herself – to think she met you in the coach and didn't even know.'

'She has a fine young man.'

'Not titled. Does a title,' Lelitia asked, strolling through the garden, 'convey a privilege to your ardours?'

'I beg your pardon?'

'Do ladies swoon, and do you take advantage?'

'I haven't held my title long enough to know.'

'There are three panting misses in the parlour – and one playing for you the sweetest laments. I'm not accomplished,' Lettie said. 'I don't play spinets, and my tapestry is a total despair. But I sit a horse well, and not always side-saddle. And I can prime and load a gun, and shoot a card at twenty paces. I can draw water, fell trees and grub potatoes —'

'And you make the most delightful Devil-on-the-Coals.'

He took her hand, intending to place his lips upon it, then changed his mind and kissed her, her lips parting unexpectedly to a soft yielding that began to lock their bodies, her body melting, straining into his. He broke away, more in surprise.

'I told you I was a tart.' Though she hadn't, not precisely.

He took a hold upon her wrist, hard enough to make her gasp. 'That will never be true.'

'Now you detest me.'

He looked for answer from her eyes shining from the stars, searching out what she wanted, what special flame was in her that made her burn so. He himself had never wanted so urgently, but the very collision between them – like comets on a savage course – compelled him to take pause.

'Lettie!' screeched Mrs Considine from the kitchen doorway. 'Where are you, love?'

'I have to go,' Lettie whispered.

But neither of them moved.

'It's all right, loov,' they heard Mr Considine in a gentler voice, 'she'll be back in a tick.'

'But she's with that man.'

'Aye, I know that.'

The door closed again. There was a din of crickets in the garden, and a soft wind from Ironbark. 'Sir Frederick...?' she said in a voice both submissive and challenging.

He leaned forward and kissed the cleft between her breasts, just above the cameo brooch. 'Where?' he said.

'No, not now.'

'When?'

'Soon.'

'Tomorrow?'

'Friday. When they go away.'

'I will make arrangements.' They turned towards the house. Even as they walked, he could hear the catch of her breath. 'Compose yourself,' he said.

She pressed her fingers to the place where he had kissed her. 'That's a devil's kiss,' she said. 'It burns right through me.'

They went inside.


In Ironbark, there was celebration of a different sort – the grim and weary revels, the ritual of hungry men up from the diggings in the lunar wasteland of the fields eight miles away. All day long they worked in the slosh, down holes and tunnels, cradling, crushing, fossicking for the bits of gold the first big rush had overlooked. The fields were done, these particular fields, they all admitted this, but a few old moles, forty, fifty of them kept burrowing with enough tunnels to stretch from here to China.

At sundown they couldn't wait. They'd hitch up horses and wagons and move into Ironbark to spend their find. Canning was used to it. He was sitting in his office, or rather Pottinger's, doing extra duty while the baronet was being fêted. Such was the luck of the aristocracy. He could hear Trooper Batchford's accordion in the yard and Micky Travers singing at the fire:

'We'll 'ave plenty o' girls, y' must mind that.
Buck-jumpin' Maggie an' Leatherhide Pat.
Stringybark Peggy an' Greenstick Trish,
Oh yes, me boys, as many as you wish!'

Canning sighed, and laboured over his report with his tongue stuck out. It would be near on midnight before he was done.

Frank Gardiner took the bottle out of Johnny Piesley's hands and told him to shove it in his saddle-bag. 'You don't need that,' he said. 'You need your wits.'

They were in a well of darkness not far from the Irish Tavern. It was very still and all the sounds were magnified.

'Well,' said Gardiner, 'might as well get on with it.'

'Frank,' yelped Piesley, 'someone'll see us.'

'I don't doubt, if you keep yellin'.'

They set off up the street towards the barracks. Gardiner was leading a horse, not his own but a working nag, all muscle, heft, and stubbornness, not bred for speed. Then he stopped in his tracks. 'Where's the doings?'

Piesley smacked his own head for the sake of his incompetence. He'd left the keg just past the Irish Tavern.

'Go and fetch it,' Gardiner said. He was beginning to have doubts himself, mostly due to his accomplice.

Piesley came up hugging the keg. They continued on their way – past the barracks, past the open passageway now without a sentry, past the windows where Canning could be plainly seen working beneath the green-shaded lamp.

'Canning's in the office!' Piesley said, stating the obvious.

'Keep down, and shut up.'

They turned the corner of the barracks, into the darkness down by the white exterior wall, to a paddock where the town ran out of buildings – and the horse and cart was there, just like old man Walsh had promised.

'Right,' said Gardiner, 'get at it.'

Piesley moistened his lips and crept across to the barracks wall where, nudged into the corner and part of the wall itself, was a solitary structure with a single window barred across the cobwebbed glass. Piesley set down the keg and began to prise it open.

'What the hell are you doing?' Gardiner said, grabbing him.

'I'm doin' what you said.'

'Not here,' Gardiner said, 'back around the passageway.'

'That's the front door,' Piesley objected.

'Now you're thinking.'

'Blow that,' Piesley said. 'I'm not sticking my neck in there.'

'Hitch this to the window,' Gardiner told him, handing him the rope. The rope was harnessed to the horse. 'And when you've hitched it good, climb aboard and hang on tight.'

'I don't get it, Frank.'

'It's all related. Like a socket in a joint . . . I'll be with you in a minute.'

Gardiner picked out the bung from the keg and started back to the street. 'Frank . . .' He heard a pathetic whine behind him. He retraced his steps and pushed his fist at Piesley. 'You get that horse harnessed to the window,' he said. 'And if you make a mess of this, I'm going to mash your face.'

'Stupid blooming business,' he heard Piesley say as he moved around the corner.

Crouching beneath Canning's window, Gardiner began to lay a trail of blasting powder. It was going to be the world's shortest fuse, but he couldn't help that. What he needed was a bang to keep the barracks busy. He wouldn't have, he reckoned, more than a minute.

Just then, a couple of lurching diggers came up from the

dark. Gardiner slumped against the wall and sat in the dirt. If they knew him, even halfway knew him, he was done.

'Which way's Mrs Richard's?' said the stout one with a sailor's roll.

Gardiner lifted his head with a look of drunken torpor.

''E's got a keg, George,' said the smaller man.

'I see that. So 'e has.'

''Ow much for the keg, feller? Act o' charity, or a punch in the beak?'

'Push off,' Gardiner said.

''E's a selfish-lookin' bugger, George.'

'Which way is Polly Richard's?' said the sailor.

'Back o' the smithie's,' Gardiner told him, 'an' welcome to the clap.'

'Hey, look here, you fellows! ...' Canning's voice came from the window, his head poked out. 'Push off before I toss you in the pot.'

Gardiner was alone again. He rolled around from where he sat and could see clean through the passageway into the barracks yard where a little fire was going, and a few lobster-tails around it, singing songs and spinning out a ration of rum. Gardiner tidied the powder trail and put the keg in place. He supposed it would make a hell of a bang, but not much more. He really wasn't a powder man.

A couple of gents went by in a spanking horse and sulky. Gardiner thought it might have been Sir Fred. He moved back along the wall, crouching once again beneath the window, to the end of the powder trail. Flint-box. Damn he'd left it in his saddle-bag.

'What the all-fired blazes do you think you're doing?' said a voice.

Gardiner turned with a start. It was the man they all called 'Boots' because that was his trade.

'Lend us a light. Come on, quick.'

'What are you doing, Frank?'

'Looking for me diamond stickpin, what do you think I'm doing?'

'Boots' took his clay pipe out of his gob and jammed the stem at Canning through the glass. 'He'd give me a year's takings for the likes of you.'

'I'd give you a bullet in the teeth. Give us your pipe.' Gardiner grabbed the pipe and sucked it hard to get a glow up.

'Hey,' said 'Boots', 'that's blasting powder, ain't it?'

Gardiner put the hot coal to the powder and ran so fast he left a hole in the air. He had a final, nightmare-like impression of the orange zizz-z-z! of powder in the darkness, and 'Boots' flinging his hands up on the run, and he reached the corner, turned it just as Canning pricked a full-stop in the page. Then the door slammed off its hinges, buckling in with a terrible hail of wind and debris, and next there was a rending, ripping detonation that tore through the length of the barracks and sent Piesley's horse rocketing with terror into the dark – until the harness snapped tight, and horse and rider plunged, dragging the bars of the window with them.

'Get the wagon!' Piesley heard Gardiner's command, but far off through the singing in his ears. He looked around and was just in time to see Gardiner's feet vanish through the opening in the window. He ran, half tipping over, to get the wagon.

Blood streaming, Canning lurched out into the ruined passageway. He'd been flung mightily against the office wall, ripped off his seat, back against the portrait of the Queen.

'Buckets!' he roared. 'Get some buckets.' Flames were lapping up the architrave. Then it struck him. There had to be a human hand in this. He raced back and found his gun.

In the passageway, a white-faced Trooper Batchford had turned up with a bucket, the nearest he could find. It was full of whitewash. 'Use it!' Canning commanded.

A slash of white spilled across the burning smoke.

'Sound the alert,' Canning cried, stepping through smashed timbers into the yard. The men were in panic, that much was clear. Some had guns, some stood stunned from sleep and shock, one oaf was even naked. Adding to the general clamour came a braying lament from the lock-up, from the prisoners who were convinced that battle had begun, that they were dead meat in the onslaught. And half the town was on the run, squealing outside the barracks walls.

'Ride and search!' Canning barked. He was a terror to behold with the blood on him, standing in the smoking ribbons of his uniform. 'Break out the guns,' he cried.

'Bullets,' Gardiner said, passing out the boxes.

'That's enough, Frank,' Piesley told him. He'd already loaded enough weapons to fight an army.

'Right. Coming out,' Gardiner said. Then the door to the Weapons Store opened behind him and a trooper pushed into the dark with a lantern held before him.

'Damn!' Gardiner said. He was caught on a spike of glass from the broken window.

'It's him!' he heard the trooper say. 'It's Frank G —'

The bullet passed through the lantern glass, snuffing the flame and the life behind it. The dead man passed into another's arms and Gardiner felt the return fire cleaving the air with a whoosh of wind across his ear.

'Get moving!' he commanded the horse as he wrenched the wagon full about and headed into Ironbark.

'Wrong way!' Piesley yelled.

'Think I can drive it blind through the bush?'

The wagon swept through town, down the main street, spilling residents aside. Piesley clung to the boards, afraid for his life. Things swept past him in a blur, lantern lights and candlelights, people crying out, gunshots, a horse rearing – Jesus, he was thinking, how did I ever get into this?

Then he heard a final voice, trailing way behind him. 'It's Gardiner, S'arnt – headin' out of town.'

But they never found them. It was too late, too dark.

Old man Walsh was sitting up when the wagon arrived with Gardiner and Piesley. He walked out to meet them. 'How did it go?' he asked.

'It went very well,' Gardiner replied. 'It damn' near took Ironbark off the map.'

'Thought it would.'

'Why didn't you tell me?'

' 'Cause I wasn't sure.'

They began to offload the haul and stack it away. At the end of it, Piesley said: 'Now what, Frank?'

Gardiner lit a cigar. 'Now we got the guns,' he said.

'Yeah, I know that.'

Gardiner started down towards his horse in the darkness, tossing his reply across his shoulder: 'Now we're gonna get the gold coach.'


## Fourteen

Despite the disastrous turn of events, Pottinger continued arrangements for his clandestine meeting with Lelitia Considine. He decided against the room at the Irish Tavern. There was far too much gossip attached to the Tavern, and urchins had been known to spy through the windows. He settled on a room at the back of Mrs Polly Richard's house, which lay a quarter-mile beyond the bridge in a copse of wattle trees. Mrs Richard was a heavy, spotted woman in a soiled chemise and blanket. She promised anonymity when he crossed her palm with gold. Then he inspected the room, a melancholy place where a child had died six years ago of a whooping strangulation, so he was informed, and certain childish things, a doll, a bonnet, had never been removed. There was a bush-bed in the room – made of saplings laced together with a straw-filled mattress on the staves – and that was about all.

'I'll fix it up real nice, yer highness,' she told him with a wobbling sort of curtsy.

He gave her some extra money. 'Get some sheets,' he said. 'Put them on the bed.'

But after all the trouble, his fair Lelitia failed to turn up at all. He waited almost two hours, passing from disappointment to vexation. He thought of riding to the homestead, and damn the embarrassment. But long experience in affairs of the heart had taught him that unrelenting pursuit was total capitulation. He gathered his cloak and said farewell to Mrs Richard.

'Oh, sich a shame,' she said with false sympathy.

He nodded and began to edge past her through the shambles of the house with all manner of feminine garments strung across the hearth.

'Let me get you a nice girl, sir. Let me get you Mary Winters. She's only married this three-month a virgin, and she needs the money.'

'I think not,' Pottinger said, grappling with the locks on the door.

'Let me get you Taffy,' she said desperately, offering the prize. 'Very clean,' she said. 'Dr Hudson makes full use of her himself.'

In all, it had been the most abysmal week. After the explosive devastation of Tuesday night, the barracks looked like a battlefield and all but half a dozen guns were gone. Though Pottinger had taken solace in the fact that his absence had been unavoidable, and that Aubrey Holliday very well knew it, it was Holliday himself who upbraided Pottinger for leaving the 'fortress' unmanned.

'May I say,' Holliday said to Pottinger, 'that this is a most slipshod way to run a military establishment?'

The upshot of it was that Captain St Clare from Bathurst was fetched to 'tighten up' Ironbark. He did so with a look of acid distaste and a terrible chill in his voice. 'Why is everything whitewashed?' he wanted to know. 'Who is growing beans against the wall? What is being done to apprehend Frank Gardiner?' There was an endless daisy-chain of questions. The more Pottinger answered with the same iced control, the more Captain St Clare fell back on his deplorable habit of tweaking the hair from his ears as he waited with what was patently disbelief or lack of interest. It all ended with the Captain sighing, 'I hope to God Sydney never gets to hear of this.'

But on the Monday a man arrived from the *Sydney Morning Herald*, a fellow by the name of Lobcock, and they went through the whole thing again – though with certain variations.

'Let me get this right,' Lobcock said as they sat in a private room at the Irish Tavern. 'It was ten o'clock at night or so,' the journalist went on with wearisome repetition, 'and these two men, under cover of darkness—'

'Four men,' St Clare corrected.

'Four?' said the journalist.

'Five,' said Pottinger, who was quick to catch the drift. 'One around the corner.'

The item, as it turned out, was given quite a splash. Pottinger came out of it looking like a jackass. 'While these events took place,' it said, 'the baronet was supping with his landed peers . . .'

Eight more days had passed. Captain St Clare took his leave of Ironbark on a dismal, rainy morning. The rain had settled with the first southerly change of wind, and fell in misty veils.

'You'll be hearing more from Gardiner,' St Clare warned from his superior height on the horse.

'We're patrolling every inch of territory,' Pottinger reminded him. It was the wildest metaphor, as both well knew – where the plains lapsed into stunted mountains, the forest rolled for miles as far as the eye could see. The only greater distance that Pottinger had ever witnessed was the ocean itself on the endless voyage from England.

They watched St Clare ride out through the misty rain – and the two men, Pottinger and Sergeant Canning, glanced at each other. There was a numbing cold within them. They would indeed hear more from Gardiner, but how it would come and which way it would come was quite beyond them.


The first man to learn of Gardiner's plans was Michael Taylor, Clara Considine's betrothed. He lodged with a family on the Blackbottle Track, and as he was setting out for church one Sunday morning, he met Frank Gardiner's gun. He threw up his hands and made an effort.

'Pretty poor pickings,' he laughed. 'You can have my wallet, the whole two pound ten of it, and as for my watch —'

'I don't want your wallet or your watch.'

'What do you want?'

'I want you, boy.'

Taylor shifted his glance, thinking to make a run for it, but two more men moved out of the trees, one of them Johnny Piesley.

'Mornin', Mr Banker,' Piesley said.

'This here other feller,' Gardiner said, 'he's Johnny Gilbert, an old mate of mine.'

Michael Taylor felt the prickle of hair at his collar. He knew about Gilbert. He was wearing a braided jacket, and strawberry-coloured vest crisscrossed with gold — which was why they called him 'Flash' – Flash Johnny Gilbert.

'Hope you're going to be agreeable,' Gilbert said. 'I never shot a banker in my whole dang' career.' He had an accent as vibrant as a zither. He was Canadian by birth.

'Now look, you fellers...' The words perished in Taylor's mouth. A watery sun fell upon his shoulders, and he was sweating as though in the heat of summer. In his heart he knew something terrible could likely happen. His whole body went rigid and his mind shut down as a horseman's shadow crossed him from behind.

'Don't get excited,' Gardiner said. 'We're going to put a bandage on your eyes.'

A black silk headband closed out the day for Michael Taylor; it was like the closing of a coffin.

They walked through the bush over rough ground for twenty minutes or more. Taylor could feel the slap of branches in his face and once or twice the splash of water. Then they came to a standstill and the blindfold was removed. Taylor looked all around at the press of bush. They might as well have dropped him in the ocean; he didn't know where he was. A terrifying thought kept pricking at him. He kept trying to suppress it, but in the end he had to get it out. He looked at Gardiner. 'Are you going to kill me? Is that what it is?'

'Not yet,' Gardiner said cheerlessly.

They kept riding deeper into mountain country. There were tree ferns way above their heads, orchids and fungus. It began to get cold; they were climbing steadily and this was a part of the mountains where winter never truly left. About noon, according to the sun, they ate and drank some raw potato liquor, and then rode into a valley pass at the end of which was a rough stringybark shelter, not quite a hut and not quite a gunyah, but a place with a chimney toppling over.

They bundled Taylor inside and Piesley got the fire going. Flash Johnny Gilbert considered their captive, and turned to Gardiner.

'Tie him up?'

'No. Where's he going to run to? You don't feel like running, do you, Michael?'

All at once Michael Taylor sagged to the dirt of the floor and sat there head in hands, weeping with abandon.

Piesley laughed, about to pull him out of it.

'Let him go,' Gardiner said. 'He'll be the better for it.'

For the rest of the day, Taylor sat slumped in a depression so deep that his captors began to treat him with a quiet consideration. As night fell, they ate again and Taylor was finally persuaded to join them. He sat at the rough table now, and they sat at the other end, their elbows on the table – Gardiner, Piesley and Gilbert – watching him.

'How old are you, Michael?' Gardiner asked.

'Twenty-two.'

'Getting married, aren't you – to that filly out of Ironbark? When are you getting married, Michael?'

'September. The end of winter.'

'Got a place to go?'

'I'm going to find a post in Sydney.'

'In a bank?'

'Yes.'

'That's been arranged?'

'Mr Perch is going to speak for me.'

'That's Henry Perch, the bank manager?'

Taylor nodded and moistened his lips.

Gardiner shoved the bottle down the table. 'Have a drink.'

Taylor shook his head. He couldn't stomach any more.

'So it's all worked out?' Gardiner said.

'What is?'

'A real, cosy, put-your-toes-up life.'

'When can I go home?' Taylor said. And then it all came out; he couldn't stop it. 'I haven't done anything. I've never said a word against you. I never will. I'll just go back and shut my mouth. You've made a mistake; that's what it is. People know you work in a bank, they think the money rubs off. I haven't got anything. I never will have. You know how much they pay a bank clerk? I make less than the smithie does.'

The three outlaws greeted this with an abysmal silence. They passed the bottle round. There was the gurgle of the liquor, the plink of a coal in the grate, and Gardiner's sigh.

'You see your situation, don't you, Michael?'

Taylor didn't answer.

'You're way up here in some nowhere place with three desperate men, and the way I see it, well,' he laughed, 'you might never even get to wed that girl. Unless . . .' he added with a weighty emphasis.

'Unless what?'

'It's a pretty simple thing, Michael. It comes in two parts. First part, you go back to town and shut your mouth – just like you say. Second part – that's the easiest part – you just pass the word along next time the gold leaves town.'

'The gold?' Taylor said stupidly.

'The gold on the coach, boy. The next haul from the diggings. It comes to the bank, don't it? It stays there overnight, and it's weighed and notarised. Next day it leaves for Bathurst. That's all I need to know, Michael – which day it is.'

'I couldn't do that!' Michael Taylor said.

The three men sat back and sighed, disgruntled.

'I mean,' said Michael, quoting his unwritten charter, 'I'm a trusted officer.'

'That's why you're here, ain't it?'

'No, I couldn't, no!' he protested, momentarily overwhelmed

by the enormity of the proposal. 'No one has ever touched the gold coach.'

'That's what I've been thinking,' Gardiner said.

'How much money-value's on that coach?' Gilbert asked.

'It . . . it all depends.'

'Take a stab.'

'Twenty thousand,' Taylor said.

Piesley whistled. Gardiner said, 'He can only count to ten. 'Well,' he said, leaning on the table, 'what about it, Michael?'

'I would die,' Michael Taylor said, 'rather than betray a sacred trust.'

In the morning, they were all lounging round the clearing. 'I seen this wild dog once,' Piesley was saying, 'got its foot all tangled up in wire. Me and Jimmy Scully found it, riding up the Narrows. When we come on that dog, he just up and ripped hisself loose, leavin' half a leg behind him. Y'know, that little piece o' leg – must've been there four, five days at least – was all shrivelled up, black as a pickle. Now you,' he said, looking at Michael Taylor, 'if you would be so kind as to take your boot off, I got here a piece of greenhide twine, and I've a mind to blacken off your toes, startin' with the big feller.'

As Taylor hurled himself headlong towards freedom, Gilbert's leg shot out and the young man spilled to the ground hard enough to shave his skin off.

'Damn' stupid thing to do,' Gardiner said.

Taylor looked up to see Piesley standing over him, the thread of leather dangling. 'Suppose I blacken off your private parts?' he said. 'Save you the cost of a weddin'?'

'You wouldn't do that, would you, Johnny?'

'Sure I would. Pull his pants off.'

'Wait a bit,' Gardiner said, getting up. 'Maybe he's changed his mind?'

'Never!' said Taylor.

'Peel his pants off.'

'No, leave it till tonight,' Gardiner said. 'We got nothing else to do tonight. We might as well have something to look forward to.'

'Tie him up?' Gilbert asked.

They tied him to a sapling like a dog, with a leash around his neck that tightened if he struggled. Most of that day the outlaws played cards, swapped yarns and drank a lot, though Gardiner drank less than the others. Taylor spoke to them only once. 'Please untie me,' he said. 'I have a call of nature.' They ignored him, and he was forced to shame himself.

Around dusk they lit a fire. The thought did not cheer Taylor. It meant they were so deeply hidden in the forest that they could abandon all caution. While the others cooked the evening meal Gardiner came and untied him. When the rope was undone, he just sat there stunned and speechless.

Gardiner crouched down beside him, his voice low and gentle. 'Listen, feller, I don't know as I can hold off these villains that much longer. They'd be two of the meanest men in the Colony. They mean every word they say.'

'I can't betray the bank,' Taylor said miserably. 'That gold is a sacred trust.'

'Gold don't belong to anyone,' Gardiner said. 'Belongs to the earth. Belongs to the man that holds it. All that money passing through your hands – like you say, it don't rub off. That ain't sacred, that's an insult.'

'I can't do it,' Taylor said. 'I won't do it.'

'Well?' said Piesley, coming from the fire.

'He won't do it,' Gardiner said.

Piesley swore. 'Did you ever meet such a stubborn cuss? He won't do it, Johnny,' he called to Gilbert.

Gilbert came over and the three men looked down on Michael Taylor. A night bird cawed somewhere in the bush, and the leaves all about shifted with the antics of inoffensive animals. There was no menace in the bush, not of that nature.

'Been thinkin' about the greenhide treatment,' Piesley said. 'Reckon it'd take us three, four days. That'd be too long.'

'You got any more ideas?' Gilbert said.

Piesley put his boot into Taylor's ribs. 'Git over on your hands and knees,' he said.

'Better do as he says,' Gardiner told him.

Shivering with cold and fear, Taylor did as he was told.

'Crawl on over to the fire.'

The three men followed Taylor to the fire where he waited dumbly on all fours. 'Please let me go,' he said. 'Please let me go.'

Piesley pulled out his knife and set it in the coals.

'Mike,' he said, 'I got me a red-hot knife here. Tell me what I'm going to do with it ... Answer me!' he said, with a shove that nearly sent Taylor into the flames.

'I don't know.'

He felt Piesley's hot breath at his ear as he rasped, 'I'm gonna poke it in your rear end, Mike.'

'Dear God, please make them let me go.'

He felt someone yank his trousers down. He felt the cool night air on his skin, the sudden approach of something hot, the first kiss of heat. And then he fainted.

He woke some hours later in the hut to the realisation that he was still locked within his nightmare. Gingerly, he felt his behind. They hadn't even touched him. And he heard their voices. Piesley sounded drunk.

'That girl of his, that Clara Considine, she'd be a virgin, wouldn't she?'

'She sure as anything looked like one.' This was Gardiner's voice.

'I'm goin' out,' Taylor heard Piesley say, 'and I'm gonna get myself a piece o' that virgin's tail.'

'It's a hell of a long way to go, Johnny.'

Then Piesley's snorting laugh. 'I'm gonna get her in the bath tub. And when I get her, I'm gonna split her up the middle, boy. I'm gonna grab those two white titties and ride her down the drainpipe. And when I'm through, boy, when I'm through ...'

There followed a string of such sickening degradations that Taylor finally shrieked, 'No!'

'He's awake, Frank.'

There was the screech of Gardiner's chair, and the outlaw

stood over him, gazing down. 'You changed your mind, Michael?'

'No.' Michael wept and prayed his way into the early hours.

At dawn, he stirred. The others were already moving about. He heard Gilbert say: 'You ever heard of the glass glove treatment?'

'No,' Piesley said, 'what's that?'

'You get this here leather glove, and you kind of mash a bottle up real fine. Then you stick honey on the glove and coat it good with bits of broken glass. That way, you can pattern a man's face up real pretty. It's like a tattoo, it never comes out.'

'Gee, I'd like to see that Johnny.'

'Or you ever hear tell,' Gilbert went on relentlessly, 'of the Kickapoo Indians, up along of Great Lakes way, and what they call the Bull Ant Banquet? What you do is string the feller out, pin the head down by the hair, and . . .'

Michael Taylor hunched back into sleep. Maybe if he ignored the light of dawn, the dawn would go away. He lapsed into a half-world of sleep and wakefulness, of dreams of Clara, ecstasies and torments, and Henry Perch declaring from some fiery prominence: 'Michael Taylor, your treason has made a bankrupt of the Colony!' Then the voices of the men impinged, and they were arguing, Piesley saying, 'I've had enough of the little twit waitin' round to change his mind.' And Gardiner's soft, insistent purr, 'Give the feller time, Johnny.' Then Gilbert's twanging rejoinder: 'I'm a mite inclined to side with Johnny, here. Whyn't we kill this'un, and go get another?'

At sun-up, they tied him to the tree again. All day no one spoke to him, not a word, not a grunt. Piesley spent a good deal of his time sharpening his knife, getting it to so fine an edge that he could slice a blade of grass right down the length of it. Gilbert kept asking what was it he planned to do with the knife, and Piesley wouldn't answer. As for Gardiner, he appeared to sleep all day, the kind of sleep aboriginals slept, akin to lizards, awake but comatose.

On the fourth day, Michael Taylor didn't know whether it was the fifth or sixth day. He lay back against the sapling, the rope about his neck, unshaven, crusted by his own filth and separated by a yawn of silence from the others. Around mid-morning he heard Piesley sharpening the knife again, and on the still morning air, asking petulantly, 'What're we gonna do, Frank?'

'I don't muchly care,' Gardiner sighed. 'Fact is, you can do as you damn' well please.'

Then the whispering sound of the knife against the rock again, and Gilbert saying, 'What're you plannin', Johnny?'

'Gonna give our friend the Wuradjeri treatment.'

'What in hell is that?'

Taylor looked around. Piesley was now smashing up a little piece of rock. 'Gonna treat him like the blacks would.'

'And how would that be?'

'Well,' said Piesley, fossicking among the broken rock, 'you see this here teeny piece o' quartz crystal?'

'Yeah, that's real nice.'

'What you do . . .' He looked around at Taylor and nodded to Gilbert, 'Come on over here.' And, when they had crossed to Taylor, 'Hold him down, Johnny, and hoist the shirt up.'

'Frank! Frank!' Taylor shouted, struggling. But Gardiner seemed oblivious.

'What you do,' Piesley continued laboriously, 'what the Wuradjeris do . . . is cut out a little piece o' kidney fat – dammit, hold him will you? – and put the crystal in its place . . .'

'Is that what they do?'

'Then you heal the cut up with a heated stone and let the feller go. Right on about three days' time, the crystal starts growing and spreading through the body and rotting up the parts . . .'

Taylor gave a tremendous heave in Gilbert's arms, but to little purpose. 'He can buck real good, this'un.'

' 'Course if they kick about at all, you take two sharpened sticks and drive 'em down along the collar-bone, and another down below the tongue – stops 'em yellin'. You think maybe we should do that?'

'No. Just cut the kidney out.'

'Now where in hell is the kidney?'

'Search me, Johnny. You might have to poke about a bit.'

'Hey Frank, you're the butcher. Come and find the banker's kidney.'

Then Michael Taylor's eyes rolled up. 'Shoot, man,' he heard Gilbert say, 'the kid's passed out.'

When Taylor woke it was night and, in the light of the embers, he thought he was alone in the clearing. Then he smelled cigar smoke and looked around, and there was Gardiner sitting right behind him, back to the same sapling.

'Been thinking on your future, Michael . . .'

Taylor explored his body and found himself intact, and began to snuffle quietly in the dark until Gardiner thumped him. 'What are you – man or boy?'

'I can't help it,' Taylor said miserably.

'I been thinking – you ain't got a future. Suppose you do get out of this? You get married, you have a family, you work in a bank. That's a future?'

'Please let me go,' Taylor said. 'I promise not to talk.'

'They're gonna give you life, boy – chained to an ink-pot, wearing specs, blotting up the figures. Nights you go back home to Clara – and damn me if she ain't fat an' fifty, saying "Loosen up me stays, darling", and boy, I tell you, when you see all that skin and meat spilled over like stew in a pot, you're gonna think back to this time when you was true, loyal and stubborn to the bank. And you're going to ask yourself, "Why did I do that? Why didn't I use the fine banking brain the good Lord give me, and see that all those figures passing through my pen . . . is loot, gold, banknotes?" I'm not saying anything, mind,' Gardiner affirmed; 'I'm just saying your future looks stony broke to me. And here you are, sitting on a fortune. You want a drag on my butt?' Gardiner asked, passing the cigar.

Taylor shook his head.

'What you have to calculate,' Gardiner went on, 'with that

fine old banker's brain o' yours, is the elements. First, there's the money. Then there's me. Then there's you. It's like a kind of arithmetic, ain't it? And then,' Gardiner said, rising, 'there's a big subtraction – those two fellers, the two Johnnies. Now, I've been holding 'em down real hard – you know that – but comes tomorrow, I'm riding out. And I'm gonna leave you here. I mean it, Mike. And the moment I'm gone – subtraction ... from you! Think about it, boy. You got till dawn.'

Taylor thought about it – all night long. He thought about it in a tidy way, yet fevered, like a man doing diabolical sums. He could tell them what they wanted – that was the two plus two of it – but he'd likely end in gaol, for who'd believe he was coerced? Behind bars, he thought sourly, no job, nothing, just his skin. He wanted his job, he'd worked for it, for the forty years in front of him. Forty years! he thought. That's nearly half a century. Don't tell them, he began again, scribbling out the figures in his head. They'll kill me, he bleated. He tossed and groaned in the limbo of his sleep. His legs shot out and punched the billy by his feet. Sat up wide awake. They'll kill me! Only crickets answered in the night, and he felt the sweat on him and the cold drench of morning air, the black, damp air of dawn. He began to pray. That didn't work. And set to examining the computations of the night, trying to balance out a spectral balance sheet. And then it came to him, a hard, cold answer. And yet, he still held back.

In the morning, Piesley and Gilbert came out. No one spoke. There was a light ground-mist about and Taylor was frozen through. He roused himself with a painful gasp to hear the forest birds and the splash of urination. He'd hardly slept. In the early hours, hallucinating, he'd thought he was losing his mind. Now everything was sharp and clear with heightened clarity, and he said straight off to Gardiner as Gardiner came walking from the hut, 'I thought about it like you said.'

Gardiner moved across to him as Piesley put the billy on.

'Untie me,' Taylor said.

Gardiner cut the rope.

'What you need,' Taylor said, 'is the name of the day the gold leaves town.'

'Right.'

'And the time. Sometimes they vary the time.'

'Yeah, we'd also need the time.'

'And the number of guns they carry.'

'Anything'd help.'

'And where you'd likely take it.'

'Don't overdo it, boy. Don't get carried away. The time and the day, that'll be enough.'

'No, it isn't.'

'It ain't?'

''Cause I'm cutting myself in,' Michael Taylor said.

Gardiner glanced at the others. 'You're doing what?'

'You need half a dozen men to take that coach. I want to be one of them.'

Gardiner laughed. 'Stick to your trade, Michael ... Tell you what, I'll pay half a hundred on the side. How'd that be?'

'I'm after three thousand three hundred pounds. That's as near as damn to a sixth of twenty thousand.'

'Yeah, I wish I had your brains.'

'Am I in?'

Gardiner blew out his cheeks. 'Wait'll I splash me boots,' he said, unbuttoning his pants.

'What's goin' on, Frank?' Piesley called.

'Negotiations.' Gardiner crossed back to Taylor. 'By golly, you done a load o' thinking, didn't you?'

Taylor nodded. 'Thought I could turn my figures into gold. Get married, set up in Sydney in a saddle shop.'

'You can ride, then?'

'I won the half-mile gallop on the Flats.'

Gardiner nodded. 'Maybe so. But you're a townie. You'd be gun-shy.'

Taylor's glance fell to the Colt Navy.

'That thing loaded?'

Gardiner thought about it, and handed him the gun, barrel first.

'What's in God's name are you doing, Frank?' Gilbert said.

Everything went very still. Taylor took the gun, slipping the butt into the palm of his hand quick as a lizard, and eased the hammer back. Piesley yelped and scrambled over backwards out of range as Taylor levelled the gun at the billy on the fire. 'Hey,' Piesley said, 'that's our boilin' water.'

The first shot sailed clean off into the scrub, whipping through the leaves.

'Bulls-eye!' Gilbert laughed.

'Step up a bit,' Gardiner advised.

Instead, Taylor backed off three paces and turned again. His second shot smacked the billy off the rocks, sending a ribbon of scalding water right across the clearing. And he kept firing, and the billy kept bouncing, leaping like a rabbit until it lay there flattened with the holes shot through it. He handed the empty gun back to Gardiner.

'Where'd you learn to shoot like that?'

'My father was a gunsmith.'

'He'd be damn' well proud of you.' And Gardiner turned to the others. 'Meet Micky Taylor,' he said. 'He's a member of the gang.'

## Fifteen

Now that he was titled, Pottinger felt constrained to attend the Sunday service. Prestige, he ruminated – while not attending to the message from the pulpit – was synonymous with responsibility; it was an equation he had hitherto avoided. 'The agonies of soul, the corrosion of the spirit is the bud that dwells within the heart of each of us...' explained the Reverend Foster as Pottinger's attention continued to wander. It was no cathedral, that much was evident. The church, put together by the faithful, was fashioned from split logs and daub with bird-droppings on the crossbeams, and a rent open to heaven in the canvas roof that let the rain weep through.

The sluggish flies, drugged by the touch of winter in the air, rhymed along with the Reverend Foster. One big chap, a blowie, the type of insect that raddled meat with maggots, had settled on Old Jack Flynn's strawberry-coloured ear, and thereon began a merry fidget with its legs. Pottinger lowered his head to a pious incline and examined the shine of his boots. Shortly, Flynn snorted awake with a stifled oath and a titter drifted through the congregation. 'Let us not admonish the wayward lest we ourselves should fall . . .' the Reverend said in a voice pitched high and nasal, and Pottinger shifted his position to observe the baker, 'Polly' Pollard, and Boots the Bootman and Farrier Jones and that other Polly – Mrs Richard – with a sprinkling of fallen damsels clustered about. In fact, he was looking everywhere but at the one single place that kept returning to his mind – the dark sheen of hair beneath the little flowered bonnet that was Lelitia Considine's. How proud she sat, he thought, as helplessly he studied her again; how well the shoulders bore the head which she kept now at a small aggressive tilt; how – when she sighed – the shoulders lifted like the drift of wings, and how, when she leaned to gather her prayer-book, the blades of the shoulders pushed against the back of her dress. He uttered a silent blasphemy and shifted his own position. That he, Pottinger, should be concerned with such trivia, having never studied shoulders in his life.

But there she sat, foursquare in the solid bosom of her family, flanked by Clara and the elder Considines. And here was he in a heat of longing four rows back, spurned, and not even with a note from her. Well, the game was played and lost. He'd lost before, many times, but never after such promise. Had she not teased him with her ardour and received a kiss, most intimate? And made assurances, a day, a time, a place? Damn the woman.

'He'd had some sleepless nights about Lelitia Considine he had to admit, wrestling not with the soul, but something more mundane. But, he prided himself, he'd not yielded – except to throw himself with honour into work. Work, a veritable storm of work – his activities had been volcanic and a misery to the men. But not without results. At one stage eight bushrangers in the logs, a cattle duffer wounded in the thigh, seven drunken miners soundly thrashed and turned out of town. By Harry, the new broom was sweeping resoundingly clean. There'd even been a piece in the papers. The baronet was not a laughing matter now.

Except for the lamentable affair of Michael Taylor. One fine day, or so the story went, the young bank clerk had set out for the church ... and was never seen again. Well, 'never' was only six days long, but long enough for the gossips to assert that either he'd absconded with fifty-seven pounds, or had gone to live with Blindeye Mary, a coloured girl of certain nubile charms despite her deficiency, or else been taken by the gold fever. All in all, a conundrum to vex the minds of Ironbark.

But it came as no true surprise to Pottinger this Sunday morning when a muddy trooper crept into the service to inform him in a cracked whisper that Taylor was outside with Sergeant Canning, who had spent the last four days tramping through the bush in search, and had now found the missing man not five miles from where he lived, on the forest side of the Blackbottle Track.

'I must have walked around in circles,' Taylor was saying, quite cheerfully in spite of his ordeal. 'I was on my way to church, and the horse took the bit and he bolted.'

'Well,' said Pottinger, as the voices rose within, 'I'm glad to see you got here.'

He led the little party to the horse trough and sat the young man down. Canning, in spite of his fatigue, kept preening himself, repeating, 'And we found him – walking through the bush – not five mile from the track.'

'We've been searching for four days,' Pottinger said to Taylor, 'up and down the valley, shouting and shooting, the very devil of a din. Didn't you hear the men?'

'I may have been delirious at one stage.'

He didn't look delirious, or even post-delirious. 'You lit no fire? Never called?'

'In fact, I think I was unconscious.'

'You think you were?'

'I'm sure I was.'

'What did you eat?' Pottinger said tartly.

'Roots and berries.'

Pottinger turned away. He didn't believe in roots and berries. It was a fiction of the bushies, and he said as much. He himself had never seen a single edible berry growing wild in the whole of New South Wales.

Canning narrowed his eyes at the drift of Pottinger's thoughts. 'Are you suggesting, sir, that something's amiss?'

'Why, what could be amiss?'

'Exactly, sir.'

But indeed, there was something wrong. The young man, despite his miserable and in some ways disgusting condition, was too glib, too polished in his explanations and, in fact, looked more alert than the dishevelled Canning who'd spent his time on horseback. But this, perhaps, was the whim of his experience; he'd seen a woman once throw a child in the fields back home and right herself within the hour to carry the squawking infant home. Though she was a lusty peasant, mother of eleven. 'Take him in,' he said. 'Give him food. And get a full report.'

'Yes, sir.' Canning awarded him with a smart salute. The man was doubtless improving – though possibly for the benefit of those who were now filing out from the church, like Eliot Considine, the sailmaker.

'Hi there, hi, Sir Frederick!' he called. 'Do me an honour, and let's repair to the local hostelry. It's the devil of a thirsty job observing the sabbath, eh?'

'I think not,' Pottinger said, observing beyond Considine the rest of the family moving towards the shaded graveyard.

'It's all right,' Considine said, seeing the direction of Pottinger's gaze. 'Moother likes to have a chat with Aunty Bess, the dead, y'know. And me,' he continued with a cheery grin that pushed the apples of his cheeks against his eyes, 'I'd like to have a chat with you.' And then, with a certain cringing glint,

'I do 'ave summat you ought to hear.'

'Really?'

'Come to the pub,' he pleaded. 'Let's do the gentlemanly thing.'

'Well?' said Pottinger after they'd settled at a table with the ale. 'What is this vital communication?'

Considine set his tankard down and left himself with a foamy moustache. 'Well then ...' he said expansively.

Two or three stockmen came into the Tavern – the brothers Hamilton, and one unknown – and slipped across to the other side as though drawn away by magnets. Pottinger was not a popular man and his presence made a certain taint. 'Go on,' he told Considine impatiently.

'Well,' said Considine with irritating evasion, 'it's like this ... I mean,' he said, 'I haven't had the gift of education, I'm a plain man, just as you see me and not accustomed, no sir,' he laughed, 'to sharing a pot with the gentry. But,' he emphasised with the pudge of his finger on the table, 'I'm a plain-spoken man and I like to drive one foot before the other, that's my style ...'

'I'm sorry,' Pottinger said, rising, 'I really must go.'

'No, wait,' the other said, almost pathetically. 'It's about the girl, y' see. You and the girl.'

'Which one?' Pottinger asked relentlessly.

'The elder. Shall we order another?' he asked, his face desperate, red above the tankard.

'What about her?'

'Now you won't take offence? I mean, a man can talk to a man, surely to God? I mean, I've been through it. Mrs Considine's my second. The other's well and truly gone, beneath the sod, and no love lost, not a tear – 'cept for the cost of digging her down. But the girl, me elder, Lettie— God save us, let's spill another'n.'

'My turn,' Pottinger said.

'The girl has taken a shine to you. But of a most ...' and he leaned in confidentially '... a most peculiar bent.'

'Oh?'

133

'A temper the like you've never seen! Smashing about the kitchen, galloping round the station. And such moods and vapours, mooning about. She won't talk to me! I'm her Dad. She acts more proper to the stable-hands.'

Pottinger smiled. It gave him a certain twinge of pleasure to think of that crystal charm 'smashing' and 'galloping'. 'I should give her a decent spanking, sir,' he teased.

'Oh no. No, she's not of that age, no, I wouldn't think so, no.'

'Why, might she strike you back?'

'Ah yes,' Considine laughed in an 'oh-hoh' way. 'You're a bit of a wag, all right. Begging your pardon,' he added quickly, 'Sir Frederick, no offence.'

'I don't doubt,' Pottinger said, examining his nails, 'that she'll get over it.'

'You underestimate yourself.'

'The mere sight of a uniform, you know, is inclined to drive some women wild.'

'No, it's you, it's you she's after. You have my word.'

Pottinger looked with a touch of contempt upon this, Papa so desperately pursuing his daughter's would-be swain, and it gave him no real pleasure to divine that his title lay at the root of it. Had he been Black Jack the Stockman, it might have been a different story.

'Look man,' said Considine imploringly, 'do me a favour. Restore the peace and quiet – come out to loonch and share the table.'

'Lunch?'

'Aye, a bit of a meal, a humble repast, you know what I mean? She'll mind her manners. She's not been reared that rough.'

'She won't throw plates, or upset the apple-pie?'

'You're a tease, you are,' he chortled.

'My hidden vice,' Pottinger said modestly.

But 'loonch' was almost as painful as he'd imagined. Lelitia could barely conceal her fury. Having spurned him with an evident finality, she felt herself now paraded as at the market-place. But Pottinger, for his part, gave no ground. He was the perfect guest, regaling them with anecdotes of the gifted and the great, what his ludship had said to his lady, and what the Queen had said of the Earl of Beaconsfield and his canary-coloured vest. He was rewarded with gales of laughter and a good madeira wine. Only half, or less than half of his stories were true, but he knew how to tell them with the proper degree of wickedness and spice. Thus had he entertained his peers at the Athenaeum years ago, and now, as he sipped his wine and Clara cleared the dishes, he thought of those days with wistfulness.

But – 'The river!' Mrs Considine shrieked. 'We must go down to the river.'

'D'you fish, sir?' Considine asked.

'Not on Sunday,' Pottinger replied mischievously.

'I have a throbbing headache,' Lettie said in expiring tones.

'Oh, poof!' her sister retorted. 'The air will do you good.' Clara, in fact, was in a jolly mood. She had rejoiced to learn from Pottinger that Michael Taylor had been salvaged, and would doubtless shortly join them. 'Did you speak with him?' she'd asked. 'The first name upon his lips,' Pottinger informed her, 'was yours.' 'Oh la!' she'd cried, and wept for joy and set to waiting in an agony of love.

'To the river!' Mrs Considine cried. It was a kind of battle cry. And doubtless, Pottinger mused, a deep conspiracy.

In any case, they left the dishes to the flies and trooped out through the garden gate – and mounted the horses which the stables (by some psychic knowledge) had thoughtfully saddled, and rode down to the nearby river.

'I leave my pole in place,' Considine said, as they approached the willow tree. 'I am addicted. Hand me the spinners, love,' he called to Clara, 'and fetch me out the gutta-percha.'

'I shall sit 'ere,' Mrs Considine announced, 'upon this rock and watch the tiddlers rise.'

'Now, Moother!' Considine said.

'Clara!' shrieked his wife. 'Where are you goin'?'

'Up the track a way,' she called, 'to see if Michael's coming.'

'That girl, that girl!'

135

Then Considine made a great, looping cast and the spinner splashed across the glitter of the water.

Pottinger looked around and Lelitia had vanished. Was he to be stuck for the afternoon with the angler and his wife?

It had turned out a rare and sparkling day with the sun bright, but benign. The river was broad enough and flowing swift, but it lacked the charm of the English waterways. All manner of native shrubs and weeds straggled behind the willows, but none was redeemed by blossom. The natural palette was exceedingly spare, the colours of verdigris and bronze as though the leaves were shaved from metal.

'Take it. Take the bait,' Considine ordered the stubborn fish.

'Angler's luck,' Pottinger laughed to Mrs Considine.

She looked up at him then, shielding her eyes against the sun. 'There's a narrow walk,' she advised, 'along the bank, that turns to a clearing by the rapids.'

'Yes,' he said, falling into the spirit of the thing. 'I may just take a stroll.'

Within moments he had reached the shaded clearing where the water, shallow here, rattled across the stones. The willow whips, all but bare of leaves, trailed the water and yellow leaves fell down from the shine of the sun in the branches. But the girl, Lelitia, was nowhere to be seen. Pottinger tossed a stone or two, then sat on a rock to watch the midges dance. And suddenly her shadow crossed his knee.

He leaped up, turning, more avidly than he might have wished.

'I suppose at the very least,' she said, 'I owe you an apology. Or an explanation.'

'Not at all,' he said graciously.

'Well,' she said, 'in any case I changed my mind.'

'That would be self-evident.'

'It was doubtless the grog,' she told him bluntly, 'and the heat of the night ... and, yes, my gratitude for your behaviour with those indecent men. Even though I still suspect your heroism.'

He inclined his head, accepting this. But, after a speech that was patently rehearsed, she turned to go.

'No, wait,' he said.

She turned to look at him. 'Our association's at an end.'

'It had no beginning.'

'I've more to do than bandy words.'

'Why, what have you to do? Sit down,' he told her. 'Talk a while. It could possibly be that I've also changed my mind.'

She smiled at this, and, as he resumed his seat upon the rock, planted herself on the long sweep of a fallen tree.

'Changed your mind?' she prompted.

'I came to this Godforsaken country a pretty shabby fellow – but with a certain understanding of the natural order of things – that the man befits his station, that good is the counterpart of bad, that grace goeth with dignity and so on, and so forth, a whole panoply of tenets and beliefs. But here, God help us, each day is an act of faith, each man is his master and I'll as likely jostle elbows with a drover as a duke. It's all topsyturvy; they make it up as they go along. And if a man,' he told her, looking deeply into her sombre eyes, 'is to survive as man, he must be a gambler and stake his throw ... and cut his losses when the cards turn sour. I'm without a woman,' he said. 'I make no apology.'

'None was asked for. I accept the blame.'

'But I was oafish. And presumptuous.'

'It was the grog ...' she began laboriously.

'Yes, yes, and the heat of the night. At least do me the honour,' he said, 'of turning me off with truth.'

She looked away. 'I prefer to discontinue this discussion.'

'Perhaps I should go?'

'Perhaps you should.'

The shift of the sun lit up the olive of her skin and the rise of her breast. He had no intention of going. She began to pick at willow leaves, the leaves lying golden against the green of her dress.

'If you're so miserable in this "Godforsaken country" why don't you pack up and go home?'

He shrugged indifferently.

'I'm sure as lord of the manor the village maids would flock?'

He observed her openly. 'They're not built so fine.' And he had the pleasure of her colouring, the flush rising.

He placed his hand gently upon hers, bidding – but not everything – on this early throw.

'Your intimacy is uninvited,' she said, with her eyes across the river.

'Lettie ... Is a man to be damned for a single act of ardour?'

'Yes.'

And he – to her surprise – removed his hand.

'As much as I damn myself,' she amended, 'for behaving like a beast in season.'

He blinked at this, still unaccustomed to her sudden forays. She wasn't merely a country girl, he thought, it wasn't that, it was ...

'Got the beggar!' came a booming voice from up the river. 'Got him, damme, what a whopper!' And there was laughter floating down from the trio at the river and bawling comments and a fine old ruction.

'That beastly man!' Lettie said suddenly, rising with a stamp of her foot.

'I beg your pardon?' Pottinger said.

'My father. My Godforsaken father.'

Pottinger quite wisely allowed the outburst to run its course, and when he moved behind her and placed his arm about her, she did not resist but turned and said, 'There's a boat further up the stream.'

Pottinger peeled his coat off when they came to the boat – a boat rough-hewn and cumbersome – and took the pole provided and launched them out across the river.

'I imagine we shall drift,' he said with some apprehension. He was no mariner.

'No,' she told him. 'Only to the further bank. I spent my childhood here.'

He looked about. They were now at the middle of the river, and drifting as she'd said. Not far off was a watery pasture of reeds with something grey trapped in it.

'What the devil's that?' he said.

'It's a sheep,' she told him. 'They drown.'

And she rested back on her elbows, eyes closed to the sun.

'Do you really go smashing about the kitchen?' he asked.

She smiled. 'Did Papa tell you that? Oh yes,' she confessed, 'there have been occasions.'

'I can hardly imagine.'

'I'm a filly with the feelings of a stallion.'

Good God, he thought, what might she say next?

Suddenly she sat erect, and told him. 'It's your blasted title, that's the trouble.'

He laughed. 'I can peel it off as lightly as a coat. I didn't earn it. It doesn't come with valour. It's a miserable joke.'

'All lies,' she said easily. 'You enjoy your station.'

'As you wish.'

'Oh Frederick!' – it was the first time she'd used his name – 'Can't you see what shabbiness Papa is up to? He wants you for his son-in-law, he wants me for a Lady. Such a sighing and wringing of hands when you came to the house! Such a fever of anticipation!'

'It's water from the back,' he shrugged.

'Not to me, it isn't – to be mated up by pedigree, as one would assign Jones's cow?'

'I hadn't thought of it quite like that.'

'I will not be put on the block,' she said, 'for the bastard to be born an aristocrat.'

'Do be sensible,' he said, irritated now. 'You talk extremes, quite childish —'

'Thank you for your understanding,' she retorted acidly.

'Good grief,' he said, 'you make such a mountain of it. Have you never dealt with men before?'

'Am I still intact, you mean?'

'Now look here!'

'Am I still a virgin, is that what you're asking?'

'I do detest,' he said, finally admitting it, 'to hear a lady speak improperly.'

'I made no claim to be a lady,' she told him.

'You need,' said Pottinger, 'a decent spanking – with a hair-brush.'

'Would you dare?' she asked coolly.

'It would be my pleasure.'

'Here? In the boat?'

'Don't tempt me, madam.'

She laughed at this in a silvery way, the laughter pealing across the water, a throaty laugh, the way a bawd laughs – she was the devil of a puzzle, no doubt about it.

Then something whipped across the back of Pottinger's head and he started, fearing some animal attack, but it was instead a trail of willows and they were drifting into a private cavern of leaves and branches where, in the shadows at the bank, green ferns and damp moss grew.

'We're aground!' he said in some alarm.

'No,' she said, lying back, gazing at him.

'Are you sure?'

'Oh yes. I've drifted this way a hundred times.'

Indeed? Then it struck him. She'd known their destination all along!

'Well,' she said, 'did you bring your hairbrush?'

He looked at her, her face agleam against the shadows in this private canopy of leaves. 'No,' he replied, 'though I came equally well prepared.'

They kissed in a gentle exploration to the drift of the boat. And, with the extremest delicacy, he lowered her dress to the place where first his lips had kissed her in the garden, and kissed her now again on the topmost rise of her breast where daylight had never dared to touch her. 'That really is enough,' she said in a dreamy way that was encouraging, so much that he began to peel her like a peach, down to the creamy skin and a darker crescent, swollen against the cloth beneath his fingers.

'Lettie!' came Clara's voice. 'Where are you? Michael's here!'

'We must go,' Lettie said, eyes shining at him.

He kissed her again, more passionately.

'No.' Her hand was pressed against him. 'There'll be another time,' she said. 'I promise.'

He examined her in a state of limpid ease, his smile sardonic. He was in love, consumed by it, for the very first time in his life.


## Sixteen

Roy Foster – Kate's husband – stoked up the kitchen fire to last the night through. It was the first time he'd had to do this for the season. It was a cold, sharp night and it was near on bed-time.

He stacked the billets carefully crosswise and set the damper. He was, at this moment, alone in the shack. Kate was out again, somewhere. She'd even left the dishes and the litter on the floor; there were the bones the dog had gnawed and the darning that she never did, and a grain sack burst open.

Roy took his clothes off, down to his longjohn underwear, and slipped into bed up against the wall. About ten minutes after, Kate came in and began to sling some clothing across the line above the hearth.

'Where you been?' he said, watching her.

'Doing the washing.'

'At night?'

'I wash when I please.'

'I never heard you do the washing.'

'Well,' she said, slapping the garments on the line, 'I never damn' well fell in the river, did I?'

'What, you did it up at Ma's place, did you?'

'Yes, I did it up at Ma's place.'

He accepted this, his mind turning laboriously through the facts that Walsh lived just across the way and there was no good reason why you couldn't wash at night, though his own Ma never had.

'You complain,' she said, 'when I don't do the washing, and then you complain when I do.'

'I'm not complaining,' he said. 'I only asked. I stacked the fire,' he went on ingratiatingly. 'It's gonna be a freezer.'

But she didn't answer. These days her mind was always somewhere else, and her eyes kept seeing something absent.

'You're dripping water on the floor,' he told her. 'Whyn't you twist the water out?'

'Why ain't you asleep, Roy?'

He turned over and faced the wall, reaching up to finger patterns in the dirty window glass. The glass had been Kate's pride when first they married; it had come to them in a round-about way and had been destined for the bank. 'See anyone?' he said to the wall.

'See anyone where?'

'At Ma and Pa's.'

'Yeah. I saw Ma and Pa.'

'How are they?'

'For God's sake, Roy, you keep making conversation!'

'Ain't I supposed to?'

He looked around – at the wrong moment. She was pulling off her dress.

'Sorry,' he said, and turned away again. He didn't know when it had started, but at some point of time not so long ago they had, by tacit agreement, begun to live more private lives.

'I ain't seen Frank, if that's what you mean,' she said.

'I know, I know. I never asked.'

'You're always asking. You never say anything, but you still ask questions.'

'Wouldn't you?' he said.

She didn't answer, and he heard her blow the lamp out and he turned again to plead or remonstrate, he didn't know which, and there she was, standing in a way that silenced him completely, standing with her back to him, night-shift raised, warming her front at the fire.

'Kate ...' he said.

She dropped the hem abruptly and sat instead, on the three-legged stool. 'I ain't seen him,' she said with her eyes on the coals, 'or heard from him or anything. Must be two, three weeks, I wouldn't know.'

'It's all right, Kate, you don't have to tell me.'

'One o' these days, he'll likely clear out altogether. He'll be gone. He's like that.' She sighed and hoisted herself from the fire, and crossed the room and said to him, 'Shift over.'

She got into bed, lying flat on her back and Roy propped himself up and gazed down on her, instructing himself: She's my wife; I'm legal married. But he didn't feel married. He felt that he was lying with someone else's woman.

'They reckon,' she said, 'he spent a week with Michael Taylor. Him, and Gilbert and Piesley.'

'Who's Michael Taylor?'

'Feller missing from the bank.'

'Missing?'

'Don't you ever know what's goin' on?'

'I don't talk to anyone. No one ever seems to talk to me.'

'Don't go feelin' sorry for yourself.'

'Well, they don't.'

'Go to sleep, Roy.'

'Kate . . .' he said softly, in the way she knew too well.

'I'm tired,' she said, using the same code.

He leaned down and brushed her ear with his lips.

'Jesus, don't!' she said. 'Put your snout somewhere else.'

'I'm your husband, ain't I? With a licence bought an' blessed.'

'You had your money's worth.'

But he ignored the sting and yielded to the urgency. 'Oh Kate, Kate darlin',' he said, and thrust himself against her.

She sprang away as though from a knife. 'And keep your pecker in your pocket.'

'I got a decent, married urge,' he said angrily.

'Go and find a randy goat.'

'Kate, I'm warnin' you —'

'All right, all right, anything to shut you up.' She spread her legs. 'Get the damn thing done with. And don't go slatherin'. I'm not in the mood . . . Well,' she said, 'what's wrong now?'

He turned away. 'I can't,' he said miserably. 'I'm all slackened up again.'

'There must be somethin' wrong with you.'

'Could you . . . could you maybe coax me on a bit?'

Abruptly she sat up in bed. 'Roy, it's no damn' use, is it? We play more damn' games in bed than ducks in a pond . . . It ain't that I have no feelings for you, but I just . . . I just feel different now.'

'You feel for him, don't you?' he said darkly.

'I'm going to sleep. I don't want to talk about it.'

'What would you do if he was lying here? What would you do if he stuck his snout in your ear?'

'He wouldn't do that.'

'Why, what would he do?'

'You couldn't imagine.'

'Well, tell me. I might as well know the right way, mightn't I? I might learn somethin' I never even heard about.'

'You're in a rotten, stupid mood, and I got a pain the size of a fist in the gut, and —'

'Why, what's wrong?'

'What's always wrong this time o' month?'

He felt a sudden pang of guilt and offered his hand above her belly. 'Let me smooth it over for you.'

'No. Just let me be.'

Roy tossed himself back into the bed and enough minutes went past for her to think that he was asleep, but then his voice came out of the darkness, angry and strangled, like a child that beats its fists against a wall. 'It isn't fair,' he said, 'that he ever come back.'

'No,' she agreed. 'It isn't easy.'

'If they give a man ten years, they ought to mean ten years.'

She didn't answer, and he felt himself further driven by her silence. 'I'm gonna do for him,' he said.

She laughed a little.

'You wait. You see. I'm gonna put him back on Cockatoo.

And I'm gonna make a wife of you if I have to chain you to the bedpost!'

Finally the silence deepened and she felt herself drifting into the night. Some embers fell in the grate and a wind sighed up the Valley. Then Kate slept with the fancy of her lover's lips upon her.

## Seventeen

On Monday morning at the bank the southern mail arrived. A trooper brought it with the news that Gardiner and his gang had struck again, taking a pair of coaches at the Gully, debagging the gents and setting them off at a lively trot, on foot, back the way they'd come. 'Then,' said the trooper, 'they done Mr Shanks, bailed up the house, the wife and the hands, and laid 'em out there on the floor and stripped the —'

'Is that the mailman?' asked Mr Perch from his little, half-walled box at the rear of the bank.

'Stripped...?' encouraged Alexander Oliver, the chief accountant and Michael Taylor's superior.

'Stripped the store and everything in it. Three months' supplies, gone in a flash.'

'Tch, tch!' said Mr Oliver.

'What has happened to the mail?' cried Mr Perch petulantly.

'Take the mail,' commanded Oliver to Michael, 'and do stop gawping about.'

Michael Taylor took the mail and sifted through it. There was a long parchment envelope with a seal upon it, and the envelope was addressed by Henry Cummings's unmistakable hand. So the gold was coming up from Fivecrown. But when?

'Come, come,' snapped Mr Perch, 'You'll read the spots off.' And, with an irritating inflexibility for first things first, put the envelope aside.

It was a quiet morning for a Monday and Michael was

assigned the task of searching for the sum of two and nine-pence missing from the month of April. He worked at a high bench desk against a dun-coloured stucco wall, sitting on a stool rather like a dunce with the top of his head at the level of the window set too high to see out; but if he pondered with his head tipped back he could see the polished blue of a cloudless sky and the shabby roof of the smithie's shelter wherein metal rang on metal, and the smithie sang laments in Welsh or gave out rounded oaths.

Michael Taylor couldn't find the two and ninepence, let alone his fingers. He had to know the contents of Cummings's letter, the weights and shapes, the time and date, and short of rifling Mr Perch's papers there seemed no way of early information.

Around 11.30 there came from the manager's corral a series of stifled gasps and cries best rendered by 'Tchah!' and 'Argh!' He was a man who liked to draw attention to his plight. 'Look at this,' he said, blundering out to Mr Oliver. 'The gold is coming Friday. We'll be here half the night.'

'What a bother,' said Mr Oliver.

'I'm supposed to be in Copper Creek. I shan't get there till Saturday.'

Taylor scratched away with his pen with a quickening excitement. He blessed Mr Perch's lament.

'And you will also be required,' Perch told Michael crossly.

'On Saturday?'

'On Friday. At least till nine o'clock. To weigh the bullion out.'


On the following day, an hour before dawn, Michael Taylor rode into Winooka Valley. The first to see him arrive was the black man, Billy Dargin, who, it was said, never slept though he rolled up by a log not far from Ben Hall's shack.

'Rouse Ben Hall,' Taylor said. 'I got to get back to the bank and it's three hours' travelling time.'

'Ben's asleep,' said Dargin.

'Well, get him out.' He got down from the horse and looked

146

at the aboriginal. All he could see in the pre-dawn dark was the moons of his eyes.

'I'll fetch him,' Dargin said.

Minutes later, Ben came out. 'What the blooming hell?' he said. 'You've set the baby bawling.'

Sure enough, there was a howling from the shack and the reluctant bloom of lantern-light and, shortly, Biddy at the window. 'What's the trouble?' she called.

'Let's walk a bit,' Taylor said. 'It isn't women's business.'

'Where's your night-eyes?' Ben said when Michael stumbled. 'How'd you ever find the place?'

'I might be in the banking business, but I was bushborn. I know what I'm doing.'

'That's far enough,' Ben said, as they came to the peppercorn tree.

Michael Taylor looked around. He could still see, a little way off, Dargin's eyes that gleamed like opals.

'He works with me,' Hall defended. 'We got no secrets. We was reared together. He's more Christian than half the townies that ever banged a bible.'

'I've got to see Frank Gardiner,' Taylor said.

'You're asking me?'

'That's what he told me to do.'

Hall turned to Dargin, but Dargin shook his head. 'I ain't seen him three days past.'

'Well, you better find him,' Taylor said, 'Him and Piesley and Gilbert, they're waiting for me, what I got to tell them.'

They must have spent an hour or more prowling up and down the Valley. Half the time Dargin rode with his head below the saddle as he searched the ground, and then would right himself, screwing up his eyes, seeing into and beyond the distance, a silence and magic about him.

What perplexed Taylor was Dargin's excitement when they reached the grass. 'There he is!' Dargin said, but to Taylor it was just dry grass, blade upon blade, acres of it.

'You believe this jiggerypokery?' he asked Ben.

147

'I thought you were a bush boy.'

Taylor watched Dargin prowling through the grass. 'My Dad shot blacks. I never spent the time of day with one.'

'He's a Christian,' Ben said.

'You think so? He'll spend eternity banging on the Pearly Gates.'

It was nearly seven o'clock when they came on a group of shacks, with smoke twining from the chimneys. 'What's this place?' Taylor said.

'Walsh's.'

Taylor looked back the way they'd come. 'Hell, we could have ridden straight on down the road.'

'Yeah, but Frankie didn't. That's how come he's stayed alive so long.'

Within ten minutes Dargin had found the site of Gardiner's camp straight down the Creek. But it was Gardiner who found them – with both guns pointing at their backs.

'You come creeping up like that again, you'll likely lose a shoulder-blade.'

'Feller wants to see you,' Ben said.

'It's the banker,' Gardiner laughed. 'It's Micky Taylor. Come and help me eat a piece of old cooked snake.'

'I've already eaten. And I've damn' near ridden to Sydney and back. I'll be late at the bank, and they'll be asking questions.'

'Hey,' Gardiner laughed, giving him an affectionate hug, 'you've hardened up, boy. You got more yap than a dingo.' They walked a little way to the ruins of the fire. 'What's the news from Ironbark?'

Taylor put his hand on Gardiner's arm. 'Am I in?'

'Course you're in. I never double back, you ought to know that.'

Taylor glanced back at Ben Hall. 'Let's talk private.'

'No need. He's in, too.'

'In what?' Ben asked.

''Cept he don't know it, yet.'

'Hey, come on, what's this? What am I in?'

Gardiner gave him the devil's wink. 'For the best damn' time of your life, boy.'

Later, when Michael Taylor had left the Valley, and Ben and Dargin had gone to sweat their backs at fencing and mending and cattle-rousting, Frank Gardiner spent the day alone lying flat out on a rock above the Creek, sheltered by an overhang. He never slept, but drifted to the edge of sleep and watched through the veil of his lashes all manner of birds and beasts and acrobatic insects flicking past. His mahogany arm lay like a branch on the rock, and once a yellow-footed mouse, a pouch-mouse, nosed against him. In the afternoon as the sun lowered, he heard the flap and splash of a platypus at play, and the distant yip-yip-yip of an unknown bird.

At four o'clock the whole forest froze to unholy stillness as a police patrol approached. With none of the arts of those they sought, they yelled instructions up and down the Valley and splashed through the creek with as much grace as a bull in a puddle – and Gardiner watched them riding right on past, the Corporal shouting, 'Shake yer tails. We're gonna miss our supper.'

At sundown, when the Walshes were at table – Ma and Pa, and Kate and Roy – Gardiner slipped in and they put a plate before him.

'Troopers been by,' Walsh said, 'up and down the Valley, wearin' out a track.'

'Yeah, I watched 'em.'

'Heard tell you was workin' down the Gully, shootin' up some coaches an' the like.'

'That's right,' Gardiner said, 'and I didn't come empty-handed.' He emptied out his pockets, laying out among the bread and stew-plates an assortment of rings, brooches, strings of beads and a snuff-box inscribed with the name of Captain Hadrian. 'Give it to the boy,' he said to Kate, of her husband Roy.

'I don't want no stolen goods,' Roy said meaningfully. 'Nor should any man.'

'My!' said Ma, taking up the rough-cut beads. 'That's real

pretty. That's blue jade, ain't it?'

'That's lapis-lazuli,' Gardiner said, 'and worth a decent whack. Keep it, Ma. I brought it for you. And I brought for you, special,' he said, turning to Walsh, 'a true gold watch with the figures of the moon.'

'Dammit, Frank, I got seven gold watches you already give me, lyin' there like fish on a plate.'

'This one plays a tune.'

Kate took up the cameo brooch, the one with lovers twined.

'Thought you'd like it,' Gardiner said.

'What the hell,' Roy said unexpectedly, 'do you keep bringing my wife presents for?'

'I got some dried-out melon pie left over,' Ma said. 'You got room on top of that stew?'

Walsh spread his legs and took his pipe out until he caught Ma's disapproving eye. 'Anyways,' he said to Gardiner, 'I thought you'd planned to rest a while, leastways till the police give over?'

'Just flexing up my muscles, training up my style.'

'Why, what deviltry are y' plannin' now?' Ma said.

'You never know what comes along tomorrow,' Gardiner said carefully, watching Roy with half an eye and sensing out the sniff of danger in the air.

'You planning something?' Kate said eagerly, and instantly regretted it. The whole air had become filled with a kind of caution, like electric lightning in the room.

'Is that the last of the melon pie?' Roy asked vexedly.

Then Walsh scraped his chair back in the silence and said, 'Come on out, Frank, and help me smell me pipe.'

The two men walked out under the shine of the stars and down by the water tubs and listened to the horses snuffling down for sleep. It was a fine, clear night and they could see the mountains cut like paper shapes against the rise of the moon. 'Somethin's goin' on,' Walsh challenged, 'that's bigger than gold chains and pocket watches.'

'Why, what makes you say a thing like that?'

'I got a nose,' Walsh said. 'And I also seen Ben Hall.'

'What's he say?'

'Nothin'. Same as you. That's what bothers me.'

Gardiner didn't say anything but stuck his foot up and scraped his boot on the edge of the water tub.

'Animals got to drink that,' Walsh said, sucking on his pipe.

These were the moments Gardiner would always remember: the seventy-two hours that were left to him, divided by days and nights like this one, with the old man and his pipe, poised on the brink of the biggest thing he'd ever done, the thing that would change his life and Kate's, a poke in the Governor's eye, and the thing – he never doubted – that would put a story in the storybooks. This was what he lived for, the animal excitement, the rare shiver of fur the dingo gets when it noses out the kill.

'If you were ten years younger, Pa, I'd count you in.'

'No, I've done my day,' the old man said. 'I've had my times.'

'You're never done,' Gardiner said, 'not till the sod's in your face.'

'Kate know about this?' Walsh asked.

'No.'

'You intend to tell her?'

'No ... Pa,' he said, 'you're dancing all around it. What's on your mind?'

'Just think you might be planning to abduct my middle-eldest daughter, that's all.'

'I'd be doing her a favour.'

'Dammit, Frank, whyn't you go off and find some decent other girl?'

'Because she's mine.'

'No. No, she ain't. She's taken up now.'

'Lend us your pipe to light my cigar,' Gardiner said and, as he leaned over the cherry glow, added so softly that Walsh could hardly hear, 'I want to tell you, Pa – good times aside – when the day comes, anyone stands between me and Kate, I'll kill 'em stone dead. And that includes yourself ... Thank you,' he said, with a good, bright light at the end of the cigar, 'much obliged.'

'I wish you hadn't said that, Frank.'

'Just so's you know, that's all.'

Then Roy stepped out from the house and emptied the kitchen scraps into the fowl bin, and both men watched him like you would watch a man heading straight out for the gallows. Roy Foster had the look of trouble on him, trouble spilling out in all directions – for both himself and everyone he laid a hand to.

'Might be I have to side with Ma,' Walsh said. ' 'Tain't right a man can take another's wife, no matter how he feels.'

Gardiner shrugged. 'Let the boy fight his own fights.'

'I'm her Dad. You forget that. It's a blood matter.'

'That's fair warning.'

'I got to tell you fairer still – I'll load the gun and put it in Roy Foster's hand if he don't load his own. I can't abide a yellowtail.'

Gardiner slapped him on the back enough to choke him on his pipe. 'Better start loading the gun, then.' And started back towards the house.

'When? How soon?' Walsh said, trotting after him.

Gardiner turned and took him by the shoulder. 'I damn' near forgot what I came about. All this gun-talk, that's what I'm looking for – three good guns. Could you place your hands on three good guns?'

'What kind of guns?'

'Ones with fellers at the other end.'

'You got good guns. You got the Johnnies – Gilbert an' Piesley – ain't that enough?'

'I need three more.'

'And Ben Hall. Ain't you got Ben Hall?'

'I still need three.'

'Holy Christopher, Frank, what are you thinking of? You gonna cart the Bathurst gaol away?'

'I tell you this, Pa . . .' Then Gardiner paused, some prickle of warning at the back of his scalp.

'Tell me what?'

Gardiner turned again to face the old man and the yellow

moon behind. He's seen what he needed to see – a blend of shadows by the house and one shape notably darker than the others. 'I'm going back to the Gully side,' he said distinctly, making it up as he went along, 'and I need a few fellers for Saturday. I'm going to clean up the Gully road, clear on back to Bathurst. Saturdays that road's as busy as a bull-ant, and I reckon I can clear a thousand or more.'

Walsh scrubbed his whiskers in the dark. 'You split the money that many ways,' he said, 'you'll hardly have enough left over to mop the plate.'

'Leave me do the worrying,' Gardiner said. 'Just get the men. And get me one good man that knows the back trails, I might have a whole heap of running to do.'

Pa Walsh stuck his pipe in his face, and nodded. He knew what he had to do.

Then briefly Gardiner put his lips to the old man's ear. 'Don't name them,' he said. 'Not to anyone.'

They strolled back inside the house, and there was Roy Foster sitting at the table, innocent, as though nailed there to the bench.


## Eighteen

'What are we doing way up here, Frank?' Piesley said in a complaining voice.

'I don't know about you, boy, but I'm looking right down on top of Ben Hall's roof.'

'Yeah, but what for?'

'Actually so's I can watch the road that passes by the back.'

'That's a helluva long ways off, Frank.'

'Yeah, that's a pretty fair comment, Johnny. I believe you're improving.'

'But what are we waiting for?'

'Oh, I don't know. I like to see the people come and go. It

gets lonely up there in the caves.'

It was the Wednesday morning, the day after Gardiner had been with the Walshes, and Saturday was getting a bit too close for comfort. They were halfway up the Valley slope above the Ironbark Passage, and they'd been there since break of day. If there was one thing Gardiner prided himself upon, it was care and caution; you could act 'flash', but you had to do the thinking first. And he'd thought a lot about Saturday, about the coachload full of gold; and Wednesday, this day, was just a part of it.

'I saw the banker feller,' Gardiner told him for the first time, 'and Saturday is getting-rich day.'

'We're gonna take the coach?'

'Monday, boy,' Gardiner said with slitted eyes, 'you can buy yourself a pair of solid golden guns.'

'Ee-yah-hoo-o-o!' Piesley yelled.

'Don't tell 'em in Ironbark,' Gardiner said. 'Let's just keep it between you and me and the whole damn' Valley you just hollered at.'

'Sorry, Frank.'

'You got a fat mouth, feller. No wonder I never talk to you.'

Piesley walked off with a grin on his face, mashing his hands together. It was like he'd just been fed a Christmas dinner. He was going to be the richest bugger in the Valley – him, that had started life with a hungry gut and a brawling, randy Dad, and his Ma saying over and over, 'I fed you at the breast, Johnny-boy, till you was doin' chores around the house, that's how poor the table was.' 'I know, Ma, you keep tellin' me,' he'd say. 'Just so's you remember, Johnny. So's when I'm gone...' And go she did – one violent winter with the Creek in flood and her delirious raving for a land he'd never seen. Rich! he thought. Bleeding rich!

'Let's go,' Gardiner said behind him.

'Now?' Piesley said. And looked around, and down. 'Who's that?' he asked, gazing at the horse and cart way off.

'That'd be Roy Foster,' Gardiner told him.

'Where's he goin'?'

'He's got a fat mouth, too,' Gardiner said, ''cept his is wrong way round.'

Piesley kept studying the dwindling figure as though the puzzle might suddenly manifest its shape, but all at once there was the thrust of a horse behind him, and Gardiner was moving off.

'Hey, Frank! Wait for me, dammit,' Piesley yelled. He hated to admit it, but from where they were he didn't know his own way home.


Roy Foster was lathered up with sweat by the time he got to Ironbark. Yet it wasn't hot; the breeze was fresh and the horse was as plodding as Walsh, the man who owned it.

'What in the blazes do you want the wagon for?' Walsh had asked.

'To go to town and buy up Ma a broiling pot.'

'She don't need a broiling pot. We'll take it to the tinsmith.'

'Going to get a broiling pot,' Roy had said, 'and a red Crimea shirt for me, and some sewing things for Kate.'

'Ma's got all the sewing things the girl'll ever need.'

'I need a shirt, anyway. I'm wearin' holes just hung together.'

'What did you do, strike gold?'

'Can I have the wagon, Pa?'

'Take the wagon, you stubborn coot, and spend your bloomin' money till it's gone.'

Now he was in Ironbark on the Wednesday morning early, standing in the bank before the young, clean-shaven fellow, Michael blooming Taylor, the reading-writing man, very churchy, stuck-up, educated, the man who hardly touched a drop of grog and was known by the Tavern toughs as 'Mr Golly-Gee'.

'Yes, sir, can I help you?' Taylor said, putting on his airs.

'Takin' out my money,' Roy said.

'All of it?'

'No, just two pound bloomin' ten of it, like I've written there.'

The two young men met each other eye to eye across the counter, and for the first time in Foster's memory – and, in fact, the only time – Taylor didn't flush or look away. What's got into him? Roy Foster thought.

'Is this your signature?' Taylor asked.

'Of course it is. I signed it.'

'Better write it down again, then. It's not the same as last time.'

'You know who I am. You've seen me a dozen times. What are you talking about?'

'Right here,' Taylor ordered, 'where I've marked it with a cross.'

'You call yourself a bank,' Roy shouted. 'You're blasted thieves. A man can't get his money.'

'Now then, now then, what's this?' said Mr Oliver stepping up. Taylor showed him the signature. 'Quite so,' said Mr Oliver. 'The F is formed in a different fashion. We are not thieves, sir,' he admonished, as Roy signed again with his tongue stuck out, 'we are responsible men – protecting your interests.'

'Yes, sir,' said Roy politely, quite convinced that if he gave more lip they'd take the blasted lot, 'I'm not too good on F's.'

'Carry on, Mr Taylor.'

Roy Foster got outside with half a dozen tiny coins clutched in the sweat of his palm. Money somehow shrank inside the bank – he'd put in notes, and it had come out coin. He blotted the sweat of his brow in the crook of his arm and looked up the yellow clay street. A couple of soldiers went in the barracks door, and there was a man outside, a sentry. He didn't know exactly who to approach, or who to tell; they might even do him down. The whole day and all the people in it – Old Jack Flynn hanging tubs outside the door, the horses pulling in and pulling out, Dr Hudson punching at his door, the door jammed, Hudson furious – took on the hard, clear, cardboard cut-out shapes of fantasy, like something dreamed in bed, and all the sounds pounding in as though through muffled blankets. Roy Foster was going to spill it all and it would put him as far removed from other men as a shooting-star on a winter's night.

Turning rat, that was the worst crime in the unwritten book, worse than buggerising animals, or shooting out a horse to even up a score. Rats were killed, drowned or stamped on. They'd found Hairy Tom the Gentleman with his head cut clean from the neck.

Roy Foster set out gamely for the barracks, but turned instead into the Irish Tavern, into the cool rum-and-sawdust smell where the twilight never changed.

'Haven't seen you in a month of moons,' Paddy Whelan said.

'Break this up,' Roy said, putting down a sovereign, 'an' gimme gin.'

'What'd you do – rob a grave?' Paddy asked.

'It's my money, ain't it?'

'I wouldn't be that sure,' Paddy said, giving the wink to the other patrons, 'I don't see no name written on it.'

'For Christ's sake, gimme the gin!'

'Marriage got you down, Roy?' said Black Harry solicitously.

'It's my weddin' money,' Roy defended. 'Given to me by Pieter Oud.'

'How's Kate?' asked the other fellow, a pimpled stable-boy, Cecil Clemens.

'Kate's all right.' He downed the gin, choked it down with water in his eyes and said, 'Gimme another.'

'You got a good handful there in Kitty Walsh,' Black Harry said.

Roy put his foot up to the bar. The gin was working him loose. 'I can handle her,' he said. 'She sauces me, she gets a backslap o' the hand.

'You're right!' said the little, crooked man, Billy No-Boots, speaking out for the first time. 'Two ways to treat a woman. One's a duty, t'other's a pleasure. And both is not done halfways.'

The knot of drinkers, drawn together by the empty yawn of the hour of day, began to warm to the moment and the drinks that Roy provided – and the talk passed from Roy's Kitty, that any man would like to get his hands on, to a gin-filled philosophising on the female sex in general, and the devilish ways they sought to treat a man. 'First night that bloomin' Kate Walsh sauced me,' Roy said, slurring, unable to get away from Kate, 'I slapped her down, up-tipped her over and, I'm tellin' you, they rang the Christmas bells in Bathurst all night long!'

Around midday, after he'd tightened his purse, he slumped out the door and leaned against the wall in the glitter of the sun. 'Go on, Roy!' he kept urging himself. 'Get it done.'

He crossed the street in a looping walk and doused his head in the horse trough, and towelled himself on a bit of blanket from the horse that was standing there. Right across the way was the dark tunnel of the barracks passageway and through this were troopers in the yard, jackets bright tomato red against the white. Roy hitched his pants and strolled across, peering in. The sentry stiffened. 'Just lookin',' Roy said, thinking: a man could go in there and never come out. 'Which is Pottie's office?' he asked. The sentry never even moved. 'Well,' said Roy casually, 'I'll be seeing you soon again, then.' And started down towards Jack Flynn's Store.

But he didn't get there. He was standing just a few doors down from the barracks, struck rigid by the problems in his head – like he had a head full of knots he couldn't untie – when he became aware of eyes boring into him with the power of a burning glass, and he shifted his gaze to see a man standing in a shadowed room beyond the street window, the window soiled, but he could see these two piggy eyes above crescent lenses, and a pasty, full, round, lemon-coloured face hazed by cobwebs and street dust, like a sick moon rising from a muddy pond. Then, with some embarrassment, Roy pulled his eyes back and saw, inscribed on the glass in peeling gold-leaf letters, 'L.T. Hancock, Solicitor-at-Law', and it came to Roy in a shot of inspiration: This time I'll get the law behind me!

'Sir . . . sir,' he said, tapping on the glass.

The window was open a little way down from the top and Roy had to stand on tiptoe to see the wrinkled, baldhead fore- head rise and the eyes appear like leadshot levelled at him.

'Sir,' Roy said, 'could I see you private about a legal, lawful matter?'

158

'Of what nature?' said Hancock sceptically.

'It's a sort of money matter.'

'Are you being dunned? Have you been improvident?'

'No,' said Roy, who'd caught the general drift, 'I believe I may come in for a bit.'

'Come inside,' Hancock told him.

Roy pushed open the street door and turned into a hallway with stairs leading up, and knocked on the door that said again 'L.T. Hancock'.

'Yes, yes,' said a muffled voice.

Roy hesitated. Everything about the place had a kind of religious air, very dim and silent, all the timbers polished and the doorknob made of brass. He could hear with some regret the world he was leaving behind him – the clatter of carts in the street and Jack Flynn calling instructions – and it seemed to Roy when he opened the door that a pedal-organ should pipe him in and a hundred faces look up from their bible books, but all he saw was a cross man sitting at his desk, his brow dewed bright with perspiration, his spectacles hooked on the tip of his nose and his eyes peering over as he fussed – the whole two hundred pounds of him in a squeaky lawyer's chair – with his parchments and papers and rolls of legal contest tied with tape, the little lives of his many clients locked therein, nesting in a box marked 'Pending'.

'I'm not a peddler in a street, sir,' the lawyer said tartly. 'I do not drum up business from the window. It is customary, sir, in fact it is mandatory — Cunningham, Cunningham, the Crown versus — Ah! What date is on the calendar? Bother! Bother and thunderation. They do not notify. They do not have the grace to — Yes, sir, mandatory – that's the word – to make a day and a proper time, as I was saying, and properly to discuss . . .'

A great weight of weariness descended on Roy, and he propped his elbow on the table and pushed his fingers through his hair.

'Are you unwell?' Hancock asked, leaping to the question from the middle of his sentence.

Roy shook his head and, hearing the shriek of the chair, looked up to see Hancock's mottled yellow face looming at him from across the desk. 'Have you been drinking?' the lawyer asked with cloves on his breath.

'I had a tot,' Roy confessed.

'That, sir, is an insult,' Hancock gasped, crashing back into his chair, 'to me and my profession. Is this the way to present yourself to a guardian of the law?'

'I'm sorry.'

'Well, sir,' Hancock said, taking in the whole, untidy specimen in the chair across the desk, 'what miserable business have you come upon? Tell me how your sheep have strayed, your fence is crooked, your water is corrupted. I don't have time for such contrary matters. The Colony is writ in matters large – legacies and slanders, contracts and conveyances . . .'

'I'm here about Frank Gardiner,' Roy blurted out.

A creaking silence filled the room as Hancock subsided in his chair. The clock on the wall ticked as loud as a tinsmith's hammer and footsteps passed in the hall outside.

'Gardiner?' said Hancock. 'The bushranger?'

'I've information leading to his arrest,' Roy said.

Two hours later by the lawyer's clock, Roy Foster was repeating the same story to none other than the Inspector of Police, Sir Frederick Pottinger and his aide, Sergeant Canning. The room was deeply shaded now, for they had prudently drawn the blinds. Roy was in the same narrow chair and the three men were standing watching him, Hancock tugging at the wrinkles of his vest and Pottinger looking straight down his nose.

'And where did you come upon this den of thieves?' he asked.

'Down by the Creek, just down from where I live.'

'And what precisely did you overhear?'

'That they're goin' up the Gully road on Saturday – to do the coaches – Gardiner, Gilbert, Piesley an' Hall, an' three other fellers.'

'Ben Hall?'

'Yes, sir.'

Pottinger looked at Canning. Hall had been in trouble before, but was a slippery fellow skating round the nether side of law. 'And three other fellows?' he said to Roy.

'Yes, sir.'

'What three?'

'I don't know, sir.'

'The Gully road . . .'

'Yes, sir.'

Pottinger turned to Canning as though Roy had vanished down a hole. 'Think he's telling the truth?'

'There's a pretty fair chance.'

'Sticking his neck out, wouldn't you say?'

'They do it for the money, sir.'

'My client,' Hancock interposed, 'would be entitled to reward.'

'I am aware of that.'

'Which I intend to collect on his behalf.'

'We may be policemen,' Pottinger said drily, 'but we're also gentlemen.'

'Can I go now, sir?' Roy said.

No one even looked his way.

'I still find the story in some ways stretched,' Pottinger was saying.

'They'll expect me home,' Roy said. 'With a broiling pot and a red Crimea shirt.'

'What's that got to do with it?' Canning said.

'I think,' said Pottinger with a deepening sigh, 'we should all sit down and get the details straight.'

'I have his statement,' Hancock said.

'We have not,' Pottinger replied.

It was half past four by the time he got away and Old Jack Flynn was closing early for lack of trade, and Roy was forced to hammer on the door and he only had enough for the shirt and a small-sized broiling pot – he's spent the rest on gin – and they'd laugh him up and down the Valley for buying something useless, but he couldn't do a thing about it. He'd spend the change at Paddy Whelan's and go home decent drunk – that would be his excuse, and the only thin protection against the terrible, shameful seed of despair that was lodged in his heart.


## Nineteen

On Thursday night there was a full-sized penny of a moon suspended in an icy sky. The men were waiting by the Stump and they waited hugging themselves against the cold. Frank Gardiner wouldn't let them light a fire.

'Dammit,' Piesley said, 'I should have brought a coat.'

'You got a coat,' Gilbert said, who was up against his horse, taking up the warmth.

'I mean another coat.'

'Someone coming,' Gardiner said from a pit of darkness.

They could hear the crunch and shuffle of the horse on shale long before it reached them. And there was another, tiny sound in the darkness as Gardiner eased back the hammer of his gun; he wasn't taking any chances.

Within minutes, Johnny Bow had reached the Stump and had pitched himself off his horse in a fancy flying leap.

'Holy Christopher it's cold,' he said. 'Whyn't you light a fire?'

'You leave that hoss,' Gilbert told him, 'like you was jumpin' off a roof. You always do that?'

'This here's Johnny Bow,' Gardiner said. 'And two more Johnnies – damn the luck, I don't know what to call you. Gilbert,' he said, 'and Johnny Piesley.'

'Yeah, I know the runt, but I never met a man who called a horse a "hoss" before.'

'He's Canadian,' Gardiner explained.

'And I ain't no runt,' Piesley said.

Gardiner told them, 'Start fighting, and you're out. That's the first rule.'

Shortly, two more riders appeared, both young, one with a dark, chiselled face as narrow as an axe blade – this was Harry Weir – and the other with a kind of dreamy look, a moongazer with hair that settled in a haze about him, the kind of hair some women liked to run their fingers through – and he was Dan Charters, the man who knew the back trails.

'How well do you know the Bathurst road and the parts about?' Gardiner asked him.

'I was born there – at my Auntie's place – in this nowhere sort of place, an' I ran as wild as a wallaby the first ten years. Ain't nothin' I don't know,' he laughed, and Gardiner didn't like the ragged, snorting laugh that was halfway to a sneeze.

'What's this damn' job, anyway,' Johnny Bow asked, ''fore I freeze to death?'

'We're one short,' Gilbert said. 'Ben Hall ain't here.'

'I been here the last five minutes,' Hall said from the darkness behind the razor grass, 'listening to you fellers complaining.'

Gardiner shook him by the hand, the only hand he'd taken that whole night. By God, Ben Hall was good. Without him, he would have had to think it through again.

'Well, what is the job?' Ben said.

They gathered round and Gardiner told them. He told them in about a minute straight, keeping the proposition bare – how they'd take the gold coach, share up the loot and vanish, eight different ways.

Harry Weir said, 'This Michael Taylor feller, is he in as well?'

'That's right,' Gardiner said.

Charters, who was chewing grass, complained, 'An eight-ways split is a lot splittin'.'

''Bout two thousand pounds apiece is what I reckon,' Gardiner said.

The money, and the thought of it, settled on them all. It bonded them; they could envisage money, but not two thousand pounds of it; it was as though Gardiner had said something holy, or magical.

'Two thousand!' whispered Johnny Bow, letting the words

slide across his tongue. Jesus, he could almost taste it.

'Shoot, man,' Gilbert said, 'I could buy myself a brothel in Toronto.'

This made them laugh, and the tension cracked and Gardiner stood back a little and watched the jokes fly – it was working all right, he was thinking; they were going to be all right. 'What's wrong?' he said quietly to Ben Hall, who was standing just beside him.

'I got a wife and a baby son,' Ben said.

'I know that.'

'If I do this thing, I won't turn back. That's the road I'll go. Same road as you, Frank.'

'Yeah, I know that, too.'

He looked at Ben in the moonlight, and Ben said, 'Anyway, that's the road I'm going. You know I have to wrap my kid in blankets against a winter's night — 'cause we don't have the shift to put him in?'

'You don't surprise me,' Gardiner said.

'You know damn' everything, Frank.'

'I'm just a family man at heart. Hey fellers,' he said, striding across, 'you sound like a cackle of geese. You want to wake Fred Pottinger?'

'He's ten mile away,' Piesley said.

'His ears are as long as his nose.'

The men laughed again, shifting about, like sticks in a pond, to make up the twos and threes of comradeship. Gardiner knew he had them now, was fusing them together; they'd work very well in a corner and they'd do, for the most part, exactly what he said.

So he outlined the plan in more detail, how they'd meet on Saturday, at dawn, and where they'd meet and where they'd do it. He made his ideas sound as simple as sunrise, so that the eight men – against the six guns they would meet – would work together like pieces of machinery. He kept telling them about the money, how they'd weigh it in the caves above Winooka and go home quietly to take up their daily chores with no one the wiser. 'Stick your money in a tree,' he advised,

164

'or bury it. Don't go spending or flashing it about – not till the spring, at least, and then you have to spend it careful, or maybe even leave Winooka.'

'What are you going to do, Frank?' Charters asked.

'I haven't exactly thought about it,' he said. But he had. He knew precisely – as he knew only too well that all shooting hell would break out once they'd done the job, and half these hungry faces around him already had the mark of death. Money would destroy them; they didn't have the brains or pocket that could hold a penny: Piesley would drink it, Weir would splash it about, Charters would talk, and Bow would buy himself something as big and foolish as the Bathurst town brass band. The others – Hall, Gilbert and maybe even Michael Taylor – might just, and only just, get clear with it. But that was the way the cards faced up; he couldn't play their hands.

'Well,' he told them, 'that's how it lies till Saturday.'

Then Gilbert dropped a bundle of trouble. 'There'll likely be some shooting,' he informed them. 'We got any nervous Nellies here?'

'Sh-shooting?' Charters said.

'Sure. Those escort guards are goldfields fellers. They're not from Ironbark. They're all trained up. They can shoot a bullet down your whistle at twenty, thirty paces.'

'Holy hogspatch!' Johnny Bow breathed.

'You never mentioned shooting, Frank,' Charters said.

So he told them then, about the guns and the good, repeating rifles, and how the escort carried muzzle loaders and if there was shooting, he'd do it and do it fair, though blood was the one thing he didn't want – it was shock, surprise and suddenness, that was the gamble. Guns could turn the narrow pass where he planned to do the job into a slaughteryard.

'Anyway,' he said, 'those troopers won't have time for shooting. And it's not their gold. Why should they fight for it?'

'I ain't afraid o' shootin',' Harry Weir said quietly.

Gardiner looked at him. 'You can shoot the sky out. That's all the shooting you're going to do.'

'Why, what are you scared of?'

165

'You, mainly. You keep right in front of me, boy. I don't want you running wild.'

Later, when Weir, Charters and Bow had ridden off – with enough noise to wake the granite in the earth – Gardiner turned to Ben Hall and said, 'Maybe eight's too many.'

'That's one too many, is that what you're thinking?'

'One or two too many.'

'Which is the other?'

'The dreamy feller – Charters.'

'You won't do better,' Ben said. 'Not in these parts.'

Gilbert and Piesley came up. 'You having second thoughts, Frank?' Gilbert asked.

'No. Are you?'

Gilbert shrugged. 'No. Nothing special.'

'Yeah. I feel the same way.' Gardiner turned and mounted his horse. 'But I never go backwards.'

'What's he talking about?' Piesley asked. 'What's goin' on?' But suddenly, he was asking questions to the empty air. 'Wait on,' he called after the shuffle of hooves. 'Wait for me.' He had night-fears of the bush to which he never confessed – and something more this time – a dread he couldn't put a name to – but it had a day, all right, and that day began with Saturday.


## Twenty

Friday morning early, Sergeant Canning had the maps out, right across Pottinger's desk. This was where experience counted. This was where he came into his own. He'd hardly slept the night before, he had his ginger up the way it used to be. 'You show him,' Bess had urged. 'You show that blooming baronet.' 'Oh, I'll show him,' Canning had told her with his hand upon her rump in bed. 'I know that Gully road, old girl, the way I know your beauty mark.' 'Now then, now then ...' she'd said. But what a bundle they'd made of the bedding! He was sixteen again; he was reborn. And she'd wept for it, and called him their courting joke: 'Old Neddy the Ready'. Wasn't that a woman for you, always shedding tears? And in the morning, she'd loved him again in a gentler way, sprucing up his uniform, dusting off the dandruff – 'You look a picture, love,' she'd said, 'you look real smart' – and he'd kissed her, right on the mouth. 'You didn't know I had it in me, eh? You thought I'd drained up dry.' 'Don't go talking dirty in the morning,' she'd said. 'Just fix that lordship Muck-It-Up.' 'Pick a cabbage for tonight,' he'd told her, 'and let's have Bubble-and-Squeak. Goodbye, Bessie,' he'd said. 'Wish me luck.' It was like going off to war.

'And what,' Pottinger said as he tramped in, 'is the nature of this total disarray?'

'Good morning, sir,' Canning said smartly, showing a shining face. 'I've something here to show you.'

'Why is my desk littered with your maps?'

'This is the map of the Gully road,' Canning said, 'where Gardiner and his gang intend to operate tomorrow. And this is a list of the coaches, three in all – two from Bathurst and one from the fields – and the points at which they'll likely pass . . .'

'And what are these . . . gumnuts doing on the map?'

The gumnuts were somewhat the source of Canning's pride. He'd gathered them – the seedpods of the eucalypts – with an air of jollity, to mark the points along the road. 'This is where,' he said, 'these four places, that I'd deploy the troops – by your leave, that is. Each place, if you care to observe the markings on the map, provides for concealment, the element of surprise, because . . .'

But Pottinger appeared more concerned with his image in the mirror.

'. . . And assuming the outlaws separate, as they surely will,' Canning concluded, 'we'll have them outnumbered three to one.'

'I have a different mode of thinking,' Pottinger said, sitting at his desk in such a way as to tip the corner of the map and send the gumnuts rolling. 'You've lost your deployments,' he said as he searched for his papers. 'Pick them up.'

Canning's face turned to a plum-coloured fury as he groped on the floor plucking up seedpods around Pottinger's boots.

'You have,' Pottinger said, peering over, 'an infinite capacity for assuming postures of indignity.'

'What's the matter with my plan?' the older man asked petulantly.

'It's quite an excellent plan.'

'Then what's the matter with it?'

Pottinger studied the document in front of his nose. 'Do be a good chap and trot across to the bank and confirm with Mr Perch that I'm cognisant of the departure of the gold coach?'

'You're ignoring my advice?' Canning said in a stifled way.

Pottinger looked up at him. How the man was ageing! How his lines, furrows and shades of red and grey betrayed him! Not a well man, he was thinking; all the iron had gone to ashes. 'We're not in a contest of command, Sergeant. I thank you for your advice, but I don't need your advice.' He leaned back in his chair. 'I am about to reveal to you errors and incomprehensions that are quite beyond your intelligence...'

'Sir —'

'If,' Pottinger said, 'you were Frank Gardiner, God forbid, and about to plunder the Gully road, how much do you think you'd get? A hundred, two hundred pounds? Divided half a dozen times among your six collaborators? To save your arithmetic, old man, that's thirty pounds apiece.'

'To those men, that's a fortune,' Canning countered.

'But not to Gardiner. Gardiner can pick up his pennies – alone – any day he chooses. Monday, Thursday, any old day. But Saturday? With six desperate men? Should we not,' he asked, leaning back to observe the ceiling, 'consider Saturday?'

Canning, in spite of himself, curled his fingers about his jaw in earnest contemplation. 'Saturday's the gold coach,' he said,

'Ah!' said Pottinger. 'A light in the darkness. And what would be your next step – if you were of the felonious ilk?'

'They wouldn't take the gold coach,' Canning said. 'Not the

gold coach. That's a hanging matter.'

'Not even with six or seven men?'

'Not a chance.'

'Not even with the armaments that you provided from the barracks store?'

Canning coloured. He had not forgotten the night this same office had been blown apart.

Pottinger sat back and watched the Sergeant. He had no more than the wildest theory, he knew this, and no one but Canning to test it on. He had no certainty, none at all. In the space of silence he heard the unpleasant workings of the Sergeant's innards.

'Look,' said Canning desperately, like a man in quicksand, 'I know these people. They wouldn't touch the gold coach. It's like your London layabout – you think he'd rob the Palace? Think of the gold coach as the Palace on wheels. No, sir,' he affirmed, 'I stand by the map and what Roy Foster told us.'

'Foster is a liar,' Pottinger said. 'And Gardiner put him up to it – to lead us astray.'

'A bit of guesswork there,' Canning laughed.

'You beg to differ?'

'Well, it's obvious.'

'On what grounds?'

Sergeant Canning knowingly tapped a finger to his temple, a gesture which Pottinger particularly abhorred.

'Well, in any case,' he said abruptly, 'you may get about your duties. Time has allowed us twenty-four hours.'

Canning straightened to attention. 'Then what's the plan, sir?'

'The plan is to get about your duties.'

'But about the Gully road, sir?'

'Canning, don't be tiresome. You are dismissed.'

Pottinger rattled through his papers, among ration sheets and requisitions. When he looked up again, Canning was gone. The plan, he thought. Indeed, what was the plan? He didn't have a plan. He thought of Saturday as two diverging roads – both as a figure and a fact – and he didn't have the men, the right sort of men, to cover both. Dear God, he prayed, and not irreverently, don't let me end up an ass.

At twenty past the hour of noon a trooper came to tell him that there was a lady for him outside.

Waiting at a little distance from the gate was Lelitia Considine, who greeted him boldly and with no sense of propriety, none at all, exactly like a soldier's tart, he thought. He was in a beastly mood, and knew it.

'Have I offended you?' she asked as they walked in the direction of the church. 'Have I behaved improperly?'

'Not at all,' he said stiffly.

'Mama is choosing buttons at the Store,' she said. 'It takes at least a full half-hour.'

'I'm delighted,' he said.

'I have upset you,' she said teasingly.

'My dear,' he said, 'I have more on my mind than buttons.'

'What a crosspatch you are. My dear, beloved Inspector Grump,' she laughed.

He relented. 'You'd tease me out of a fury.' And offered his arm. 'Though I have to admit you're the most delightful event of a singularly dismal morning.'

They took what was known as the Graveyard Walk. It was a grassy, winding track that skirted not only the church but the hallowed ground it was named for, but on this occasion Pottinger opened the wicket gate and ushered her in. 'Let us take the short way.'

He stood looking down at tilting slabs and crosses, some with names scrawled on, and fading. 'Henry Williams, Free at Last, 1823.' 'Brian Crawley Amos, Captain, Beloved' – and the entire Amos family, all of them, dead for twenty years – Gregory, George, Isabel, Kathleen and 'Little Hester' – 'Murdered by the Blacks' – and a phalanx of proper, good people – Rumsey, Nives, Lismore, Patterson – flanked in the shady part among weeds and thornbush, by those whom the church had redeemed in death, the pickpockets and poachers, the strayed and fallen who had come such an anguished way to die in irons.

'Prisoners,' said Pottinger, 'all of them. Prisoners of Ironbark, of this wretched Colony.'

They strolled on.

They left the graveyard and walked to a fine-toothed brush of stunted trees with narrow leaves as sharp as needles, the whole array decked with blood-red flowers, but contorted like slivers of flesh. Even the blossom, he thought, was contrary.

He spread his jacket for her and she sat on the brown winter grass. 'I hate to see you sad,' she told him.

He dismissed this with a wave, turning his gaze to the roof-tops of the town spread below, the rooftops crooked, pitched, and tilting, most of them made from rough, red, hairy bark.

'I never did believe,' he said dreamily, 'that I'd come to relish the thought of England. Of course, it's a punishment,' he added, with irony, 'for turning my back on the dubious benefits of birth. One loathed the whole, prolific tribe of Pottingers. There was no sense of humour. There was dust in the veins. I was such an unnatural fellow, rather on the frisky side, not quite stuffed with the proper pomp. But equipped, I should imagine, for rather more than this' – and his hand took in perhaps a thousand thousand miles of misty forest beyond the town of Ironbark – 'which is the setting for a parlour game of Find the Felon – a type that breeds with the fecundity of swine.'

'Oh, Freddie, don't!' she said suddenly.

'Don't? Don't what?'

'Go on like this.'

'I see,' he said remotely.

Then impetuously, she took his hand and turned upon him a limpid, defenceless gaze of such intensity that he felt ashamed and chastened; he loved her, and had no right to this moody display. 'My dear . . .' he said.

'I do so love you,' she told him.

He kissed her with tenderness.

'If I should ever leave here,' he asked, 'to take my place in England – would you come?'

'To England?' she said.

'As my wife?'

She lowered her eyes at this and her full lips parted.

'Would you,' he persisted, 'be my wife?' And took her hand between his. 'I'm an oaf,' he said apologetically. 'I've asked you like a stablehand – without proper grace or decent courtship. But I knew long ago, the first time – when first I saw you with your Devil-on-the-Coals – with flour up to your elbows, your hair untied and the heat of the stove in your face. I loved you then – irrationally. And I thereon renounced from that moment a whole tangle of wicked ways and improper diversions. I admit I've been a reckless fellow – unworthy, unrepentant. But I promise to make a shine of myself. We'll depart, the two of us, with garlands of honour – to England, our home. Because I love you, Lettie, on my knees I love you.' And so saying, he fell to a suppliant position on the grass above the graveyard, so that she felt constrained to reach out, to touch him, his hair, his face, seeing beyond him the town and forest and hazy air, everything locked in a wintry stillness, the birds suspended above the Pass, the township huddled, glittering, the sunlight trapped in the central wink of Baker's Pond, and all the chimneys sending up a lazy twine of smoke.

'How can I go to England?' she said to a distance far beyond him.

'As my Lady,' he laughed.

'Yes,' she said so softly he didn't even hear.

He straightened and kissed her hand. 'You'd liven up the old ancestral home no end. They believe all colonials are hairy Hodmadods.'

'Is your home very large?' she asked.

'Not particularly.'

'How many bedrooms are there?'

'Quite enough for the two of us. Fifteen, I believe.'

'And servants?'

'Half a score at least.'

She was silent for a time, watching Ned the Tinker's cart winding through the streets of Ironbark – if you listened hard enough, you could hear the tinkle of his pots and pans. 'Where you live,' she said, 'does it snow?'

'With depressing regularity. And there's a pond across the county where they skate on ice among the woods.'

'It must be miserably cold,' she said.

He laughed. 'There's ice in Ironbark. Or will be.'

'Only a puddle or two.'

'Anyway,' he said, 'what's a bit of winter cold? Apsley Chase has a hearth the size of a house. Time was, the servants slept within – stacked on a shelf like muffins in the oven.' He looked at her, grinning, with a great love. But there were tears in her eyes. 'My dear,' he laughed, 'what's the tragedy?'

She shook her head.

'Have I said some stupid thing?'

'No, of course not.'

'I suppose I've gone at a bit of a gallop,' he lamented, 'but that's my style. I should have sent you notes and allowed you time to dwell on them. And brought you flowers, plucked along the way. And poetry! I should have written —'

'Don't mock me,' she said.

'Was I? Was I mocking?' He sighed. 'I hadn't meant to. I'm not such a dab hand at proposing. I flop and flounder about. I've only asked a lady once before. That was my Aunt Gracie, and I was twelve years old. There . . .' he cupped her chin – 'that's a pretty smile.'

But gently she took his hand. 'I don't want to go to England.'

'Oh, what rubbish, of course you do.'

'I don't, Freddie. I can't.'

'Can't?'

'I can't leave here.'

'Why not? What on earth would keep you here? Look,' he told her in a kind of desperation, 'think about it through the winter. Give me time to make a mark. Then we'll go – in springtime – and take Clara with us, if you wish, Clara and the Taylor boy. Put it to her. Let's all of us go.'

She looked again down at the town as though it were already fading – it was such a tiny, insubstantial place, but she'd seen it grow, or the most of it, beside the Creek, seen them felling trees, splitting timber, building houses, stores and churches, and this year, Mr Sefton said, there'd be a school with a proper mistress and she'd foolishly, dreamily thought that one day she'd have children to attend. The town itself was like a gangling child to her, and she could not explain – or even understand – her love for sticks and bark, and cartwheel tracks in the yellow clay. But it was a love – of a different kind.

'I can't go to England,' she said. 'I belong here.'

'Belong?' he said waspishly. 'This is where thieves and assassins belong.'

She leaped to her feet. 'You don't understand!'

'Lettie . . .' he pleaded.

Then she ran, and he called her name again. And when she turned and faltered, 'You haven't answered,' he complained. 'You gave no answer. Will you marry me?'

'Ask me again,' Lettie tossed at him, then she was gone and he watched her departure with a rapture, the dance of her body descending the slope, the tilt of her shoulders, the bob of her head – then all that was left was the glint of sun on a waver of grass.

He gathered his jacket and shook out the dirt. He was not amused by the mischief she had made. What that missy needed, he was thinking, was a decent, home-made spanking.


When Sergeant Canning dropped by the office at half past seven in the dark of night, he discovered his commanding officer in a most extraordinary state.

'Sitting in the dark, sir?' Canning laughed.

'So it would seem.'

'Shall I light the lamp, sir?'

'There is no oil in the lamp.'

'I'll fetch some.'

'Sit down, Sergeant.'

'Yes, sir.'

'There's a candle on the cupboard. Let's light that.'

Canning lit the candle, just the stub of a candle and set it on the desk. 'Bit more cheery, don't you think?' he said as he slyly observed the bottle and the glass.

174

'As you can see, Sergeant,' Pottinger said with the greatest control, 'I'm pitched-over, blind-stupid drunk.'

'Oh no, sir, never.'

'And if you wish to share my abysmal state, you may help yourself to the grog. This fateful hour, as I lurch in my cups in disgrace, is quite, oh, completely off the record, I'm sure you understand?'

'Of course, sir,' Canning said, pouring himself a gin.

'There are times when the greatest of men lapse into the trivia of common vice.'

'Quite so, sir. Your health, sir.'

'Is the town,' Pottinger said, 'still completely intact?'

'Oh, yes. Everything in order.'

'It hasn't been blown away? Or devoured by termites?'

Canning laughed. 'I can see you're in a rare old mood.'

'There's a light in the bank,' Pottinger said. 'What is that light in the bank?'

'They'd be weighing out the gold, sir.'

'Ah yes, the gold. Let us drink to the gold.'

They drained the gin that had the burn of acid.

Pottinger pushed himself up from the desk and crossed to the window. The windows of the bank were orange-bright with the light of the lamps within. He leaned against the cool of the glass to feel the winter night come through. It was less than half a dozen hours to midnight, to Saturday morning, and nothing could stop the wheel of the stars. 'We shall need,' he said, turning to the small grey man in the stutter of candlelight, 'a high-sided wagon of the kind that carries hay. And four of the best from the lamentable dross of your troopers.'

'Sir . . .'

'Do not impugn my sobriety, Sergeant. My most courageous plans are laid while drunk.' He took up the bottle and drained it from the neck. 'In order to allay your fears, Corporal Lovatt will take a small detachment to patrol the Gully road . . .'

'Corporal Lovatt?'

'Is he incapable?'

'Well no, sir, but – but what's the wagon for?'

'To disguise our intentions.'

'What intentions?'

'I intend to escort the escort. We – you and I, and four good troopers – will precede the gold coach, concealed.'

Good grief, Canning thought, he's drunker than I thought. 'Don't you think, sir,' he said, rising, 'that a mounted show of strength would be more in order than crouching in a cart?'

'Do it, Sergeant. You have eleven hours till morning.'

But all the same, it gave Pottinger pause for thought. It was the first time he'd faced the nature of his planned deception: it was Gardiner that concerned him, not the gold. And Gardiner had become a special kind of hunger. He would make, he thought, when stuffed in a box, a rather fitting sort of wedding gift.

## Twenty-one

Frank Gardiner was the first to turn up at the Rocks. He'd not only turned up, he'd slept there, alone on a winter's night. The closer he came to the game, the more he liked to be alone.

The dawn woke him. There was an icing of frost across the straw-coloured grass, and the sun came up at this place, Eugowra, like a fuming sphere of molten gold across the unmarked plain, the sphere bursting at the seams and spilling out through ribbons of cloud, igniting the whole eastern sky.

Johnny Piesley was plainly put out when he rode in from the forest. He'd had a bad, wakeful night thinking of the day, this day, Saturday and listening to the creepies in the dark. 'You call yourself a mate,' he accused. 'I hardly ever see you.'

'I never said I was a mate.'

They cooked up some breakfast on a little fire among the rocks. Gardiner said there wasn't any risk, not this early.

'What time are you expecting?' Piesley asked, gnawing on something he didn't like the look of.

'Ten past ten,' Gardiner said.

'What's so special about this place?'

'They have to slow up for the turn. That, and the hill.'

After that they didn't talk for some few minutes. There was something wrong with the Eugowra Rocks, Piesley was thinking, something you couldn't put a finger to. The Rocks loomed up large behind them, big as houses, big as a church, great, sleeping, thinking things with their snouts buried in the clay. Not another rock for miles around – like they'd ploughed their way there from some swampy, haunted place and were maybe resting, waiting, smooth and stretched as the belly of a beast in bloat. And the aboriginals knew. They wouldn't come anywhere near the place.

'What time's the others coming?' Piesley asked, his voice sounding high and skinny on the crystal air.

Gardiner shrugged. 'When they get here.'

'Eight of us,' Piesley lamented.

'You feel outnumbered?'

'I will when we split the loot.'

'You won't if the troopers start shooting.'

'You think they will, Frank?'

'Whyn't you wash the pans out? There's a little creek back up the way.'

'I'll shoot the beggars dead,' Piesley said. 'I'll shoot 'em double-dead.'

'You know you've got a real sweat up, and it's freezing cold?'

'I've been ridin', ain't I?'

'It's not that kind of sweat.'

'I'm not scared, Frank.'

'That's good, Johnny.'

'I'm just all excited up, that's all.'

'Well, go and wash the pans out.'

The sun was up by thirty minutes now, steadily shrinking the shadows of the trees. There was a blue metallic haze right across the plain to the icy distance where the mountains turned again, and the birds were wheeling there, flashing back

177

the sun each time they swung about. The morning was of such a frozen stillness that it seemed you could hear the cry of those birds from all those miles away, but Gardiner who had his head down, seemingly at rest against the rocks, was hearing also a dozen different sounds, paring them apart as he listened in his head – the Piesley sounds, the horse sounds, the bush sounds, and riders drumming maybe half a mile or more away. That's two men, he was thinking; that's Charters and Bow, or Hall and Gilbert – Gilbert planned to rendezvous with Hall, and had maybe started early.

In any case, it turned out Charters and Bow, which reassured Gardiner. You never knew with men like them, they could drink themselves into a funk, or simply change their minds. He needed all the men, every single one of them. There was going to be an almighty shooting, which the half of him didn't want to face. But those men from Bathurst, they were trained to give their lives, and his own ragged crew, or some of them, would likely have to put their blood upon the road.

Ten minutes later, Harry Weir turned up. He arrived quietly, silent as a snake.

'Where's your horse?' Gardiner asked him.

'Back along with yours.'

Weir didn't talk much, hardly acknowledging the others. He'd come well prepared – with food, water and guns.

'What the hell kind of guns are they?' Gardiner said.

'Tranters. Double-action, five-shot.' They were chunky, squared-off handguns with a pitched-back grip, and good to look at. 'This here's a Spencer.'

Gardiner took up the carbine which was nearly as long as his arm, and sighted down to get the feel of it.

'Shoots seven hundred yards,' Weir said quietly. 'A seven-shot repeater. It'll blow a barn apart.'

'Seven hundred yards?'

'Shoots just as good at seven yards; what's the difference?'

'The difference is I'm not that keen about it.'

'You counted me in, Frank,' Weir said with his eyes closed down to slits, 'but you never guaranteed you'd get me out. I reckon that part's up to me.'

'I intend to take this coach without a shot.'

Weir grinned. 'That's what you tell the other fellers. Don't try tellin' me.'

Gardiner looked across at Piesley, Charters and Bow. They were sitting yarning in a group, oblivious. 'How do you make your money, Harry?'

'I'm a stockman, ain't I?'

'I'm asking you.'

'Don't ask me, Frank. You'll get your money's worth.'

'I can believe it,' Gardiner said. 'Just don't hand me more than I asked for.'

Weir began to clean his guns, the blue of the metal shining into the blue of his unshaven jaw, the guns as mean and deadly-looking as his deadly-looking face, and Gardiner knew with an unpleasant certainty that some marriage had taken place, a union of a kind between man and metal, so that talking to the gunman was like talking to the gun.

'I hope you hear me, Harry,' Gardiner said.

'I hear a horseman coming down the road.'

Gardiner turned about, chastened by his own lapse.

'What the hell did you come riding down the road for?' he asked. It was Michael Taylor.

The young man dismounted, looking cold and pinched and with such a shine of innocence about him. 'No one saw me,' he defended.

'You better hope not. You bring some guns?'

'Pair of six-shots. Present from my Dad.'

Gardiner took his hand. 'Well, anyways, you're welcome, boy. I never thought you'd make it.'

'Said I'd be here.'

'So you did. Come and meet the others.'

'He should be here,' said Henry Perch petulantly. 'I'll take him to task for this, indeed I will.'

Pottinger turned from the aggrieved bank manager to resume his supervision. He was not concerned with Michael Taylor's lapse of duty; he was more concerned that every grain of gold and every farthing left the bank intact.

The coach stood in the deserted street, looking grand and red and gold, with a pair of fine mounts, everything glossy and splendid. They did take a pride; there was that to be said. And the guard itself was equally splendid-looking, even to a Guardsman. They stood like twin vermilion sculptures at either side of the doorway to the bank, and a further pair was already mounted in position to the rear of the coach. Fine men, the four of them, under the impassive and silent command of the Escort Sergeant Quillan. Soldiers, Pottinger was thinking, real soldiers, not like the Tom-and-Dick platoon that occupied the barracks. What he wouldn't give ... he thought, but thought again. It was winter, and he had his lady, and he wanted to be home.

'Mr Oliver should not be grappling with such weights,' Perch said, as the senior clerk came staggering out with the coinage bags. 'That's Taylor's job.'

Finally, out of the bank came Aubrey Holliday and Henry Cummings, whose responsibility the gold was. Holliday had up a fine morning flush, but Cummings looked as though he might be better for some bed.

'Almost twenty thousand pounds,' Holliday declared, loud enough to wake the tombstones. 'Three thousand thirty ounces gold, and thirty-seven hundred pounds in notes and coin.' And thereon both men – Holliday and Cummings – signed for receipt.

'Where is the driver?' Holliday asked Sergeant Quillan.

'In the Tavern, sir.'

'Tippling?'

'No, sir, he slept in the loft.'

'Better roust him out, then. It's five to eight.'

Pottinger turned at that moment to see a horse and wagon coming at a spanking clip out of Crooked Lane and up the street towards them. 'Someone coming,' he said.

'It's Mr Pirie,' said Henry Perch, 'doubtless with some tale of woe. Michael lodges with the Piries.'

Pirie, it proved, had a letter of excuse from Michael Taylor, written in Taylor's hand. 'Ill!' he exclaimed. 'He claims to be ill. What a morning to be ill.'

'I'd thought to fetch it along at opening time,' Pirie said, 'but I came straight up instead.'

Now Pottinger read the letter, and followed Pirie to his wagon. 'What time did you leave the house?

'At six o'clock. Why? Does it matter?'

'Was Michael up then?'

'No. He was groaning in his bed.'

'Had he had his breakfast?'

'No. Nor me. I took what they gave at the Craigs'. I had my business there.'

Pottinger thanked him and studied the letter again.

*I am unable to attend the Bank*, it said. *I have had the misfortune to bring my breakfast up* ...

Curious, thought Pottinger, that Taylor should anticipate his illness, unless of course he was playing the simple sluggard's game?

'I'm Fagan, sir,' said a shrunken man with wrinkled skin. 'I'm the driver. Do you have the duty mail?'

Pottinger handed him the letters and reports for Captain St Clare.

'I usually deal with Sergeant Canning, sir,' he said with a tilt of his head and both eyes squeezed up as though against the sun.

'Sergeant Canning is absent.'

'Sick?' said the wizened man.

'You have but a minute to eight, Mr Fagan.'

'I'm as British as a silver shilling,' Fagan declared.

'I'm delighted to hear it.'

'And naught to do with Mr Dickens's Fagin which is spelled different – his with an "I" and mine with an "A". Names do be important, sir,' he rattled on, stuffing papers into his coat, 'and there's some as makes merry with mine as they do, no doubt,' he laughed in a particularly distasteful way, 'with yours, Sir Frederick.'

'Do climb up,' Holliday said hastily. 'You're late.'

'Pottin*ginger*!' Fagan murmured as he took up the reins.

'A very good driver,' Holliday apologised.

Then Quillan offered the salute. And in the moment of delay, Pottinger thought: I should warn him, tell him my suspicions. But he saluted anyway. What did he have to go on?

'A job well done,' Holliday said, stepping back. 'A minute past, but he'll pick it up.'

And the coach was away with a flurry and jingle to stir the heart, the wheels twinkling in the still-early light, and the flame of the troopers' coats dancing in the saddles of the rear-guard as the gold, the boxes of it, slumbered within the coach, secure beneath six good guns.

While Corporal Lovatt was patrolling the desert of the Gully Road and detaining all sorts of unlikely suspects in the zeal of his first command, Sergeant Canning was bivouacked with troopers Merrett, Batchford, Travers and Hardy – and a hay wagon – nine miles or so from the Eugowra Rocks. The location was no mere accident; it was a Pottinger gamble which they'd argued out in the early hours. There was, Pottinger had asserted, only one decent place to ambush a coach on the nether side of Bathurst, and that was the stretch be-tween Battle Creek and Crossroads. It was a narrow ribbon of wretched track – allegedly the highway – he had good reason to remember, for it was here or shortly after that Mrs Con-sidine had pinned 'Onepot' Wally Higgins through the throat. And along this stretch, where brigands plundered almost daily, it was impossible to pass or overtake. The plan, in its impu-dence, was to block the gold coach, to precede it and thus enforce an escort unbeknown. At least, such was the plan until they reached the Rocks. After the Rocks there was Crossroads, where they changed the horses, and after that – and what a blessing – it was no longer the Western Division or Pottinger's command.

'You're mistaken,' Canning had said, scrubbing his face. He felt so weary his eyes were hanging out. 'They'll do it at Cob-bler's Bend.'

'Too close to Ironbark.'

'Or on the climb.'

'Too exposed.'

'Or Stringy Flats, now there's a stretch.'

'An indefensible position.'

'They won't do it,' Canning said with finality.

'They will do it,' Pottinger affirmed, 'between Battle Creek and Crossroads.'

They'd had this discussion in the earliest hours and there'd been a degree of unaccustomed intimacy promoted by the grog.

'Tell you what,' Pottinger had said. 'Put a shilling on it.'

They'd put a shilling on it, and now it was all too ridiculous standing here in the scrub, and he, Sergeant Canning, having to explain to the men exactly what they were about.

'Hide in the cart, Sergeant? Concealed in the cart?' Merrett had reiterated.

'That's what I just said.'

'Like the Trojan Horse,' Batchford offered.

'Like the what?' Travers asked. Everything had to be explained to Travers.

Batchford was the scholar. An older man who'd earned his ticket, he'd been sent out for forging, signing a docket for sixpence, a monstrous act from a position of trust and not to be forgiven.

'Be a darn sight easier to ride a horse than ride a cart,' Merrett lamented.

Exactly, thought Canning. 'Just do as you're told,' he said. 'Hardy,' he called, 'd'you see anything?' He'd posted a scout up on a rock, young Hardy, the barracks wit and a good man with a gun.

'Party of wallabies, sarn't, fossicking about.'

'Might be Gardiner in disguise,' Travers yelled.

'Now then, now then,' Canning said, 'it's not for your amusement.' He was waiting for Pottinger's appearance.

The baronet had planned to leave right after the coach and

cross the country half an hour ahead to reach the meeting place. If he doesn't get lost, Canning thought. He wasn't in the best of moods. It's not the blasted horse and hounds, he thought. And there was an underlying nightmare – that he'd step along the road in some unlikely place, and all because of Pottinger's whim, would meet his bullet fair in the chest, fair in the heart.

'Keep back,' he ordered the men. 'Keep under cover.' He didn't want to spoil the show, it might just work, you never knew. Between Pottinger's wits and his own experience . . .

'Feller coming in a cart,' Hardy called.

They all fell back behind the trees and watched. It was a man and his family travelling early – kids, dogs, pots and pans, the lot – then Canning gave the signal, breathing easy, as they moved out again to watch the cart joggling down the road, the troopers making comments. But Canning looked down at his hand, embarrassed. His gun was in his hand and the hammer was back. He replaced it carefully. That had been a stupid thing to do. He was as nervous as a green boy on his first parade.

Shortly after nine o'clock, Gilbert turned up with Ben Hall. Gardiner went down to meet them. 'What kept you?' he said.

'He had trouble with his wife,' Gilbert told him. 'You know what women are.'

Ben didn't speak. He took the horses back behind the trees and returned with his guns, his face set, all his movements thought about, like a craftsman squaring to his job.

'What's the trouble, Ben?' Gardiner asked.

'No trouble. I'm here, ain't I?'

'No, come on, feller, what's it all about?'

Ben was laying out his guns and checking on the chambers, the free spin of the bullets passing round. 'Biddy knows,' he said.

'Knows about the job?'

'Knows there is a job, not what job it is. And,' he said, sighting, balancing the gun easy in his hand, 'she doesn't like it.'

'Did you tell her?'

'What do you take me for? Women know these things; they don't have to be told. I got a baby boy. She can see me swinging in and out the window and the troopers coming through the door. For ever, that is. No goin' back.'

'She could be right, Ben.'

'Could be.'

'You can pull out if you want.'

'Oh, go and blow your nose, Frank, what am I doin' here?'

Then for just a moment, everything went crazy. Johnny Bow came galloping over the rise, yelling in a hoarse, strangulated voice, 'It's them! It's them!'

And even as Gardiner whipped about to size the situation, what he saw dismayed him. His men, this fine, well-drilled, professional gang was running round like rabbits with their brains blown out, people falling over guns and spilling pannikins with enough clatter to match the bells of Bathurst as they sought to take positions only half-understood – Bow himself making a fine, standing target, Charters with his rear stuck out, and Taylor – damn that Taylor – wandering in a dream. 'Get down!' Gardiner yelled. 'And stay down till I tell you.'

Sure enough, in a minute's time, the horse and wagon that Canning had seen came toiling past, the children brawling and the mother laying into them. Just the thing, Gardiner thought, to give this murderous gang the high fandangles.

He went up to Bow when the wagon had passed and punched him in the face. 'No false alarms, you ninny!'

'Aw gee, Frank,' Bow said from his seat in the dirt.

'I give up,' Gardiner said. 'I give the game away. You fellers take the coach.'

'Don't be like that,' Charters pleaded.

'I mean it. I'm walkin' out.'

He let them persuade him. And told them – again – the coach would come at ten past ten, that they'd be ready, in concealment, that he'd give the signal and they'd rush the coach, no shooting. 'You hear me, Harry Weir?' he said.

'Right. No shooting.'

'Just so's you hear me.'

Gardiner went back to the rock by Gilbert and Ben Hall, and lit a cigar.

'You're doin' a power of smokin',' Gilbert said. 'That's the second stogie you got goin'.'

Gardiner didn't answer. There was an unpleasant creep upon his skin. If that had been the coach, he likely wouldn't even be alive.


About this time, Pottinger arrived from Ironbark. He was brisk and precise in his commands. He'd never truly been under concerted fire before and he rather thought he might be. Painstaking and plodding in detail, he had them tether the horses a quarter-mile away, and there was a deal of waiting and tramping through the brush before the men, the six of them, moved to the hay wagon.

'Is this the best you could do, Sergeant?' Pottinger asked.

'I thought, sir, under the circumstances, we should rather ignore the plush.'

'Is that a jest?'

'Not quite, sir.'

Pottinger peered through the slats of the high-sided wagon. 'Did you not think to clean it?'

'Clean it, sir?'

'It has droppings in it.'

'So it has, sir. Must be livestock.'

'Climb aboard, you chaps, and keep concealed. Where's the driver?' he asked Canning.

'Merrett's driving, sir.'

'In a redcoat? In uniform?'

Sergeant Canning flushed. It was just the sort of stupid detail that one overlooked. 'Of course not,' he said quickly. 'Strip your jacket, Merrett.'

'I trust he arrived here in mufti,' Pottinger said.

'Oh yes, sir. Naturally.'

'And the hat, you idiot,' Pottinger said to the trooper. Chances were that it was not intended to be his finest hour.

But shortly, they were bouncing down the road. 'Slow down,' Pottinger instructed. 'It's not a race.' They were a mile or so from Battle Creek and the coach was not yet to be seen. It was all a matter of timing, Pottinger thought. They had to be at the narrow road by 9.2o, give or take, in order to take the lead. Pottinger looked at his watch. It was eleven minutes past the hour. 'What time do you make it?' he asked Canning.

'Make it ... just on nine o'clock.'

'You're wrong. Batchford?'

'Twenty after, sir. Or twenty two.'

'I've got ten to eleven,' Hardy said.

'I haven't got a watch,' Travers said. 'I lost it in the kitchen stew.'

All this while, the coach was making good and steady time and Fagan, as adept as his reputation claimed him, was easing the horses at an undemanding clip, saving them for the climb and turns ahead. He was informing Sergeant Quillan of the origins of his name, which he'd gone to no end of trouble to discover, explaining the middle-Englishness of 'Fage' and how the honour had been handed on. But Quillan had been through it all before. He'd ridden with Fagan many times and the man had a gift, if that was what it was, for repetition. So he watched the dance of the road unwind, and the sparkle of the sun through the shifting leaves. The truth was, he was somewhat less than alert. People didn't touch the gold coach, there was that kind of respect — no more than a bushranger would ever touch a woman, or so the legend went.

'There's a family of Fagans in Market Drayton,' Fagan was explaining, 'which is just at the bottomside of Stoke on Trent, which has a crest, sir, stuck on the wall, which has certain ancient derivations ...'

Quillan turned in his seat with a nod or a grunt and saw with satisfaction his men — Blythe and Harrow — following on behind. He liked to do this periodically, it gave him reassurance to see their grim, forward-looking faces. He had his best men to the rear, since attacks invariably came from the tail, and they were as steady as clockwork.

His gun he now drew to him as a source of comfort. It was a hybrid-looking brute and permitted to him by a special dispensation – a Beaumont-Adams gun, of which but a score had been made. It was a six-shot revolver-carbine fitted with a handsome stock. Fagan, for his part, had a double-barrelled shotgun slotted beneath the seat, but by God, Quillan thought, you wouldn't trust a thing like that.

'All tidy?' he called, banging on the roof of the coach. It was his usual turn of phrase.

'All in order,' came the reply – from Fawcett, he supposed. If he knew which way was up; the other, Clemens, was almost certainly nodding off.

Thank goodness, he thought, there's one awake.

By twenty past the hour of nine – when Pottinger had lurched his wagon across Battle Creek – Frank Gardiner had his men positioned. He had three anchors to the general drift of things – himself, Gilbert and Hall – whom he'd spaced among the others in a line of closure that would spring to attack on his word. He'd outlined the plan again, perhaps for the fourth time, but there were some among them, as he knew, who still had but the cloudiest notion. One of them – Dan Charters, the youth with the silky hair – he'd dispensed with and told to wait by the horses, and to bring up the horses at the sound of attack. He supposed that Charters was capable and had the stomach for it. Gardiner had seen a vision briefly in which he himself was running with a box of gold and they were shooting his pants out.

He took a breath and cleared his mind. His mind was like a sheet of white, ready to be written on. No fear, no feelings. He'd waited for this, not planned it, but waited for a sign to come, some hint of destiny, something stunning in his span of life. And remembered Cockatoo, stone walls and bars, the footsteps on the flagging, ten to the corner, ten to the door, rhyming with his pulse-beat, written into his blood.

A bird shrieked overhead, went swooping through the up-draught.

'That's a carrion bird, ain't it?' Piesley asked in a squeaky voice.

No one answered. Johnny Gilbert was tossing pebbles at a rock. Ben Hall was squatting with his guns laid out, kind of listening with his eyes far off. Maybe, thought Gardiner, he's hearing the cry of that babe. He didn't know about such things. Right beside him he'd placed Harry Weir, for the reason Harry knew too well. He was under the thumb where he was, but, damn the man, Gardiner was thinking, it's my life he's pitching into the ring. On Gardiner's right hand was the bank clerk, and Gardiner looked at him. Michael Taylor was having trouble with his buttons, a button hanging by a thread and Taylor twisting at it. 'I'm all right,' Taylor said, looking up. 'I get pitched up, that's all. But I'm hard as a boot inside.' I don't believe a word of it, Gardiner thought, but best to leave the boy alone; he'd come out shining more than Charters would.

The sun was getting higher now, and they'd dressed too warm. The weather had the feel of ten o'clock, but damn if it wasn't only half past nine. Forty minutes more, Gardiner thought, but he wanted them ready, on edge, keen, sharp as knives. Let them sweat it out, he thought. They'll move as fast as fleas when I give the word.

'Frank. Hey, Frank.' Piesley called.

Gardiner slid his eyes across.

'I gotta go and wet the rocks, Frank.'

'Wet your pants instead.'

There was the slow humming zizz of insects and the stealthy lift of leaves, and then the silence deeper and more consuming than before, each man drawn into it like men being drawn by the suck of their graves. The silence crept over them with a kind of suffocation until all that was left was the little chink of someone's gun grating on a rock, and Gilbert whistling through the gap in his teeth. 'Cut it out,' said Johnny Bow. 'You give me goose-bumps.'

They began to watch the silence and the stillness as though a dream had settled on them. It was so still that the yellow landscape clear to the far horizon looked like a picture in a stained-glass window, all the pieces and fragments – the rocks and trees and hills and streams – laid out in circlets and slivers as though a hand had put them there. All the birds had gone now, and the sky was shiny as a plate. The men, some of them, watched Gardiner watching. You couldn't escape him; he drew you in. He sat with the cigar stuck between his teeth, and the thin smoke went straight up, and then an inch of ash fell off and rolled away. Excepting for the flick of his eye he could have been dead.

'I don't hear that coach,' Harry Weir said.

Gardiner didn't answer.

'Going on for ten to ten,' said Harry Weir.

'It'll be here.'

'That coach is late. It ain't even halfways here. Where is it?'

'I don't run the coach,' Gardiner said.

'Be kinda stupid if we missed it.'

'Hey Frank,' Piesley yelled.

'Yeah, what's the trouble, Johnny?'

'The coach is gettin' sort of late, ain't it?'

Gardiner sighed. He felt like getting up and going home.


'Late!' croaked Fagan. 'I've never been late before. I have my pride. I have my reputation.' The one thing he didn't have was a timepiece, but there was no need. The clock was in his head and he knew by the feel of it that ten minutes at least had gone against him – for there on the road ahead, on the worst possible stretch, was the insulting, swaying rump of a wretched wagon not even loaded. 'Pull over!' he shouted. 'Clear the way!'

'He can't pull over,' Quillan said.

'He's obstructing the road. He has no right.'

'Be patient,' Quillan instructed. 'We'll make up the time.'

'Never. No chance. We'll lose a quarter-hour.' And alternately he thrashed the horses, then reined them in, he couldn't decide to go or stay, he'd all but lost control.

'Give over, man!' Quillan shouted. 'I'll vouch for the delay.'

'I'll be the joke of the Coach and Wheel. I'll never hear the end of it.'

Quillan sat back in despair, and held on. He had the impression, to look at the frenzy of the driver, that they were dashing for dear life itself, and he wasn't sure that Fagan might not try the impossible – like climbing the cliffs or sailing through the air.

'Pull over, pull over!' the coachman yelled.

'Enough!' cried Quillan with threat in his voice. 'Now that is enough.' And he saw Fagan choke back a sob, like a man who's missed the gates of heaven at closing time.

But in the hay wagon that occupied the road ahead, there was much concealed amusement. Hardy was maintaining a regular watch through the slats at the rear, and was passing back the information. 'He's doing a dance in his seat ... He's going purple in the face ... He's belting up the horses – no, he's putting on the brake!'

'Give up, Hardy,' Pottinger commanded.

'You should see him, sir.'

'Give up and sit down!'

Wagon and coach slashed through the crowding trees. To one side, screened by a press of saplings, was a rocky gully, to the other ditches and a random pitch of rocks beneath a sandstone cliff-face.

'Sit down, Hardy,' Pottinger repeated as he rolled on the floor and clung to the nearest support.

'Sit down,' shouted Canning.

All had the sinking feeling now that their mission had taken a comic turn and would, if the news leaked out, provide the journalists with much hilarity. Pottinger, with a growing dismay for his folly, peered at the road ahead. There were dips and turns and plenty of them, but in the shadowed stillness not the slightest sign of an evil deed.

'Looks like a wild goose chase,' Canning said, not without a trace of malice.

'Speed up, move on!' came Fagan's demented cry.

'How much further?' asked Pottinger.

'A hop and a skip,' said Canning. 'Perhaps a mile before they overtake.'

'Still time,' said Pottinger grimly. He looked at his troops, who'd lost the scent of the game, mere youths, the three of them, and Batchford who was chewing on a fingernail.

'They'll likely take the lead before the Rocks,' Canning said, 'where the road swings wide.'

Pottinger nodded. He knew all this.

'Should have put men at the Rocks,' Canning said, more to himself.

Pottinger turned away. Didn't he know this, too? What else was the sickness at his stomach?


'I hear the coach,' Harry Weir murmured, seconds after Gardiner heard it.

'It's in your head,' Gardiner told him. 'So keep it to yourself.'

'You scared, or somethin'?'

'I'm scared of you scaring them.' He looked at the others getting restive. Five minutes more and he wouldn't have a gang, just a bunch of fellows.

Then, 'Hey, hey now . . .' Piesley said.

And Taylor and Bow were halfway to their feet.

'Get down,' Gardiner said.

'That's the coach, Frank.'

But Gardiner was listening to the sound, the sound washing distantly in tides with less noise than it takes a leaf to fall. 'That's more'n just a single coach,' he said.

'That's maybe half a dozen troopers more,' Weir said.

'It's another coach, a wagon, maybe.'

'I see a little glint there, Frank, right off through the trees.' It was Gilbert, who had the vantage point.

'How many's on the road?'

They had to wait a minute more. 'See the coach, and I see a wagon. Wagon's up the front.'

'Fellers in the wagon?'

'Just the wagon.'

'What you gonna do, Frank?' Piesley asked.

The sound began to seep from the forest like a tide approaching. And shortly they could pick out the special mix of the sound – the hammering of hooves and the turn of wheels, the jingle of harness and the clash of stones, stones bounding from the wheels and the wheels striking sparks as the wagons spilled a searing path through rocks and rubble, funneling dust behind.

'I see 'em. I see 'em good and plain,' said Johnny Bow.

Ben Hall grabbed him by the collar. 'Sit back,' he told him, 'before they see you first.'

And finally Gardiner saw the first wink of colour in the trees, the flash of red and gold and the twinkle of the horses' hooves, and for that brief second his stomach knotted and he had to flex his fingers slowly to remove the iron of fear in his blood. Dammit, he thought, I'm as skittish as a newborn foal. What's wrong with me? Then he took up the cool, clean metal of the matching Colts, and they came into his hands as natural as babes to a mother, cradled by the bed of his palms, his hands not loose or tight, but a comfort to the guns, and both his thumbs without instruction took back the hammers so smoothly that the two sounds made a single sound, not a whisper overlapping. I'm ready, he thought. I'm all right.

And down the road and along by the bend, the clash and thunder of the wheels spilled out, and seconds after, a hay wagon driven by a beardless youth and close behind, whip cracking, calling oaths and curses, the coach-driver driving like some devil at the Styx, eyes bulging white and hair spilling wild, his voice in a screech of impatience, warning, 'Coming through!'

The coach suddenly paced out and swung to the wide, pulling ahead at a furious rate and clipping near enough to the lurch of the wagon to turn the driver white as the escort guards thundered on behind. 'Blooming madman!' Merrett yelled.

But Fagan was beyond hearing, and already wrestling the climb. He didn't have the speed, not nearly enough, and now he was wild with the whip, setting the horses to a lather.

'You'll turn the coach!' Quillan cried, feeling, for one reckless second, inches of air beneath his breeches. 'Gad!' he yelled as he hit the boards. But none the less they were making the grade and he saw to his relief the crest of the rise at the Rocks, the Rocks rising up like a cluster of moons, the shadows black and still, as clean-cut as the spill of ink. 'I shall report this,' he said, though no one heard him. 'I prefer to be alive than early.'

Now the wheels were grinding slow, crunching and skittering the shale. And Fagan took the opportunity to shake his fist at the wagon dwindling to the rear. 'Sluggard!' he yelled. 'You Timothy Turtle!'

'Do give up,' Quillan sighed, and in the equal instant the revolver-carbine was in his hands, the chamber spinning and the fat, soft-lead bullets were smacking into rocks, three of them, the explosions rending at his ears. 'Attack!' he was crying in warning or command he didn't know, but 'Attack, attack!' he was shouting as he pitched out of his seat and on to the ground, hearing – how many? – ten, twenty guns, he couldn't tell. But four bullets at least ripped out the seat where he'd been, and Fagan, less than a wink after Quillan, had reached for the shotgun, then flung up his arms shotgun and all, and leaped into space and now was running on his stumpy legs for the shelter of the scrub. 'Come back,' Quillan yelled. And he heard a voice above or behind him – 'Jump for it!' the voice was crying – and Quillan twisted about to look through the wheels of the coach to see the escort horses tossing and Blythe and Harrow blasting with their carbines. Then suddenly, like a blanket descending, some shadow swooped upon the Sergeant from above, and even as he sought to shield himself the shadow took on bulk, and a trooper – it was Fawcett – crashed upon him. 'Get off, you oaf,' he said, and couldn't believe as he shoved him aside, he thought he was hallucinating as his hand pushed into Fawcett's chest, the hand plunging right into the chest, into broken bone and blood. 'Oh, my God!' he murmured. And Fawcett looked at him with a childish innocence and uttered a word, incomprehensible, the word emerging in a bright red skin of blood. There followed, then, the sting of dust in Quillan's eyes and he saw bullets spouting through the dirt and rolled himself among the thresh of hooves and wheels seeing eight, perhaps a dozen men dotted through the Rocks, and one, Frank Gardiner almost certainly, crying hopelessly, 'Hold your fire!'

It had been hopeless from the start. From the moment Weir had shot the trooper, and shot him with the Spencer carbine, the lads had opened fire to a man, tossing everything they had at the inoffensive coach, everything but boots. The coach stood there receiving the bullets, tossing on its springs as the bullets shredded the timbers and pulverised the glass. There's a man in that coach, Gardiner observed, a man flat out on the floor – and the man was Trooper Clemens who'd slept the journey all the way from Ironbark and had woken to see Fawcett die from Harry Weir's gun; and Clemens was lying prostrate on the floor, saying prayers, the simple prayers of childhood with his body wedged between the boxes he'd been assigned to give his life for.

'Frank! Back down the road,' Gilbert instructed.

Gardiner turned. There were troopers running from the hay wagon, half-a-dozen of them, and damned if the one with the beard and the snout wasn't Pottinger, himself! 'Johnny!' Gardiner yelled, and three Johnnies – Piesley, Gilbert and Bow – turned as one and started shooting at the running men who split apart and dived for cover. We're eight against a dozen, Gardiner thought, as he backed himself against the comfort of the rocks – not the kind of arithmetic he liked. 'Damn!' he said aloud. 'Double damn and blast him!' There was stupid, dreamy Charters obeying orders to the letter, and fetching down the horses. 'Go back!' he yelled. 'It isn't time.' But what the hell, there were horses everywhere, bucking, dancing to the gunfire. Charters couldn't hold them. There were horses looping round in circles, thrashing, skittish, and Charters swinging in a dusty pirouette. 'I can't hold 'em, Frank.'

Something hot and singing whipped past Gardiner's ear. He glanced across to see Sir blooming Frederick, and now Sergeant Canning, deploying the men, the four of them. Have to pin them down, Gardiner thought. Have to do it the hard way. And the guns, the matching Colts, without his bidding, fastened on the foremost troopers, on the scarlet of their coats, and the guns bucked in Gardiner's hands, leaping alive, and two men dropped, crumpling down upon their shadows as though some-one had cut a cord from above – and one was Batchford who'd earned his freedom to accept a bullet, the other, Travers, twenty-two years old.

'Let's git the gold!' Piesley yelped.

'Stay down!' Gardiner commanded.

But Piesley was whooping halfway down to the coach when the two Sergeants – Canning and Quillan – fired less than a second apart, and the shots took Piesley on the run, jolting his body with a doublehanded slap, the kind of teasing slap you'd give a friend, and Piesley stood there stunned, and then abruptly fell as though his legs were severed at the knees. 'I'm hit, Frank,' he lamented in a wheedling voice. 'I'm shot. They got me, Frank.'

There was of a sudden, a stunning silence, the silence of reloading, both sides feverish, but in the stillness of the morning, in the golden sunlight and purity of winter air, more like the silence of contemplation. But two or three guns remained constantly firing, the shots exploding idly like a lazy refrain, and Gardiner realised that the silence, or what he'd held to be the silence, was principally illusion.

'Hey, Pottinger,' he called. 'We got the guns, an' we got the cover...'

'You're outnumbered,' he heard Pottinger inform him.

'Call a halt, or we shoot the lot.' He looked at Gilbert and Hall, at Weir and Bow, at Michael Taylor, his whole face white with a sheen of sweat, at Charters crouching like a turtle and the horses waiting dumbly, shivers at their flanks. Out-numbered, he thought. Yes, they were.

A sudden rage of bullets began again, the most from Quillan emptying the revolver-carbine, the bullets clipping rocks, sending up a hail of pebbles, the fat lead slugs razoring the grass, flicking leaves and whining through the empty air.

'I think they mean it, Frank,' said Gilbert, right up close beside him.

'Roy Foster!' Gardiner said it like an oath.

'Roy what?'

'He shopped us. I shoulda killed him dead.'

Two bullets breezed across their heads.

'I wonder how it is along the Gully Road?' Gilbert said.

'Pretty damn' quiet. Something went wrong.'

'You play it too damn' clever, Frank.'

They saw, down at the coach, Quillan's hand reach out as sneaky as a ferret, reaching out towards the shotgun on the road, Fagan's double-barrelled shotgun. 'No, this'un's mine,' Weir said with a lopsided grin. And he brought the Tranter up as, 'Watch it,' Gilbert warned, and they all saw, the three of them, Dan Charters's snowy, cloudy hair as he darted from his cover – and next, the Tranter sent out a hard and slamming shot, and Charters turned an acrobatic somersault and pitched down hard upon his face.

'Holy hell!' Gilbert told Weir .'You just shot Danny Charters.'

'Like hell I did.'

'You know you did.'

'I only —'

Gardiner had the Colt jammed hard against the back of Weir's skull. 'I ought to blow your head off.'

'Easy, Frank,' Weir said, going green. 'Easy up, now.'

Gardiner moved the gun away. Charters was down there on his knees, both hands clasped to his head, his hands patterned red and white like coloured gloves, the smoky haze of his hair speckled with rubies glistening red. 'Flatten down, Danny,' Gardiner yelled, but couldn't even hear himself, didn't even hear the bullet that raked along his arm.

'You're shot, Frank,' Gilbert told him.

'Keep shooting, and mind your business.'

'I got Frank Gardiner!' Pottinger crowed. 'I creased him.'

'Take more than that, sir,' Canning responded bitterly, he wasn't enjoying this, not a bit.

'I shot Frank Gardiner,' he repeated; he couldn't believe it; he'd drawn the beggar's blood!

They were shooting side by side, each gun like an echo to the other, and Pottinger had found his courage and his confidence; it was the rage of crisis he'd waited for all his life, and he thought illogically of the tinkle of the dinner table at Apsley Chase, and himself in two places at once: the one saying to his father, 'Not bad for a nitwit son, d'you think?' and the other offering breezily to Canning, 'I believe we've turned the tide, old man.' And as he sought to rally his troops, thinking to make a reckless charge, he saw a bullet sweep Hardy, the barracks wit, tease and practical joker, clean off his feet, the whole body lifting inches as the bullet plunged through his throat so that, even as he fell, a twine of blood uncoiled across the air and stayed suspended, there to fall with a dusty patter on the road. 'God help us!' Pottinger breathed, and turned from the sight, but the body in its paroxysm pursued him, the heels thumping at his side, asking for attention.

'Keep down!' Canning barked at his commander, and pulled Pottinger to cover – and they both saw Quillan's blind, mad run, the man beside himself with the battle's heat, running with Fagan's shotgun, the big twin barrels spilling Hall and Bow and Gilbert into deeper cover even as the bullets began to jolt the running man, but he couldn't feel them, or felt something like a child's fist and heard the smack of bullets at his flesh as he ran, his mind no longer his – and then his finger pulled the trigger at the closest range, and it was the action of a dead man, a man dead on his feet, and all that Gilbert saw was the spreading orange flash and the double charge ripped away his face, his chest, the emerald-coloured jacket with the true gold threads, ripped it all aside to the meat beneath, and the man, his jokes, his laughing good looks that had charmed the girls across the world, was gone for ever.

'Charge them! Charge!' Pottinger cried, leaping to his feet. 'Charge the beggars!' But no one came to the cry, and there was none to match his foolish valour. He looked around – at Canning's puzzled, plaintive face, at Quillan dead, at Fawcett,

Travers, Hardy dead, all dead. Where, oh God, where, he accused, are my troops? His troops were Batchford huddled nodding down across his wounds – and the missing escort, Blythe and Harrow. 'Come on!' he urged the stubborn Canning and, as the lazy shots stitched across the ground before him, he turned to fire at the bandits running to the coach, and emptied his gun, shot after shot, hitting one, one at least he was sure he had. 'I got one,' he said grimly, and slumped beside Canning, done up and drained.

'Get out of the coach,' Gardiner said to Clemens, who'd burrowed like a wombat down among the boxes. 'Get your tail out of there.'

'Don't touch me,' Clemens said, pushing up his head.

'Get out,' Gardiner said. 'We want those boxes.'

Clemens began a long, continuous shudder as though in fever. 'Don't shoot me,' he said.

'We got a little problem here,' Gardiner said.

'Just leave me grab his legs,' Johnny Bow began, but Clemens straightened to a crouch, his hands defensive, pushed out front.

'Come on, feller,' Ben Hall said. 'The shootin's done, you're safe now. He don't know what in hell he's doin', Frank.'

'I know what he's doin',' Weir said from half a dozen feet behind. 'He's holdin' up the gettin' of the gold.'

Gardiner gave the nod to Ben and they both moved to gather Clemens, as Clemens, terrified beyond all reason, straightened in the coach, hunched down like a man at the brink of the grave.

'Trooper . . .' said Gardiner gently.

And a great roaring rip of fire punched past his face, enough to blind him, and he saw the bullet, the seven-hundred-yard bullet collect Clemens like a puppet pulled off-stage, the body leaping back and up and sprawling half a dozen feet away on rocks and yellow grass.

'That'un got him out, I reckon,' Weir laughed – then Gardiner's gun smashed his teeth out.

'You could be dead,' Gardiner said, gazing down. 'I never felt so keen to kill a man.'

'Let's get the gold,' Ben said, easing off the situation.

'I should shoot you damn' well dead.'

'The gold, Frank.'

They reached into the coach and began to hoist the boxes out. Gardiner slid them out one by one. 'Take this,' he said to Michael Taylor – and looked at him. The boy was white as saltlick in the sun. 'What's wrong?' he asked. 'You hurt, or something?'

'I'm all right,' Taylor said, reaching for the box.

'Too much killin',' Ben Hall said. 'He ain't used to it.'

'Nor me,' Gardiner said.

But as Taylor took the full weight of the box, the box itself dragged him to the ground, Taylor plunging with it.

'So much for banker's muscles,' Bow laughed.

'He's hurt, Frank,' Ben Hall said. 'Bullet's ripped his back out.'

'Get him over to a horse. And see to Johnny Piesley.'

They continued working at the gold, the boxes thumping down, heavy with the wealth they'd only dreamed of.

Pottinger, who'd been keeping low, now stuck his head up, his hand on Canning's arm. 'That's the one,' he said. 'That's the one I shot. That's Michael Taylor from the bank.'

'Small comfort,' Canning said.

They remained crouched there in the ditch while the outlaws worked, with only Merrett for comfort. Merrett had lost the contents of his stomach and was lying back, sick and all but lifeless. 'All right now?' Canning asked him. 'Feel all right?' He had a feeling for the boy he'd never expressed. It wasn't the sort of thing he would have wished a lad to see. They trained them up to believe that death was clean and valiant, not that death had guts and innards.

'How's Batchford?' Merrett asked.

'Alive and well,' Canning told him, but to what degree he couldn't answer.

'Poor old Batch,' Merrett said.

Poor old all of us, Canning thought.

'We shall rush them,' Pottinger said with renewed vigour, 'while their hands are full.'

'The three of us?' Canning asked dismally.

'Great heaven, man,' Pottinger said, conjuring up his outrage, 'that's the gold they're taking.'

Canning rolled on his side and gazed across the battlefield. 'Let 'em keep it,' he said. They were taking it, right enough – Gardiner, Hall, Weir and Bow – the only ones intact. The desperado Piesley was lying with his eyes wide open, shocked; he couldn't move his legs. Taylor was piling on to the nearest horse. And the other, the one with the fuzz of hair, was standing watching, dumb, his whole face now dissected with blood like the roots of a tree growing down.

'There's just the four of them,' Pottinger remonstrated, 'against the three of us.'

'Don't be foolish, sir.'

'Sergeant, I am never foolish.' And yet his lips refused to offer the command; there was a stubborn, growing fear in him.

But unexpectedly Merrett said beside him, 'I'm for it, sir – for Travers and Hardy, let's do it.'

'Now look, lad . . .' Canning warned him.

'Just fifteen yards to the horses,' Merrett said.

'I tell you this . . .' Canning began. I'm not going, was what he'd intended to say, but was saved from shame by Pottinger's urgent whisper.

'Reinforcements!'

At the further distance, in the scrub behind the Rocks, Blythe and Harrow had reappeared, mounted high upon their horses, unscathed, ready.

'By God, that's it, then,' Pottinger said, and abandoning all caution, scrambled from the ditch and waved.

'What the bloomin' hell's he waving at?' Ben Hall asked.

'Strap that tight,' Gardiner told him, 'and let's get going.'

Gardiner moved from the packhorses that he and Ben would lead and signalled the others to mount. They were leaving quite a picture. The same stillness had returned, the cry of birds, the brush of leaves, everything. The same glass window, he thought – with some red splashed on and some figures in the foreground lying twisted in impossible contortions beneath the drifting veils of powder smoke, the veils lying each across the other, like the covers and colours of mourning. He looked back to see the men on the horses, and crossed to Johnny Piesley.

'Gonna heft to you to horse,' he said. 'And I'll have to be quick about it.'

'I knew you wouldn't leave me, Frank.'

But when Gardiner tried to gather him there was such a shriek of pain that crows sprang out of the trees.

'Where's the trouble?' Gardiner asked.

'It's me legs, Frank. They shot me legs out.'

'This is gonna hurt, Johnny ...'

'Don't touch me!'

'Dammit, man, don't you see the troopers?'

'You have to leave me, Frank,' Piesley said.

Gardiner could see Pottinger and Canning mounting up. There wouldn't be time to heft this man to a horse. 'Reckon you might be right, Johnny.'

'Right about what?'

'Might have to leave you.'

'Don't leave me!'

'Hell and dammit, I can't do both.'

But when he tried to lift the wounded man again ... 'Oh, no. Oh, please. Oh, don't.'

'Sorry, Johnny,' he said.

'Come on, Frank,' Ben Hall yelled.

'Yeah, I'm coming.'

'Leave us a gun,' Piesley said. 'I'm gonna shoot my brains out.'

'You got a gun. Right down there in your belt.'

Gardiner took the gun out and put it in his hand.

Piesley's hand went up to Gardiner's sleeve. 'You tell 'em Frank – I never shed a tear or nothin'.'

'I'll tell 'em, boy.'

Then the shooting started and Gardiner was running for his life, and his boot was in the stirrup and he was moving off before he ever hit the saddle.

Piesley screwed his face up in a kind of grief at their departure, and turned to see Pottinger, Canning and the trooper thundering down, and yelled, though they never heard him, 'You won't take me alive!' And cringed into himself as a dozen hooves flashed past his face, then took the gun up and opened his mouth and bit down on the barrel. May the good Lord receive me, he thought. I never killed a man in anger. And he waited for the rip of the bullet that would lift off the back of his skull, but his hand, his own damned hand wouldn't pull the trigger. 'Do it!' he said to his hand – and in the same instant hurled the gun clean away, right across the lump that was left of Johnny Gilbert's body.

This is the finish, he thought, what a rotten way to finish. The finish for the lot of them, and all for the sake of gold when the good times were still going strong up and down the roads – where the watches, wallets, guns and girls were – the best times, and he hadn't ever known it. 'Damned luck!' he said. 'I never should have left it.'

And heard the drumming of the hooves retreating from him, and the staccato crackle of gunfire, the sounds of chase and escape from the games the big boys played.

*Twenty-two*

'This way!' Charters shouted, plunging ahead into the deepening forest that left the plains to the rear. Obediently, they followed – Gardiner and Hall with the packhorses, Johnny Bow coaxing Michael Taylor – Taylor drifting in his saddle, losing blood, the blood spilling from the saddle – and Weir riding skewed to the rear, the Tranter in his hand. Right behind them, just a second or two from actual sight, were the five pursuers urged along by Pottinger.

'Through here!' Charters shouted.

'Stop yelling,' Gardiner told him. 'We're practically on your tail.'

He looked at Charters, the craziest phantom rider he'd ever seen, the eyes wild and bright, his hair matted with his blood, the blood on his face a tangled mosaic, the kind of crazy man, Gardiner was thinking, you needed six bullets to kill.

'I see them,' he heard Pottinger cry.

Hell and blazes, Gardiner thought, dragging on the rope; he'd piled too much on the packhorse; he'd underestimated and the beasts were acting mulish. 'Git! Git!' he yelled.

They began all but rolling down the slope, the hooves slipping, striking stones and the horses snorting their dislike.

'They're catching up,' Ben said.

A shot went wild among the trees, chipping off the bark.

'Move, damn you,' Gardiner said to Bow.

'Taylor's near but done.'

'Move, move!'

They crashed deeper, blindly into the forest, the gully arrowing down to the wink of water where tree ferns were, the ferns spraying out in lacy fronds clear above their heads, and the air was icy cool and the rocks brilliant green with moss, the water dripping, splashing from the rocks in twists of deep green watergrowth.

'Not the creek,' Gardiner said. 'They'll follow the creek.'

So they stumbled instead on a lateral climb, entering a true timber forest, the trees growing little more than a horse-width apart and the earth dank with an umber overlay, and vines hanging down in a sweet green growing darkness. There they paused at Gardiner's sign and listened for the troopers.

'This ain't the way, Frank,' Charters said in a husky whisper.

Shortly they heard the troopers splashing in the creek, and silence, and discussion so close it seemed, you could reach through a veil of leaves and tweak the speaker's beard.

'Vanished, blast it!' came Pottinger's voice.

'They're somewhere hereabouts,' Canning said.

'Go back,' Pottinger said to Merrett, 'and alert the guard at Crossroads.'

'Which way do you fancy?' Canning asked as the unseen horseman moved away.

'Downstream,' Pottinger said.

And there came a crashing and splashing, growing fainter, safer. 'Good thinking, Frank,' Ben said.

'Let's split the gold,' Weir said.

'I'll split your head if you say that again.' It was the second time he'd said it since they'd waited by. He was as hungry as a bank.

'I want my cut,' Weir said. 'There's a six-ways cut o' gold an' I want mine.'

'This feller needs a doctor,' Ben Hall said of Taylor.

Gardiner walked a little way alone among the trees. There was a throb in his head and a flame along his wounded arm he didn't dare to admit to. Damn, he was thinking, now it's done they all want something different – but he was thinking also of the dead men, those ripped carcasses; they did it cleaner in a slaughteryard. Next thing, Ben was there beside him. 'I reckon we got four, five minutes before they double back,' he said. 'Give Johnny Bow my packhorse, and I'll take Taylor back to Winooka, back to the Valley.'

'That's not the plan,' Gardiner said. 'We're gonna go where Charters takes us, ain't we, and hide up a spell?'

'A dying man ain't the plan, either.'

'When you fellers are through . . .' they heard Weir say.

They walked the horses back to Charters. 'How far's this place you're taking us to?' Gardiner asked him.

'It's just across the way, Frank.'

'How far across the way?'

'Couple of hours or so. Place called Yellowbottle Creek, where my Auntie used to live. About ten mile across from Ironbark.'

Gardiner looked into the sombre forest as though he could see through trees. 'It's all uncharted country there,' he said.

'Gees,' laughed Charters through the cracked dried blood on his face. 'It's like a map in me mind. What are you worrying about?'

'Split the gold and let's split up,' Weir said.

'That ain't the plan.'

'I'm sick of hearin' about the —'

'Troopers!' Johnny Bow said, and the six men plunged on again, hearing Canning's cry behind them – 'Here, sir! They've left the creek,' – as they pushed without choice into the deepening forest.

'Go back!' Gardiner said. There was a wall of green ahead they couldn't penetrate, the forest opening to a clearing and the wall beginning dense, rising from the native grass like the trails of a velvet cloak suspended from the branches. 'Through there. Down along the gully,' he said.

They spilled back through the forest in untidy formation, passing from sunlight to shade and back again, and they saw as they dipped from the rise, the flash of troopers' coats among the green. Then there were the rocks of the deepening gully, great polished slabs of rocks flung there at random, and the horses thrashed at the treacherous path, nostrils flaring, sides foaming with a sweaty fear. Gardiner began to lash at the horse, dragging on the rope. The packhorse wouldn't go much further, the load was slipping, dragging down. He lashed and coaxed the horse, the horse spilling down the tumble of the rocks, snorting and thrashing as the rocks rolled beneath the hooves.

'Keep going,' he told the others. They had reached a meandering trickle of water at the bottom of the gully, and Gardiner was intent to try the same old trick again – troopers, by the very nature of the beast, would always take the easier path, and he had to go where troopers wouldn't.

'Frank, we ain't gonna make this,' Bow said, gazing up at the climb through the trees.

'We're dead if we don't.'

They began to climb the lee side of the gully, which was steeper, denser with ferns and daisy-chains of hanging vines, and it was necessary now to drive the horses hard as cruelty, to cut the flanks to a gloss of blood, to drive them savage into deepening cover so that men and vines and speckled shadow merged and covered. 'That's it,' Gardiner said. 'Stay still as a stick.'

There was a gradual, settling shuffle and they could hear in their immediate containment the wheezing of the horses, the rattle of foam at the bits, see the lungs pumping and the eyes wide to the whites. 'Easy, feller,' Gardiner said, caressing the horse, and now saw below, at easy bullet-range, the troopers tramping through the stream, and Pottinger pausing, looking round, 'Blast if I know,' he was saying.

'Should have a tracker,' Canning said.

'Should have half a hundred men.'

'Can't hear them,' Canning said. 'They could be on our tails.'

The four men – Pottinger, Canning, Blythe and Harrow – looked all around, and Gardiner felt a sting of apprehension as Pottinger, for sure, it seemed, looked right at him through the dappled leaves, right into his eyes, right into his head, and it was such a certain thing that he had the Colt in his hand and the hammer back.

'Think they'd pull that trick again?' Pottinger said.

'Not with the packhorses, no,' Canning said.

When the last hoofbeat had faded, Gardiner dismounted. 'We'll do it your way,' he said to Weir.

Immediately, Weir had out the knife.

'Whose throat are you aiming for?'

'I'm aiming to cut those boxes down,' he said, gazing through eyes red and sunken in the yellow, blue-jowelled flesh.

The men, all but Taylor, dismounted as Weir slashed through the tie-ropes and the boxes thudded to a pad of leaves. Then they got the boxes open, all but two of them, and lugged the bags out. There were four bags to a box, six boxes open. It made it easy now with Gilbert and Piesley out of the count.

'Get them other two,' Weir said.

'Those two are mine,' Gardiner said.

Weir's hand dropped loosely to the Tranter. 'That's not the way I understand it.'

'That's the way I told it to you. That's my bonus.'

'That's the way he said it, Harry,' Ben said. 'The way we all heard it.'

'Damn, you wouldn't be here if it wasn't for my shootin'.'

'Split the bags up, boy, before the troopers come.'

'Why don't you do it?' Ben said, with his gun in his hand.

Weir looked at them, the sweat on his face, his hair wild, some kind of insanity deep behind his eyes. 'That the way you understand it?' he asked Charters and Bow.

'Split the bags up,' Bow said, and they all fell to until Charters straightened and scrubbed the mop of his hair. 'I got here twenty-four bags,' he said, 'going for the five of us. How many's that – not countin' Frank?'

'Keep it moving, will you?' Gardiner said. He had a bad feeling about this. It wasn't the time for dickering.

'I make that four and four-fifths bags apiece,' Bow said.

'Hold it,' Weir said. 'These bags is only goin' four ways, ain't they?' And he looked at Michael Taylor, all but unconscious in the saddle.

'He ain't dead yet,' Ben Hall said.

'But he will be.'

'Take the money,' Gardiner said irritably. 'Make it up with money ... I hear them,' he said breathlessly, and they all heard them, perhaps four minutes away.

'I'm splitting off,' Ben Hall said to Gardiner as he stuffed his bags away, 'and I'm taking Taylor with me.'

'You won't make time with a wounded man,' Gardiner told him.

'Sure I will,' Ben said. ''Cause you fellers are going to lead the troopers off.'

Gardiner grinned. 'I hadn't thought of that.'

'See you in the Valley,' Ben said.

'Where's he going?' Charters asked. 'No!' he called after Ben. 'Valley's up along the other way.'

'Valley's west,' Bow said.

'No, it ain't, it's — Gees, I dunno, it's somewhere hereabout.'

'Put your hat on,' Gardiner told him. 'That bullet blowed

your brains out.' And he turned to Weir, 'What the hell are you doing?'

Weir among the lot of them was still down there in the dirt, his fingers feverish at the drawstrings of the bags between his knees.

'Harry!' Bow yelled.

'We're going,' Gardiner said, and set the horse to a shuffle, more to alert the absentminded Weir.

Now Weir looked up, a puzzlement on his sallow face, his brows drawn down to an arrowhead. 'How do I know they give me gold?' he asked.

'It ain't chaff, you idjut.'

'How do I know you ain't double-dealt me?' And his fingers plunged into the bag, and his hand came up with a glitter of alluvial metal, about the purest gold on God's good earth.

'You satisfied?' Gardiner said.

Then the bullets began slapping through the leaves, and Gardiner felt the twist of his saddle-bag as a bullet flying wild whipped past his leg. He didn't have to give the order. They were off, he and Charters and Bow – and he was dragging the packhorse behind, the horse working better now with just two boxes, one aside from the other. 'Harry!' he heard Bow calling as they spilled down the slope. Damn Harry, he thought; it was Harry's damn' fault that they'd delayed.

They whipped across the bottom stream and up the other side mere seconds before the troopers rounded the turn, and Gardiner paused by a high, flat rock and looked back, pausing long enough to see Canning gesturing to Weir's cover – and Weir bursting out from cover, horseless, running wild, with gold and money-bags, demented by the fever of his wealth, running down towards the stream, the horses closing all about him. Then Weir tripped and fell flying from a rock, and the spilled gold rayed out over him, glittering like powder burning in the air, a yellow, incandescent rainbow falling, raining down.

'There's the others!' Canning yelled, and Pottinger and Blythe and Harrow were halfway down to the stream.

Gardiner, Charters and Bow swept back to the forest again, back into the twilight damp – the forest was something you couldn't escape; and Charters, for every step they took, felt a growing numbness, a despair. Although he knew the country, he didn't know it at a random ride. 'Just let me get me bearings, Frank,' he said, as they came to a dead-end avenue of trees.

'You mean you're lost,' Gardiner accused.

'I ain't lost. I'm just thinkin'.'

They pressed on another way and found a trail, perhaps some bullock's trail, and Gardiner took the chance. He had to make time to extend the gap between the troopers. Then, in a clearing, Charters suddenly said with a shine to his eyes, 'Hey, I know where I am!'

'That's more'n I do,' Bow said glumly. 'Stop crowing and get us out of this.'

'This here is Binty's Camp. And that'd be the Razortop down there. At least,' he said, scrubbing through his hair, 'it looks that way. Thing is, we've come around the other way, and —'

'Danny,' Gardiner sighed. 'Leave out the ifs an' buts. Do you know where you damn' well are?'

'Yeah, 'bout five miles from my Auntie's place.'

'Auntie put the billy on,' Bow sighed.

'Right through here!' Charters said, galloping off, and they piled in after him, going down another trail, the path widening and the trees pulling back, getting smaller, the forest yielding to saplings and yellow grass again. And as the ridges rolled across Gardiner's gaze, he saw the wink of flatland in between, the land spreading miles across as he'd seen it hours before when he'd sat by the Rocks waiting and dreaming of the coach plunging down the road towards them. Don't I know this place? he asked himself. And something drew him back as Bow and Charters pulled ahead, and the something was a kind of dream that shouldn't be there – for the track had widened to a road, and up along the road was a cluster of dwellings, a shanty pub, a barn, a stable.

'Pull back!' he yelled, but much too late.

Even as the foremost riders reared their horses, Gardiner could see the detachment of troopers led by Merrett, ten, a dozen troopers fresh and frisky – that thickhead Danny Charters had led them straight to Crossroads!

Now he was alone. He was alone in the forest again, him, the horses and the gold, and he felt better for it, not being the kind to team with men – it was men that made a muck of things. But he wasn't out of it, not yet. Each time he paused, there were troopers crashing round, but now he dismounted and led the horses silently into the thick of trees, the trunks pressing up so close that they grazed the horses' sides. But this was the way to beat the baronet; there was no damned tally-ho in the bush, and if a man could think like a beast and move like a beast, a man could be invisible.

He moved this way right into the afternoon, not hurrying, not thinking of gold or guns nor even of tomorrow, moving where his tracks were negligible, sometimes pausing to erase his tracks, scrubbing out the spoor with branches or rearranging leaves – because by now they'd have the trackers out, but he was lost, deliberately lost; that was the cleverest thing. Because trackers – and presumably baronets – rested on the faith that a hunted man always had a place to go, a destination, and he could afford a day or two in limbo. He had no fear of being lost, had never shared the townsman's fear. How could he truly be lost, he reasoned. This was the land where he lived.

At the brink of sundown, he permitted rest for himself and the horses. There was a wondrous forest silence in the late of afternoon, and a hugely molten sun ignited the air and slanted in the purest gold through colonnades of trees. He gave the horses water, and piled leaves beneath a tree and lay down dead dog-tired, peeling back his sleeve for the first time to see where the bullet had furrowed. That'll keep, he thought, and closed his eyes.

He would let perhaps a week lie idle on his hands before he moved from the forest, and then he'd simply track the sun to

Winooka Valley. All told, he thought – and God rest the dead – not a bad day's work. He had the gold now, and now it was time to quit.

## Twenty-three

For five whole nights Kate Foster hadn't dreamed of Gardiner. Each night – it was a ritual – she'd settle in the dark and place him in her mind, but dreams were absent and her head was emptied out. On the sixth night she had the dream and in the dark, unbeknown to her, he was moving through the wash of moonlight in the shack.

The news of the biggest theft in New South Wales, in the Colony, in all the world perhaps, had come to Kate with the sudden, savage drumming of the troopers' horses. They had come to search the Valley, convinced that in one of these old tumbledowns, or in the forest, or along the streams, Frank Gardiner was hiding out assisted by his friends. The troopers ripped through every house in the Valley, and when they came to Biddy's house, to Ben Hall's house, they turned her out and put the torch to it. Overnight, the law had turned its teeth upon them, smashing, breaking, cussing up and down the trails, and they'd placed £4,000 upon her lover's head, enough to buy a palace for the turncoat.

But it gave Kate Foster no satisfaction, none at all. Pa Walsh had put his hand across her shoulders, and told her: 'He's gone, love. He wouldn't dare to show his beak in here.' And McGuire said: 'Best you forget him. Men like him, they come and go as sudden as the weather.' And Roy told her on the sixth night: 'I reckon he's dead, and they won't never find him.' On this, she'd slept and dreamed about him, idle, inconsequential dreams that took no account of the fact that he was in the room and gathering her clothes and the things she'd need, or he thought she'd need, into a saddle-bag.

He took the dresses that she liked, just one or two – he knew them all – and some warmer things drying by the fire. And shoes, she'd need some shoes and shifts and things – damned if a woman didn't need so many things. He stuffed them in the bag, the garments and a hairbrush and a lacquered trinket box, enough to keep her going. Then he went to the bed where the two of them lay spilled across each other, she on her back and innocent with sleep, and he sleeping with a windy sigh, dead to the world. He felt sorry for Roy, but even more for his emptiness, his follies and weakness that would trail him to the grave.

He put his hand on Kate, and she stirred and opened her eyes almost as though she'd expected him.

'Get up,' he whispered. 'We're going.'

'But Frank —'

He clapped his hand across her lips. 'Get moving,' he said, and drew her warm from the bed into his arms, hoisting her right off the cold of the floor as he kissed her, tasting the breath and the life of her.

'I thought you'd up and died,' she said, her head against him.

He lowered her and told her to dress, thrusting garments at her, not watching her but the windows and the door. There was a batch of troopers camped halfway down the Valley, and with them, corralled into duty, was the best tracker in the business, and that was Billy Dargin.

'My woolly underbreeches ...' she complained, searching for them.

'They're in the bag,' he told her, and then he had to rifle through the bag to find the stupidest garment a woman ever wore, like something comic in a campfire joke.

'They're wet,' she said.

'Kate ...' he pleaded, as she held them to the fire.

'Where are we going?' she asked him.

Roy turned with a terrible snort and slammed his knuckles against the wall.

They moved outside into the ice of a brilliant, moonlit night. Down there in the shadows were the horses, two of them, one of them borrowed from Danny Charters, who wouldn't have the need.

'I don't believe it,' she whispered at him in the stillness. 'I don't believe it.' And she was half-laughing, half weeping in his arms, clinging to him in a fierce embrace.

He took her by the shoulders and held her hard. 'No tears,' he said. 'None of that. We have to ride through hell. If you were any other woman, I wouldn't take you. I wouldn't go.'

'I'm ready,' she said, pushing the tears away.

'We could maybe never get there,' he warned her.

'I don't care. I'm going anyway.'

'That's good enough for me,' he said.

But less than ten paces towards the horses, Gardiner heard the little, tumbling metal sound that lives were lost upon. He gripped her arm and held her by him. Someone had cocked a piece at them from the shadows of the house.

'You moved real quiet, Roy,' he said turning.

'I'm gonna blow your tail out, Frank,' Foster said, moving into moonlight. 'You clear on out, Kate, else I take you with him.'

Gardiner looked at this lunar apparition in its nightshirt, with the howdah, the ancient horse-pistol, in both its bone-taut hands.

'Is that thing loaded, Roy?'

'In seconds flat, you'll find out good.'

'You put that damn' thing down, Roy,' Kate said. 'It'll likely blow your arm off.'

'You shut your mouth,' he told her. 'I'm gonna get myself four thousand pounds o' dead man ... You thought to take me for a momma's boy,' he suddenly thrust at Gardiner, 'walkin' in, playin' fancy with my woman ...'

'You lost me the day we married,' she said.

'... threatenin' me, tellin' me you'd shoot my big fat toe. I don't forget. I'm gonna blow you straight across the fencepost, Frank ...'

Gardiner put Kate aside, shedding her aside and offered his empty hands to Roy. 'We're evened out, ain't that the truth?

214

Didn't you play the rat on me and tell that baronet policeman? You bet your life you did. And the way it was it ended up a slaughter. We're even score, Roy. I'll take the girl, or I'll take your life, whichever way you want it.'

'Stop dancin' round,' Roy said, 'and keep your fingers from that gun.'

Gardiner's hand was almost at the guns, the ones on either side, and left or right he knew he could take Roy Foster easily and stitch a line of bullets through him long before he could pull the heavy trigger of the howdah. But he removed his hand and turned it empty. 'I suppose I do owe you the satisfaction Roy,' he said.

The single shot ripped across the stillness of the air, straight across the yard and into and out of old man Walsh's house, jangling at the pewter pots strung across the stove. 'Japers!' Walsh cried, leaping out of bed.

'Mount up,' Gardiner told Kate. 'We're gonna see some troopers if we stand here long enough.'

'What's this, then?' Walsh said from the doorway. Then he and Ma came out sleepstruck, like a pair of ancient elves in nightshirts, and Kate was in their arms and saying, repeating, 'I'm going, I have to go, Pa.'

'That's your lawful husband standin' there,' Ma said.

'I can't help myself,' Kate said dumbly.

'There'll be a judgement on you, Kate,' they told her.

'Get back inside,' Roy said, and it was like the bleating of a lamb and no one took the least blind bit of notice.

'Piece of advice,' Gardiner told him. 'Get yourself clear of the Valley. I could have shot you dead for what you done – and there's others will. They'll seek you out, boy, and they won't give you a standing shot like I did. Ain't no place here for a turncoat. You better get you gone.'

'I'll fend for meself,' Roy said. 'I don't need your advice.'

'Then you're a dead man.'

They mounted up, Gardiner and Kate. And Kate held Ma's hand – Ma standing on the tiptoe of her naked feet, a long, hard road of whips and chains behind her, the kind of life that gave you pause and knowing. 'It's Satan's work is what you're doing,' she said, 'but bless you both, and God help you in his wisdom.'

'Treat her decent, Frank,' Pa said, even as they heard the distant shuffle of hooves in the crystal stillness of the night. 'That's troopers, ain't it?' he said querulously.

'Ain't the wedding march,' Gardiner said.

They thrust into the shadows of the night, down through the feathery glade where the melaleucas grew. Shortly the troopers arrived and Sergeant Canning said, 'What's going on?'

'Through there!' Roy Foster burst out. 'They went through there.'

'Gardiner?' said Canning as though he didn't believe it.

'And my wife,' said Roy in a husky voice.

They stood there as the troopers moved away, Roy and Pa and Ma; and Ma folded her arms about herself and said, 'I got the shivers,' she said. 'I'm gonna poke up the fire a bit.'

'Get off my land,' Walsh told Roy. 'And don't you never come back.'

'Pa . . .' said the woman.

'If you're here at sun-up, you'll leave the Valley in a box.'

He put his arm about his woman, the one he'd bought for the going price, the good stout woman who'd seen him through the hardest journey of his life, and took her inside and slammed the door and put the shaft across it as Roy turned from the night's deepening silence and went back to the 'love-nest', as they'd called it, to gather up his things.

Gardiner and Kate rode the whole night through, moving back to the forest that he'd recently learned, back past the site of the slaughter, with the troopers growing tired and lost and hopeless, though Canning drove them on to the point of folly and had Dargin tracking moonbeams. But the forest defeated them, and when the Sergeant finally called a bitter halt, there was just an inky silence studded by the cry of mopokes in the dark, and he knew it was his wretched fate to have lost the world's most wanted man.

'Is this the place?' Kate asked as they crossed the road at a certain point. 'Is this where you took the coach?'

'No,' he told her. 'It was back along the other way.'

But he could see the bullet casings glinting in the dust. They rode at an easy pace past the slumbering Rocks, the Rocks touched now with a dread that would always remain, and he thought for a moment he heard a man cry out – some neglected corpse perhaps, clawing back to life – but it was just a night-bird, one he couldn't recognise. After this, they continued up the road to Crossroads, the little staging outpost that didn't even boast a dog.

She nodded sleepily and they left the road to take the one through the wilderness that was marked out only by the stars, and the way turned north to a landscape that neither one had ever seen before, and in the night it went on for ever with moonlit horizons for ever darkening, one ridge upon the other, but gently placed like veils of night in shades of indigo and inky green.


## Twenty-four

'Have you seen the newspapers?' said Captain St Clare in a cracked and angry voice. 'And the letters to the press?'

He tossed off his travelling cloak and threw it at Canning as he pushed past Pottinger and sat in his chair.

'Yes,' said Pottinger, 'I've not only seen the papers, but I've heard them quoted at me every time I step outside ... Get another chair,' he told Canning. 'The local wits have invented ditties at the Tavern,' he said to St Clare, 'which they chant as I go home, and there is a variety of epithets scrawled on my walls, some of which would scorch your ears to hear ...'

'Yes, yes,' said the Captain impatiently, perusing the papers on the desk and tweaking at his hairs. 'A policeman sometimes has a burden, but —'

'I am cognisant,' Pottinger said sharply, 'of my failures, my frustrations, my dimwitted, stumblefooted —'

'Now then, now then.'

'And I don't need salt and vinegar to sharpen my despair. Yes, I've lost Frank Gardiner, I've lost him – as what man wouldn't? But I'm not a dunderhead, and I refuse to be a scapegoat.'

'But you tracked him?' St Clare prodded. 'Did you not track him?'

'Sergeant Canning tracked him.'

'As far as Crossroads. Thence to the bush.'

'And lost him?'

'Except for several twenty miles or so. But the man's as smart as a tracker himself – using creekbeds, trailing branches and the like.'

'But he has a woman with him?'

'It appears to make no difference, sir.'

'First time,' St Clare said, 'a tracker's failed?'

'Oh no, sir, not the first time.'

'Whom did you use?' St Clare asked, his eyes as chill as the winter in the room.

'Dargin,' said Pottinger. 'Reputedly the best.'

'Is there not some curious relationship, some blood brothership or something between the black man and Ben Hall?'

'He once dossed with Hall,' Canning said. 'That's all finished.'

'And hasn't Ben Hall since gone to the bad?'

Both men, Pottinger and Canning, left the thrust unanswered.

'Perhaps I should roust up a pot of tea?' Canning said.

St Clare turned upon him his frozen eyes, then said to Pottinger, 'Whom do you have for trial?'

'The names are on the sheet beneath your hand.'

St Clare looked down. 'Ben Hall is absent.'

'You know where he is. You just observed it.'

'And Michael Taylor, the young man from the bank?'

'There's some doubt about him.'

'But you shot him. So you reported.'

'I shot a youngish fellow, presumably Taylor.'

'Who's since deserted the bank?'

'So it would appear.'

St Clare rose from the desk and turned his attention to the speckled window, his hands clasped behind his back. 'I find your attitude ambiguous,' he said.

Pottinger paused long enough for St Clare to turn about. Pottinger said, 'I couldn't swear it was Taylor, not in a court of law.'

'Was he named by the offenders?'

'Not by Charters, no. Charters named the others, not Taylor.'

'So much consideration for a first offender?'

'That remains to be proved, Captain.'

'So of the eight, you have but three?'

'Four,' said Canning. 'We acquired Bow the morning after.'

'And Gilbert dead is five.'

'Five,' murmured St Clare. 'I suppose it could be worse. But be it known, Sir Frederick,' he said, his voice unpleasantly soft, 'that Gardiner alive is a stain on us all, that you, by indolence or incompetence, have allowed a felon, a murderer, to cock a snoot at Her Majesty's men, and have set this Colony on a course of infamy that makes of us, of me, of you, but a cuckold in the eyes of decent men. That, sir, is my brief, that I'm pledged to tell you by men who reside in the sanctity of government. You will find Frank Gardiner, sir, or leave your name in tatters.'

'Am I dismissed?' Pottinger said. And, upon the other's silence, dismissed himself.

Pottinger took the road out of town with neither haste nor leisure, and within the morning came upon the wintry spread of Considine's with the river full in view, the willows now bare and lacy in the clarity of winter light. There were men working in the fields, either burning off or ploughing, and the whole environ was one of ochre shades, russets and umbers, even to the foothills whose forests never changed their look of faded green. His romance had not been going well of late, not since that tiff in the churchyard. They had not precisely parted, but they had strayed. And there was more. There was his battle at the Rocks, the letting of blood, his cruel initiation that had somewhat scarred his character. He was not now the same man, nor could ever be, so his face was set grim as he passed through the gate and even grimmer, perhaps when Lelitia Considine came out, and yet he'd never seen her look so fine. There was a passion in her that had departed from his own soul. Her eyes were bright and skin clear, her body moulded to perfection, to a provocative thrust beneath the simple shawl and woollens that she wore against the cold.

She took his hands as he dismounted and kissed him fully, shamelessly in the full vision of the yard. 'Dearest Fred,' she said, 'I thought you'd deserted me. Was I all that adamant,' she asked, 'when you implored me to go to England?'

'You're looking very . . . elegant,' he said.

'I'm in rags,' she laughed. 'Do come inside. We're alone,' she coaxed. 'Which may outrage your sense of propriety, but I'm not feeling elegant, not a bit. I'm feeling — I mustn't say it,' she said wickedly. 'You must forgive me, I feel as gauche as a filly. I'm so glad you came.'

'Alone?' he asked abstractedly, gazing into the smoky silences of morning where the men were burning grass.

'I've missed you more than you could know,' she murmured to him. 'Missed you to the point of shamelessness.'

'You flatter me.' But he paused at the garden gate, beneath the branching rose. 'Where's Clara?' he asked.

'She's visiting,' she told him after a slight pause. 'You must tell me about your adventures,' she hurried on. 'Were you truly in the thick of it? Was your life endangered?'

Despite her patent attempt to guide him away, he chose to sit on the bench by the water tank, where the vines grew, and rows of winter cabbages were planted neatly out.

'At least come into the kitchen,' she pleaded.

'Who is Clara visiting?' he asked.

'Oh, a fig for Clara,' she said. 'You never cared twopence for Clara. Or threepence,' she laughed, trying to make light of it. 'She's visiting Mrs Rossiter,' she said at last. 'What it is to love a policeman!' She sat primly by him, close by him and arranged her skirts. 'I've been in a torment ... There was no news, and the wildest rumours. Then Papa heard the news from town, and ...'.

'I was galloping about,' he said wearily, 'hither and yon, and largely to no purpose. The men I wanted were nowhere nearabouts.'

'I thought you'd made a capture?'

'Except for Hall and Gardiner. And another fellow.'

At this she fell silent. He was quick to sense the awkwardness that fell suddenly between them, and a new and gauzy distrust that he was loathe to penetrate. He took her hand and pressed it to his lips. 'Is it true,' he asked, 'that women commit their blindest follies when driven by compassion?'

'It may be.'

'Or love?'

'I've spoken to Papa,' she said, ignoring his drift, and straightening on the bench, her bosom bold against the cloth, 'and Mama as well, and both have chided me. I believe,' she laughed, 'they're enamoured of your title. And they take me to task for being far too headstrong – which I am – and inform me that a woman should bow to the will of her spouse, or spouse-to-be should I say?'

'Where are your parents?' he asked with a bleak detachment, as though he had her in a witness box.

'Freddie!' she pouted. 'You're not listening to a word I say.'

'Where are they?'

'In the field, of course.'

He looked through the thicket of English shrubs that fringed the garden, across the rutted yard to the woolshed, the barns and little shanties dotted thereabouts. 'I'm here on a miserable duty,' he told her. 'You know why I'm here.'

'I love you,' she said.

He felt for the first time a threat to their love. He pulled her abruptly to her feet and put his lips to hers; there was half of him that would take her where she stood, his hand searching at her flanks, feeling there the firmness and the tremors of the flesh, moving hard against her so that she was forced to gasp. 'Oh God,' she uttered, her eyes wide and startled by her own rough surge of responding passion, her knees folding stupidly so that he held her totally, his hand exploring the cloth of her dress where his hand had never ventured. 'Please...' she pleaded with him, and he looked down at the dark glitter of her eyes and saw a wildness there, molten and consuming.

'Not now,' he said. 'Not yet.'

'Now!' she commanded.

'We shall have done with this thing,' he told her. And, to her wide-eyed look, half reproof, half puzzlement, 'I will not have this thing between us. Will you show me,' he said, moving to the gate, 'or will I make my own reconnaissance?'

'Would you jeopardise our love?' she asked.

'Haven't you already done so?'

They moved into the yard, where the crooked fences passed down to the huts and the handling yards, and stood there in a warm caress of sunlight by the shadow of the woolshed. 'Where do you suggest I start?' he asked.

'Please, Freddie...' she clung to him, '... must you be so wretched?'

'Should I begin with the barn, or what you call the woolshed?'

'I do so love you, and I spoke to Papa like I said, and —'

'Or that little patchwork shed, standing by itself? What would your father keep in there?'

'Freddie, please.'

'I believe,' he said, drawing away from her, 'that I'd be well advised to terminate your agony.' And so saying, he drew his gun and shot a bullet at a cloud.

There was such a rending of the silence that Lelitia clapped her hands too late to her ears, and a confetti of birds spilled up from the trees, and, in the moment after, Clara Considine wrenched open the door of the paperbark shed.

'Good morning,' said Pottinger. 'How unexpected.' He began to march towards the shed, aware that he was penetrating a field of vision between the sisters, made almost tangible by the revelation of their guilt.

'May I step inside?' he asked Clara.

But she refused him entry. 'I'm tending a sheep,' she said. 'The sheep is laid up sick.'

'Isn't there a stall or stable more appropriate?'

'It's a pet sheep,' she said.

'Injured in the back?' he asked. 'By a wayward bullet?'

He turned to look at Lelitia. 'Does this Considine conspiracy,' he asked, 'also involve the parents? I should hate to see them end in twenty years of irons.'

She looked at him, her head held high, her features set in a flush of pride – at least she wore her guilt better than her falsehoods – and told him firmly, without hesitation, 'I am to tell you, Papa said, as I've tried to tell you twice times over already this morning, that I'm willing to accept your hand, as well as your home in England.'

'No, Lettie! I won't let you,' Clara cried.

'It's done,' Lettie said. 'It's what I want. I make no sacrifice.'

Pottinger sighed. It was also what he most desired, but not in this fashion. 'Step aside,' he ordered Clara, and moved towards the doorway as she also moved, with a cry, to obstruct him. He looked once at her, and once within, there to see the 'sheep', or the five human toes of it lying in the straw. 'Damn you for your stupidity,' he accused Clara. 'And please forgive my language.' At which he allowed himself to be drawn half willingly by Lettie from the shadows into the sunlight. 'My position is perfectly untenable,' he complained.

But she put her fingers to his face, tracing out the worry-lines; and the pride in her own face was gone, though in its place was another bloom of something deeper. 'Do you not understand love?' she asked. 'That our stupidity is love?'

He sighed and turned away with the weight of weeks upon him, of St Clare's icy contempt, of Gardiner's slippery escape. And now, when he had Michael Taylor, a certain prize, half a dozen feet away, was he to renounce his victory and his own salvation?

'I'll never leave you,' she told him. 'I may have committed my follies, have offered you a form of barter and the insult to your uniform. But I'll accompany you through life though we're a thousand miles apart. You owe me nothing. I owe you everything —'

He sighed aloud a second time and pushed his fingers through his hair, gazing now at the two of them, these breathless, innocent, contrary sisters, the partners in the crime. Then he felt something heavy in his hand, and put the gun away and buckled up the holster.

'Miss Clara . . .' he began. She stood there with her lips apart. 'I would advise,' he said finally, 'that you set the sheep on the road. And follow it, if you have to, a good long way from Ironbark – before its teeth grow long enough to bite the hand that tends it.'

'Oh my,' she said in a swell of emotion, 'you are a lovely man!' And she clung to him and kissed him.

'Now, now, that's enough,' he said, colouring, whether from pleasure or the guilt of his compliance, he didn't know; but when he walked with Lettie to his horse, there was a certain sag in his spirit that she soon detected.

'That was wise and courageous,' she told him, 'and I love you doubly for it.'

He looked back at the little, shabby hut. 'Which is the sheep and which is the lamb?' he said.

'He renounced the gold,' she informed him. 'There is no gold.'

'I fail to hear you,' he said. 'I've gone deaf in the field of conscience. My whole life long,' he sighed as he mounted up, 'is spent departing the ruins of my battlefields.'

'But you love me,' she said boldly, fearing that he might have changed his position.

'That much is surely proven,' he said. And he looked down at her. 'There's a devil in my lady. What a fiery bride she'll make.'

'When?' she implored him. 'When will it be?'

'When I drop the rope on Gardiner's neck.'

And he was gone, the horse merely plodding through the gate, the rider's shoulders slumped, his head to one side nodding, a philosopher in scarlet as he turned now to the major task of salvaging the tatters of his family name and honour.

## Twenty-five

Gardiner was taking Kate to the brink and the end of the earth, where the land, she was prepared to swear, must surely falter into a deep abyss of demons. Or so she dreamed on these successive nights as they rode by the stars, with her half-nodding asleep in the saddle, to be wakened by the clash of pans and the billy steaming in the dark, and Gardiner bringing tea and food to her, urging her to waken and promising reprieve when once the sun showed through; and there'd be a cave, or a pile of mouldering logs, or tiers of dreaming leaves with the dance of the sun shining through. She came to know more of the land than she'd ever known before, living close to the land, to the fruity perfume of the forest floor, and the smouldering aromas of fungus and lichen, strange fruits and roots – the wild figs, conkaberries and quondongs – the *mangari* as the black men called it, the kitchen garden of the bush yielding food from the spike rush and the pods of waterlilies growing wild.

For days upon days he refused to approach the settlements, preferring to live wild and as nocturnal as an owl. And she could see in him, her man, a change to peace and a calm tranquillity as they moved forever north from Ironbark. 'How do you know where we're going?' she asked as they lay on ferns with the water splashing by.

'I just follow the nose on my face,' he said, and they resumed a coupling in the forest, joining like beasts at play, but with laughter and love, the entire edge of uncertainty gone, and in its place an idyll, a time of loving that could never be as sweet again. She studied him by firelight, mulling over the scars and punishment that his body had received, his whole history written on his skin, from the accident of a knacker's blade to his face being peppered by the window-glass at Considine's, to the bullet that had sheared his arm at the Rocks. She kissed the scar to bring a blessing to it.

'It'll pass,' he said. 'It's nothing.'

'It'll leave a furrow,' she told him.

He laughed and hauled her up across the hardness of his belly. 'So's you'll know me in the dark.'

A week or ten days north, he showed his face at a staging post for the first time in the light of day. It was just two or three bark shanties where the coach pulled by, and a place to buy your feed and grain.

'I haven't seen you through these parts,' said Owen Evans, who ran the store.

'I doubt you would,' said Gardiner.

'Owen Evans,' said the storeman and stuck his hand out.

'Christie,' said Gardiner. 'Frank Christie.' It was his rightful name, or one of them. He'd picked up names along the trail from birth. 'Just fill me up some foodstuffs,' he said, tossing down the sack. 'I'm going north.'

'How far you going?'

'How far does it go?'

'Just keeps going, so they tell me. Is that your woman by the hitchin' post?'

'That's my wife,' Gardiner said.

'No offence, Mr Christie.'

'None taken.'

'She's a fine-lookin' lady as ever I seen.'

'Just watch the peas, boy, and give me a full, fair pound.'

And shortly, just before he left, he cashed some gold.

'Where'd you get this gold?' Evans asked.

'That'd be telling. I just struck it lucky.'

'You surely did. That's the best-lookin' gold as ever I seen.'

'That's education,' Gardiner said, stuffing the notes away. 'Gold and women, I know 'em both.'

'You surely do, sir. You surely do.'

They began at last to travel by day, but not by the roads, not yet. It was bitterly cold but Kate never complained. She'd wash out her things by some flowing stream and often wear them wet. 'Let me wash that shirt out, Frank,' she'd say, 'and dry it by the fire.' 'No,' he'd tell her, 'leave it till it peels away; then I'll buy another.' He could be the most mule-headed man, and though he took it easy now, and was sweet to get along with, he never relaxed, he was for ever obliterating the ashes of the fire, or sweeping out their tracks, or removing horse-droppings, some damn' thing.

One morning it rained. It was the kind of rain that was alien to Kate, born of a warm north air and the chill of mountain passes, heavy, straight-down, steaming rain that had him rousting her with a grin as wide as a slip-rail gate. 'Now we'll make some time,' he said.

'In this?' she complained. But she shortly understood from the swill of mud they left behind them that there'd be no tracks, that no tracker in the world could follow water. 'What tracker?' she complained again. 'You think they'll follow all the way from Ironbark?' She'd begun to think with a wistful regret of the little town and the lovely Valley she'd left; it always came with pictures in her mind of sunlight and birds and a silver glitter on the creek. She rode with her head down through sheets of rain. The rain was warm to the skin, running down her body. He found a bush track, something made by the northern cattlemen, and he took the chance and they made good time, all right, better than they'd ever done before.

That night she had a fever and a harsh, dry, racking cough. Immediately he was all guilt and regret. He built a shelter, a gunyah, and put a stuttering fire beneath. The rain continued right through the night and into the following day. He vanished halfway through the morning and returned with a man who said he was a doctor. She never knew where he'd found the man, but that was the way it was with Frank; he'd find a snowflake in a desert if that was your heart's desire. The man, who had some old bucket-gin steaming from his breath, unpeeled her dress and massaged stinking oils into her chest –

working with a dedication far beyond his line of trade, she thought – and gave her quinine and Bewick's Blessing, so the label said, a painkiller stiff with opiates that sent her into raging dreams, gross nightmares and forays into terror from which she woke weak and sweating in another place entirely.

'Where am I?' she said.

They were in 'Trumper's Shack', so Gardiner told her, and shortly toothless, one-leg Billy Trumper turned up with provisions, having rented out his shelter to the travellers and dossed by himself in a ditch. Trumper was a travelling man, a fossicker, full of worn out sayings : 'Gold is where you find it' – 'It never rains but that it pours.'

'Where are we?' she asked again while Gardiner was tending the fire.

'You're in Queensland, missus,' said the ancient, hobbling about in a clutch of greasy rags.

'I never heard of Queensland.'

'That's the north of New South Wales,' he said. 'This here's the Colony of Queensland. And right across the way – damn' if I know how many miles – is Port Danger.'

'I can believe it,' she said.

'Port Danger is the sea,' he said.

She thought about the sea, the thing that Ma and Pa had talked about, and, thinking about the old folk, she wept a little. She would never see them again. They could even now be dead. 'Go on, get out of here,' she told Billy Trumper. 'I'm getting up.'

'By golly,' said Billy Trumper to Gardiner at the fire, 'if I was only ten years younger!'

'That's right, dad, you'd even have your teeth again.'

Thirty, forty miles to the north again, Gardiner took his second chance, playing out his possibilities with all the care of a man at cards. They came, in the late afternoon on a lonely track, to a small log shelter built stouter and firmer than the usual settler's shanty, and tacked across the door was a sign that read in scrawled-up letters 'Illingdale Police'.

'For God's sake, Frank,' she said, 'what are you doing?'

There was a bluecoat constable in the yard, scrubbing up his horse. Gardiner walked straight past him and stood by the door reading the 'Wanted' posters, names and desperadoes he'd never heard of.

'Which one do you fancy?' said Constable Sharman, strolling up with the horsebrush in his hand.

'Christie,' said Gardiner turning, offering his hand.

'Don't believe we've met,' Sharman said with a smile that went past Gardiner to the lady on the horse. 'I reckon I'd remember.'

'We've just come up from Brisbane way – place is getting too damn' crowded.'

Sharman laughed. 'It's all solid land from here to the top,' he said, 'and hardly a man has marked it.'

'Thinking of cattle,' said Gardiner lighting his cigar.

'Same as the others. 'Cept gold. There's a speck or two of gold, but we don't want it. Gold is trouble. Lookit they got in New South Wales.'

Gardiner nodded and gazed at the posters. 'There's enough trouble in this lot.'

'No, them's Brisbane. You've left 'em behind. No pickings in this neck o' the world.'

'I'm pleased to hear it. I'd hate to meet up with some damn' Frank Gardiner, the Darkie.'

'Who's Frank Gardiner?'

'Feller from the south.'

'South's a long way from here, Mr Christie. Don't you worry. Me and Jack've got it all our way. We don't brook no trouble in these parts.'

Gardiner shook his hand again and expressed his gratitude for the constable's reassurance. The constable wandered with him to the horses.

'Whyn't you stay for supper, ma'am?' Sharman asked hospitably.

'We're moving on,' Gardiner said, 'to the first water we can find.'

'That'd be Shelley Creek, up a ways.'

'Much obliged,' Gardiner said, and they continued up the track and met the Creek, and sheared away from it, moving to a steeper climb and the soft, sheltering trees of deep green foothills, the foliage heavier here, and lusher than they'd known. They camped and ate their dinner cold. He'd made his play, and made it to his satisfaction, and wouldn't, at the moment anyway, take further chances.

As they continued north, reverting to meandering tracks, they met a sequence of cattlemen and drovers, Gardiner observing the fat, rich beasts were better than he'd seen down south. She smiled at him as he gazed at them with a good professional eye. 'This'd maybe be the place,' he said, 'to take up the trade again.'

'Butchering?' she said.

'Got to do something.'

She reined in, there on the track. 'Frank,' she said, 'we could live for the rest of our lives on what you got.'

'I hate to be bone idle.'

'But butchering!'

'What's wrong with it?' – and when she turned away in a sulk – 'What's wrong with butchering?' he pursued.

'I didn't come a thousand rotten miles,' she told him, 'to be a butcher's woman!'

' 'Tisn't a thousand miles, anyway. It's five hundred, maybe, more or less.'

'Go butcher yourself,' she said.

'All right, all right,' he told her, anything for peace, 'I'll think o' somethin' else.'

They rode on bickering for ten miles more and camped by cascading water, and in the night she came to him, relenting, and they made love in the forest, on the leaves, by the water.

Three days later, they came on a man banging a peg in a tree. 'What's this for, feller?' Gardiner asked him.

'This here's the railroad track that'll likely run from Ipswich to Grandchester.'

'Railroad?' said Kate. 'What's a railroad?'

'For the trains to run on,' said the man, who was a Government man, of education.

No one in Winooka had ever heard of trains, or seen a train, or seen a picture of a train.

'Train's a thing that runs on wheels,' the man explained, 'the whole thing pushed by steam.'

'What's wrong with horses?' Gardiner asked.

'Train's as good as a hundred horses. Take people and goods, take anything.'

'I don't like the sound of that,' Gardiner said. 'That'll bring a pack of people living round.'

'You better hope so. You're paying for it.'

'I ain't paying anything.'

'Paying taxes, aren't you?'

So they kept moving north, up along the foremost finger of the Continent, moving, though neither knew it, towards the Tropic of Capricorn where the air was balmy even now in winter, and the forests increasingly dense and often laden with unsuspected blossom.

'This is far enough, Frank,' she said one night. 'How far you 'tending to go?'

'I don't know,' he said, drawing on the thin cigar, 'I like to see the country anyway.'

'I've seen enough damn' country to last a life. If you keep going, Frank, God knows where we'll end. There's blooming China somewhere up the top – Pa said so – and it's full of Chinamen.'

'China's right across the water.'

'How do you know?'

'I've seen a map.'

She didn't trust maps any more than she trusted this alien country. It wasn't right to be so far from home. 'I'm getting tired,' she told him. 'I want to settle somewhere.'

'We'll settle,' he assured her. 'But I want a whole wide world between me and that blooming baronet. I don't trust him. He's a foxy-looking gent and he won't give up easy.'

'He couldn't find his way past the pimple on his nose,' she said.

They laughed at this, made a joke of it, and he chased her **through the** trees, Kate shrieking, laughing till he tackled her and brought her down and tickled her to a gasp of breathless passion, and later, when things were soft and sweet with them, she begged him, 'Settle down, Frank. Let's have us a home...'

But there were six more days of it before he relented. They were riding early one evening – the sky still blue with ribbons of yellow and green – when the jolt of hooves settled into something softer, yielding, and Kate looked down, and there was sand between the tussocks, the grass yielding to open dunes of sand unmarked and gleaming gold in the setting of the sun.

'Where are we?' she called to Gardiner. 'Where are you taking us?'

There was a heavy moisture in the air and a new, musky smell. 'This way,' he called, and she looked up to see him atop a rise of sand, etched black, a silhouette against the furnace colours of the sky. When she walked the horse to join him, the rim of sand sank lower in her gaze, and there was beyond it, gradually unfolding, an immensity, a molten plain that swept almost further than the eye could travel to the bloated bubble of the sun balanced on a cauldron. Her heart leaped and she was speechless.

'This is the sea,' he said, as though he'd conjured it up himself.

She got down off the horse as the sun slipped away, hearing now the secret shuffling of the water sliding there in lacy crinolines across the sand, and she walked straight down as the darkness gathered, and crossed the beach and let the water lap about her ankles.

'Thought you'd like it,' Gardiner said, moving up behind her.

'It tastes rotten,' she laughed, as she tested the water.

'It's not for drinking.'

'How far does it go?' she asked.

'Across the world.'

She looked up at the fading lemon colour of the sky and contemplated, for the first time, the world. There was altogether too much of it, she was thinking. It was three times bigger than they'd ever told her.

'What are you weeping for?' he asked.

'I'm not bloody weeping.'

He put his arm about her and they stood there in the drifting swill of ocean, and she laid her head upon him and, thinking of space, eternity and the like, asked him to swear that he would never leave her, that they would take the longest journey to the future hand-in-hand.

'It's for ever, you and me,' he said. 'I done some terrible things,' he reflected, watching the waves slide in and out, 'and I done 'em for you, so's we could be together. And damme if I come this far,' he laughed, 'to turn you back. You're stuck with the Darkie, like it or not.'

'I like it,' she said dreamily. 'Can we live here by the water?'

In any case, they moved up the coast a few miles by daylight and came to Rockhampton, the settlement which was not to his taste, then cut back inland a little, into forest and the things he knew and understood.

By midday there was a bunch of shacks and shanties on the track, and there was a store marked 'Aphis Creek'. The man who owned the store was a man called Chivers, who stood as straight and skinny as a stick. 'I cracked my back a year ago,' said Chivers, 'and I'm strapped so tight I can hardly move.'

'How'd you do a thing like that?'

'I fell down a hole.'

'What kind of hole was that?'

'Up the Creek. Up the diggings.'

'There's gold up there?'

'None I ever found. And never likely to. If I had my way, I'd pack my bag and settle on my sister, which is Brisbane and where my wife ran to.'

'Your wife run out?' Gardiner asked.

'Mister, if I started on my troubles, you'd stand there long enough to root your boot in the ground. If troubles was profits,

I'd be the richest man you ever met ... Is that your wife out there?'

'Yeah, that's my wife.'

'Then you're a rich man already ... I got a nice line here in ladies' clothing. Whyn't you buy her something pretty?'

'What I mostly had in mind,' Gardiner said, fingering the counter, 'was how much you'd take for the blooming lot?'

'This?' asked Chivers, taking in the tangle of his stock, the boots and nails, treacle, rum, food and grain, racks and stacks and lines pegged out with diggers' clothing. 'All this?'.

'The whole store. How much would you want?'

Chivers showed his rotten teeth in a sickly grin, leaning forward on the counter. 'How'd you like to tweak my ear?'

But minutes later, Gardiner came out and said to Kate, 'How do you like it?'

She looked at the store. 'It's a frowsty-lookin' place, why'd you ask?'

'I bought it,' he said. 'It's home.'

She looked again in a new and melting light. This wretched, white-ant ridden hovel with half the timbers sinking to their haunches was their home.

'You bought it?' she said.

'Hope you like it,' he told her.

She laughed so hard she toppled off the horse and into his arms. He swept her around in a pirouette dance and she was laughing, crying. 'You stupid, mad galoot,' she called him, and he carried her across the creaking threshold.

It was near as damn to being married, anyway.


## Twenty-six

Some few weeks after the disastrous attack on the gold coach, Pottinger was one day taking the sun at the police office door, watching the dismal return of Sergeant Canning and his patrol, when he saw arriving down the street the Considines in their first concerted public appearance, the four of them dressed to the nines for shopping, sitting proud and straight behind Eliot Considine at the reins. It had been widely rumoured that they had sheltered at least one of the outlaws and that the younger girl was enamoured; certainly Michael Taylor had left his position at the bank, or was abducted or dead, and the Considines were therefore treated with everything from smirks to outright condemnation. Even so, there were sympathisers, and many of them. The police were jackals, the gold was fair game, and when Ben Hall rose like a phoenix to take the fit of Gardiner's boots there was even celebration at the Irish Tavern. The press itself had indulged in a high old chuckle, and Lobcock had even crept from his inky warren in Sydney Town to get the proper slant of outrage on the alleged facts. None of it had gone down well with Pottinger. He had been unrelenting in his pursuit of Gardiner, had even travelled to unearthly places with Dargin and a brace of men, exhorting the tracker to the extremest efforts, until Dargin became sullen and even menacing. All this had resulted in Pottinger's increasing isolation in Ironbark and the feeling that he was now merely haunting this outpost of the plains. Yet he endured threats and brickbats and various lampoons, some of them published privately.

> There was a young feller called Fred,
> Who vowed to get Frank Gardiner dead;
> But a man with a nose
> That obscures his own toes
> Couldn't find his own whistle in bed.

And there was an even chillier side, originating presumably from Captain St Clare in Bathurst and blowing an unpleasant draught all the way to Sydney – an allegation that the baronet was no longer fit to hold his post. So arctic was the winter of officialdom that Pottinger felt his days to be numbered and the total disappearance of Gardiner, and the impudence of Ben Hall, condemned him all the more. Now, he was thinking, standing in the doorway, it was all but hopeless – finding the

Darkie was like finding a pea in a pumpkin field. And, Disgrace, he was thinking. Disgrace was the ultimate. It would be back to Fivecrown, he supposed, grubbing in the dirt or finding some further, hopeless town, there to drink himself to extinction. Dark days, he was thinking, the winter's end, the worst time.

'What luck?' he said, stepping out to meet the Sergeant, whose muddy, grass-stained uniform revealed the rigours of patrol.

'None at all, sir,' Canning said.

'Well done, Sergeant,' Pottinger told him, passing on the acid of his own ill-humour.

'No news of Hall, none of Gardiner. Plenty of complaints. Stores robbed, squatters outraged —'

'Spare me, please.'

'Bogged a horse,' Canning added gratuitously. 'Trooper Kenning got the dysentery. May we rest up, sir?'

'Reports come first, Sergeant. And in detail. These reports are read in Bathurst. We're on trial. And then by all means,' he said, gazing pointedly at his watch, 'put your men to bed. In preparation for a further sally in the afternoon ... Good morning, ladies, Mr Considine.'

'Coom and share a pot,' Considine said when his lady declared her intention of trying on hats and bonnets.

'I'm addicted to my 'ats,' said Mrs Considine. 'My only indulgence.' And, with a touch at his arm, 'We 'aven't seen you for a long time. We'd 'oped you'd come and share our table.'

'I've been flitting through the forests,' he said, 'in pursuit of fireflies.'

'All work! ...' she wagged her finger, and, with a shriek as she stepped across the street, 'Buy yourself an 'at!'

Pottinger sighed. It was all too tiresome, and his feelings for the Considines were ambiguous. Had they not sheltered Michael Taylor?

'Look man,' Considine said, drawing him aside. 'I don't know how to phrase this —'

'Perhaps it's best you don't.'

'It's just that me and moother have been something in the

dark, y'know about the up and down of things, but putting two and two together— Well, it's all done now, is what I say. The die's cast, the blighter's gone ...'

'Which "blighter" would that be?' Pottinger asked.

'No, come on now, you know what I'm at. You twigged it weeks ago.'

'Please,' said Pottinger, 'do not drag me into your schemes and explanations.'

'When I found out,' Considine continued, oblivious, 'I put my hand to the gel good and proper. I had my suspicions, mind, I don't mind admitting, and I may have erred on the human side, or lapsed a bit in matters of public duty, but I did not harbour knowingly. I did not sanction —'

'You'll shortly say too much,' Pottinger told him. 'Confessions – in a public street – are not necessarily purgative, and could be classed as criminal, you follow?'

'It's my own good name,' Considine said, puffing up the ruby colour of his face, 'I want it clear, I want it white.'

'Then don't soil it. Please,' he urged, 'go and refresh your thirst like a decent chap.' And stepped past the unfortunate man to the girls who remained at the carriage.

'Did he instruct you,' Clara asked, 'how despicable I am?'

Pottinger dismissed the question with a gesture. Gazing at the girl's wan face, the eyes wider, darker, he asked her as lightly as he could, 'What's become of the poor sheep in the shed?'

'He's gone,' Lettie said.

'For ever,' Clara added miserably.

'That's not true, Clara. You know where he is. I mean,' Lettie said to Pottinger, 'she has a notion, enough to sustain her, that's all.'

'And I shall follow him,' Clara asserted, 'when the coast is clear, despite Papa, despite everyone.'

'That wouldn't be advisable,' Pottinger felt constrained to offer. 'His description is enjoying the widest currency. And if you do know where he is, so much the worse.'

'I love him,' Clara said. 'I'd die for him.'

'Is there nothing can be done?' Lettie asked.

'Short of submitting himself to the mercy of the court, I doubt it. They may see fit to offer clemency. He could always claim coercion or duress.'

'You don't know Michael!' Clara said sharply.

Which, Pottinger thought, when he recalled the shine of innocence to Taylor's face, was patently obvious. 'Shall we take a stroll?' he said to Lettie, who in turn instructed Clara to follow after Mrs Considine to ensure that her hats were neither too youthful nor extreme.

'I shall sit in the carriage,' Clara said. 'I'm not ashamed.'

'She isn't well,' Lettie said, accepting the offer of Pottinger's arm. 'She doesn't eat. She keeps to her room.'

'Has it been too unendurable?' he asked in a kinder tone.

'Without you, yes.'

'For your sister,' he amended.

'She's not the girl she used to be. Nor living in the house what it used to be. We keep the curtains drawn. We eat in silence. Papa speaks of going home. He won't, of course, but baits us with the threat.'

'Was he aware of Taylor's presence?'

'How do I know?' she asked. 'That's the one secret he'll take to the grave.' And then she burst out, 'I wish I'd never heard of gold or banks or blasted Gardiner. It really is too cruel.' They were standing now at the bridge, at the Creek, flowing sluggishly and muddied by the winter rains. 'We might have been married,' she said, 'but we drift on.'

'You fell in love with a policeman,' he said.

'I love you,' she said, ignoring a tinker and his cart rattling across the logs, 'I want to be your wife.'

'You will be.'

'But when? Fix a date at the very least.'

'Let us not stand about,' he said, ever-conscious of watchful eyes, and as he took her arm, offered, 'In the spring, in October, we shall marry in October, that's a promise.'

She looked up at him, her face alight. 'Do you mean that?'

'My dear, I never make an idle promise.'

'October,' she breathed, 'October ... Will you come to the

house, tell Papa, bring some happiness?'

He hesitated. 'I have to go away . . .' he told her.

They were standing by the horseyard, where horses were bought and sold, and just beyond in the little shanty schoolhouse, children were chanting poetry:

> 'I bless thee, Lord, because I grow
> Among the trees, which in a row
> To thee both fruit and order owe . . .'

'Away?' said Lettie plaintively. 'For a week, a month, or what?'

'I can't say. I don't know.'

'It's that man again,' she said. 'It's Frank Gardiner.' She turned to look at flowers growing wild. 'Can't you understand,' she told him, 'that I'd go with you as a pauper, in disgrace if I had to.'

'You might,' he said. 'I can't. There's a man on the Sydney side of Bathurst, several men who claim to have seen Gardiner. It's a possibility I can't ignore.'

'When do you leave?' she asked dumbly.

'Tomorrow.'

'Alone?'

'Yes.'

'May I see you tonight?'

He took her hand. To think he had reduced her to these craven entreaties! 'We shall meet when I return,' he told her, 'and plan the wedding. We shall marry in Bathurst, quite a fine affair. And I shall present you with boat tickets to London.'

He peered at her as he offered these compensations, but her head was turned and he saw that she was weeping. He put his hand on her solicitously, not understanding her complexity, not dreaming of the ache she had for him, of how it had sustained her in the terrible weeks when Michael Taylor had split apart her family. He was not much good at this sort of thing; women had always served him, and rarely for more than a span of weeks. 'What on earth is wrong?' he asked, making it worse.

239

All at once she fled from him, and he turned to see the horsedealer, Channing, watching his dismay with a wide and knowing grin. 'You'll end up saddle-sore on that'un,' Channing said.

'Do mind your manners,' Pottinger told him and marched straight back to the barracks, there to put his affairs in order for tomorrow's journey. But he was not to go, as he had planned, to the Sydney side of Bathurst. He was to go where fate and Captain St Clare directed, to the tropical north of Australia, almost seven hundred miles away, into and beyond October.

## Twenty-seven

'It is a matter,' said St Clare, with a tweak and sniff, 'of the utmost secrecy.' They were standing, St Clare and Pottinger, in the bitter cold and darkness, outside the tiny lodging room, the annexe to the Irish Tavern, the lights of which glowed orange in the densest night. St Clare set the door ajar for Pottinger to enter.

There was a small man sitting in a large wickerwork chair with the fire behind in the otherwise darkened room. The man had no more features than a cardboard cutout shape; his face was masked in darkness.

'This is Sir Frederick,' St Clare said, closing the door reverently behind him, 'the pride of Ironbark.'

Was his superior officer lapsing into satire? He did not know. So small was the room, with the big double bed, the tables, chairs, mirrors and so forth, that they were nearly jostling elbows.

'Delighted,' said the man in the chair. 'I understand you've sniffed out yet another trail?'

'Frank Gardiner's trail,' St Clare supplied.

'One of several,' Pottinger said.

'This one substantiated?'

'As usual.'

'Quite.'

'May I know to whom I'm speaking? May we even strike a light?' Pottinger asked with a vexed edge.

'Do sit down,' said the man in the chair.

They sat, after jockeying about, on the edge of the double bed. 'May I introduce,' St Clare said, 'a fellow officer from Sydney, Inspector Edward Millard?'

'My pleasure,' said Pottinger politely, not moving a muscle.

'The same,' said this shadowy man, shifting now for the first time with the creak of the wickerwork beneath him.

St Clare continued, 'Edward – as he prefers to be known, and as you should henceforth call him – is no ordinary policeman, no mere run-of-the-mill policeman . . .'

'My speciality is detection. My forte is invisibility. We are,' he said, rising at last to fetch his pipe from the mantelpiece, 'part of a small and growing band of thieftakers – a sure sign that this Colony has come of age, that it's lapsing, sir, into criminal sophistication. It is a sad fact,' he said, lighting his pipe with a taper, 'that as the criminal becomes more devious, the law must proceed with a hop and a skip to set itself a pace ahead. Do not think,' he began as Pottinger audibly sighed, 'do not think that your efforts are not appreciated. But the cult of thrust-and-parry, cut-and-run, is better suited to more gallant times. The criminal mind, as you would understand it, and this is borne out by the study of phrenology . . .'

Who is this ass? Pottinger was thinking, observing now the man as his eyes adjusted and the firelight lit up the speaker's face. And Edward Millard, his stubby fingers clenched about the bowl of his steaming pipe, swam out from the shadows of the room, a nuggety, thick and uncultured-looking man with bumps on his nose, the head too big, and brow too deep, the eyes cavernous – not a bit like a policeman, lacking both the height and manner, built more like a bargeman, his accent overlaid with education of a kind.

'Could we perhaps open a window?' Pottinger suggested as

241

the smoke-stench drifted from the pipe in stagnant layers.

'I must not be seen,' Millard said. 'I arrived in darkness, and we leave in darkness.'

'We?' asked Pottinger with sinking spirits.

'Inspector Millard is here to assist you with your investigations,' St Clare offered hastily.

'We shall get him, you and I,' Millard said with the greatest relish, and laughed. 'We have the noses for it, eh?'

Pottinger ignored this impertinence. 'I doubt that I need assistance. I expect to make my own arrest by the week's end. Somewhere out of Bathurst.'

'No, no, not Bathurst,' Millard said. 'Somewhere to the north.'

'North? Gardiner doesn't even know the north.'

'That,' said Millard, 'is the general trend of my investigation.'

'How long has this been going on?' Pottinger asked St Clare.

'I've been working,' Millard cut in, 'with my colleague Brompton for some few weeks on the instruction of —'

'This is quite improper.'

'— Mr Aubrey Holliday.'

Pottinger subsided on the bed. His entire authority had been undermined. He was disgraced.

'You have no alternative,' St Clare said with a rustle of paper, 'other than to accompany Edward.'

'Edward?' – then he dismally remembered, taking the paper from Captain St Clare, the paper duly authorised, signed and sealed.

'That,' said St Clare needlessly, 'is the Governor's signature.'

'You will see by my attire,' Millard went on, 'that I'm dressed as a traveller of no considerable note. You'll also dress accordingly and I, for the purpose of this exercise, will call you, by your leave, Fred. The whiskers,' he said, examining Pottinger's face, 'will need to be trimmed, and clothing – of the proper kind – should alter your appearance. But the nose...' it was his little joke '... I doubt we can alter the nose.'

'Is my presence absolutely necessary?'

'You're familiar with Gardiner. He also may have altered his appearance. And we'll need,' Millard said, shaking out the dottle in a spray of molten-coloured droplets, 'a man from the ranks, from the barracks, trustworthy, reliable – which matter I leave to you.'

'You're too kind.'

'Come, come now, Fred,' Millard said, 'we must be chums. You know, a pair of travelling stockmen, we could be weeks together.'

'You won't find him,' Pottinger said, 'not in the north.'

'I've a card or two up the proverbial sleeve.'

'None that I haven't. I've followed every possibly lead,' Pottinger said tartly. 'No stone unturned, proverbial or otherwise.'

'That's it. Precisely. Yes. Yes, I know. Knocking on doors, rousting people out. Looking for the swarthy, hairy man. "Have you seen Frank Gardiner?" "No, zur, no, I never 'ave." As, indeed, it may be true. Every man is hairy in the bush, every man is tanned a treat. But,' he said, thrusting forward, stubby finger poised, 'there's one thing they won't forget. Once seen, forever imprinted . . .'

'What's that?' St Clare supplied, since Pottinger wouldn't.

'The woman,' Millard told them in a particularly unpleasant papery voice. 'Kate Foster. Don't they say she's a raving beauty?'

In the darkness before dawn the three men – Pottinger, Millard, and Trooper Merrett in baggy shirt and breeches – rode out of Ironbark at a walking gait, with stealth – a dramatic indulgence, Pottinger thought – bound for Crossroads.

And of course from Millard: 'Would it not be better to pursue the line of the Creek?'

'We'll meet the Creek at Crossroads.'

'Ah, but let us consider the possibilities . . .'

The horses padded through the dusty night, past the blacksmith's, past the bank. 'Should we perhaps muffle the hooves?' Pottinger teased.

They rode to Crossroads, and out past Crossroads into a density of bush such as Pottinger had hardly ever seen. 'Do you expect to find him in a thicket?' he asked.

'One endeavours,' Millard said, 'to enter the criminal persuasion of mind...' Within the first twelve hours of their meeting, Pottinger had come to recognise Millard's peculiar, strangled, classroom voice, as though enunciating from the lectern. And he began to learn devious ways of not asking questions, of sealing off the avenues of conversation. But around mid-afternoon he was forced to call a halt. 'We're lost,' he said bluntly. 'We should have kept to the road.'

'No, sir,' Millard said with something of a flourish. 'I have a map, and I have a compass.' And he spread out the map, incomplete at best but which none the less revealed roads and tracks and settlers' huts and shanties.

'Where did you get this?' Pottinger asked.

'My colleague Brompton is a qualified cartographer.'

'I would have sold my soul for a map like this.'

'Ah, but let us consider the possibilities. Suppose the map were to fall into improper hands, Fred...'

They camped by a considerable river and Pottinger was forced to admit that Millard made a very good fist of it. He was enterprising and innovative. Only Merrett dared to suggest, 'Mightn't there be snakes, sir, in grass this long, and close to the water?'

'There are no snakes in this area.'

But when it came time for retirement, Millard was heard to let out a howl. There was a snake, three feet of it, residing in his blanket. 'That's a copperhead,' Millard said whitefaced; he had a fear of snakes.

'It's just an old water snake,' Merrett said, and disposed of the offender.

'I shall retreat to higher ground,' Millard said.

Later, Merrett shared a final mug of tea with Pottinger. There was something about these vast oceans of the night that drew them together – the wink of the embers, the shift and cry of animals unseen, the slow vaulting of the stars. 'Is that man really a policeman?' Merrett asked.

'Yes, he is,' Pottinger said heavily.

Merrett blew on his tea and sent the steam rising. 'He reminds me of my father,' he said.

The first few weeks of Millard were merely abrasive. Thereafter every day was almost unendurable. Time had just toppled over into September and there were balmy days of early springtime. 'I believe we should retrace our steps to Turranbar,' Millard said one morning.

'But we've been there.'

'None the less, we should consider —'

'Yes, yes, by all means let us go to Turranbar.'

'Why are we going back to Turranbar?' Merrett asked, as he fell in easily beside Millard's horse.

'The criminal mind...' Millard began in the tone of voice that would take him for a mile or two, and Pottinger allowed himself to fall behind. They were clearly getting nowhere – excepting north, perhaps – and no one had the slightest information about either Gardiner or his woman.

They came to Turranbar in the early part of afternoon, and Millard went to turn some stone he'd left unturned. He'd developed as an obsessive, infinitely patient man, a man transfixed by every seeming irrelevance. Was the country good for cattle? Were they troubled by the tick? What was the nature of the gin? Was the rum imported? Every time he asked a question Pottinger felt a prickle at his scalp and if he lingered, developed headaches and the pressing need to punch that bumpy, twice-broken nose.

Pottinger tramped the dusty layout of Turranbar which, lacking streets, was no bigger than a parade ground. But there were several dwellings, perhaps a score of them. It was something more than a staging stop, an embryonic town. He had long since given up inquiries – 'May I suggest, Fred, that you leave the questions to me? Your tone of accent, you know, rather gives the disguise away.' He felt that he was being eroded by some immense, grinding force, reduced to something called 'Fred', faceless, now voiceless, twiddling his thumbs in a dusty limbo with pigs and fowls running wild, and a naked child turning his tail to defecate. My God, it was worse than medieval times.

That night, they camped on the outskirts, Millard and Merrett sitting together across the campfire, Pottinger slapping at mosquitoes and brushing at moths. 'I perceive, Tom,' Millard said with a nudge, 'that a certain gent is in a certain mood.' They'd formed an alliance against him, a father and son.

'I'm leaving you,' Pottinger said suddenly, 'tomorrow morning. I'm going back to Ironbark.'

'Now then, don't be downcast.'

'We're almost there, sir,' Merrett said encouragingly.

'Almost where?'

'The north.'

The 'north' to Pottinger had become some kind of mystical sphere for ever bouncing backwards on the far horizon, and he despaired of it.

'I've asked you to call him Fred, Tom.'

'Sorry, I keep forgetting.'

'You have a ladyfriend in Ironbark, don't you?' Millard said in that distressing, papery voice.

'I beg your pardon?'

'Your betrothed. I always make inquiries,' he laughed, 'consider the possibilities. And this is one possibility I did consider. You miss her, that's natural.'

'You have an infernal cheek, sir.'

'Tom is also betrothed. Did you know that? Thought not. Alas, we're all three men without our women.'

'Please exclude me from your solicitations.'

'And,' said Millard rising, 'having considered this particular contretemps, I've made certain ... arrangements, shall we say, with a certain tavernkeeper's daughter not fifty yards from where you sit.'

'Now look here ...' Pottinger began.

'What's she like?' Merrett said eagerly.

'Oh ...' said Millard, describing shapes in the air.

'Golly!' breathed Merrett.

246

'Shall we hie, then, gentlemen?'

'Just a moment,' Pottinger said, astonishing even himself.
'Would you have it on your conscience, sir, to lead this lad
astray – you, an inspector at law, a man who should consider
responsibility?'

'Tom's fully twenty years a man.'

'And betrothed. Have you no shame?'

'Best he keeps in trim, then.'

'I'm for it,' Merrett said laughing.

'I forbid it,' said Pottinger.

'Oh come on, Tom,' Millard said, 'let's leave him brood about
it.'

'Trooper,' Pottinger said abruptly, 'you're on duty and under
my command. If you set foot outside this firelight, I'll have you
on a charge.'

'Fact is,' said Millard in a soft, low voice, 'I'm in charge.'

'I would dispute that.'

'You've seen the paper.'

'It offered no such right.'

'You're not in Apsley Chase now, old boy.'

'I made no mention of my title.'

'I thought you would eventually.'

'Fact is,' Millard said with a certain bunching of his shoulders, 'I'm more baronet than you are, being as I'm baronet of
all the bush, a title that I earned by sweat and wits. You gentry
here have no such rights. This is not the village green. This is
the land of equal men. Which I command as the arm of law.
All this,' he said, his body hunching, his voice pitched lower,
eyes bright with firelight in their sockets, 'a kingdom, mine,' he
said, 'and I command.'

'You do not,' Pottinger said.

'Sir —' said Merrett nervously.

'Don't tell me what I do or don't!'

'Get yourself to bed. You're drunk.'

'Drunk, am I?' Millard said, beginning to stamp about like
some stubborn-booted animal. 'Drunk? Am I drunk?'

'Oh, for goodness' sake!' And Pottinger, half turning by

design, allowed Millard the initiative, and half saw, or rather felt, the bulk of the smaller man rushing through the darkness, and made a stoop of his body that pitched the man aside, and sent him reeling with a hard, foul blow to the lower back, something not approved of, but damned effective, so that as Millard presented himself half standing, twisting with pain, the several blows to his face took a greater effort – but the man refused to fall. He was tough and built of rocks. I must not lose my temper, Pottinger was instructing himself on the one hand, while some wretched part of his mind was prompting, The nose, crack the blasted nose! as his knuckles continued a satisfying and repeated crunch, slipping on a stream of blood until Millard, like a boulder toppling, went sailing over and thudding to the ground.

'Cor,' said Merrett, 'where did you learn to fight like that?'

In the goldfields was the real answer, but instead he lamented, 'I damn' near broke my hand.'

'You broke his face all right,' Merrett said, examining Inspector Millard on the ground.

'Oh . . . oh . . .' groaned Millard.

'Get some water,' Pottinger told Merrett. He crouched beside Millard. 'Let that be a lesson to you,' he said. 'Never underestimate the aristocracy.' And he took the pan of water and sloshed it in Millard's face.

'Does he need a doctor?' Merrett asked breathlessly.

'Leave him. Go to bed.'

'But Fred . . .'

'If ever,' said Pottinger, 'you call me that again, I'll punch your own face in.'

'Yes, sir!'

'Go to bed. And don't let me find you creeping from the camp . . . Can you manipulate the jaw?' he asked Millard.

'I'll report this,' Millard said from a puffy face.

'You'll have every opportunity,' Pottinger assured him. 'We're going home tomorrow.'

That night Pottinger dreamed of Lelitia Considine, confusing her in the dream with the tavernkeeper's daughter, dreaming that she sat astride him, skirts hoisted, indecent, and he woke in a sweat in the middle of the night.

The journey south, as it turned out, was swifter and more agreeable. Millard hardly spoke. About two weeks out of Iron-bark, they rested at a staging-post and Pottinger, by weary custom, asked his weary chain of questions. No, no hairy, swarthy man had passed this way. Nor with a woman, no. Not even a woman of such charms as Pottinger described, nor had he heard of Gardiner, Christie, Foster. The man was adamant, and was by name Owen Evans.

'Which way are you heading?' Evans asked.

'South. Ten or fourteen days away.'

'To Bathurst?'

'Ironbark,' Pottinger said.

'I've got a letter for Ironbark,' Evans said, 'waiting for the coach. Would you care to drop it off?'

'I'm not a postman,' Pottinger said.

'Thought you might be passing by the door. Name of Walsh, you know them?'

Pottinger snatched the letter from Evans. There in a clumsy scrawl were the words 'Mrs Walsh, Winooka'.

'You can't do that,' cried Evans as Pottinger wrenched the letter open. *Dear Ma*, it began, *So's you know I'm still alive* ...

'From your lady?' Millard asked, sauntering in.

*Your Loving, Wayward Daughter, Kate*, the letter said.

'Where's Aphis Creek?' Pottinger asked, unable to control the tremor in his hand.

'North,' said Evans. 'About a month away.'

'At what pace?'

'Twenty miles a day.'

'Two weeks,' Pottinger said, turning to Millard. 'Two weeks, and we've got him!'

## Twenty-eight

'Lookit your shirt,' said Kate. 'That was fresh on yesterday.'

'I just been shifting flour bags,' Gardiner said.

'Then whyn't you go and change, then?'

' 'Cause you wouldn't have nothing to complain about. What keeps a woman happy, is complaining,' he said with a wink to George Jeffers and Jack Connors, timbergetters both and men who came to share the morning often in the store with a pot of Gardiner's rum. Christie's, as the store was known, had become the best damn' place on the mountain slopes, where a man could ravel out his weariness and feast his eyes on womanflesh of the kind you only got to talk about. And Christie's woman never seemed to mind. She was a girl in great good humour – and she was also Christie's girl. You couldn't put a shred of paperbark between them so close they were, even when a yard or two apart.

'Seen Dave Erickson up the top,' Jeffers said, turning the subject around.

'Is he getting any good stuff?' Gardiner asked.

'He's sloshed himself a speckle or two,' Connors said.

'I got a bundle for him in the tank,' Gardiner told them. 'He's doing all right for a new chum.'

'Beginners' luck,' Jeffers said, downing the pot.

Erickson was a new chum fossicker who'd struck a secret golden rivulet somewhere in the slopes. Each week or so he'd come down in his clomping boots and add his pittance, stashed in a lucifer tin, to the store in Gardiner's 'tank' – which was a dried-out cistern, padlocked, where Gardiner put the fossickers' treasures until such time as they took it out to spend it. Frank Christie was known throughout as an honest man, a man you could trust your life to.

'Get movin',' Jeffers said to Connors, and Connors abandoned his stool with a sigh.

'See you later, missus,' Connors said with a downward sweep of his eyes.

'You're seein' enough already,' Kate said.

Connors laughed. 'Frank,' he said, 'any time you're tired, she can warm my blanket anytime.'

'I'll warm your hide for your trouble,' she called after them, and Gardiner slid his arm about her. She stood there lost for a moment, gazing out into the sunstruck forest with sandmites flitting, and listening to the buzz of flies among the steamy smells of rum and grain and kitchen herbs. She grew them now, right along the storefront, the oreganos and the sage and Lad's Love growing tall. 'It's a good place,' she said. 'We've got a good place.'

'Showing profit, too,' he said.

'Damn the profit,' she told him. 'It's the life I like.'

'You happy, Katie?' he asked, for what must have been the fiftieth time.

She nodded and took up the broom. 'Gonna sweep out.'

'Again?'

'Your splawfooted friends have tramped in the mud.'

'Gonna make a boardwalk,' he told her, 'soon as I rip down the wall.' The wall was white-anted, the last one left. The rest of it he'd reconstructed as bright as a pin.

They cooked and slept in the room at the back of the store. He'd lie in bed on those velvet, moist nights and look through the window built specially low so that he could see the stable – almost the second structure he'd erected – with the horses, Baronet and Duchess the gelding, shifting in the darkness. How he loved those horses! He was not a man without his horse.

'Do you miss the roads, Frank?' she asked, lying awake, covered only by the thinnest cotton, beautiful to look at in the blaze of moonlight.

'What do you think?'

'I don't know. I'm asking.'

'No, I don't miss the roads, why should I?'

'Excitement.'

'I'm thirty-four years old,' he said. 'That's half my natural span. I've had enough excitement. I look back,' he said, 'to that day at the Rocks, and that's become my one damned regret. Not the gold – the gold's the thing that got us here – but all those men, all that blood . . .'

'Don't think like that. No profit in regret.'

'Would have done it different, now. Would have planned it better. Could maybe have done it at Crossroads – with half the lobsters in the pub, and the horses changing in the stables. Could have done it with half the men. I didn't plan it like I should.'

'Sometimes I think of the gold,' she said, 'lying down there in the tank.'

'For gold,' he said, 'underground's a good place.'

'How much have we used?'

' 'Bout a handful.'

'You need never have touched that coach. We could have ridden out of Ironbark and made our own way. I put you wrong.'

'We wouldn't be here,' he said. 'We would never have left.' And it was true. They'd needed the gold to prise them loose from all the things that had held them fast.

They lay there listening to the croak of frogs and the tinkling call of night birds. She shifted on his arm and felt the prickle of his face. 'Whyn't we build some lodging rooms?' she said with her eyes on the daub of the ceiling. 'You can make a decent price from lodging.'

'Are we intending to stay that long?'

She pushed herself up on one elbow. 'Why, where are we going?'

'Nowhere,' he said, 'I just asked.'

'Where else would we want to go? What for?'

'Don't get excited,' he told her. 'I was only thinking. I was thinking,' he went on, 'now that it's safe, we could move out almost anywheres. Across the water, across the ocean, if you felt that way.'

'On a boat?'

'I ain't walking.'

'Where to?' she said.

'England, America.'

'I'm not going to no blooming England.'

'That's your Ma's place.'

'That's where they shopped her.'

'Serves her right if she was caught.'

She thumped him and they wrestled in the dark, and he hoisted her garment aside and nuzzled her deep in the belly so that she got the giggles and twisted, slippery as a snake, and got him down and held him.

'No, listen,' he said. 'No, wait a minute...'

She hesitated over him, knees astride him, breasts swinging.

'Listen,' he said. 'I want to tell you. If anything should happen —'

'Happen? What should happen?'

'You won't listen!' And when she'd relaxed contritely, 'If anything bad should ever happen, and we're ... you know, split apart...'

'Oh don't, Frank.'

'...You take that money – hear me? – take the gold and git. Not back to the Valley, not anywhere near Ironbark. Get down the coast – Newcastle, maybe – and get a boat and go.'

'I don't hear you. I don't hear a word.'

'Get a boat,' he told her. 'Get a ticket to California, some-place. You'll make a good life there.' And from her silence he knew her to be weeping in the dark. 'You'd have to forget me, Kate. These things have to be said. If it comes, won't be no time to say it then, you hear me?'

'Yes,' she said. 'I hear you.'

'Just so's you know,' he told her.

And she fell upon him. 'Oh Frank, why'd you have to say it?'

'Some things have to be said, that's all,' he said gently. 'Plans have to be made. I want the good life for you, Kate, that's all I want.'

He held her close and she curled like a child and he caressed her, his hand gliding, just grazing like a shadow to stir the hairs along her arms, moving to her breasts to linger there, enclosing

253

the warmth and the weight of her breasts as she unfolded turning, her legs widening to the gentle kiss of night.

They made love by moonlight, a gentler, old accustomed love, a deepening sweetness to it, the moonlight washing down in golden tones as he gentled her, murmured to her, loving both the child and then the woman, 'Kate, Kate, how I love thee Kate,' the words and jokes and parodies in turns an aphrodisiac, a comfort to her. She had not been loved like this before and she would love him for a lifetime – till death, she was thinking, being born again, renewed by storms of passion.

In the morning when she unlocked the door and set it back with the door-stop, a man came in to buy tobacco.

'You're bright and early,' she said. 'I just got out of bed.'

'I'm travelling,' the man said. 'Got a way to go.'

She weighed the tobacco fair and saw him looking not at the scales, as they usually did, but at her. But she smiled, she was used to this.

'How far you come?' she asked.

'Too far to remember.' He was a short, thick-set, nuggety man – could be a fossicker, a smithie, anything. 'Got a lame horse outside,' he said; 'could be a pebble or a shoe. Would your man maybe have a look?'

'He's beat you to it,' she said. Gardiner was already in the yard beside the horse, running his hand along the flanks. 'What you looking at?' Kate asked of the short man's silent contemplation.

'Just considering the possibilities, ma'am.'

Next thing she saw a wink of something through the nearby press of trees. 'Frank!' she yelled. And as Gardiner spun about Millard locked his arm about her throat tight enough to cut the wind. Then two men exploded through the trees, both with guns, running with force enough to storm a gate, and Gardiner for a moment stunned solid, gazed at her through the open door as the entire world solidified, the buzz of morning flies suspended, the trees, mid-breeze, congealing, the sky glazing to a crystal, and she could hear Frank Gardiner thinking like voice in her head, 'The shotgun. Fifteen paces to the shotgun.

254

But suddenly, the older, taller man — and blast if it wasn't the baronet! — also caught the drift and cried out, 'Don't try it!' Yet even then, Gardiner, ready to die where he stood, felt the charge of life pass through him, nerves and muscles responding until the rasp of Millard's voice: 'Move, and I'll spread her brains across the wall!' She felt the hard nub of the pocket pistol against her skull, the metal biting hard enough to pierce the skin, and then, at the sound of Gardiner's easy, glad-to-know-you voice, she sank in the squat man's arms, and Millard let her slide, sliding to her knees.

'Got to hand it to you,' she heard Gardiner say. 'You fellers earn your medals.'


## Twenty-nine

Pottinger, who was skewering at the inward growth of his toenails sat bolt upright, incredulous as he heard a voice outside his door proclaim, 'Coom on, now, mind them trunks, or you'll fetch a clout about the ear'ole.'

And another voice shrieking, 'Mind my 'atbox,' followed by a rumpus and a clatter such as no decent hotel, let alone the Tales of Chaucer tavern, should endure. Then just across the hallway the rattle of a doorlock and a crashing shriek of bedsprings and the female uttering, 'Oh! Ah! That's better. Oh, my goodness, oh!' And within minutes there was a tapping at his door.

'Devil take it,' he said, peering out through an inch or two. 'I don't believe it.'

'The mountain of the Considines has come to Sydney,' said Lelitia Considine. 'Let me in.'

'You can't come in. I'm not dressed.'

'Let me in, anyway. I look indecent in the hall ... Very handsome,' she said of him mockingly as she closed the door. He was dressed in a ruby velvet jacket and — thank God he had his breeches on! – no shoes, no stockings, just naked, knobbly feet, embarrassing. Yet he kissed her fervently; she was exactly what he needed, a springtime to this torpid mugginess of early summer, this December by the harbour.

'My darling Potts,' she breathed in his arms. And suddenly springing from his grasp and leaning halfway from the window: 'You have a view!'

'What on earth are you doing here?' he asked.

'How pretty!' she said. The day was darkening even as they watched, the sweep of water glossed with fiery colours to the deep viridians of the furthest shore, and they gazed, lightly pressed against each other, through a lacework of ships' rigging, the populace strolling by beneath the gas laps, gigs and broughams clattering past, streetsellers, fishmongers closing stalls and barrows.

'What are you doing here?' he said again.

'Salvaging my bridal gown,' she said.

He sighed, partly from a twinge of guilt. Their wedding, or the promise of it, was two months gone. 'I wrote to you ...' he began.

'That's why I'm here. We were called to Sydney, and I thought, what better place than a seaside hotel?'

'You suggested it?'

'Of course.'

'You are a cheeky girl ... And Clara?' he asked politely.

She turned aside as the darkness settled in the room. 'She's left us. Gone,' she said. 'Without word.'

'Did you make inquiries?' He sighed, and let the matter drop. Gravely, he took her hands in his. 'What can I say? I've failed you. I travel a thousand miles or more to deck myself with laurels, and yet I fail you. We'll wed, I promise, as soon as the task is done.'

'Don't promise, Freddie. Better not to promise.'

'But I promise. Monday, we take the villain up for trial. A month from then, they'll hang him. And I'm done. It's done,' he said, turning back to the evening sparkle of the waters, not truly believing that the sea could then convey him and his bride to England, home. 'And I must dress,' he said, turning back. 'I'm to dine with Aubrey Holliday.'

'Then I shall dress you,' she said mischievously, turning back his jacket.

'My dear,' he laughed, 'I'm in my undershirt.'

He was, she thought as he submitted, a fine, upstanding figure of a man, built straight and wiry, and the thousand miles that he'd endured had toughened him – she thought back to that first time in the kitchen with the Devil-on-the-Coals, and how she'd resented that foppish trooper with his condescending ways. It was something that she'd never tell him, never, that she'd thought him a prig and a laughable snob. Now she loved him and he, presumably, loved her . . .

'Have you been faithful?' she asked, smoothing down the ruffles of his shirt.

'What an extraordinary question.'

'Have you?'

'Lamentably faithful, yes. One used to be such a rake,' he said, smoothing his hair in the mirror, a brush in either hand.

'Did you have women in your room?'

'Never more than two at once.'

'You're teasing.'

'One has not been monkish,' he told her. 'A fact to be regretted.'

'I find it challenging.'

'Madam,' he said. 'Do not seduce me. It takes me half an hour to dress.'

It was seven o'clock by the time he left – as chastely as he'd started. He was late and there was no conveyance at the rank, not a thing on wheels. He paced there, chafing, consulting his watch beneath the stutter of the gas flare, waylaid once at least by a beggar with both feet bundled in a stench of rags, and by some dreadful and persistent harridan more than twice his age. He began to think somewhat wistfully of Ironbark and its placid ways. Then a hand clamped down upon him from behind.

'Sir Frederick!' said Considine. 'This is a coincidence.'

257

'Mr Considine,' he nodded.

'No, no, it's Eliot. You never called me Eliot. Or "Father",
should it be, eh, hm, what d'you say? What say you coom and
put a pot down, eh?'

'I have an appointment.'

'Where are you staying?' – and when Pottinger gave a negli-
gent wave to the formidable bulk of the tavern standing
straight behind them, 'That is a coincidence. Wait till I tell
Moother.'

'She's well?' Pottinger asked politely, scanning the street and
the tangle of lanes and byways.

'She leaves for England in three days' time. Her sister has
been stricken.'

'Leaving?'

'Aye,' said Considine with a hangdog look. 'And I'll be desolate without her.'

'I'm sorry,' Pottinger told him with a touch of true com-
miseration, 'I hadn't realised.'

'Be gone at least twelve or eighteen months, depending as it
does on the lady's condition. There's five children. She's a
widow.'

'Life has its sorrows,' Pottinger said as people jostled past.

'First Clara, then Moother. My fortunes have taken a rotten
turn.'

'Where is Clara?' Pottinger asked.

'Gone,' said Considine with an airy wave and a somewhat
shifty look. 'Gone. This is no country for a gel, let alone the
young folk. That Michael Taylor, now, you would have took
him for a decent lad ...'

'Hi, there!' Pottinger called, leaping out across the puddles.
'Must go,' he called to Considine and, by way of compensation,
'We'll share a pot tomorrow. Macquarie Street,' he told the
driver – it was a 'jingle', a dismal conveyance in which one
shared the driver's bench and paid a shilling for a mile. 'Tomorrow,' he waved, watching Considine's forlorn figure in the gas
light dwindling as the swirling humours of the waterfront
came up in mists and eddies of damp.

At ten o'clock the dinner was done and the gentlemen were in the drawing-room, an elegant assembly drawn together to determine in advance the fate of Her Majesty's most singular Colonial enemy. There was not only the host, the Governor's man, Aubrey Holliday, but Henry Cummings and two or three legal gentlemen, the assistant to the Attorney-General, Richard Mayhew, the eminent barrister-at-law, D. G. Clarence Coppard, and a Parliamentary man introduced as 'Pritchard'. The proceedings began on a mundane note, discussing the fish they'd sampled at dinner. There then began a spirited discussion as to the general state of the weather. Pottinger suppressed a sigh for these meanderings; it had taken months to arrest Frank Gardiner, surely it needed no more than minutes to despatch him?

'It isn't quite that simple,' Mayhew finally admitted. He was an elderly man and ashamed of it, and wore a girdle of a kind which was plain to see beneath his waistcoat, and his eyes were bloodshot, and he was tired. 'And I am advised that we should proceed with the utmost caution.'

'Caution?' blurted Pottinger. 'The man's committed murder. I saw it with my own eyes.'

'The Crown,' said Clarence Coppard in tones as crisp as a biscuit cracking, 'does not have a case.' Pottinger set his glass down, unable to believe his ears. 'Your own testimony,' he heard himself instructed, 'will not stand up, at least, I doubt it.'

'But it's supported by Canning and Merrett.'

'Both policemen.'

'Thank God for that.'

'More wine?' Holliday asked.

'A police testimony,' Mayhew said, rising and turning to warm his seat at the fire, 'by very nature requires corroboration, a witness, a civilian.'

'The only civilians,' Pottinger said drily, 'were outlaws.'

'Could we not call again on Charters?' Henry Cummings asked.

'He has refused,' Holliday said. 'Having named several names and craved the Queen's indulgence, he now refuses to in criminate the leader.'

'Am I to understand,' Pottinger said, 'that Gardiner is to get away with it? That I set my life in the balance, and the lives of my officers so that he can kick his heels up in our faces?'

'Harrumph,' offered Holliday, or something like it. There was a plain embarrassment in the padded, polished room, the lamps reflecting brassy colours and speckless highlights.

'It is the mode of judicial attack that concerns us,' Coppard said.

'Ways and means of hanging, that's all I care about.'

'Now, now,' Holliday admonished, 'I fear you've spent too long in roughish climes. We're, after all, concerned with justice. We're not rogues or executioners.'

'I saw that man commit a murder.'

'Ah, but did you?' Coppard asked.

'I was there, dammit.'

'But did you see the act itself, or the consequence of several bullets flying wild?'

'I will not amend my testimony,' Pottinger said.

There was a silence at this, marked by the clopping of a horse and carriage in the warm, damp night outside, and the surreptitious tinkle made by Cummings as he charged the glasses. He had been instructed by Holliday – with whom he lived, though not so graciously, occupying a damp stone room below – to lubricate the evening; it was bound to be vexing, and there was a private fear that Pottinger might turn difficult.

Finally, 'You will not be called upon,' Coppard said.

'That's outrageous. And improper.'

'Now, now . . .' said Holliday.

There was a mouselike rustle in the room and the Parliamentary man – Pritchard – looked up for the first time and closed the pages of the notes in his lap. 'The Governor has empowered me,' he said like a man rehearsed, 'to enjoin your patience and consideration, Sir Frederick. It is to our regret that the police in this Colony are in somewhat baddish odour. Such testimony as you could offer could be held as bias, and the accused can offer witnesses to such effect. The upshot could very well be a government on trial by press and public which, at this particular stage, we wish to avoid. You, sir, are a realist, you will understand. But mark me, the echoes of Ironbark will reflect in Whitehall. These are difficult times,' he sighed.

'Difficult for me,' Pottinger said.

'We – and I use the word advisedly – do not wish to make of bushranging a popular sport, nor to suggest that the gold of the realm is a sportsman's challenge. We've already hanged our bushrangers to no effect, offered substantial rewards. A certain fellow – Mad Dog Morgan – was taken only recently, scalped as a trophy, and decapitated in the interests of science for examination in Melbourne. May I remind you that the press made much of this? And the press, if you take my point, is populated quite frequently by journalists who once were felons themselves. Let me finish,' he said, raising his hand, 'and regard all of this as never uttered. It is to be regretted that we're somewhat less than men of government – we're gaolers, wardens of security. Freedom is a fiction when it rises from the chains. Emancipation, yes, but how long, how many generations before the corruption departs? No, sir, we will not eulogise Frank Gardiner, Christie, whomsoever; we will not make of him a legend. The coach is taken. The gold is gone. We will treat him instead, as the very commonest of criminals.'

'What will you do?' Pottinger asked acidly. 'Grant him ticket-of-leave? Again?'

'Your remarks do not become you,' Coppard said.

'I'm wasting my time,' Pottinger said, getting to his feet.

'No, no,' said Holliday, 'look, do have some wine.'

'Pottinger . . .' Pritchard said with a lingering and commanding pause. 'You won't be a problem?' It was more a statement than a question.

'I've dealt with a variety of levels of society,' Pottinger said. 'I understand completely.'

'Good chap!' Holliday said with a beaming glance that took in the room. 'Do stay, Sir Frederick. This is not the note to leave us on.'

'It's late. I must offer my apologies.'

There was a general move towards the door involving Holliday and Cummings and, lastly, Mayhew who, as they stood in the hallway above the stairs, advised, 'He won't get away with it, you know. We're not that benign.' Pottinger looked at him as he fastened his cape. 'Gardiner will be tried on the count of Bill Henry, storekeeper, Barton's Crossing, last December.'

'Bill Henry? I've never heard of him.'

'Attempted murder, old man. And grievous bodily harm. A charge that'll stick rather firm, I believe.'

'Barton's Crossing,' said Pottinger, 'is outside my jurisdiction.'

'So I understand.'

'Then I shall get no credit?'

'Nor blame. You must learn to count your blessings. If Gardiner were to defeat you in the witness-box . . .' His hand clasped Pottinger's, his other falling like a weight upon his shoulder.

'Henry will run you home,' Holliday said at the glass-panelled door.

'I shall walk,' Pottinger said.

'It isn't safe, not this hour of night.'

'I doubt that worse could happen to me.'

He walked through the swirl of harbour fog, his footsteps ringing where the way was paved, and then thudding into mud and the creep of slime oozing from the rocks. There was a little bookshop and printhouse crabbed into a corner not far from the Tales of Chaucer, and through the glass by the gaslight he saw ranks of paper printed books, twopence each, entitled *The Romance of Frank Gardiner*, and beside them several engravings, some of them framed, of the outlaw himself, though nothing like a likeness. Dimly he began to recount Pritchard's words, to understand in just what corner of the globe he was, and how he, not them – the creeping denizens of the shanty town that clustered to the foreshores – was the alien, the exile.

He let himself into his room and shed his cape where he stood. His cape was wet with fog, the fog clinging with a brackish, seaside smell. And he stripped off his jacket, sighing for the melancholy of his fate. There was through the window a green and sodden moon arising, the merest baleful hue behind the mist, and he thought at the moment to pitch himself straightforward into bed, dressed as he was and numbed by port and too much talk, when he saw on the bed an apparition rising up, and it was his betrothed waking from the deepest sleep. She came to him, a sleep-walker, her head tilted ruefully, the softest smile on her lips, her eyes still deep with sleep as a child might come, resting her hands across his shoulders.

He drew her warm and fragile into his arms and placed his lips to hers, feeling the softness and the yielding and tasting the night-breath, the musk of sleep. He set her standing there, and she waited. He saw her mellowed, small in the wash of moonlight, the light becoming phosphorescent, sifting through the clouds, and saw that she was wearing some hand-fashioned chemise or sleeping-gown, of a kind that was gathered to the throat by a drawstring in a bow.

He reached out, with her eyes upon him, and took the tail of the bow between finger and thumb, and disrobed her like a statue. 'Lettie,' he said, and took in her gilded shape, the hair streaming across the domes of her shoulders, each crested by the gleam of light and echoed at the breasts, the breasts high and youthful, pointed hard. 'Oh, my love,' he murmured, and dropped to his knees and buried his lips at the nest of her thighs.

'I fell asleep,' she confessed as she peeled his clothes away. It was as though they'd done it many times and were now together, by appointment, enacting rituals. 'I thought I dreamed, but didn't. I've such a torment for you.' She stepped back when she was done, and asked him, 'Do I please you?' And as he sought to take her up, to carry her, she leaped upon him, arms locked behind his head, legs about his shanks and ground her body to him, the flesh both silken and adhesive and so persuasive that 'Wait, wait!' he cried, and then, shamefaced, 'Great damn,' he said, 'I've spilled myself,' and they capsized on to the bed, stifling laughter, murmurings and sighs as she coaxed him to a further strength deviously and mischievously, her eyes bright in the dark, proclaiming, 'Am I not a wicked wench?' and 'Am I not better than some hairy bawd?' And when he asked – 'Oh!' – of her experience, she replied that rutting was of common nature to her 'as any common farmer knows'. 'Next time,' he said, 'I'm in the field, I must pay more attention.' But as her body closed upon him, she yielded utterly and there was no more mocking, and the cry she gave was so deeply embedded that it seemed like her soul leaping out.


## Thirty

Lobcock was submerged in his papers, books and files, the files tottering up to the ceiling in erratic, multicoloured pillars, as his pen scratched out the inky allegations – 'Sydney Streets a Quagmire', 'Electrical Illumination No More Than a Myth' – when Mary Gallant, the junior copyreader, ushered in the lady, removed the volumes of encyclopaedic reference and sat her on the lame-legged chair.

'Time and patience,' the journalist waved from his warren. '*Tempus fugit.*' Then he spied a veritably rhapsodic ankle. 'My dear,' he said leaping up to obtain a birds-eye view. 'Delighted,' he said, surging forward and spilling out the inkpot. 'No mind, no matter,' he continued from the floor as he mopped away, 'plenty more where that came from. I just open up my veins and ink flies out. I didn't catch your name,' he said across the wiring of his spectacles. 'We must firstly deal in names.'

'I'm Kate Foster,' she said.

'Foster, Foster, that rings a bell.' Gerald Foster's girl, perhaps, the one with . . .?

'I'm Frank Gardiner's woman,' she said bluntly.

The office went so still she heard him suck in his breath. He shut the door with a soft and secret click. Sat down. Got up. Removed some clothing from a lie-back chair. 'Be comfortable,' he said.

'I'm all right where I am.'

'Kate Foster, quite so. Indubitably so.'

'I want you,' she said, taking a scrawl from the depths of her purse, 'to print this in your paper.'

He read the words: 'Frank Gardiner is Innocent'. And put the paper down.

'And I want you to get him out of gaol.'

'Two impossibilities,' he said, slumping in his chair.

And it was as though, there in the dun and brown coloured room, he'd lit a fuse. 'You can do it!' she blazed. 'Don't you sit there and deny me. He never done no more'n the others. He done less. And he went straight. For months and months he lived a proper, legal way. And if they'd have let him be —'

'Yes, yes, quite so. Shush, now, shush. The walls, you know, have ears, you know. Let us keep it for the moment confidential and proceed with the proper attack.'

'I won't be put off,' she said. 'I want that printed.'

'Quite so,' he said. 'Have you seen him? Have you seen Frank?'

'I don't even know where he is. They won't tell me, they won't talk to me. I've tramped these bloody streets for three whole weeks —'

'Yes, yes, I know. I'm not surprised. You need a little jostle in the right direction, that's all. He's in Darlinghurst,' he said, 'being held in Darlinghurst, the debtors' prison . . .'

'He never owed a penny.'

'. . . on remand, you follow me? Awaiting trial. You have some weeks in hand,' he said, looking at the calendar, 'and a weight of public opinion – quite surprising – in his favour.'

'He went straight,' she repeated. 'I won't be put off.'

'You need a lawyer,' he told her.

'Which one?' she said.

'That's a prickly question.'

'Then which is the best?'

'The best is Wright and Haversteen.'

'They'll do,' she said. 'How much?'

He smiled. 'A mite too much.'

265

'How much?' she said, her jaw jutting out. And showed him a bundle of money he would have sold his life for.

'Come with me,' he said.

Kate discovered that almost all of Sydney was for sale. The lawyers – when she paid – fell about themselves. The printer – Lobcock's friend – knew a fellow-writer, a man of political aspiration, and he obliged, for a fee, by writing a fluent diatribe absolving, if not canonising, Gardiner in the most persuasive terms. The pamphlets soon littered the streets and found their way to the most august desks.

*The Romance of Frank Gardiner* was reprinted twice over, and an enterprising gentleman offered a waxworks likeness, sixpence a look.

But it was money, always money that opened the doors; and it was hard, cold cash that bribed the warder who let her into Darlinghurst. He let her in by a small rear gate, past the stables, past the horses and into darkened corridors, down the steps worn smooth, until she faced him through the door.

'You got five minutes,' the warder said, and crept back to keep nick at the corner.

'Oh, Frank . . .' she said. They'd shaved him, cut his whiskers off, cut his hair. He looked younger, but thinner, sallow in the light.

'You shouldn't have come,' he said.

'I'm going to get you out.'

'I wouldn't think so. They got me going for Bill Henry. I hardly even touched him.'

'Who's Bill Henry?'

'What they'll get me for. I got 'em beat on the gold coach, but they'll get me for Bill Henry.'

'I got lawyers, Frank. The best there is.'

'You need some money?'

'I used the money from the store.'

'What about the other?' he said.

'I got it safe. I won't touch it.'

'Use it,' he said, reaching through the bars, 'use it like I told you.'

'Don't you go sendin' me away,' she said. 'I ain't goin'. I'm gonna get you out.'

'Put your face up,' he told her. 'Give us a kiss.'

He kissed her with the bars pressing down beside her face. 'Makes it all worthwhile,' he told her.

'Still love you, Frank.'

'Still love you, Kate.'

'Frank . . .'

'Now you hear me,' he said with a grip that hurt her arm. 'You get going like I told you. If you stay, they'll grind you down. They don't forgive, this lot. They'll get you the same as me.'

'I ain't going,' she said.

'Will you just stop saying that . . .'

They heard the footsteps of the warder. 'That'll do y',' he said.

'Come on, Mr Jolly,' Gardiner said. 'Let's have our money's worth.'

'Out,' said the warder to Kate.

'I'll be back,' she told him, and went with Jolly, walking backwards, the tears coming to her eyes as she prayed to God he couldn't see her in the half-light; he wouldn't want her crying.

'What'll he get?' she asked the warder at the gate.

'Whatever's coming,' he said. The gate closed, and she was out and Frank was in, her whole world was cut across the middle, and she started down towards the sea again ready to fight, to continue the struggle, but there was no one to fight and nothing of any shape to fight against.

## Thirty-one

The 'miscarriage' of justice that Pottinger feared did not take
place, though the mode of attack did nothing for his own good
name. He looked at the man in the dock and listened to the line
of accusation, and it could have been Jack Frost the Body-
snatcher there on trial so alien did the proceedings seem, and so
unlike himself did Gardiner appear.

But the press and the public had sniffed out blood and land-
slide assault, and were packed together sweating in the heat,
edging forward, mouths agape to see blind justice slip the noose.
The Crown, with polite ferocity, decked up its charges against
the accused who, despite his tonsured head and the drape of
the prison clothes, was recognisably Gardiner, accepting the
assault with a cock-eyed grin and a sparkle to his eyes as he
inscribed his first initial with his thumbnail in the bench.

He greeted his thespian defence with the same equanimity;
he liked this play of words about him. Had he not gone
'straight' as Kate had said? Was he not the most trusted man in
Aphis Creek? He had repented, this much was plain to see;
there was contrition in this man – though the judge for the life
of him could only see a man showing impudent enjoyment
with his eyes upon the ceiling.

And was it not known, the defence continued, and witness
Mad Dog Morgan, that the Crown created its own monsters
merely to rejoice in conquest?

Order, order, went the cry. The whole court rustled forward,
voices raised, ex-convicts braying 'Justice!' with hairy chins
and gap-toothed jaws stuck out.

And did not, cried the defence, reaching true heights of
theatricality, did not the Crown maintain its own mad-dog
bloodhounds, the police, some titled, to pursue the hapless
quarry? What chance did Gardiner have against the aristoc-

racy? 'Down with 'is ludship!' came the cry. 'Down with 'is mudship!' came another. Laughter. And 'Order!' And 'Objection!' The press scribbling furiously. Kate on her feet, hands dragging her down.

At this point, Pottinger blundered from the gallery; he'd heard enough. The courts, the entire judicial system was a vampire sucking the blood from the very stain of crime, permitting a gross and improper defence that merely stirred the blood of what passed for the 'people'. Yet he himself had seen men die, their innards spilling; what was the meaning of this courtroom Punch and Judy show?

But none the less the charges mounted, and when Mayhew saw that they were properly stacked above the accused, he saw to it that the ropes were cut: fifteen years' hard labour, two in irons for Bill Henry, ten for Horsington, seven for Hewitt – the latter two dredged up from a fair-sized list to which the prisoner threw himself upon the mercy of the court. Thirty-two years – concurrent. At this, the public broke loose, fists raised, trampling, beyond control, the jury looking stunned and whitefaced as missiles fell, Lobcock warding off his fellow-journalists from Kate Foster, Kate sitting numbed as rock unable to believe the verdict and the sentence – thirty-two years! – and doing her arithmetic; he'd be sixty-six years old! And people pushing, trampling – 'Get off!' she yelled, and when the pink-faced gent informed her, 'It's a judgement,' she smashed him with her bag and smashed his glasses on his face. 'Out,' said Lobcock, hastily propelling her. 'We'll continue the fight in the press.'

But the press was not to be so willing. '*We do not welcome the public outcry in the courtroom,*' it said two days later: '*We honour the jury and believe them fair. If every trial is to become a plaything of the public . . .*'

Lobcock was not quite in disgrace, but chastened, and there was other news, the perpetual unfolding of news in the ferment of Sydney: a man had drowned his offspring in a horse trough . . . 'The die is cast,' he said to Kate. 'You must accept his fate.'

'It was a mis-trial,' she countered, having picked up some of the jargon. 'They didn't do him fair.'

'It's late,' he said, floundering about. 'It's raining. I have to greet the steam train. Where's my umbrella?'

'I'll see the Governor,' she said. 'I'll shove it in his blooming face!'

The rain persisted into February, the most trying time of year. It came from as far away as Queensland, the remnants of a cyclone, and settled in a baleful fug along the southern coast. It rained for days, and it would rain for weeks. It was the time that certain quarters thought about as 'Quack's Delight' and the sale of curatives and nostrums soared – for it was widely known that the dysentery, for example, was caused by the dampening of the feet or wearing thin-soled shoes. And sure enough, Eliot Considine came down with Colonial Fever, almost to the day that Frank Gardiner received his sentence.

He had stood in the rain with Lelitia and Pottinger watching his dear wife depart. Never having valued her in latter years particularly, he now felt the first twinges of twelve months' separation, missing her nagging stridency, her riding at his side, lamenting the loss of the dip in the bed, her wheezing snore, the elbow in his ribs. Dear woman, a burden and his only love.

That night, the fever had struck. He lay tossing, bright-eyed, seeing again and again the departing boat. 'Goodbye, love. Goodbye.' And he returned abruptly from the fever to the hotel room, the rain on the roof, the water in the pipes, and Lelitia, his only daughter left, sponging his brow, and the baronet pacing, saying, 'He needs a doctor.'

'It's a bit of ague, that's all it is.'

Then the sick man heard them murmuring beneath the shaded lamp. 'I have to get back to Ironbark,' Pottinger said.

'Then we'll postpone,' she said.

'Again?'

'Get married, for God's sake,' Considine cried. 'Do you think I don't know what's going on? For decency's sake, get married.'

'Papa,' she said, kneeling by the bed, 'when you're on your feet again.'

'Oh Lord,' groaned Considine, blaspheming more than usual, 'what's happened to my daughters? Clara!' he burst out. 'Tell Clara.'

'Yes,' she comforted.

'Find Clara.'

'I'll tell her.' She looked at Pottinger. There was this thing between them that they didn't dare talk about.

'I shall endeavour,' said Pottinger, 'to obtain a stay of duty.'

Days passed with the fume of rain outside the window. They plied the invalid with Weston's Wizard Oil and Bosisto's Syrup of the Red Gum and a variety of stomach oils and plasters. 'Here's one,' Lelitia said, reading from the paper, 'Aborigines' Sacred Bark Liver Tonic. Do you think...?' she asked Pottinger.

He shook his head, and the upshot of it was that Considine was bundled off to Water Springs for a course in hydropathic treatment, bouncing in the train to Campbelltown and lurching in the steam tram to Camden, there to be placed in the care of Monsieur Trieste, with water sheets and douche baths and internal draughts of tonic water – which Considine survived, but more due to his constitution. For the 'Colonial Fever' was the typhoid.

In the end, Pottinger was forced to pack. There was such a thing as duty. Lettie came to his room chastely in the late of day to see him well prepared. 'I shall make for Parramatta,' he said, 'and spend the evening there. Captain St Clare will collect me in the morning.'

'Don't say goodbye,' she said with her arms about him. 'We'll be back in Ironbark by the turn of the month.'

'What a sorry pair,' he said, observing their image in the mirror.

'Do you have regrets?'

'None,' he said, 'except for our fatal sense of duty.'

'Our time will come,' she told him, 'when the Lord wills it.'

271

She kissed him, and was gone. Well, he thought, summer will pass into autumn, and autumn into winter. He hadn't imagined that he could stay so long in love, that it could run so deeply. Love fitted him now, like accustomed clothing; he wouldn't be himself without it. He gathered his baggage by the door and turned again to appraise the empty room and the things he might have left. He had an hour to spare and time for a glass to fill it. He crossed the room and took up his cape, gazing as well at the misery of the window, the rain weeping down, the harbour waters grey as metal, ships drowning, people huddling, splashing by the drains as night drew in earlier than usual, the sun obscured, the daylight fading. Then unexpectedly, he saw Lelitia Considine turning into Chandler's Lane.

By the time Pottinger hurried out the door, she was nowhere to be seen. It was not the first time he'd noted absences, and it vexed him somewhat that she had another, secret life. He tramped down the laneway across running puddles and came to a mews of a kind with streets diverging. He spent fifteen minutes or more between one and the other, peering through the grey of sodden twilight as the lamps were lit, one here, one there, as random beacons across the town.

In a dismal quarter disgraced by Potter's Alley, he caught a glimpse of her, he thought, dancing across the swill of water between two tipsy buildings, a stable and a storehouse. He went down the Alley between the press of stone and brickwork fences, past snapping dogs and surly louts lurching home from the gin shops, and turned into yet another winding lane with a scattering of shops, a baker, an apothecary. He gathered his cape and walked more at seeming leisure until he came at last to a tiny store with a bow-front window, a light within and a youngish man weighing out tobacco on the scales. He looked at the man through the speckled window, at the warmth within, the lamplight golden, the tones russet in the light, the tobacco piled like a treasure on the pan. He stepped back from the window to read the inscription above: 'Michael McNaught, Tobacconist', and turned and walked away. McNaught he may be now, he thought, but he knew him as Taylor.

## Thirty-two

'That's right, missus,' said the surly man in the house along the Tank Stream, 'they done Frank Gardiner dirty. They done the same to me. Fourteen years they give me – for a bleedin' pheasant! And a hundred stripes, beside. Cut the cords o' me back, they did. I can't bend but halfways over.'

'Thirty-two years they give my man,' Kate Foster said. 'There ain't enough crimes in the book.'

'They'd hang him half-a-dozen times if he'd wriggle long enough.'

'Would you sign, then, to set him loose?'

'Gimme that there writing-stick!'

'Many thanks,' she said.

'Bless you, missus,' he told her. 'Try next door, but not across the street – he's a bleedin' trooper.'

Fourteen hundred signatures she'd taken on the dog-eared scroll she carried, and by God she'd double it by the time she was done. Signatures and letters, it had become her life – letters written for her, to the papers, to the Governor, and just occasionally, hardly ever, a stir of answers. She carried the answers in her bag, along with clippings from the papers. Money wouldn't buy her what she wanted now, and there was precious little left. But the gold was still intact. She wouldn't touch the gold, not to save her life. She tramped through leaves. It was autumn and the winter would be hard.

Often in the afternoons she made her way to the high point above the harbour and sat beneath the Moreton Bays chewing on a knob of bread and salted beef, there to gaze across the waters to the island of Cockatoo. It was one of eight such islands in Port Jackson – the largest, about forty acres of it, an almost solid block of sandstone. It was here that Frank Gardiner lived in chains, chipping chunks of rock to repair the

273

Circular Quay, handsome with its stonework, the finest in the world. She thought she could see him sometimes, but she couldn't be sure. There were some that hobbled when they walked from the irons about their ankles, and he'd be one of them. She couldn't visit; they allowed no visitors. She'd spent fifteen pounds on futile bribes – to the man with the boat, the warder on his shore-leave and they'd betrayed her, taken her for a fool.

At nights she went back to her house. It was a ruined house, abandoned, two rooms falling down. There, she taught herself to write, copying out the letters, the same letters written for her, tracing out the intricate slopes and curlicues, inscribing 'His Excellency, the Governor', and beginning, her tongue stuck out with the labour, 'I wish to draw your attention to a Gross Miscarriage of Justice . . .' Her house, her bed, her life was filled with the rustle of paper. Paper was a talisman, magic, words of indignation forming on it. In Ironbark, in Winooka no one cared a damn for the flick of paper; a punch in the beak was the shortest remonstrance.

She spent her last ten pounds on Wright and Haversteen, the defending lawyers. They were not unsympathetic. There was a stir in the upper levels of government that she didn't know about. It was being stated, and sometimes openly, that Gardiner was more truly serving time for the case that never came to court, that he'd been savaged by a justice somewhat less than blind because he'd robbed – it was alleged – the gold coach.

'It's a fine and delicate point,' said Haversteen from the comfort of his leather chair, framed by a window in Gothic style.

'But can you get him off, then?' Kate asked.

'One might do better to broach the matter of Horsington and Hewitt, to which he pleaded guilty.'

'It was that or fifty years,' she said.

'The Crown was devious, and deviously clever. On the score of which we might wriggle in a plea? One might even dare to suggest,' he said, 'a mis-trial which, though it would never wash, could cause a nasty twinge. Though on the other hand . . .'

He thought aloud, and the more he thought aloud, the more Kate lost the trend; she couldn't fathom the legal turn of mind. He saw her to the door, his arm about her. He was an older man, paternal, his hair light and insubstantial as floss. 'Are you cared for?' he asked. 'Are you well looked after?'

'I'm doin' all right,' she said.

'Your tenacity does you credit.'

'I'm going to get him off,' she said, an old refrain.

'Your activities have not gone unnoticed,' he assured her. 'When one is in the fray, too close to the attack, one tends to be in ignorance of the effect. Government is chafing somewhat. There are letters to the press, gossip in the clubs.'

'I got a petition,' she said. 'Will you sign it?'

'As your representing lawyer, that would not be in your interests.' But he examined the tattered scrolls and the variety of signatures, scrawls and crosses and nodded at them, quite impressed.

'I'm going to fetch it to the Governor,' she told him.

'Alas, I doubt he'd even sight it.'

'He's a good, fair man they tell me.'

'With a good, fair number in between. It's a sad fact of life,' he said, 'that the upper echelons of power are far removed in cloudy realms. Though there is a certain gentleman . . .' he mused, thinking of a certain chap who'd done him down in cards; he owed him one and serve him right. 'You could always go and knock him up one night . . .'

It was from this advice that she gained access to Aubrey Holliday's house in Macquarie Street, standing in the hallway with Henry Cummings insisting that the good gentleman was visiting in Parramatta, and would madam leave her name or come back later?

'You know who I am,' she said. 'I'm Frank Gardiner's woman.'

He looked at her more closely, at the sadness of her clothes, and took pity. 'Come in for a moment,' he said, ushering her

275

towards the reception room.

'Is that a fire down there?' she asked.

'That's my quarters,' he said.

'That'll do,' she said, and started down towards the glow.

'You can't go in there,' he protested.

She paused on the flagging, looking back. 'I haven't seen a fire these last three weeks.'

He took her in, gave her rum – and blast the look of it. He was all alone in his warren. He never had visitors. He had no friends to speak of.

'Oh my,' she said, spreading her fingers to the fire, 'that's better.'

'I saw you in the courtroom,' he confessed.

'I don't doubt you did.'

'I thought you'd gone home.'

'My home's where he is,' she said, not troubling to identify the 'he'.

He filled her glass and poked the fire in a flutter of self-consciousness – he'd never had a woman in this room, and never had there been a woman in his life. His lot was to serve, to perfect his penmanship, his fluency. Every second Wednesday night he attended a literary coterie – which Holliday mocked – there to read aloud his clumsy poetry. And now there was a woman at his fire. He'd written of women, their 'dimpling cheeks, their velvet lashes, and la! the snowy pastures that mine eyes do dwell upon,' but he had never seen a woman such as this, whose fire matched the fire she stood at, whose blaze of – what was it, passion, wildness, madness? – lit up the pallor of her skin and set agleam the bony structure of her face.

'Will you eat?' he asked. 'I've nothing fancy, a piece of cottage pie, a bit of pumpkin and the like. I cook, you see – my secret vice.'

He watched her eat as others watch a woman disrobe. His eyes – as he'd later set it down in bouncing rhyme – devoured her; he'd dwell and dine on her memory for the rest of his life; for all he knew, marriage was not in his cards. Later, they sat across the table and he told her of his life, telling her things that he'd never related before, ending with an anecdote he made amusing: 'I met Frank Gardiner once – at gunpoint, though he was quite the gentleman about it. It was his first hold-up.'

The fire burned low and the lamplight stuttered. 'I must shortly turn you out,' he said.

She gave him the petition and explained it. 'Will you fetch it to the Governor for me?'

He sighed, 'I have no sway with Governor, I'm afraid.'

'But they told me—'

'Mr Holliday,' he said, 'is in the Governor's confidence. And Mr Holliday...' He broke off at the sudden sag of her defeat.

'Then who can I turn to?' she asked. She had come to the end of a desolate road to reach this room, and the scrolls lay there on the table in among the plates and papers, a thousand muted voices twice times over that would never get a hearing. 'I'll come back,' she said. 'When will your master be back?'

'He isn't my master,' he said. 'I'm more of a . . .' What was he – secretary, companion, parasite or whipping-post? Perhaps a little of each of these.

'Will you help me?' she asked directly. 'Say it yes or no.'

He sighed, in fact thinking of various manipulations that would help him place the woman's papers on the desk of government; but the woman, Kate, read him otherwise and stood abruptly, turned away, and began to work her fingers at her buttons.

'Good God, no,' he said. 'What are you doing?'

'What has to be done,' she told him. 'It's little enough.'

'Do, please, I beg of you . . .' he said. 'No, stop that. Good grief,' he told her, 'that's not required.'

'Don't you want me?'

He couldn't answer.

'Do I offend you? Then get your duds off. Do it!' she commanded. 'I'm not some old bat or tart that's wandered in. I'm Kate Foster-should-be Gardiner, and I don't go pitching my tail for the fun of it nor for sixpence in a laneway. But I know

277

what you want. And you know what I want. And that's a fair trade, ain't it?'

'Kate...' he said gently, using her name as a lover would and touching her shoulder. 'I shall serve you with honour – for the honour of it.' She was weeping, as he could plainly see, and he had never been touched so deeply before. God willing that he might be loved like this one day. 'Fasten your clothes,' he told her, though his hand dwelt – only for a moment – on the warm roundness of her shoulder. He kissed her shoulder, and turned about. 'Fasten your clothes. Do not demean yourself. Do it, do it!' he said.

Her fingers flew to her buttons. 'I'm sorry. I didn't mean to offend you.'

'Some of us have pride and dignity,' he said.

'I'm sorry.'

'As well you might be.'

Shortly she stood at the doorway. 'What's your name?' she asked. He told her. She looked at him, searching his face. 'Goodnight, Henry,' she said, and kissed him on the lips.

'Goodnight,' he breathed as her footsteps faded in the street. And he turned, imbued with the resolve to beard the Governor in his den, and botheration to Aubrey Holliday! He would put his own career, Henry Cummings would, his life, his aspirations in the balance. For a woman, he sighed, leaning lovesick in the doorway. So this was love, this sweet sickness? What flowers of rhyme his pen would spill!

## Thirty-three

'There, sir,' said Pottinger stamping round the barracks office, bumping the desk, upsetting the tinpot vase of wild boronia, 'you have my resignation!'

'No, no,' Canning demurred, 'that's not the way, sir.'

'Take the desk, take the chair, have done with it.'

'I've no such aspirations,' Canning laughed, half rising guiltily.

'Sit down. It's yours. For ever.'

'Sir . . .' Canning began.

'Have you seen the Sydney papers?'

'Not lately,' Canning lied.

'Thoughtfully supplied by some anonymous benefactor? Have you seen the tack they've taken with my name? Am I to blame for vagaries of government? She's as fickle as a woman. She can't tell her head from her tail. Look, sir, look,' he said thumping down the paper and spearing the item enough to smudge the print, 'look at this rot!'

'Tch, tch!' said Canning, his head twisted round.

'He's to be released. They're going to release him.'

'Yes, sir, I see that. A general amnesty, I see.'

'They might as well reward him, knight him, anoint him.'

'I note there are twenty-seven others,' Canning offered mildly. 'It isn't Gardier alone.'

'Heaven help us,' Pottinger sighed. 'Why did we bother, why did we shed blood?' And he sat down in the chair in which Canning had first placed him all that time ago when he'd arrived in Ironbark. 'Why are we infested with boronia?' he asked.

'My good wife Bess thought it might brighten the office.'

'It reeks like a twopenny tart.'

'I thought it rather pleasant.'

'Why did they release him?' he shouted, his fist smiting the desk.

'It explains, I believe, sir, that there's a turn of tide in the Colony, that bushranging is – what shall we say? – an old nag that's had its day.'

'They'd like to think so.'

'Pickings are rather lean these days. People send their money written down on paper honoured by the banks.'

'Have you informed Ben Hall of that innovation?'

'He's rather a different case.'

'He's a progeny of Gardiner's. What will he do now – assas-

279

sinate this office and ask for amnesty?'

'We'll get him, sir. Don't you worry.'

'I'm not worried, Sergeant,' Pottinger said, getting to his feet, 'I'm not worried in the least. You have my resignation at your elbow.'

Canning touched the paper lightly as though it was unreal. 'It's not for me to accept,' he said.

'Then pass it on to our friend St Clare.'

'As you wish, sir.'

'Or better still, I will.' His hand clawed up the resignation angrily, then paused. 'Or better yet I'll take it down to Sydney – and see the villain when they turn him loose. That memory at least I should bear to the grave.'

'You have a week,' said Canning, referring to the newspaper, 'before he leaves the country.'

'Leaving, is he?'

'That, sir, appears to be the stipulation. He's to be banished.'

'Cruel fate,' said Pottinger satirically. 'That they should do the same for me.'

Sergeant Canning stood to watch him go, ostensibly an honour to the officer of his command, but more to catch a vision of Sir Freddie mounting up and leaving – leaving! Canning breathed and grabbed his hat. 'Take over, Corporal!' he cried to Lovatt as he, himself strode out – it was only minutes down the way – to tell his wife, 'I'm reinstated!' or better, more wisely, 'I've won the day, my love,' and stick his feet up, confident and jocular, master of himself again, lord of Iron-bark, king within his kingdom. 'I saw him out,' he crowed to himself as he strode through the town, 'I did him down.'

'Good morning, Sergeant,' they called, acknowledging his confidence.

'Good morning!' he replied. His face was shining, his jaw stuck out, he seemed a dozen years the younger. 'Blooming baronet,' he laughed, 'a marshmallow man!'

The baronet was helping himself to Considine's decanter. Of recent months, he'd taken on his unofficial role as son-of-the-estate, for Considine himself was laid up by the ravage of the typhoid, spending his days in a chair by the window, a shadow of his former bulk, cheeks sunken, eyes glazed by a brightness that was far from health. And yet he could still summon up a yell from his position of command: 'Yard those horses, Watson! Three men slouching, Merrick!' He controlled the general drift of labour, but not his health. 'What month is it?' he'd ask plaintively. 'What day?' He watched the days through Lelitia to the time when 'Moother' would return.

'I have business in Sydney,' Pottinger said, tasting what was a passable port, 'and I wondered would you spare Lettie for a week or so?'

'That barn is falling down,' Considine said. 'How many times have I told about it?'

'Sir . . .' Pottinger persisted. So often these days the sick man failed to hear or else ignored the affairs of those about him.

'Tell Merrick!' said Considine, 'or else I'll have him flogged.'

'I fear that day has passed.' At which point, Lettie came in and Pottinger imperceptibly shook his head at her. They had devised a system of discretions which conveyed the patient's state of health.

'How are you, Papa?' she asked.

'The barn is falling down,' he said.

'I was hoping to take you to Sydney,' Pottinger told her, 'before the winter sets, for a change of climate, a little sea air.'

'I can't leave him,' she said. 'How can I leave him?'

'Surely Mrs Watson would oblige?'

'She's not to be trusted.'

'Then she should be dismissed.'

'And lose her husband's services?'

'My dear, if you can't get away for a week . . .'

'We waited a month, then three, then six —'

'Yes, yes,' he said. 'We each have our duties, I'm sure.'

He drained his wine and stepped outside, and soon she joined him. 'If you can't spend ten days in Sydney,' he told her tartly, 'I can hardly see you in residence at Apsley Chase.'

'Mama will be back by then.'

'Yes,' he said, 'so she will.'

'Oh Freddie, don't be difficult.'

'Was I being difficult? How extraordinary.'

They were standing outside the kitchen door watching the clouds passing over, the shadows sliding across the winter pastures, the water fowl dancing at the distant swamp.

'You go,' she told him. 'I'll wait here.'

'Very well,' he said, 'I'll go.' And when she uttered his name, a plea, 'It makes so little difference, anyway. One becomes accustomed to our abstinence.'

'That's a rotten thing to say.'

'I want to marry you,' he said. 'I am prepared. Now you provide the obstructions.'

'October was the month you named.'

'I will not wear the guilt, madam, not for your convenience.'

'Oh go, go,' she cried, and suddenly was in his arms and pressed against him. 'Come back,' she murmured. 'I'd die without you.' It had become a litany. They had somehow missed the anchorage of marriage as though it were a stormy cape obscured by night. They would marry, oh yes, they kept affirming this, but there were many reefs and lost directions, and the return to marriage was longer than the journey.

'When I return...' he began, but desisted from what was now a parody of promises. He moved to his horse and mounted and waved from the saddle. She signalled back to him, then was still, watching his departure, the shadows slipping down the road as he travelled, and he saw her ultimately from the turn of the road still standing there motionless against the house, and so small she seemed, so stricken that he felt a twinge of guilt and love commingled.

But his journey, and the motivation for it, was far from done. They had slipped Frank Gardiner out in the dead of night, the row-boat rocking through the inky waters, and taken him by coach with curtains drawn seventy miles to the north, to Newcastle, away from the rage of protest and peppery gentlemen fulminating in the clubs, and prying journalists, and malcontents, and petitioners, clean and clear away, for government had its own good reasons, and not the least of these was to sweep the offence beneath the carpet before it began to breed. 'Be him gone and forgotten,' went the collective sigh.

But even Kate had missed her lover. 'Where is he?' she cried. She'd been up and down the length and breadth of Sydney asking, but Gardiner was something worse than dead, he was obliterated, effaced from earth. 'Where is he?' she repeated. 'What have you done with him?' They were walking, or she was trotting, more or less, down Macquarie Street – with Aubrey Holliday and Henry Cummings on the way to Government House – and Holliday was saying, plucking off her fingers, 'Do get away, madam, or I shall call the constable.'

'Where is he?' she said again.

'Who is this wretched woman, Cummings?'

'Sir ...' said Cummings, and, 'Watch out!' as a wagon-load of ale nearly ran them down.

'You see?' Holliday said to her. 'You almost had me killed.'

'Tell me where Frank Gardiner is,' she said, standing on the corner.

'Never so much as heard of the man. Come along, Cummings, we shall be late.'

She watched them go, her last thin chance. 'Henry,' she called.

'Henry?' said Holliday. 'Did she call you Henry?'

'Must have read my name,' he explained. 'In the papers.'

'Have you been in the papers?'

'Newcastle,' he called to her. 'They've fetched him off to —'

'Good Gad, sir,' Holliday roared, 'have you lost your wits as well as your tongue?'

Kate fled across the town and reached at last the coaching-stop. 'I told you, lady,' the stablemaster said, 'the coach is gone this past two hour ago.'

'I'll pay,' she said. 'In gold.'

He looked down at her rags and grinned. 'Clear off,' he told her, 'before you're trampled under.'

Big, sleek-bodied horses clattered past and she stood there ignoring the brush of their flanks. Frank was sailing out from

Newcastle somewhere to the north, some day, some time, this much she knew, and she could see him in her mind this very moment departing across that ocean vastness that she'd only dipped her toes in, and if a man was taken by the ocean, swallowed up, he was gone for ever, for the world was larger than the heavens you could see. But there was gold, and gold could buy the world. She kneeled down on the cobblestones and began to unlace the bag she'd lugged across the town and back again, when suddenly behind her a voice said, 'Going north, by any chance?'

She looked around and up at Pottinger, and hastily closed the bag.

'They tell me he's leaving this afternoon.'

'Leave me alone,' she said.

'Delighted.'

He crossed to the stablemaster and quick as wink they had a coach, the duty coach held by for dignitaries, and baronets presumably. 'We shall have to go like blazes,' Pottinger said. 'It's one event we can't repeat.'

'Be there at sundown,' the coachie said.

'A pound note says it's four o'clock.'

'Board up, sir. I can have you at the Pearly Gates for less.'

Pottinger set foot on the step and turned by afterthought to look at Kate. 'Jolly bad luck,' he said. He looked down at the dismal woman standing in the unrelenting grey of watered cobblestones, her clothing grey as iron, the big bag an untidy heap at her feet. 'Were you intending to travel with him?'

'I was,' she said.

'Pity. Perhaps you'll track him down some other time.' She turned away, her head hung down. 'Unless you could lower your dignity?'

'I won't beg,' she said.

'You might have to.'

'Time's tickin' on, sir,' the coachie said.

'I never begged once in my whole damn' life.'

'That was more a matter of fortune than circumstance. You're lucky you're not in the female prison. You were hard enough

284

at Gardiner's heels.'

'Give him my love,' she told him, hoisting the bag.

'Hold on,' Pottinger told the coachie. He went to Kate, and turned her with his touch. 'What a very foolish girl you are.'

'I have my pride.'

'They should write that on your tombstone.'

'I won't beg,' she said, the tears filling her eyes.

He sighed. 'Then I must demean myself. Madam,' he said, 'would you do me the honour . . . ?'

They went rollicking up the road so fast she was hanging on to the window-frame, and he was watching her, this somewhat more than incredible woman – a woman with a fire not unlike Lelitia's, though would *she* follow him so unremittingly? And it was all written there in Kate's face, not merely the hunger and the long, abrasive grief, but the time she'd served alongside Frank, the prison-time, he on the Island, she on the streets, so real it had been that at night her ankles chafed.

'I'd much prefer to see him hang,' he told her bluntly.

'I know that.'

'As he'd prefer to see me dead.'

'You flatter yourself.'

'Did he speak of me at Aphis Creek?'

'Never.'

'I do flatter myself.'

They bounced across a sequence of roads and splashed across the creeks. The coachie's oaths drifted by on the winter air and birds spilled out of the forests as they passed.

'I saw your husband in Ironbark not three days ago,' he offered, not in the kindest spirit.

'Oh? How is he?'

'Tippling, rather. Drunk, to be exact.'

'Poor Roy.'

'That would just about describe it.'

'I'm not proud of what I done,' she said, 'but I done it and I'd do it again. I made my mistake and I patched it over.'

'You what?' he asked over the crash of wheels on skittering shale.

285

'I have to do it,' she shouted. 'I'm part of him, I'm part of Frank.'

'Oh yes,' he said. 'I quite imagine so.'

'God help me,' she uttered.

'Say again?' he shouted, but they rounded a bend and she was tipped almost into his arms.

'What's in that bag?' he asked after a further handful of miles.

'That's my things.'

'Heavy,' he said, giving it a poke.

'My worldly goods.'

'Including the smithie's iron?'

It was the gold, of course, it had to be, from the biggest theft in New South Wales, or some of the gold at least. And he could almost feel it from where he sat, as though the metal glowed with a dull, illicit heat.

'What else would it be?' she asked.

'*Bon voyage*,' he sighed. 'I suppose you've earned it in a roughshod way.'

In the later part of afternoon they crashed across the outer twist of roads that was the further spread of Newcastle made prosperous by coal, past Four Mile Creek and the unpleasant spill of mines, and down through avenues of silver-bark trees, the leaves hanging, smacking at the roof until they thundered through the town towards the ocean, the water brilliant with the flick of light between the buildings, down the alleyways.

He thought at first that some fair or festive celebration was in progress, for they had suddenly plunged into a press of people, some with ribbons, streamers and festooned hats, some moving trippingly, he thought, as upon a May Day, towards the swill of water that was the rise of a stubborn, lazy tide. He stuck his head out. 'Push on,' he ordered the coachie.

'Clear a path!' the coachie cried. 'Stand back, official coach.'

'Don't advertise,' Pottinger instructed. He now saw people by the hundred, a great drift and press of people, and heard – he couldn't believe it – a brass band playing raggedly. Next, they were at a standstill, stuck fast by the mob. Had they come

erhaps on the wrong day? Was royalty departing? Then he
aw a banner dancing past. 'Good Luck, Frankie' it read in
rimson letters. 'Good grief!' Pottinger said. The news, it
ppeared, had leaked out despite all efforts. Frank Gardiner was
) board the *Charlotte Andrews*, a three-mast workstained
arque bound for some damn-all destination.

'There he is!' someone yelled.

The entire crowd turned about, and now in hundreds, more
aan hundreds, they streamed towards a little knot of men –
olicemen dressed in pointless disguise – closing hard about the
anished man, ordered to see that he walked the plank, the one
rom shore to ship, never to return.

'Frank!' Kate cried, and tore away from Pottinger. He saw
er briefly swallowed by the crowd and buffeted about, then he
imself was swept along, striking out at hairy miners pressed
gainst him, ignoring cries of, 'Justice for the Darkie!' 'A fig
or Guvvinment!'

'Hands off, sir, hands off!' he cried, pushing through. 'Hang
he felon!' yelled a fellow out of tune, and when last seen by
ottinger was being pummeled to the ground, fists and legs
ying, the pumpkin-coloured vest beneath a storm of boots.
nd once again, now borne by the crowd, he saw Kate and
ate's man, Frank – Gardiner clearly searching for her through
he crowd, his face tanned by the sun and shackled labour, but
hin and sharp, more youthful than remembered.

'Let me through!' Kate yelled, and Pottinger followed after.

Gardiner saw her then. He pushed back past the stomachs of
our policemen, their hands grasping, faces apprehensive, and a
ranny cried, 'Oh, bless y', Frank!' and fainted even as the
overs joined, and he swept her up with a grin for the whole
lamn' world to see.

'Make way,' cried the voices of command, hands shoving,
rying to peel them apart.

'She's going with me, you idjut.'

'She hasn't got a ticket.'

'Then I ain't going.'

'Board up, board up,' cried the Sergeant-in-command. 'Back,

287

sir,' he said, planting a paw in Pottinger's chest.

'Friend of mine,' said Gardiner intervening. 'Nice to se
you, Fred.'

'My kingdom for a gun.'

'No hard feelings, eh?'

'All hard feelings, old boy.' And a touch of envy? he aske
himself. He began to think of his own blind fate as he stoo
there in the swirl of the crowd, of his wretched ethics, h
honour, his name – but this was not the time for musing, an
his toes were being trampled. 'We'll meet again,' he cried – i
threat or truce, he didn't know.

'Come shooting,' Gardiner called, then he and Kate wer
bundled aboard.

They sailed on the lift of the tide, drifting out as the sail
billowed, the voices fading, the band playing with limpin
rhythms. The drummer was drunk as a prince.

'Which way are we heading to?' she asked as the afternoo
drew down with a purpling of clouds.

'Hong Kong, they tell me.'

'Isn't that in China?'

'Some damn' place.'

'I don't want to go to China, Frank.'

'We're going to San Francisco, to America.'

'That's another country, ain't it?'

'We'll get another boat,' he said. 'We'll buy a boat.'

'Oh, look,' she cried. 'What's that?'

'Them's sea birds.'

'Oh, my,' she said and leaned against him, watching th
spiral of the gulls. 'Oh, gosh!' she breathed. She had just seer
the sea opening out in viridians and distant inky tones, an
there was no land there, the land was back a way, back ther
where'd they'd come from – a little shadow-line of land, lik
some child had drawn it with a crayon.

'All right?' he asked solicitously.

She nodded and nestled to him. But she was scared, dead
scared – and alive with the whole damned world before her.